"What do we know of this Andronicus?" asked Kiren-Jool.

"He was the Royal Life Mage before Revi," Aubrey explained, "but he died before he could pass on all his knowledge."

"A pity," noted Aldus Hearn. "His understanding of the arcane arts was rumoured to have been vast."

"According to Revi, Andronicus went mad in his final years," said Aubrey. She was about to say more but paused unexpectedly, her face betraying her mind at work. "Saxnor's beard," she cried out, "he went mad, just like Revi, don't you see?"

"I fail to see the connection," said Aldus Hearn. "Andronicus was just old."

"No," said Aubrey, "you forget, I apprenticed under Revi. He told me that his master became quite erratic in his last few months. Revi wasn't even properly trained."

"And now you think the same thing was happening to Revi?" said Albreda.

"Yes," Aubrey continued, "he was always driven to discover new things, but lately he seemed obsessed. He was even short with the queen."

"I can't see how that explains his absence," said Hearn. "In any event, they're two unrelated things, aren't they?"

"Are they?" said Albreda. "Perhaps not."

"What do you mean?" asked Aubrey.

"Revi was once a prisoner of the Dark Queen," she said.

"Yes," agreed Aubrey, "but he managed to escape."

"He did," Albreda continued, "but do you remember what the Dark Queen wanted with him?"

"The location of the Tower of Andronicus," said Aubrey. "Of course, I should have realized sooner!"

"I'm afraid I'm not following," said Aldus Hearn.

"Come along, Aldus, pay attention," said Albreda, "this is not difficult. Please continue, Aubrey."

The young Life Mage thought it over a moment before speaking. "Revi must have been searching for the tower."

Also by Paul J Bennett

DEFENDER OF THE CROWN

Heir to the Crown: Book Seven

PAUL J BENNETT

Dedication

To educators everywhere who give the gift of knowledge and inspire a lifelong love of learning.

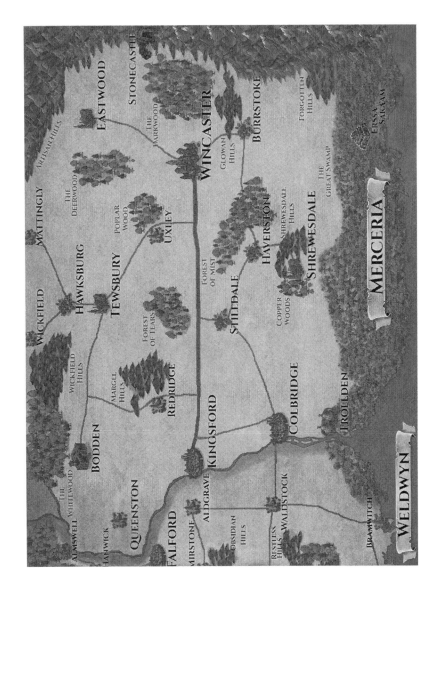

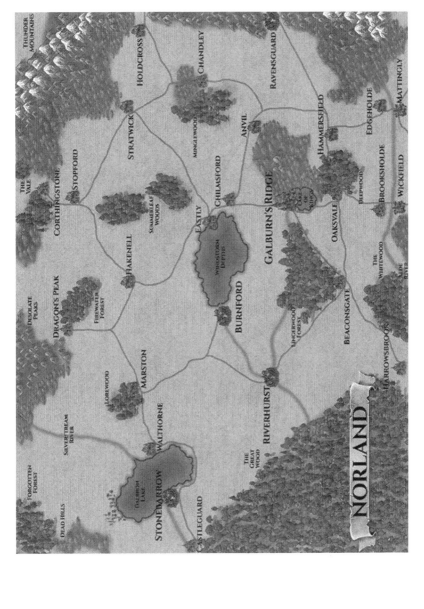

NORLAND

ONE

The Missing Mage

Summer 964 MC*
(*Mercerian Calendar)

A lbreda, Mistress of the Whitewood, entered the room only to notice that the other mages were already gathered.

"I see everyone is present," she said, taking her seat.

"Everyone except for Master Revi Bloom," corrected Aubrey.

"Yes," Albreda agreed, "the very subject of this emergency meeting." She looked at each mage in turn. It was a small council, consisting of only four members now that the Royal Life Mage had gone missing, a reminder that magic only existed in Merceria by a most tenuous thread.

"Queen Anna has asked Albreda to oversee this council in Revi's absence," explained Aubrey.

"Fine by me," remarked Aldus Hearn, the elderly Earth Mage.

"As it should be," agreed the Kurathian Enchanter, Kiren-Jool.

"I should start by saying that we keenly feel Revi's absence," said Albreda, "even though he was often distracted by his studies of late. I understand that he was last seen by you, Aubrey, is this correct?"

"It is," Aubrey replied. "I visited his house in Wincaster when I was researching the shapeshifting bartoks."

"Tell us what you recall of that meeting," Albreda urged.

"I went to his house to make use of his library," Aubrey explained. "When I opened the door, I expected him to be inside, but he was nowhere to be seen. I called out, but there was no answer. Then, I heard the sound of shuffling feet coming from upstairs, which I assumed was Revi, as his casting room is up there. However, I didn't want to disturb him."

"So you didn't, in fact, see him?" asked Aldus Hearn.

"No, not right away," said Aubrey, "but when I headed into his library to search for books, I heard another noise and wondered if he might need some help. I made my way upstairs, where I heard him muttering."

"Is this something he did a lot?" asked Kiren-Jool.

"Yes," said Aubrey, "he would often mutter while experimenting, I think it helped his thought processes. Believing he might be deep in thought, I opened the door quietly to peek inside, hoping not to disturb him."

"And that's when you saw him?" prompted Aldus Hearn.

"Yes, he was standing in the middle of the room, examining a full-length mirror."

Kiren-Jool suddenly sat up straight. "A mirror, you say?"

"Yes," Aubrey confirmed, "it was mounted on a wooden frame that allowed it to flip on its centre axis."

"Did it have runes on it," asked the Kurathian, "perchance on the frame?"

"I didn't examine it closely at the time," said Aubrey, "however, I've looked at it since. There is some intricate scrollwork around the border, but I haven't examined it at length. Why, does that mean something to you?"

"The tradition of magical mirrors is not unheard of amongst my people," said Kiren-Jool. "It is said that between the Princes of Kurathia, there are many such items."

"And what do these mirrors do?" asked Aldus Hearn.

"Some are used for scrying," said Kiren-Jool, "but others are said to be even more powerful."

"Meaning?" prompted Albreda.

"Meaning that they may be used as portals," the Kurathian mage replied.

"Isn't it more likely that he used a spell of recall?" asked Aldus.

"Unlikely," said Aubrey, "Albreda and I are the only people here that can cast such a spell. Revi hadn't learned it yet, said he was too busy."

"It sounds like he managed to unlock this mirror," said Aldus Hearn, "but surely he would have told someone before he attempted to use it?"

"He's been erratic of late," said Aubrey, "and Hayley admitted as much."

"Hayley Chambers? The High Ranger?" said Aldus.

"Of course," said Albreda. "Where have you been these past months, Aldus, under a rock?"

The old mage flushed with embarrassment, "I have been rather busy of late in the north."

"That's no excuse," said Albreda. "You really should try to speak to others on occasion."

"Can we focus on Revi?" interrupted Aubrey.

"Yes, of course," said Albreda, "you're right, we cannot afford to get distracted. Kiren-Jool, you're an Enchanter, tell us what you can about these mirrors."

The Kurathian leaned forward, resting his hands on the table. "As I said, there are many types," he began, "but it sounds as though he found one that acts as a portal."

"A portal to where?" asked Aubrey.

"Well, that's the hard part," he admitted, "we have no way of knowing."

"So he could be anywhere?" asked Albreda.

"No," said Kiren-Jool, "he's definitely in one place. We just don't know where that place is."

The Kurathian took a deep breath. "Mirrors of this type always work in pairs," he explained. "If it is such a device, the location of the other mirror will tell us where he went."

"I fail to see how that helps us," said Albreda. "We still have no idea where that might be."

"True," said Aubrey, "but Revi must have discovered how to use it. Possibly we can too."

"Where did the mirror come from?" asked the Kurathian.

"He's always had it," said Aubrey. "I believe it belonged to his master, Andronicus."

"What do we know of this Andronicus?" asked Kiren-Jool.

"He was the Royal Life Mage before Revi," Aubrey explained, "but he died before he could pass on all his knowledge."

"A pity," noted Aldus Hearn. "His understanding of the arcane arts was rumoured to have been vast."

"According to Revi, Andronicus went mad in his final years," said Aubrey. She was about to say more but paused unexpectedly, her face betraying her mind at work. "Saxnor's beard," she cried out, "he went mad, just like Revi, don't you see?"

"I fail to see the connection," said Aldus Hearn. "Andronicus was just old."

"No," said Aubrey, "you forget, I apprenticed under Revi. He told me that his master became quite erratic in his last few months. Revi wasn't even properly trained."

"And now you think the same thing was happening to Revi?" said Albreda.

"Yes," Aubrey continued, "he was always driven to discover new things, but lately he seemed obsessed. He was even short with the queen."

"I can't see how that explains his absence," said Hearn. "In any event, they're two unrelated things, aren't they?"

"Are they?" said Albreda. "Perhaps not."

"What do you mean?" asked Aubrey.

"Revi was once a prisoner of the Dark Queen," she said.

"Yes," agreed Aubrey, "but he managed to escape."

"He did," Albreda continued, "but do you remember what the Dark Queen wanted with him?"

"The location of the Tower of Andronicus," said Aubrey. "Of course, I should have realized sooner!"

"I'm afraid I'm not following," said Aldus Hearn.

"Come along, Aldus, pay attention," said Albreda, "this is not difficult. Please continue, Aubrey."

The young Life Mage thought it over a moment before speaking. "Revi must have been searching for the tower."

"And his quest led him to the mirror," added Kiren-Jool.

"I see," said Aldus Hearn, "but that still doesn't tell us where it's located."

"No," agreed the Kurathian, "but it would explain his interest in the mirror. It was likely his method of getting there."

"Would a mirror have any kind of range limitation?" asked Albreda.

"I should think so," said Kiren-Jool, "but I can't say for certain. It would definitely require a spell caster to use it, though."

"So only a mage could use such a device?" asked Aldus Hearn. "Does that mean your Kurathian princes are all mages?"

"No," said Kiren-Jool, "but a mage would have to activate the device. This would be similar to using the magical flame, requiring a sequence of magical letters to power the portal."

"If I understand you correctly," said Albreda, "then there's a chance we could decipher that sequence."

"We could," said the Enchanter, "but we have no idea how many magical words of power are required to activate it, and the number of possible combinations would be tremendous."

"Then I suggest we get started as soon as possible," said Albreda. "Revi seems to have managed it somehow, and if he could do it, so can we."

"But he's had years to study that mirror," said Aldus Hearn.

"No," said Aubrey, "likely only a few months. We travelled to Weldwyn, and then we fled the capital after we escaped. All of his research would have been here, in Wincaster."

"Yes," agreed Albreda, "and Revi is a highly focused individual, I doubt he'd research more than one thing at a time."

"I'd agree with that assessment," said Aubrey.

"So how do we explore this further?" asked Aldus Hearn.

Albreda looked around the room before answering, "I would suggest that Kiren-Jool and Aubrey examine the mirror. It's obviously an enchantment, but Aubrey has a keen insight into Revi's way of thinking, having been his apprentice."

"And the rest of us?" asked Aldus Hearn.

"First of all," said Albreda, "there's only the two of us left. I'd like you to take a look through his library, Aldus, you might find something of value that could help us."

"And you?" asked the Earth Mage.

"With the queen's permission, I'll recall to Summersgate. I'm hoping the mages of Weldwyn could be of some assistance."

"And if we find anything?" asked Kiren-Jool.

"Since I may be away for some time, I'll appoint Aubrey as the person in charge," said Albreda. "Report anything you find to her, and I'll catch up on my return. Any other questions?"

They all shook their heads.

"Very well, then," Albreda continued, "let's get to work. We have few enough mages as it is, we can't afford to lose even one."

That very afternoon found Aubrey and Kiren-Jool entering Revi's house.

"Watch your step," said Aubrey, "Revi's not the neatest person."

"There are books piled everywhere," said Kiren-Jool.

"Yes," Aubrey agreed, "and Aldus can start with those when he arrives, but we have more important things to do. Follow me, and I'll show you his casting room."

She led him upstairs to the top floor, where a door stood open.

"This is it," she declared.

He poked his head in, noting the absence of any furniture save the mirror.

"Is it always like this?" he asked.

"Yes," she replied, "he liked to keep things simple, said it helped him focus."

Kiren-Jool moved to stand before the mirror. "It looks fancy enough."

"Fancy?" said Aubrey. "What do you mean?"

"Magical items must be crafted of the finest materials," explained the Kurathian. "This mirror would certainly fall into that category."

"But it's only a wooden frame," said Aubrey.

"This is no ordinary wood," he explained, "it's shadowbark."

"I've never heard of it," said Aubrey.

"It is from a tree not seen in these parts," explained Kiren-Jool, "imported at great expense."

"Imported? You mean from the Continent?"

"Unless you know somewhere else that would have such trees?" he asked.

"But Merceria has been cut off from the sea for centuries," she said.

"This mirror is likely far older than Merceria," he noted. "I suspect it is elder magic."

"You mean crafted by Elves?" asked Aubrey.

"They are usually the ones responsible for artifacts like this. It is said that before the coming of man, magic was far more commonplace."

"Then how did Andronicus come to own it?" Aubrey asked.

"I have no idea. Maybe he discovered it somewhere? Either that, or it was handed down by his predecessors."

A noise downstairs announced the arrival of Aldus Hearn. Aubrey leaned out of the doorway and shouted, "Up here, Aldus!"

His footsteps echoed as he climbed the stairs, slowing when he reached the top.

"Those steps are steeper than I would have liked," said the Earth Mage.

"I'll be sure to mention that to Revi when we find him," said Aubrey.

"Is this the mirror?" he asked.

"It is," said Kiren-Jool. "Aubrey and I were just discussing it. We think it might have been discovered by one of Revi's predecessors."

"Did Revi maintain any notes?" asked Hearn.

"He did," said Aubrey, "but his writing is difficult to discern."

"What about those that came before him?" said the druid.

"A good place to start, I suppose," said Aubrey. "Andronicus was the Royal Life Mage before Revi, and I believe before that, it was someone named Corvus."

"Ah, yes," said Hearn, "I recognize the name. I'll start searching through Revi's books, shall I? With some luck, I might find a journal of whoever discovered this mirror." He turned around and made his way back down the stairs.

Aubrey returned her gaze to Kiren-Jool, who had already started examining the ornate frame of the mirror.

"You said you thought this might be elder magic?" she said.

"Yes, that's correct," he replied, "likely created by Elves."

"Maybe we can enlist some help," said Aubrey.

"From who? The entire Mages Council knows of this already, unless you're talking about the mages of Weldwyn? I thought Albreda was going to consult with them."

"She is," said Aubrey, "but that's not what I mean. Lord Arandil Greycloak is coming to Wincaster for the Royal Wedding. Maybe we can enlist his help?"

"Do you think he would assist us?" asked Kiren-Jool. "I'm not familiar with him other than by reputation, and the Elves are notorious for not sharing the secrets of their magic."

"The least we can do is ask," said Aubrey. "He served with Revi during the first rebellion, so the two have met."

"Let us hope he can be of assistance," said Kiren-Jool.

TWO

The Queen

Summer 964 MC

G erald opened the door, only to be greeted by a loud bark. Queen Anna, the ruler of Merceria, sat on a chair as her personal maid, Sophie, arranged her hair.

"Come in, Gerald," Anna said, her back to the door.

"How did you know it was me?"

"Tempus," she said, "need I say more?"

The huge mastiff rose from his position beside her, trotting over to him for a pet.

He scratched the great beast's head. "I hope I'm not interrupting?"

"You could never interrupt," she replied. "Come in and sit down. Sophie is experimenting with my hair."

Gerald moved closer, examining the ornately arranged blonde locks.

"You have a gift, Sophie," he said.

"Thank you, Gerald," the young maid replied.

"Well?" said Anna. "What do you think?"

"I think it looks very pretty," he remarked. "Is that how you're going to wear it for the wedding?"

"I haven't decided yet," she replied.

"This is the third style we've tried," added Sophie.

"Well," said Gerald, "this one looks very regal, a good choice for a young queen."

"You'd say that even if it was a mess," admonished Anna.

"True," he replied, "but in this case, I mean it."

"Tell me," she said, "did you come just to see my hair, or is this an official visit?"

"A little of both, to be honest," he said. "I came to let you know a few more delegates have arrived."

"Oh?" she said. "Tell me more."

"The Dwarves have sent Herdwin back to us as their official representative."

"Herdwin has lived in Wincaster for so many years," said Anna, "I'm surprised they'd pick him to represent them."

"It makes sense if you think about it," said Gerald. "After all, he knows you well and is familiar with the kingdom."

"I suppose that's true," she said. "Has King Leofric arrived yet?"

"No," said Gerald, "but he's expected by the end of the week. We already received word that he crossed the border at Kingsford."

"Alric will be pleased," said Anna. "He hasn't seen his father for some time."

"Not quite true," said Gerald, blushing. "He arranged for his father to pay my fine, remember?"

"Oh, yes," she added, "I'd quite forgotten that. Is he bringing the family with him?"

"Queen Igraine, certainly, and I'm led to believe that the princesses are coming as well, but he's left Alstan to look after the kingdom while he's away. I also understand he's bringing a mage or two with him."

"Likely Mistress Fortuna," said Anna, "she's their Life Mage. Any word on the Saurians?"

"Not yet, but there's still plenty of time. Aubrey delivered the invitation in person more than a week ago, so we know they received it. Lily sends her best regards, by the way."

"Lily spoke to Aubrey?" asked Anna. "I didn't know our mage could speak Saurian?"

Gerald chuckled, "She doesn't. She took the Enchanter, Kiren-Jool, with her. He used the spell of tongues."

"I can't wait to see her again," said Anna.

"Apparently, Lily's been enjoying her time in Erssa-Saka'am, learning all about her people."

"I have to admit, they were quite fascinating," said Anna. "I very much enjoyed my time with them."

"We were fleeing for our lives at the time, Anna, did you forget that?"

"No, of course not, but learning about the Saurians was fascinating, all the same. Have you any other news for me? Any word on Revi?"

"Not as yet," said Gerald, "but the Mages Council is looking into it, though I'm led to believe it will likely take some time to find him."

"How is Hayley taking it?" asked Anna.

"As well as can be expected, given the circumstances, but she knows the mages are the best equipped to find him. Aubrey is in charge of the search, and she'll report back if they find anything."

"Aubrey? Not Albreda?"

"Yes," said Gerald. "Albreda wants to go to Summersgate to see if the mages of Weldwyn can help. She was going to talk to you in person but knows how busy you are with all these arrangements you have to take care of, so she asked me to mention it to you."

"I see no problem," said Anna. "Perhaps while she's there, she can teach a few more of them to use the spell of recall." "I'll let her know," promised Gerald.

"What of the north?"

"We still have reports of people fleeing Norland," said Gerald. "It appears unrest is growing."

"Their king is old," said Anna, "and if I'm not mistaken, he is without an heir. When he dies, there'll be a bloody fight for the throne."

"Let's hope it doesn't spill over into Merceria," said Gerald. "We still haven't fully recovered our strength."

Sophie stood back, examining the back of Anna's head. "There you are, Majesty, all done."

Anna rose from her seat, moving closer to a large mirror to take a look for herself. Sophie followed, holding a small hand mirror to allow the queen to see the back of her head.

"Marvellous," Anna declared, "I think we'll go for this one."

She turned to face Gerald. "Have you seen my wedding dress?"

"No," he replied, "but I have a feeling I'm about to."

"Yes," said Anna, "come and take a look."

She led him across the room, halting at a dressing screen.

"Here it is," she declared.

He moved around the edge of the screen to view the green dress, noticing that it was richly decorated with jewels and lace.

"Mercerian green," he noted, "how appropriate." He leaned closer, examining the details. "This embroidery is spectacular."

"Isn't it, though? The lace was my idea."

"Is that Elvish script?" he asked.

"It is," she replied, "sewn into the hem, along with Orc runes and Dwarvish letters. There's even some Saurian in there."

"Nothing for the Trolls?" said Gerald.

"They don't use a written language," said Anna, "other than ours, that is."

"You seem to have thought of everything," he noted.

"I did," she said, grinning.

Gerald noticed the excitement in her eyes. "Go ahead, then, tell me what it is that has you so worked up."

"Look here," she said, pointing, "I had them embroider something special."

He examined the area to note a plant of some sort. "Is that a weed?"

"No," she replied, "it's a Weldwyn Clover."

"We feed our horses clover," said Gerald.

"Hush now," she replied, "it's featured on their coat of arms. We must get used to the strange customs of our newest ally."

"They're not our allies yet," said Gerald. "You still have to get married, remember?"

"I could hardly forget," she said. "Oh, that reminds me, have you seen Beverly?"

"The last time I saw her, she was arranging the guards for the wedding."

"I need to go over the ceremony with her. I'd like her suggestions on how we might best use the Knights of the Hound."

"Those things have all been taken care of, Anna. You need to slow down and relax a little. Are you nervous?"

"Yes," she replied, "can't you tell?"

"There's nothing to be nervous about," he soothed. "You and Alric both love each other. There's naught to worry about."

"But what if..." she said.

"If what?" he replied.

"What if we're not...you know?"

"No, I don't know," he said.

"Well, what if, as a man, he and I are...incompatible?"

Gerald laughed, "Is that what you're afraid of? Don't worry, Anna, things will sort themselves out. I think you'll find that, come your wedding night, you'll figure out what to do."

"Are you sure?"

"I am," he replied, "but I think you need a woman's perspective. I'll send Beverly to see you. As a recently married woman, I think she can set your mind at ease."

"Thank you," said Anna, then she moved closer, hugging him.

"What's that for?"

"For being you and understanding," she replied, finally releasing him from her grasp. "Now remember, you are an important part of the ceremony. I want you looking your best."

"Already taken care of," chimed in Sophie. "I have a seamstress working on it as we speak."

"Ah, Sophie, thank you," said Anna. "What would I do without you?"

"It's my pleasure, Majesty," the maid replied.

Dame Hayley Chambers, Baroness of Queenston and High Ranger, pulled back on the bowstring then let fly. The arrow sailed downrange, striking the distant target.

Her aide, Gorath, looked off into the distance, his keen Orc eyes taking it all in.

"Your aim is off," he said. "You appear distracted."

"I am," she replied. "Revi has been missing for almost a week, and we're still no closer to finding him."

"These things take time," said Gorath. "You must trust that they will do all they can to help."

"I know," she said, "and I do, but I feel like I should be doing more."

"Are you familiar with magic?" asked the Orc.

"Not really," she replied.

"Then there is little you can do. In the meantime, we still have to assess this warbow."

"You're right, of course," Hayley replied. "Go ahead, let fly and let's see how you do."

The Orc raised the bow, nocking an arrow, and then drew back the string to his ear. He held it only a moment before letting it go to produce a soft whiffing noise as the arrow flew true. A distant thud announced a strike to the target, and he and Hayley began moving towards it.

"You're an excellent archer, Gorath. You're closer to the centre of the target than me."

"I have been practising," he replied, "and I find this warbow easier to use."

"Kraloch said it was designed by a Human," said Hayley.

"It is true," said Gorath. "It was first introduced to the Orcs of the Red Hand."

"I'm not familiar with them," said Hayley, "are they somewhere nearby?"

"No," said the Orc, "they are on the Continent. What you would call 'the old land'."

"I find it interesting that a Human would develop such a weapon for Orcs," continued Hayley. "There must be more to this story."

"If there is," said Gorath, "it is a story for someone else to tell. I only know that this bow was built for Orcs."

They continued their way to the target, arriving to find Gorath's arrow deeply embedded. Hayley pulled it free, grunting with the effort.

"That's quite the power behind it," she said. "I wonder how it might fare against the Elven longbows?"

"Should we talk to Telethial?" asked the Orc.

"Maybe we're better off keeping it to ourselves for the time being," suggested Hayley.

Dame Beverly Fitzwilliam watched as the cavalry rode past, stirrup to stirrup, tightly organized into their battle formation. When they reached the end of the field, they began to turn, but next came the most challenging part. The riders on the outside would have to increase their pace even as those on the inside had to shorten theirs.

She held her breath as they executed the manoeuvre, only letting it out as they flawlessly came out of the turn in unison. Beverly heard their sergeant bellowing orders, and then the column resumed its forward momentum, trotting towards the other end of the field.

As they thundered past, leaving a cloud of dust in their wake, Beverly, trying not to cough, averted her gaze and noticed a pair of familiar-looking riders approaching. She waited until they were close enough then turned Lightning to meet them.

"Your Highness," she said, "Lord Jack. What brings you to the practise field this day?"

Lord Jack Marlowe grinned, "Do we need an excuse just to see you, Dame Beverly?"

Beverly ignored the man, turning instead to Prince Alric.

"Is everything all right?" she asked.

"Everything is fine," said Alric. "We came because I was curious as to how you train the Guard Cavalry." He gazed out at the horsemen, admiring the rigidness of their lines. "Do you do this every day?"

"Whenever I can," she replied, "but that's usually only two or three times a week."

"I'm surprised you can find even that amount of time," noted Jack. "After all, you're the Commander of Cavalry, and these fellows are only one company. Do you train the rest as you do this lot?"

"No," she replied, "but the Guard Cavalry are the queen's own horsemen."

"You've done a magnificent job with them," said Alric, "and that's the real reason why I'm here."

"To train with the guard?" said Beverly.

"No," the prince replied, "but as you know, I have two companies of horsemen that my father sent from Weldwyn."

"Yes," said Beverly, "your own guard, but what has that to do with me?"

"I was hoping you might give my men some extra training. You wouldn't have to do it yourself, of course, you're far too busy for that, but I wondered if you might share your techniques."

"I'd be happy to," said Beverly, "but with your wedding so close, it will be difficult. We're practising for the ceremony, you see."

"After the wedding would be fine," said Alric, "I'm in no hurry. Eventually, I'd like to see them equipped much as the Guard Cavalry, but we'll have to wait on horses. Our Weldwyn Chargers lack the strength for such heavy armour."

"I'll have to put you in touch with my cousin," said Beverly. "Aubrey's the one raising our Mercerian Chargers these days."

"You think she'd let us have some?" said Jack.

"I'm afraid the entire herd is spoken for," said Beverly, "but possibly it's time we step up the breeding program."

"That doesn't sound promising," said Jack.

"Your men could still benefit from the training," offered Beverly, "even if they don't have the heavier armour of the Guard Cavalry."

"Excellent," said Alric, "then I'll leave it to you. Let me know when things have calmed down a bit, and we'll start making arrangements."

"Very well, Your Highness," replied Beverly.

Prince Alric wheeled around, Jack following suit. They trotted from the field, leaving Beverly to return her gaze to the company drilling before her.

"I don't see why our men need more training. They're some of the finest horsemen in Weldwyn."

"Agreed," said Alric, "but they don't fight as a cohesive unit, Jack. You saw the discipline of Beverly's troops. Think what a difference such training could make to our own men."

"They're a Royal Bodyguard. Do you really think more training is what they need?"

"We're in Merceria now, a nation of warriors. We can learn a lot from them."

"If you say so," said the cavalier, "but to be honest, some of their ideas are quite...radical."

"Why," asked Alric, "because they train commoners as heavy cavalry?"

"It just isn't right," said Jack. "They're not born to the saddle like the upper class."

"And yet they distinguished themselves during the war," said Alric. "You need to let go of your prejudices. This is not our fathers' generation."

They rode in silence, trotting down the street towards the Weldwyn Embassy.

"You like the Mercerians," declared Jack.

"I have to admit I do," the prince replied. "There's a certain vigour to them as if old habits have been brushed away like cobwebs. They're full of new ideas and not afraid to try them. It's strange to think that we feared them for so long."

"With good cause," said Jack, "they did try to invade us."

Alric chuckled, "Yes, more than once, in fact, but that's all in the past now. This is a new world now, Jack. Once Anna and I are married, it will cement an alliance between our two kingdoms, and bring safety and security to both our peoples."

"I doubt that. We'll certainly be better off, of that I have no doubt, but there's still the Twelve Clans, not to mention the Norlanders, they're no end of trouble to the Mercerians."

"Yes," agreed Alric, "but now we'll be united in our defence, effectively doubling the size of our army. Who would dare invade us now?"

"The Clans," repeated Jack.

"I very much doubt that," replied the prince. "We defeated them with only a handful of Mercerians. What could they do against both our combined armies?"

"War is not always about making smart decisions," said the cavalier. "The Clans have attacked at worse odds."

"I suppose they have," said Alric, "but at least we have allies now."

"Well, we will," said Jack, "just as soon as you two are married."

THREE

The North

Summer 964 MC

Sir Heward patted his mount's neck as he waited while behind him, the men of the Wincaster Light Horse mounted up.

It was a chilly morning, but he knew that come noon, the sun would have done its work, heating them up into an uncomfortable sweat. Looking north to where the great river ran to the west, he knew that just beyond its banks lay Norland, the land of his enemy. Heward's duty this day, and that of his men, was to patrol the border, watching for any sign of activity on the far side, a task he had done often enough over the past few months.

Being a Knight of the Hound, one of the celebrated few that held Queen Anna's confidence, he took his oath seriously. As commander of the northern region, he was responsible for keeping the land safe from Norland aggression, and though he could have remained securely ensconced in Hawksburg, his presence here would have a much more significant effect.

"All set, Captain?" he called out.

"Yes, sir," Captain Carlson replied.

Heward peered back down the line to see Sergeant Gardner keeping an eye at the rear of the column.

"Very well," said the knight, "let's get moving."

When he was a knight in Shrewesdale, he had borne the burden of maintaining his horse all by himself, necessitating a much lighter mount, but now, by Royal Proclamation, the Knights of the Hound were funded entirely from the Royal Pocket. Heward smiled, realizing just how lucky he was to have a Mercerian Charger to ride, for such a horse would have been far too expensive for him to own otherwise.

He urged his mount forward, trotting along the southern bank and leading his men eastward, all the while keeping the north shore in sight. Here, the ground was relatively flat, but the occasional hill provided an excellent vantage point. And so, around noon, as they stopped to water the horses, he sent two riders up one such rise, the better to view the northern bank while the rest slaked their thirst.

Heward dug into his pack, extracting a cheesecloth and pulling forth some Stilldale White. He had just taken a bite of the cheese when he spotted Sergeant Gardner riding towards him, along with one of the sentries.

"Problem?" asked Heward.

"Wilkins has seen something, sir," said Gardner.

Heward let his gaze wander over to the young horseman. "Well, what is it?"

"A small group of riders," the man replied.

"Give him the details, man," ordered Gardner.

"Four men all told," added Wilkins, "and they're carrying a flag."

"A flag?" said Heward. "What kind of flag?"

"A yellow one, my lord," said Wilkins.

"I'm not a lord," said Heward, "I'm a knight. You address me as 'Sir'."

"Yes, sir. Sorry, sir."

"A yellow flag," said Gardner. "It appears they want to talk."

"So it does," said Heward.

"Are you sure, sir?" said Wilkins. "Perhaps it's a trap?"

"With four riders?" said Heward. "I think not."

"Orders, sir?" asked the sergeant.

Heward looked over at his men. Many had just dismounted, but it appeared their respite would be short-lived.

"Captain?" he called out.

Captain Carlson walked over. "Sir?"

"We've spotted some riders on the northern bank. It appears they want to parley."

"I'll mount up," offered the captain.

"No, I'm leaving you here to command the men," said Heward. "I'll take Sergeant Gardner and Wilkins here."

"Me, sir?" said the young recruit.

Heward turned to him in surprise. "Unless you know of another horseman named Wilkins?"

"No, sir," the man replied.

Sergeant Gardner leaned in close to the new recruit. "I can see that you and I are going to have a long chat after this, Wilkins."

"Yes, Sergeant," the young man replied.

"All set, Sergeant," asked Heward, "or do you need more time to calm the young recruit?"

"He'll be fine," the sergeant responded.

"Where's the nearest ford?" asked the knight.

Gardner looked around, taking his bearings. "Just east of here, sir, past that elm tree."

"Very well," said Heward, "then we'll leave the rest of the horsemen here. I shouldn't like to frighten away our visitors."

They trotted eastward, the ford soon coming into sight. Heward's mount splashed into the river, the water rising to his boot tops as he made his way across to the other bank. Gardner and Wilkins followed, though their smaller mounts had a harder time of it. The knight exited the river, halting as the others caught up.

"Where did you see these riders?" he asked.

"They should be northwest of us, sir," said Wilkins.

Heward pressed on, riding northward to find a better vantage point. He soon found it, a slight rise that gave him a commanding view of the surrounding countryside. Sure enough, off in the distance, he spotted the riders.

"Have you a flag?" asked Heward.

"Here, sir," said Gardner, pulling a yellow flag from his bag. He handed one end to Wilkins, and they rode side by side, draping the cloth between them.

Heward could tell they had been spotted, for the unknown horsemen changed their course, heading straight for them at a sedate pace. As they drew closer, the knight took a hard look at their equipment.

"Raiders?" asked the sergeant.

"No," said Heward, "they're too well-armed for that. These look more like professionals."

"Here, on the border, sir?" said Wilkins.

"It is unusual," said Heward, "I'll give you that."

"What do you think they want?" asked Gardner.

Heward halted, indicating with his hand for the others to do likewise. "I have no idea," he said, "but we'll let them come to us. Keep your hands away from your weapons. We don't want to antagonize them."

The riders continued until they were only a couple of horse lengths away. Here they halted, looking at one of their number, an elderly man, apparently their leader.

"Greetings," the man called out. "I am Lord Wilfrid of Hansley, representative of His Majesty, King Halfan of Norland. To whom do I have the honour of addressing?"

"I am Sir Heward, Knight of the Hound and commander of the Mercerian forces in this area. My men saw your offer of parley. Might I enquire as to the reason for this act?"

"I have come at the express order of my sovereign," said Lord Wilfrid. "King Halfan wishes there to be peace between our peoples."

"Peace?" said Heward. "Our nations have been at war for centuries, why now?"

"The king is ailing," replied the Norlander, "and wants the realm to prosper. This war that we have fought for so long is draining both our kingdoms. The time to end our hostilities has come."

"Does that mean he renounces his claim to the Mercerian crown?" asked Heward.

"His Majesty wishes me to assure you that such is the case."

"I take it you have an official request of some type?" asked Heward.

"I do," said Lord Wilfrid. "In fact, I am charged with delivering the message directly to your queen."

Heward looked over the man carefully, trying to ascertain if this were some sort of trap, but he could detect no sign of deceit on the Norlander's face.

"Very well," he replied. "You may ride with us across the river. There, we will join my company and return to Wickfield. I'm afraid you'll have to remain there until we get Royal Approval to take you to Wincaster."

"That," said Lord Wilfrid, "is much as I suspected it would be. Lead on, Sir Heward, and together, let us forge a new future for our two realms."

Heward led them south across the river, sending Wilkins ahead to warn the captain of their unexpected guests. By the time they rejoined the company, the rest of the men were ready to ride. Heward led the way, travelling beside Lord Wilfrid while the rest of the men, under Captain Carlson, brought up the rear.

By late afternoon, Wickfield was in sight, with a small crowd gathered as they rode into the village. Living on the frontier, the villagers were used to soldiers, but to see Norlanders who weren't intent on killing them was an altogether different experience. They gaped at the delegation riding by as if they were some strange kind of creature never before seen. Heward halted before the village's church and climbed down from the saddle.

"Come inside," he beckoned, "and we'll give you some food."

"In a church?" asked Lord Wilfrid.

"I'm afraid there's no inn in Wickfield to house you," said Heward, "but we can offer you a modest repast. I'll send word on to Hawksburg of your arrival, but until I receive instructions, I'm afraid you'll have to make do with the lodgings we can provide."

"I understand," the Norland lord replied, dismounting. "It's a curious thing," he continued, "to be standing here, among our traditional enemies."

"I could say the same," said Heward, "but the truth is that we are not so different, you and I, we both want to live in peace."

"As does my king," declared Lord Wilfrid, "of that, you can be assured."

"It is not me that must be convinced," said Heward, "but Queen Anna. Only she can speak for the realm."

Heward led them inside, where a small group of soldiers stood ready.

"These men will see to your wellbeing," said Heward. "I fear the locals here hold you in some contempt. Many have lost loved ones due to the privations of your raiders."

"As have we," said Lord Wilfrid, "but we must see our way forward if we are to live in peace."

"It will take some time to get word to Wincaster," said Heward, "and even more time to get a response. I'm afraid you'll likely be in for a long stay."

"Understood," said the Norland delegate. "Wincaster is some distance away, and we cannot change the laws of nature."

"Captain Carlson will see to your lodgings," continued Heward, "but I'm afraid I'll have to leave you if this letter is to be sent off before nightfall."

"Of course," said Lord Wilfrid, "and thank you for being so gracious. You know, when I set out on this mission, we had no idea if you'd even let us into your kingdom. Half the court was sure you'd kill us on sight."

"I think you'll find us much more reasonable than that," said Heward. "Good day, Lord Wilfrid."

Heward bowed, then turned and left. He was already forming the report in his mind as he exited the building.

Kraloch, Orc Shaman of the Black Arrow Clan, examined the note, then returned his gaze to the dispatch rider.

"When did this Norland delegation arrive?"

"Two days ago," the courier explained. "Sir Heward insisted I ride out as soon as possible."

"I can imagine," said the Orc. "Are you aware of its contents?"

"No," the rider replied, "but I was told to return with an answer as soon as practical."

"Your mount must rest," said Kraloch, "but we will send a reply first thing tomorrow morning. I shall hold onto this until the arrival of Lady Aubrey. She is due this very evening."

"The baroness is coming here?" asked the rider.

"Of course," said Kraloch. "It is her city, and the magic circle makes such travel easy for her."

"Should I not change horses and head back to Wickfield, then?"

"You would do better to wait," said the Orc, "for Lady Aubrey may have other messages for you to carry. Now come rest and get yourself something to eat from the kitchen. I shall take it from here."

The courier nodded his head and made his way into the manor house that served as the army's headquarters.

Kraloch read the message again, trying to glean more information from its contents. It was clear that the Norlanders wanted to negotiate something, but would the plight of his people be addressed? The Norlanders had been brutal in their subjugation of Orcs, and he wondered what Queen Anna might make of such things, but then shook his head. The queen had an alliance with the Orcs. Surely she would not abandon them.

He gazed skyward, judging the time of day. It was still mid-afternoon, plenty of time to commune with the Ancestors.

The magic circle glowed brightly, then a solid wall of light sprang upward, almost blinding Kraloch as he watched. Moments later, the light faded, revealing Lady Aubrey, Beverly, and Aldwin.

"Kraloch," said Aubrey, "I didn't expect you to greet us. Is something wrong?"

"I have received word from the frontier," said the Orc. "It appears a Norland delegation has arrived seeking an audience with the queen."

"For what purpose?" asked Beverly.

"To negotiate a peace, apparently," said the Orc.

"Peace?" repeated Aldwin.

"Yes," said Beverly, turning to her husband. "Technically, we've been at war with them since their founding."

"What brought that on, I wonder?" said Aldwin.

"Sir Heward says that the Norland King, Halfan, is ailing," said Kraloch.

"He likely wants to leave a legacy," offered Aubrey.

"This is important," said Beverly, "we'd best get it to the queen as quickly as possible."

"We'll have to eat first," said Aubrey. "I need to regain my strength after using my magic, but then we can recall back to Wincaster."

"And here I was expecting a nice uninterrupted evening," said Aldwin.

"We can still do that back in the capital," said Beverly.

"I doubt that," said Aldwin. "It's not every day that the Norlanders send a message like that. You'll likely have to spend half the night at the Palace."

"Sorry," said Beverly, "but I must do my duty."

"And I wouldn't have it any other way," said Aldwin. "Don't worry, we'll make time later, I have to work on my sketches anyway."

"Sketches?" said Aubrey. "Now you have me intrigued, Aldwin. What are you drawing?"

"I've been going over some designs for the next magic circle," he said. "Queen Anna wants them in all the cities of Merceria, eventually."

"I thought all the circles were the same," offered Kraloch.

"Each is unique to its school of magic," said Aldwin. "Albreda explained everything to me."

"Yes," said Beverly, "and Aldwin has already been immortalized."

"That's right," said Aubrey, "he put his maker's mark onto the circle in Wincaster, didn't he. You'll have to study the one here, Aldwin, it might give you some ideas."

"That's an excellent idea, Aubrey," said Aldwin. "You're a handy person to have around."

"It runs in the family," the Life Mage replied. "Isn't that right, cousin?"

Beverly laughed. "It is," she admitted, "but I think we'd best spend our time poring over Heward's dispatch."

"You go ahead," said Aldwin, "I'll follow Aubrey's advice and examine the Hawksburg circle in more detail."

"All right," said Aubrey, "but don't be late for dinner."

"Don't worry," said Beverly, "I've never known him to miss a meal."

"Oh, I don't know," said Aldwin, "I seem to recall missing a meal or two on occasion."

Beverly blushed, "That was different, husband mine. Now get to work before I get distracted."

Kraloch led them from the building. The Hawksburg circle had been built in the cellar of the old manor house by Aubrey's great-grandmother and had only recently been rediscovered. It had taken a great deal of work to make it more usable, resulting in significant renovations to the old structure. Now it was guarded, day and night, by Orc hunters from Kraloch's tribe.

"Remind me to teach you the recall spell," said Aubrey.

"I shall," said Kraloch, "though I'm not sure the queen would allow me to study the Wincaster circle."

"Nonsense," added Beverly, "I'm sure she'd have no objection."

"There is something that I need to bring to your attention," said Kraloch, "a matter of some import."

Aubrey halted, turning to face the green-skinned Orc. "What is it, Kraloch? You can tell me anything."

The shaman looked at Beverly, deep in thought for a moment. "These Norlanders," he said at last, "there's something you need to know about them."

"Which is?" asked Aubrey.

"They have not been kind to my people," said Kraloch.

"Can you be more specific?" pressed Beverly.

"As you know, the Orcs once lived in great cities," the shaman began. "There are even ruins of one in the eastern part of their kingdom."

"I assume that means there are still Orcs in the region," said Aubrey.

"There are," agreed the shaman, "but they have been ruthlessly hunted down by the Norlanders."

"I shall bring this to the attention of the queen," promised Beverly. "I can assure you that we will honour our alliance with the Orcs. When we needed help, your people, all of your people, came to our aid. We will not abandon them now. Any negotiation with the Norlanders will have to include provisions for the Orcs."

"Definitely," agreed Aubrey, "and I'm sure Queen Anna will agree."

"It would not be the first time the Orcs were used and then discarded," cautioned Kraloch.

"That will not happen!" declared Aubrey.

"And yet," said the Orc, "we still have no representation on the Nobles Council."

"You're right," said Beverly, "but I can assure you it's never far from the queen's mind. Her main problem is dealing with the existing nobles."

"I understand," said Kraloch, "for your ways have become familiar to me, but there are some among my people that are not so patient."

"I shall do what I can to bring your plight to Her Majesty's attention," promised Aubrey.

"I greatly appreciate it," said Kraloch. "Now, when are you going to let me teach you how to spirit talk?"

"Spirit talk?" said Beverly. "What's that?"

"Kraloch has been teaching me some new spells," said Aubrey. "Spirit talk would let us communicate over great distances."

"Sounds like a useful spell," said Beverly. "Does it work for anyone?"

"It's a Life Magic spell," said Aubrey, "and it only allows us to send messages to people we know well."

"Still quite useful," said Beverly. "You should learn it as soon as you can."

"I have been quite busy," said Aubrey, "overseeing the rebuilding of Hawksburg, not to mention helping out at court."

"I hear you, cousin," said Beverly. "You'd think we'd all have more time now that the war's over, but life just seems to get busier and busier."

"I miss the old days," said Aubrey. "Remember when you first visited Hawksburg?"

"Of course, how could I forget, your parents were so welcoming."

Aubrey fell silent.

"Something wrong, Aubrey?"

"I miss them, Beverly. I never got to say goodbye, and Valmar is still out there, somewhere, unpunished."

"You let me worry about Valmar," said Beverly. "I promise you he'll meet the end he deserves for his treachery."

"I know," said Aubrey, "but all of this," she waved her hands around, indicating the town, "it can just be so overwhelming at times."

"We're here to help," said Beverly. "You can always lean on Aldwin and me for support." She stepped forward, hugging her cousin.

"As are we," said Kraloch. "Despite what some may say, the Orcs are loyal to the Baroness of Hawksburg. Your people have welcomed us with open arms."

"Thank you," said Aubrey, standing back, "I suppose I just needed to hear that."

"Now come," said Kraloch, "food is prepared, for I have been expecting you."

"You'd best tell Aldwin," Aubrey remarked.

"Did someone mention food?" came a distant call.

"See," said Beverly, "what did I tell you?"

FOUR

The Royal Visitors

Summer 964 MC

K ing Leofric of Weldwyn looked out the carriage window to see the looming walls of Wincaster.

"Impressive, isn't it," said his Queen, Igraine.

"It is, indeed, a sight to behold," said the king as he sat back, looking at her in affection. "Whoever thought we'd be here, deep in the belly of our enemy."

"They're not our enemy anymore," she chided. "In fact, they're our allies now."

"Allies," said Leofric, "I like the sound of that."

"How many soldiers do they have?" interjected a child's voice.

The king turned to his youngest daughter. "More than us, Edwina," he said, "so be sure to mind your manners."

"Will Alric be there?" asked Althea, the older sister. She was almost the same age as Anna, but Leofric always thought of the Mercerian Queen as being much older.

"Of course," said Igraine, "he'll be waiting at the gate to welcome us."

"Is Anna really the queen now?" asked Edwina.

"She is," said the king.

"Does that mean that Alric will be king?" the young girl asked.

Leofric looked at his queen. "No," he finally said.

"Why not?" asked Edwina.

"Alric cannot rule Merceria," said Igraine. "That right is Anna's alone, but he will still be a Prince of Weldwyn."

"Yes," added Leofric, "and one day, their child shall rule this land."

"They have to get married first," said Althea.

"That's why we're here," said the king.

Unexpectedly, the carriage rumbled to a stop. King Leofric opened the door and called out, "Problem?"

A nearby rider came closer. "We're just waiting for the escort, Your Majesty. They're coming now."

Leofric poked his head out, looking towards the distant gates of the city.

"Can you see them?" asked Igraine.

"Yes," said the king, "and Alric is leading them."

"Is Anna with them?" she asked.

"No," he replied, "but I can see Lord Marlowe's son, and the Mercerian Marshal, Gerald."

"He's the Duke of Wincaster now," Igraine reminded him.

"Yes, that's right," he agreed. "The rest appear to be soldiers."

Opening the door fully, he stepped down to stretch his legs. Alric saw him immediately.

"Father," he called out.

"Alric," said the king, "so good to see you again, son."

"My, but you've filled out," added Queen Igraine as she joined Leofric. "You look so much taller. You're almost the size of your brother, Alstan."

"The Mercerian air appears to have done well for you," noted Leofric.

"Your Majesty," said Lord Jack, bowing respectfully.

"How fare you, my young cavalier?"

"Well," said Jack, "the food here is not all that different from home."

"Father," said Alric, "you remember His Grace, the Duke of Wincaster, Marshal Gerald Matheson?"

"I can't forget the debt we owe you, Your Grace," said Leofric.

"Please, call me Gerald, Your Majesty," the marshal replied. "And as to the debt, well, it is I that am indebted to you."

"Enough of these pleasantries," said Igraine. "Where is my future daughter-in-law?"

"She regrets that she cannot be here in person," said Gerald, "but has sent me to assure you that she awaits your arrival at the Palace."

"Well, in that case," said the king, climbing back into the carriage, "let us be on our way!"

Alric led them through the gates of the city, where guards stood by, their weapons at the salute. Soon, they were rumbling through the narrow streets of Wincaster, the wheels making a clacking noise on the cobblestones.

Igraine peered out the window. "Such narrow streets," she noted.

"Yes," the king agreed, "but they say Wincaster was originally a fortress."

"Really?" piped in Althea.

"Yes," said Leofric, "your brother tells me that when the Mercerians migrated eastward, they ran into the Elves and war broke out. Wincaster was built as a frontier base from which to conduct that war."

"Fascinating," said Althea, "did they have lady warriors back then, too?"

"I would suppose they must have," said Leofric. "I'm told it's not unknown here."

"Why don't we have them in Weldwyn?" asked Althea.

Queen Igraine smiled, "That is simply not our tradition, dear. Women in Weldwyn are not trained to fight."

"Why not?" pressed Edwina.

"They are more suited to less demanding roles," offered Leofric.

Althea looked at him with defiance, a look he was becoming all too familiar with recently. "Perhaps it's time we changed that," she said.

"Let's concentrate on the visit here first, shall we?" suggested the king.

"Yes," agreed Igraine. "Now, remember to mind your manners. They have different traditions here in Merceria, and we don't want to cause offense."

Leofric sat back, closing his eyes and listening to the clack of the wheels and the nearby sounds of horseshoes on stone.

"We must be close," he observed, "the sounds are different."

Igraine looked out the window again. "The houses are much nicer looking, and the streets are wider," she said. "Oh, it's quite pleasant here."

"We must be in the wealthier part of town," noted the king.

He heard the distinctive sound of the marshal calling out to the guards, and then they rolled through an ornate metal gate, entering the Palace grounds. The carriage soon halted, and then Alric was there, opening the door.

"Father," he said, "Mother, welcome to the Palace."

Leofric stepped down from the carriage to be greeted by horns sounding his arrival. He held his hand out, allowing his queen to follow. Guards were there, and he was pleased to see his son's men on one side while the Mercerians were on the other.

Casting his eyes towards the Palace itself, he noticed Anna standing there with her massive hound beside her, along with Gerald.

"Tempus!" called out Edwina, eliciting a bark from the mighty beast.

The king's two youngest children exited the carriage, falling in behind their parents while Alric led them towards the reigning Monarch of Merceria.

"Your Majesties," said Anna in greeting, "it is so good to see you both."

"The pleasure is all ours," said Leofric, bowing slightly.

Queen Igraine, apparently more overcome with emotion, moved closer, embracing the young queen. The guards looked fearful, but a wave from the marshal's hand soon put them at ease.

"It's so good to see you," said Igraine, "and look at this place, it's simply marvellous!"

"Thank you," said Anna. "Now, shall we go inside? I thought we might share a private meal and allow you to settle in before you meet all the nobles."

"An excellent idea," said Igraine, "don't you think so, dear?"

"Yes, very fine," said Leofric.

Edwina moved forward, fascinated by Tempus, who simply wagged his tail.

"He remembers you," offered Gerald.

"He does?" said Edwina. "Can I pet him?"

"Of course," said Anna, "he likes you."

The princess reached forward, placing her hand gingerly on his head. Tempus sat still the entire time, his tail wagging up a storm.

"Let's go inside, shall we?" said Anna.

Gerald turned, nodding to one of the servants. The doors opened, and they all made their way inside.

Gerald reached across the table, selecting a thick cut of meat and dropping it onto his plate.

"This beef is quite good," he commented.

"Yes," agreed King Leofric, "and very tender."

"It's a special recipe of the Palace cook," said Anna. "I'm led to believe it was a favourite of King Andred."

"Your father?" asked Leofric.

"I count Gerald as my father," said Anna. "King Andred was loath to acknowledge me."

"Was it not he that sent you to Weldwyn?" asked Igraine.

"It was," Anna replied, "but that was simply politics. The king's mistress wanted me out of the way so that she could advance her plans."

"Ah, yes," said Leofric, "the Dark Queen. Whatever happened to her?"

"I'm afraid she escaped," said Gerald, "though we tried hard to stop her."

"Well," said Igraine, "at least her plans were foiled. Let's hope she's learned her lesson, and we'll never see her again."

"I doubt that," said Anna. "She took my sister Margaret with her."

"Oh, dear," said Igraine, "I had no idea."

"What will you do about it?" asked Althea.

"There's nothing that we can do," said Anna, "but our guards are always on alert, and we watch our borders carefully."

"Well," said Leofric, "you won't have to watch the Weldwyn border for much longer. Once we're allies, we can both redeploy troops to more troublesome areas."

"I look forward to it," said Gerald.

"Tell me," said the king, "how is life as a duke?"

"Rather strange," said Gerald. "I wasn't born to this life, and it's been quite an adjustment."

"I've heard the Weldwyn Embassy is quite large," the king remarked. "How did you arrange it on such short notice?"

"It was the duke's estate," said Alric. "I'm sure I told you that."

"I think I would have remembered," noted Leofric.

"But isn't that Gerald's home?" said Igraine.

"No," said Gerald, "I never wanted it. I live at the Palace, that's my home now."

"But with these two married, won't Alric live at the Palace?" asked Igraine.

"Of course," said Anna, "but we'll maintain the estate for your ambassador and his staff."

"An excellent idea," said Leofric. "You know I was talking to Tyrell Caracticus about a similar matter just before I left."

"Oh, yes?" said Anna. "I know him well, we've corresponded for years."

"He's the head of the mages, isn't he?" asked Gerald.

"No, he's the chief administrator," said the king. "He and I were discussing how we might work closer with Merceria in terms of magic. I understand you have a magic circle now."

"We have," said Anna, "and our mages are learning how to travel great distances using it."

"That's how I came to visit you," said Alric. "I had Albreda bring me to the Dome."

"I should think it beneficial to teach other mages this skill," noted Leofric.

"Of course," said Anna, "and I can assure you it's a priority, we've just been busy with the transition of power."

"I brought a couple of mages with me," said Leofric. "I thought that you might grant them access to this circle of yours?"

"Of course," said Anna. "I'll have Gerald inform the guards that they are allowed access."

"Guards?" said Igraine.

"Yes," said Anna. "We don't want undesirables studying our circle. It could be used against us."

"Undesirables?" said Althea.

"She means the Dark Queen or her people," said Gerald. "They've already tried to kill me and Anna."

"You mean Her Majesty," corrected Edwina.

Anna chuckled. "No," she said, "Gerald is allowed to call me Anna."

"Why is that?" asked the young princess.

"He raised me," Anna replied. "I consider him my father."

"But, I thought the king was your father?"

"Were you not listening earlier?" chided Althea. "Honestly, Edwina, sometimes I think you're as thick as a post."

"Children," said Igraine, "that's enough of that. What did I tell you about behaving?"

They both turned sullenly silent.

King Leofric looked at Gerald. "Was Queen Anna ever like this?"

In answer, Gerald looked at Anna, who waited for his reply.

"No," he said, "she was quite well behaved, although she did manage to steal pastries from the cook from time to time."

Anna blushed but still managed a smile.

"I must say," said Igraine, "that for someone with such informal training, you've done remarkably well for yourself."

"Mother!" said Alric.

"What?" said Igraine. "I meant no disrespect."

"You have just insulted my future bride!"

"It's all right," said Anna, "I know your mother meant no offense." She turned to the Queen of Weldwyn, "I never had a formal education, that much is true, but I've always been blessed with an outstanding memory. In some ways, it's a bit of a curse, but I can remember everything."

"You know," said Gerald, "King Andred once tried to send her a tutor."

"That's right," said Anna, "a weaselly man by the name of Renfrew."

"I can't imagine he would have been welcomed," said Alric.

"No," said Gerald, "he wasn't, but Anna put him in his place."

"What happened to the man?" asked Igraine.

"He's still in Uxley," said Anna, "living off a Royal Stipend."

"He ended up being a pretty decent fellow," said Gerald, "once he got over himself, that is."

"Yes," said Anna, "he proved most helpful when we ran across that ranger."

"I sense an interesting tale," said Leofric, "but I fear it shall have to wait on another day. The trip has been long, and we have two young princesses to put to bed."

"Father," said Althea, "I'm almost the same age as Queen Anna. I'm not a child anymore."

"Your father's right," said Anna, "and I, myself, am somewhat fatigued." She rose, signifying the end of the meal. "Alric, perhaps you'd like to escort your family to the estate?"

"Of course," the prince replied, "I would be delighted."

King Leofric rose, indicating that his family should do likewise. "The meal was most excellent," he said, "and the company delightful. I look forward to our next meeting, Your Majesty."

"As do I," said Anna.

Alric led his family from the room, leaving Anna, Gerald and Tempus behind.

"I'll let you get off to bed, then," said Gerald.

"I'm not tired," she said, "I was merely being polite."

"Very well," said Gerald, "then what do you say we take Tempus here for a late evening walk?"

Tempus sat up, his tail wagging once more.

Anna laughed. "Very well," she said, "the Palace gardens are particularly pleasing this time of year."

"Yes," Gerald agreed, "and safely guarded."

Alric led his father out to the courtyard. "Shall I call for a carriage?"

"It is a warm night," said Leofric, "let's walk, shall we?"

"Very well," said Alric as he nodded to the guards, who fell in behind the Weldwyn Royal Family. They exited the courtyard, into the street that ran the length of the Palace.

"It's only two blocks down," said Alric, "on the left. I had the baggage sent on ahead, and Jack is overseeing everything."

"You look fit," noted Leofric.

"I've been kept busy," Alric replied. He looked behind briefly to make sure his mother and sisters were following along.

"So I've heard. Tell me, how are they treating you?"

"Quite well," said the prince, "why do you ask?"

"You are an outsider here, Alric. Something that many will object to."

"You're speaking of the Mercerian nobles?"

"I am," Leofric confirmed. "You are in a precarious position, politically speaking. You must strive to find your place when you do not rule."

"I've been doing that my entire life," said Alric. "I've always been the third son."

"It is different now," the king continued. "Before, the Marshal, Gerald, was advising Queen Anna, but now you, as her husband, will need to take on that role."

"I will not stand between Anna and Gerald," said Alric, "they are family."

"No," said Leofric, "they are not, despite what they might say. Gerald is a commoner born and bred. He cannot fathom what it means to be a royal. You, on the other hand, have been a royal your entire life. When the queen needs advice, it should be you that she turns to."

"Anna has many advisors," protested Alric.

"True," said the king, "but only a few, I'll wager, that she can be honest with. She is a young queen, and she needs guidance."

"And you think that's now my responsibility?"

"Think of it, Alric. Who is my most trusted advisor?"

"Mother," the prince replied.

"Exactly. We are a team, you see. I can always count on your mother to support me through thick and thin. She will not betray me or try to usurp my powers, nor use my influence for political gain."

"And you think Gerald would?" said Alric.

"I think it inevitable," said Leofric. "I like the man, but he is out of his depth here in the capital."

"He is the Marshal of the Army," noted Alric, "and a very competent leader."

"I'm not talking about his military ability," said Leofric, "but rather his political power."

"He has NO political ambitions," said Alric.

"Are you sure of that?"

"Yes," Alric replied, "I know it for a fact."

"Then he is the exception," said Leofric. "Perchance I am wrong about him."

"Have you any other words of wisdom for me?"

"Yes," said Leofric, "but I do not wish to give offense."

"Then speak plainly," said Alric.

His father walked in silence for a few steps as he framed his words. Alric looked behind to see his mother and sisters, trailing along at some distance, chatting with the guards.

"It is quite clear that you and Anna are fond of each other," the king said at last.

"We love each other," Alric declared.

"Of course," Leofric continued, "but the passion of youth fades with age."

"Just because your passion faded, doesn't mean that ours will," said Alric. "I love Anna, and I always will. Any further discussion on the matter will get you nowhere."

"I apologize, my boy, I merely meant that you must find something to give you a purpose."

"I already have," said Alric.

"You have?" said Leofric. "You should have said so earlier, instead of letting me ramble on at length. Tell me, what is this passion of yours?"

"I shall be helping with the army," said Alric.

"The army? What does that mean, exactly? Will you command it?"

"No, at least not right away. Gerald has promised to take me under his wing."

"Take you under his wing? You're a Royal Prince, Alric, you can't serve a commoner!"

Alric bristled, "He's not a commoner, he's a duke, and the marshal of the entire army, not to mention a veteran of countless battles. I can learn a lot from him."

"You're obviously quite fond of the man," said Leofric.

"As you would be if you knew him better," said Alric. "Gerald is a very humble man, and nothing I've seen has changed my opinion of him. He was a damn sight better to me than Cuthbert ever was."

"Let us not mention your brother," said Leofric. "The mere thought of his betrayal makes me sick."

"I'm sorry, Father. I know you took it hard when he died."

"It was not your fault, Alric, you did what had to be done."

The manor came into view, its well-lit gate manned by Weldwyn guards.

"I have lived a long life," said the king, "and seen more than you can imagine. I want a long and happy life for you, Alric, but I know people. The people of Merceria might like their queen at the moment, but they can be fickle creatures, one misstep, and the whole thing will come crashing down around her. You must watch over her and keep her safe."

"I shall be her eyes and ears," Alric promised.

"Good," said his father, "that is all that I ask."

As they drew closer to their destination, they noticed the two guards, wearing the blue surcoats of Weldwyn, standing watch by the gate.

"This is the manor I was telling you about," said Alric. "I think you'll find it quite luxurious."

"You're not coming in?" asked Leofric.

"I'll be along later," said Alric, "I have some things to attend to first. As you know, we're preparing for my wedding, and there's lots to be done."

"Very well," said Leofric, "but make sure you say goodnight to your mother. You know how she misses you."

The king left him, passing the guards who stood to attention at the gate. Queen Igraine and his sisters halted before him.

"Never mind him," said the queen, "he's just trying to be fatherly."

"I can appreciate that," said Alric, "but by the same token, I must find my own way."

His mother put her hand on his cheek, "You have grown so much, Alric. You're not the young lad that tried to avoid dancing at court anymore."

Alric kissed his mother on the cheek. "Good night, Mother."

Next, he turned to Althea and Edwina, "And as for you two, I'll see you in the morning."

"You will?" asked Althea.

"Of course," said Alric, "I have to show you Wincaster!"

FIVE

Word Arrives

Summer 964 MC

A nna took a bite of a pastry as she relaxed on a lounge chair, her feet propped up on a cushion while a book sat haphazardly across her lap. The fireplace in the Royal Suite kept her warm along with Gerald, who sat next to her with a tankard of cider while Tempus dozed at her side.

"What did you think of the dinner?" asked Anna.

"It was delicious," said Gerald. "One of the finer meals I've had of late."

Anna giggled, "No, I mean, how did the visit go, in your opinion."

"Well," he said, "I'm no expert, but it seemed to go well. Why? Is something bothering you?"

"I feel nervous for some reason," she confided.

"That's only natural," said Gerald. "After all, you're about to be married. I imagine it must be quite intimidating meeting Alric's parents."

"I've met them before, silly."

"Yes, but that was before you were engaged. Now, you want them to like you."

"I suppose I do," she confessed.

"They already like you, Anna. If they didn't, they wouldn't have agreed to the wedding. That was a masterful stroke, by the way."

"What was?"

"Telling everyone you were tired," said Gerald.

"I felt sorry for Alric's sisters," said Anna. "They must feel so out of their depth here in Merceria."

"Then we'll just have to make them feel welcome."

"Did you make sure to invite them to the wedding ball?" asked Anna.

"I did," said Gerald, "and I went out of my way to find some other guests their ages as well."

The door opened, revealing Sophie. "Lady Beverly to see you, Your Majesty."

"Beverly?" said Anna. "She wasn't supposed to be back until tomorrow."

"She said it was important," said Sophie.

Anna looked at Gerald, who simply shrugged.

"Send her in," said Anna.

Sophie beckoned the knight forward.

"Your Majesty," said Beverly, "I bring word from the north."

"Please tell me it's not an invasion," said Anna.

"It's not," said Beverly, "but it is strange news."

Anna sat up, her book all but forgotten. "Strange, is it? You have me intrigued."

"We have been approached by a Norland delegation," explained Beverly. "They wish to negotiate a lasting peace with Merceria."

"Peace?" said Anna. "Are you sure?"

"Their envoy was most emphatic," said the knight, consulting her notes. "His name is Lord Wilfrid, and he claims to be a close advisor to King Halfan of Norland."

"Did he mention any details?" asked Anna.

"He wishes to meet with you in person, Your Majesty."

"Where is he now?"

"In Wickfield," said Beverly. "Sir Heward is keeping an eye on him, along with his entourage."

"We shall have to bring them to Wincaster," said Anna.

"By using recall?" suggested Gerald.

"No," said Anna, "let's keep that to ourselves for the time being."

"Do you wish me to escort them?" asked Beverly.

"Yes," said Anna, "but I'm afraid it means you'll miss the wedding."

"Then who will lead the procession?" the knight asked.

"I'll have Hayley take your place," said Anna. "I'd prefer you to look after things with this delegation. Have Aubrey recall you to Hawksburg, along with a few of the Guard Cavalry. From there, you can ride to Wickfield to meet these Norlanders."

"And then I escort them back to Wincaster?"

"Yes," said Anna, "but make sure nothing is said of the gates. How long will that take, do you think?"

"A week to ten days," said Beverly, "depending on the Norlander's horses."

"Very well," said Anna. "Send a rider off when you reach Uxley so we can arrange a welcome for them."

"I'll leave immediately," said Beverly.

"The morning will do," said Anna. "I know Aubrey will have used a fair amount of energy taking you to Hawksburg and back, best if she's had time to rest first."

"Yes, Your Majesty."

"I'm sorry it interfered with your visit to Hawksburg," said Anna, "I know you were looking forward to it."

"There'll be plenty of time for that in the future," said Beverly.

"Get some rest. It'll be a long day tomorrow," said the queen.

Beverly bowed, then exited, leaving Anna to ponder the situation.

"That was unexpected," said Gerald.

"Yes," said Anna, "but I can't help but wonder if something else is going on here."

"A trap of some sort?"

"Possibly," Anna replied, "but the timing is interesting."

"You don't think they knew about the wedding, do you?" asked Gerald.

"I think it's precisely the reason for their visit," she responded. "A Merceria-Weldwyn alliance would be a threat to them. They likely want peace before we send an army."

"Are we sending an army?"

"No, not unless they give us cause. We will treat this envoy with all proper courtesy and respect. If it is a legitimate attempt at peace, we will welcome it."

"And how do we tell if it's real?"

"That's the difficult part," she said. "I'll have to give it some thought."

"Is there some way we could use magic to our advantage?" asked Gerald.

"How?"

"I don't know. Can Aubrey use a spell to tell if someone is lying?"

"Not that I know of," said Anna, "and in any case, we can't just have her walk up to the envoy and cast a spell. That would be seen as a hostile move. We shall have to learn the character of this Lord Wilfrid fellow."

"And if he's a pawn?" asked Gerald.

"Then there's little we can do about it. We'll just have to trust him."

"That's putting a lot of trust in a stranger."

"It is," she agreed, "but it wouldn't be the first time. We were in the same situation when we visited Weldwyn, and that turned out well for us. We'll just have to hope for the best."

"And prepare for the worst," added Gerald.

"See," said Anna, "I knew I could count on you to help think things through."

Gerald smiled, "So, what precautions do we take?"

"We shall keep our mages secret for now, and no mention of the recall spell."

"We can't just hide them away," said Gerald, "their names are bound to come up."

"True," she agreed, "but we'll refrain from talking about their capabilities. The less they know about our mages, the better."

"Very well, I'll pass the word. Anything else?"

"Yes," she continued, "we'll have them escorted everywhere they go, I don't want them poking their noses in where they're not wanted."

"Will we put them up in the Palace?" asked Gerald.

"No, they're not due for over a week. I have a feeling King Leofric will be gone by then, in which case we'll host them at the Weldwyn Embassy. I'm sure Alric wouldn't mind."

"It sounds like you've thought of everything," he said.

"Not quite," she responded, "but by tomorrow night, I'll have it all sorted out."

Tyrell Caracticus, High Mage of Weldwyn, sat at a table, perusing a tome that was set before him. He was in the great casting room of the Grand Edifice of the Arcane Wizards Council, better known as 'the Dome', for its enchanted copper roof.

He was turning a page, intent on his studies when one of the runes inlaid into the stone floor suddenly glowed. Looking up in surprise, he noticed as others began to light up, and then the entire circle started to hum with energy. Suddenly, a cylinder of light sprang up, blocking his view of the circle's centre, then it dissipated, revealing a woman, who staggered slightly.

"Mistress Albreda?" said Tyrell.

Albreda fell to her knees, steadying herself by placing a hand upon the floor.

"Are you all right?" he called out in concern.

"I'll be fine," the druid replied, "I'm just short of energy."

"Why?" he asked. "What's happened?"

"I have just recalled from Wincaster," she said.

"Wincaster? But that must be close to five hundred miles?"

"More like four hundred and fifty, actually," she replied. "I wasn't sure if I'd be able to do it."

"Come and sit down," said Tyrell. "I'll have someone fetch you something to eat. You need to replenish your strength."

He walked over to her, offering his arm for support, a gesture that she welcomed. Albreda let him lead her to the table where she sat down heavily.

"That was quite remarkable," he said.

"I would have found it easier a year or two ago," she explained, "but I gave up part of my magical energy when I empowered Nature's Fury."

"Nature's Fury?" said Tyrell. "What's that?"

"A weapon of great power," she explained. "It now holds the magic of the earth."

"I hope it's in the possession of someone worthy," said Tyrell. "I'd hate to think what such a weapon could do in the wrong hands."

"Have no fear on that score," said Albreda. "Lady Beverly is more than deserving of such a creation."

"I take it, it's a hammer?"

"Yes," she said, "how did you know?"

"Earth weapons always seem to be such. I think it's the Dwarven influence. Might I ask who fashioned it?"

"A very unique smith named Aldwin," said Albreda, "who also happens to be Lady Beverly's husband."

"How curious," said Tyrell. "Was this before or after he made Nature's Fury?"

"They were married after," she replied. "He also helped us create the circle in Wincaster, though I now wish we'd put a higher empowerment on it. I could have used the extra boost."

"Ah," said Tyrell, "but then the mage that empowered it would be depleted even further."

"I suppose there is that," said Albreda. "Oh well, I shall just have to return to my studies and increase my power once more. Then again, perhaps I'm getting too old for all of this."

"Nonsense," said Tyrell, "with age comes wisdom. Are you not the most powerful mage in Merceria?"

"Possibly," she replied, "but I don't feel like it at this precise moment. Quite frankly, I'm more inclined to take a nap."

"I can arrange a room for you if you like," said Tyrell, "but first tell me, why did you come?"

"To find out about magic mirrors," she said. "Have you anyone with such expertise?"

"You'd have to speak to Gretchen Harwell," he said. "She's the expert in enchantments. Shall I go and fetch her for you?"

"She's here?" asked Albreda.

"Yes, I saw her only this morning. She's been practising her recall. When I noticed the circle lighting up, I half expected her to arrive. Instead, it was you."

"If you would be so kind," she said. "I need to talk to her with some urgency."

"Very well," said Tyrell, "I'll send a servant to fetch you some food while I hunt down Gretchen."

"Thank you," said Albreda, "that will do nicely."

Tyrell made his way from the room, turning into the circular corridor that ran around the perimeter of the building. Apprentices watched in fascination as the Grand Mage rushed past, intent on some task that likely was beyond their understanding.

Gretchen Harwell was sitting in a small study room, sipping soup from a bowl set before her. She looked up as the door opened, revealing the Dome's head administrator.

"Something wrong, Tyrell?" she asked.

"Albreda has returned," he said.

"The Wild Mage?"

"Yes," he continued, "and she wants to see you."

"Me? I thought she was an Earth Mage? Wouldn't Aegryth be of more use to her."

"Aegryth is with the king, as you well know," said Tyrell. "And in any case, she's here to find out about magic mirrors, not Earth Magic."

"Mirrors?" Said Gretchen. "Now you have my attention. Lead on and be quick about it."

"But your soup?" said Tyrell.

"My soup can wait until later," she said. "This promises to be of much greater interest."

She pushed the bowl away from her, then rose and smoothed down the front of her dress. "Where is she?" she asked.

"In the casting room," said Tyrell. "Shall I take you there?"

"I think I'm more than capable of finding my own way," said Gretchen, "unless, of course, you're interested in what she might have to say?"

"The thought had crossed my mind," said Tyrell.

"Well, come along then," she said, pushing past him, "we haven't a moment to waste."

Tyrell rushed to catch up. Despite Gretchen's small stature, she set a brisk pace. They arrived to find Albreda eating some bread.

"One of your apprentices just dropped this off," she said. "I hope you don't mind."

"Not at all," said Tyrell. He pointed to his companion. "This is Gretchen Harwell, the Enchanter I told you about."

"Pleased to meet you, I am Albreda, Mistress of the Whitewood."

Gretchen stared at her a moment.

"Something wrong?" asked Albreda.

"Sorry, I've just never met a wild mage before," said Gretchen.

"Don't worry," said the druid, "I don't bite...much." The look of worry on the Enchanter's face told her all she needed to know. "Sorry," said Albreda, "it was merely a jest. I'm much like any of you. Come, sit, we have much to discuss, you and I."

Gretchen pulled out a chair opposite, sitting and watching as Albreda rooted through a small satchel.

"I have it here somewhere," the druid muttered. "Ah, here it is." She pulled forth a paper, depositing it on the table after unfolding it.

"This is a sketch I had made of the mirror in question."

Gretchen turned the paper to examine it in detail. "This is quite good," she said. "Is it accurate?"

"Yes," said Albreda, "I had Lady Aubrey make it. It shows a mirror that was found in the residence of Revi Bloom."

"The Royal Life Mage?" said Gretchen. "If it was his, then surely he could tell you more."

"I wish it were that easy," said Albreda, "but the truth is that Master Revi has disappeared. We think he used this mirror to travel somewhere."

"Where?"

"Well, if we knew that, I wouldn't be here now. We were hoping you might give us some insight."

Gretchen pointed at the ornate border of the mirror. "These runes are the key," she said. "If we can determine the order of activation, it should be a simple matter to follow."

"Yes," said Albreda, "but how do we go about doing that? The number of possible combinations is unimaginable."

"It's not quite as complex as you might think," said Gretchen. "There's usually what we call a preamble."

"A preamble? What's that?" asked Albreda.

"It's a small sequence of runes that wakes the magic up, so to speak. Typically, it's only three or four magical letters."

"Are these standard?"

"There are a few variations, but the creators of these objects often get lazy. As a consequence, there are only seven preambles, at least as far as I know."

"Shall I get some paper and ink?" offered Tyrell.

"Yes, thank you," said Gretchen. She returned her attention to the drawing. "This scrollwork around the edge is most unique. I don't think I've seen it's like before. What is the frame made of? Metal?"

"No," said Albreda, "it's wood. Something called shadowbark. I'm not familiar with it myself, are you?"

"I've heard of shadowbark, but I believe it's only found on the Continent. That being the case, I would surmise that this mirror is very old."

"Magic circles have a maker's mark," said Albreda. "Is the same true of mirrors like this?"

"Quite possibly," said Gretchen, "though I doubt that would help, our records from the Continent are woefully inadequate. In any case, once Tyrell gets back, I'll write down the preambles for you. It shouldn't take long to try them."

"And then?" asked Albreda. "How do we continue?"

"Once the preamble is complete, the runes will glow briefly. Pay attention to those whose light lingers, they will be the key runes. After that, you simply have to try them in combinations."

"You make it sound easy," said Albreda.

"It's still time consuming," said Gretchen, "but the number of possible combinations is greatly reduced. You also have to wait for a time before trying to activate them again."

"How much time?"

"It varies," said Gretchen, "but typically, the magic of the runes lingers for a little while, so you have to let it dissipate before you try another combination. Otherwise, it will think it's a continuation of the original sequence."

"I don't suppose I could convince you to return to Wincaster with me?" said Albreda.

Gretchen sat back in surprise. "Me? Go to Wincaster?"

"Why not? Tyrell tells me you've been practising the spell of recall."

"Why not, indeed," said Gretchen. "You know, I think I just might take you up on that offer, this mirror sounds fascinating. When would we leave?"

"Not until tomorrow," said Albreda. "I used up most of my power getting here, and I need to rest and recover."

"Then you're going to need something a little more filling than bread," said Gretchen. "Come on, I'll take you to a nice tavern that's close by. They have a delicious stew they serve about this time of day."

"Excellent," said Albreda, as she started folding up the drawing, "then let's get going."

Aubrey stood in the middle of the Wincaster circle as Beverly brought Lighting in by the reins. Behind her, two men followed, each leading their own mounts.

"Are you sure you can do this?" asked Beverly. "We've never taken so many horses before."

"Three horses along with the riders? I should be able to handle it."

"And if not?" asked Beverly.

"Then the spell simply won't work. Don't worry, we don't just disappear or anything. I'll know as soon as I begin the ritual. Once we're through, I'll return and bring the others."

"Won't that tire you?"

"It will, but I can rest up at Hawksburg once I'm done."

"But yesterday, you were tired just taking Aldwin and me."

"Yes," said Aubrey, "but I'd been casting all day, I didn't have much energy left. Today, I'm well-rested and ready to go. Mind you, I'll likely end up sleeping half the afternoon away, but you'll be on your way with a small escort."

"Very well," said Beverly, "where do you want us to stand?"

"Bring the horses closer," said Aubrey, "and make sure they're inside the circle, or they'll be left behind."

Once they were close enough, Lightning stood calmly, but the other two looked nervous.

"Cover their eyes," suggested Aubrey. "It will help if they can't see the light when I cast."

The horsemen did as they were bid, then Aubrey began casting the spell. She raised her arms and closed her eyes as the words of power started issuing from her mouth. One by one, the inlaid magic runes began to glow, and then a cylinder of light rose from the circle, blocking their view of the rest of the chamber. Moments later, it rescinded, revealing the wooden structure of the old Hawksburg manor.

"All done," said Aubrey.

The horsemen walked their mounts from the circle and up the ramp that led outside. Lightning, likely sensing that he was near the place of his birth, simply swished his tail and nuzzled into Beverly.

"You're getting faster at this," said Beverly.

"Am I?" said Aubrey. "That surprises me. I just assumed it always took the same amount of time to cast."

"The words seemed to spill out faster," said Beverly.

"I suppose that's just because I've cast it so many times."

"How soon till you return?" asked Beverly.

"I'll come up to the manor and have a light snack, then I'll return to Wincaster. I should have the other riders here before too long. Don't worry, you'll have a dozen riders by morning."

"A dozen?" said Beverly. "But that's four trips. You'll be dead tired!"

"Yes, cousin, but then I'll be able to sleep away the rest of tomorrow."

"Will you be back in time for the wedding?"

"Of course. Now go and see to your men, their horses are likely feeling a little disoriented."

"Very well," said Beverly, "but you keep a close eye on your energy levels. I don't need you collapsing out of exhaustion."

"Don't worry," said Aubrey, "I'll be fine."

She waited as Beverly led Lighting up the ramp, then followed, deep in thought. As she reached the top, she noticed Kraloch. The old Orc shaman was a constant fixture here at Hawksburg, and he was bearing a small tray as he came towards her.

"When word came that the circle was lit, I knew it would be you. Here, I have brought you some food."

"Thank you, Kraloch," she said, picking a strawberry from the tray.

"I take it, you have news?" asked Kraloch.

"Yes," said Aubrey. "Beverly is riding to Wickfield in the morning, along with an escort."

"So Queen Anna has agreed to meet with the Norlanders?"

"She has," said Aubrey, "but we brought your concerns to her, and I can assure you that she hasn't forgotten the Orcs."

"Thank you," said Kraloch, "that couldn't have been easy."

"Truthfully, it was very easy," said Aubrey. "It's never been a problem talking to the queen."

"That is because she is your friend," said Kraloch.

"So are you," said Aubrey. "Speaking of which, how would you like to learn the spell of recall?"

"Right now?" he said. "You surprise me."

"I have an ulterior motive," she said. "With you helping, I can transport the other riders much quicker."

"Very well," he said, "where shall we begin?"

"First, I will finish eating this," she said, taking the tray from his hands. "Then, I will show you how to commit the Hawksburg circle to memory."

SIX

The Royal Wedding

Summer 964 MC

Gerald walked down the corridor, a spring in his step, while Tempus padded along beside him. He paused at the double doors as one of the guards standing there knocked on his behalf. The door opened to reveal Sophie smiling at the sight of the old warrior.

"Is the bride ready?" asked Gerald.

"Almost," said Sophie, "I just have to adjust her hair."

"Why," said Gerald, "I thought it was all done?"

"It's the crown, it won't sit properly."

"It's my fault," called out Anna. "I forgot all about the silly thing."

"You'd best come in," said Sophie, opening the door the rest of the way.

Anna sat on a low-backed chair, looking radiant in her formal wedding dress. The warrior's crown, however, was balanced precariously upon her head at an unusual angle.

"It seems the Kings of Merceria all had big heads," said Anna, trying to straighten it yet again.

Gerald moved closer, walking around her to examine the problem in more detail.

"I don't suppose you could do without it?" he enquired.

"No," said Anna, "not with King Leofric and Queen Igraine in attendance. How would it look?"

"You'll have to change your hair, then," he decided. "Maybe, instead of piling it all up, you could somehow wrap it around the top of your head, then the crown could sit upon that?"

"Could you do that, Sophie?" asked Anna.

"Let's see, shall we," said the maid. She began undoing the ornate hair, carefully removing the metal pins.

"What are those?" asked Gerald.

Sophie held one up, "These? They're hairpins. We use them to hold the hair in place. Have you never seen one before?"

"Why would I have ever seen them?" he responded.

"He has a point," said Anna. "It's not as if he would have used them himself."

"Yes," agreed Gerald, "and my wife would just braid her hair."

"What was she like?" wondered Anna.

"She was wonderful," said Gerald. "You would have liked Meredith. She was so full of life."

Anna turned to Sophie, "She saved his life, you know."

"I sense a story here," said Sophie as she combed out Anna's hair.

"It's not much of a story," said Gerald, blushing. "She jumped on the back of a raider to save me."

"After Gerald attacked the man with a knife," added Anna.

"Well, he is a warrior," said Sophie, intent on her job.

"Yes," said Anna, "but he was only thirteen at the time, weren't you, Gerald?"

"That's true." He watched as Sophie laid down the brush, then handed him the crown and began rearranging Anna's hair.

He felt the iron in his hands, noting the dents and scratches that had accumulated over the years. It truly was a warrior's crown and had been worn in numerous battles.

"It really is quite heavy," he said.

"Even more so when it's been in place for some time," said Anna. "I swear I must be shorter after wearing it for official ceremonies."

"You should have a new one made," he said.

"A new one?" said Anna.

"Yes, there's no reason why you can't have more than one crown. This could be used for coronations, but why not make a smaller one for other occasions? Something lighter, perhaps."

"That's an excellent idea," said Anna, "though I think it'll be some time before we can afford it."

"I thought the treasury was doing well?" he said.

"'Well' is a relative term," she said. "We're no longer spending more than what's coming in, but there's not much in reserve. Thankfully, trade will increase now that the river's been cleared by the Trolls, but we likely won't see any of that till next year."

"At least we have peace," said Gerald.

A knock on the door interrupted them.

"Who is it?" called out Anna.

"The Master of Heralds," came the reply.

"I'll get it," said Gerald as he strode to the door, opening it to see the man standing before him.

"Something wrong?" asked Gerald.

"I was just about to ask the same thing," said the Herald. "The ceremony is waiting on the queen."

Gerald glanced back at Sophie, who, just finishing pinning Anna's hair in place, looked at him expectantly. He wondered what was wrong.

"The crown?" said Sophie.

"Oh, yes," said Gerald. He stepped closer, handing it back to the maid, who placed it firmly upon Anna's head.

"There we go," she announced, "all done, Your Majesty."

Anna rose, looking very regal.

"Please inform the Master of Heralds that we are ready," said the queen.

Gerald turned to address the man, but he nodded his understanding and was already striding down the hall to announce his news.

"Shall we begin?" asked Anna.

Gerald took his position to her right, holding out his arm for her to place her hand upon. Sophie held the door open, while the great mastiff watched intently.

"Come along, Sophie," said Anna. "You too, Tempus."

Gerald led her out into the hallway, while Tempus and Sophie followed. The guards at the door stood to attention as she passed, but Anna's eyes were on the distant corridor that led to the great hall.

The ceremony, of course, would be held in Wincaster's Cathedral, but the wedding party would assemble at the Palace first. The doors opened at their approach, revealing a small group of people. By tradition, the bride's family would have been present, but Anna, having no blood relatives remaining in Merceria, had opted to have her friends stand-in.

Lady Aubrey Brandon was the first to greet her, bowing respectfully. "Your Majesty," she said, "you look quite lovely."

"Thank you, Aubrey," said Anna. "It feels so good to have you here. I'm sorry Beverly couldn't be here as well, but events in the north needed her attention."

"Understandable," said Aubrey, "but Aldwin is here, along with Lord Richard."

"And Hayley?" asked Anna.

"Outside with the escort," said Aubrey. "We had to make a few minor adjustments for Beverly's absence."

Lord Richard bowed gracefully, extending his leg in the old-fashioned way. "Your Majesty," he said, "our best wishes to you this day."

"Thank you, Baron," said Anna. "Has Albreda returned from Summersgate?"

"She has," said Fitz, "but not, I fear, in time to greet you this morning. Rest assured, though, she will join us at the Cathedral."

Anna moved further into the room where the grey-eyed young man looked out of place.

"Lord Aldwin," said Anna, "I'm sorry Beverly couldn't be here. I trust you're well?"

"I am, Your Majesty," said the smith, "though I'm still not sure why I'm here."

"You're Beverly's husband," said the queen, "and as such, I consider you family. Don't look so worried, I shan't expect you to give a speech."

Aldwin looked relieved, "Thank you, Your Majesty."

"Where is Lord Arnim?" Anna called out.

"Here, Majesty," came the knight's voice. He approached, leading his wife, Lady Nicole.

"How are the twins?" asked the queen.

"They are both doing well," said Nicole. "Thank you for asking."

"I hear there was an incident at the birth," said Gerald.

"Oh," said Anna, "do tell."

Arnim blushed, "It was nothing, Majesty."

"That's not what I heard," said Gerald.

Anna turned to Nicole. "Would you care to explain, Nikki?"

Lady Nicole beamed, "It seems my husband, fearless warrior that he is, took the birth of twins in a very unexpected way."

"What way is that?" asked Anna.

"He fainted!" she replied.

Anna laughed while Lord Arnim turned beet red. "It was the shock," he mumbled.

"And so," said Gerald, "instead a son, you have both a son and daughter!"

"You look very happy," Anna said to Nikki.

"It's what I've always wanted," said Nicole, "but today is about you, Majesty, not us and our children."

"So it is," said Gerald, "and we need to keep moving if we're to make it to the Cathedral in time."

"Nonsense," said Anna, "it's not as if they can have the ceremony without me."

"Might I remind you that Alric is also waiting?"

Anna paused for a moment. "So he is," she finally said. "Very well, let us be on our way."

Gerald nodded to the Master of Heralds, who stood nearby. At his command, horns sounded announcing Queen Anna was soon to exit the Palace. Guards opened the doors to the great hall, and they walked out into the courtyard where the carriages waited.

Anna climbed into the most ornate of these, Tempus jumping up to sit at her feet. Gerald helped Sophie in, then climbed up to sit opposite Anna.

"Well," he said, a tear coming to his eyes, "here we are. Who would have thought, all those years ago, that we'd end up here?"

She leaned forward, grasping his hand. "We got here together, Gerald. I couldn't have done it without you."

"I shall miss you," he said.

"Miss me? I'm not going anywhere," she said. "Nor are you. You'll still be living at the Palace, and I'm just next door."

"Yes," he said, "but you'll be married. I doubt you'll have time for me."

"Nonsense," she said, "and besides, once Alric and I are finally married, we'll have children, and they'll need their grandfather."

Gerald could feel the emotions welling within him, and, conscious of those around them, he coughed to hide his embarrassment.

"I'm so proud of you," he said at last.

"As I am of you," she said. "As I said before, I wouldn't be here if it wasn't for you."

She sat back as the carriage began moving.

"I wonder if Alric is as nervous as I am?" said Anna.

"Likely," offered Gerald.

They rolled out of the courtyard, past the iron gates that stood open. A formation of horsemen waited beyond, Hayley at their head. The high ranger gave the command, and the riders started moving, clearing the way for the Royal Procession to follow.

"How odd to see Hayley wearing knightly armour," said Gerald. "I still think of her as a ranger."

"And so she is," said Anna, "but she's also a Knight of the Hound."

"Yes," said Gerald, "and she was only the second person to be inducted. It seems like a lifetime ago."

"It does, doesn't it," said Anna.

Cheering erupted from the gathered crowd as they made their way south. Gerald couldn't help but smile, for the people of Wincaster loved their queen. He saw the waving flags, the red bar over the green, and a thought came to him.

"We're still flying the rebel flag," he said.

"Yes," said Anna, "but it's our flag now."

"But red signifies rebellion."

"Yes, it does, and it shall always serve to remind us of the terrible cost of lives we paid to restore the kingdom. I intend to keep the flag as it is."

He smiled, "No wonder the people love you."

"Yes," she replied, "but as many have said before, the people can be fickle. I'm popular now, but I must keep their interests close to my heart or I might lose their loyalty forever."

"You'll do right by them," said Gerald.

"I'll certainly try," she agreed, "and with people like you beside me, I know we can make a difference in their lives."

Distant horns sounded, announcing that Alric and his procession were about to leave the Weldwyn Embassy.

"Shouldn't be much farther now," said Gerald.

Anna peered behind them, but the procession of carriages following hid any view of her soon to be husband.

"I think every carriage in Wincaster is here," she said.

"Yes, and why not? It's not every day that someone gets to ride in a Royal Procession like this."

Anna waved as they passed by the commoners. Gerald fell silent, enjoying the look of utter bliss upon her face.

Eventually, the procession turned westward, and Gerald's thoughts turned to memories of her coronation. The route, of course, was the very same, but somehow there were even more people in attendance today. He spotted Weldwyn troops among the Mercerian soldiers that lined the road, keeping the commoners at bay. It was good to have allies, he thought.

As the Cathedral came into view, the carriage slowed, for the square before the great edifice was overrun with well-wishers, and the cavalry struggled to push them back.

"This doesn't look good," said Gerald, as they stopped entirely. "What do we do now?"

Anna suddenly stood up. "We walk," she announced.

"Walk?" said Gerald.

"Unless you have another way of getting there?" said Anna. She turned to her maid, "Sophie, I'll need you to watch the back of my dress, so I don't trip."

"Yes, Majesty."

As Gerald stood to get a better view of the crowd, he spotted Hayley's aide, Gorath, and waved him over.

"Yes, Marshal?" the Orc called out over the roar of the crowd.

"Gather some troops," said Gerald, "the queen will walk to the Cathedral."

"Certainly," replied Gorath.

He pushed his way through the crowd, heading for some nearby soldiers while Anna waved to the commoners. Gorath soon reappeared, a dozen soldiers and four Orcs following.

"Orcs in front," said Gerald, "so we can keep the commoners at bay. Soldiers to either side of the queen, and four to the rear."

"Yes, Marshal," replied Gorath.

They took up positions beside the carriage and waited as Anna descended. Tempus, excited by the crowd, let out a howl that cut through the noise, announcing to everyone that the queen was present.

Gerald climbed down, taking Anna's arm and waited while Sophie saw to Anna's dress, lifting the train to keep the queen from tripping.

Anna nodded, and the small group began making their way down the street. They were soon joined by Sir Preston, the newest Knight of the Hound.

"Dame Hayley sent me," the knight explained, yelling loudly.

"You mean Lady Hayley," corrected Gerald. "She's a baroness now, remember?"

Sir Preston moved closer, obviously having difficulty hearing over the roar of the crowd.

"Pardon?" he called out.

"Never mind," said Gerald, at a loss as to how to be heard.

They moved slowly, the well-wishers backing off respectfully to allow them to pass. Finally, the entourage arrived at the Cathedral. Gerald let out a sigh of relief as they made their way into the atrium, and the noise of the crowd was muffled as the door was closed behind them.

"Well, I must say," said Gerald, "that was quite unexpected."

"Shall I let the Bishop Supreme know you're here?" asked Sir Preston.

"No," said Gerald, "let Gorath do that. We'll need you to lead the queen."

"Me?" said Sir Preston. "Isn't that Dame Hayley's responsibility?"

"The baroness," corrected Gerald, "is otherwise occupied, and we're already late as it is."

"Don't we have to wait on the prince?" said the knight.

"Alric is taking a different route," said Anna. "If all is going according to plan, he's already here."

Gerald moved to the door, the guard stepping aside to give him room to peer out into the Cathedral proper.

"Any sign of him?" she asked.

"I see him," said Gerald. "He's waiting up front."

"Very well," said Anna. "Gorath, if you'd be so kind?"

"Yes, Majesty," the Orc replied, slipping out the door.

Anna took up her position, smoothing away imaginary wrinkles on her dress. Gerald moved up beside her, his arm held out, as Sophie and Tempus fell in behind. The great beast, most likely sensing the solemnity of the occasion, was quiet for once, although his tail still wagged.

Horns sounded, and as the double doors swung open, a choir began to sing. Gerald led Anna down the nave to where Alric stood beside the Bishop Supreme. Jack Marlowe was there, standing beside his prince and looking quite proud, a grin splitting his features.

The onlookers fell silent as they drew close to the altar and then halted. Gerald looked on with wry amusement as everyone stared at the Bishop Supreme. The old warrior knew there had been a big discussion about the ceremony, for the Bishop Supreme had sent word to the queen. Never before had a reigning queen wed while she sat on the throne, and it had caused them no end of concern. It was not fitting for the ruler of Merceria to pledge obedience to a foreign prince, nor, had the Holy Man said, was it fitting that a Queen of Merceria be given away, even if it was only symbolic.

Anna had ended all discussion by ordering them to rework the cere- mony until she was satisfied with the results. Now the Bishop Supreme stood, shuffling his feet nervously as the choir ended their song. He stepped forward slightly, looking as if he was preparing to address the crowd.

"Who speaks for the bride?"

"I do, Lord Gerald Matheson, Duke of Wincaster."

"And do you pledge that she is strong, that Saxnor may see fit to support this union?"

Gerald drew his sword and knelt, placing it, point down before him, his hands on the pommel. "By all that is holy," he said, "I pledge that there is none stronger."

The Bishop Supreme nodded slightly, and Gerald rose, his knees protesting at the strain.

"And who deems the groom to be worthy," the Bishop Supreme called out.

Gerald's eyes moved to the front row of the magnificent Cathedral as a single man stood.

"I, King Leofric of Weldwyn, do pronounce him worthy."

"And is he strong?" asked the Bishop Supreme.

"He has the strength of Saxnor and the wisdom of Malin," replied the king.

Gerald saw a flicker of annoyance cross the Bishop Supreme's face, an action that also did not go unnoticed by Anna. The man had objected quite strongly to the inclusion of Malin in the ceremony but had relented under the insistence of the queen.

"The Gods have seen fit to bring these two people together," the man continued, "so let them now kneel in prayer."

Anna and Alric moved to stand before the Bishop Supreme. Alric drew his slender Weldwyn sword while Anna pulled forth her Dwarven short sword, its blade catching the morning light that was streaming through the windows.

Two children came forth, bearing cushions that they set before the Royal Couple, then disappeared from sight. Anna and Alric knelt, their swords before them, much as Gerald's had been.

They both took a breath, then Anna glanced briefly at Alric, who nodded, and together, they began to intone the prayer.

"Saxnor, bless us that we may find strength in this union, and we call upon Malin to grant us the wisdom to lead us forward."

"You may both rise," said the Bishop Supreme, again with that flicker of annoyance.

Gerald watched them get to their feet and scabbard their blades as the children reappeared, carrying off the cushions.

"We now call upon the gifts to be exchanged," intoned the Bishop Supreme.

Hayley, who had finally arrived, rose from her seat in the front row, a scabbard and sword held reverently in her arms. She halted before Anna, who took them, turning to Alric, a small smile playing upon her face.

"I give you this sword," she began, "that you may defend our hearth and home."

Alric raised his arms, allowing her to strap the belt around his waist. It was a little clumsy, for he now wore two swords, but he waited patiently as Anna finally completed the task, stepping back to admire her handiwork.

Hayley, her task now concluded, returned to her seat as Jack stepped forward, holding a ceremonial mace decorated with silver and gold and littered with jewels, which he handed to Prince Alric.

"I give you this mace," said Alric, "heirloom of the Royal House of Weldwyn, symbolic of the great trust between our people."

Anna took the mace, cradling it in her arms. They were both smiling now, though Gerald could still see some nervousness. They turned back to face the Bishop Supreme, who was holding a thin golden cord.

"Take each other's hand," the Holy Man requested.

Anna passed the mace to Gerald, then placed her hand in Alric's, extending them both before the Bishop Supreme, who then wrapped the cord around their entwined hands.

"Let this rope signify the holy bond that is formed this day. By the grace of Saxnor, I now pronounce the union of Prince Alric and Queen Anna of Merceria." He turned his head upward as if seeking some sign from above. "Erylor, Goddess of Fertility, we call upon you to bless this union, that the throne may endure!"

The choir erupted once more into song, their voices echoing throughout the Cathedral as Anna and Alric turned to face the gathered crowd.

Gerald waited for the hymn to end, then moved forward slightly, calling on his battle-hardened voice to be heard clearly.

"I give you, Her Majesty, Queen Anna," he proclaimed, "and Prince Alric of Merceria."

Gerald watched as a server set down a massive plate of meat onto the table. Beside him, Tempus, roused from his slumber, raised his head, sniffing the air.

"This is quite the meal," said King Leofric.

"Indeed, Your Majesty," said Baron Fitzwilliam. "I can't remember the last time we had such a fine feast."

"Wasn't the coronation just as festive?" asked the king.

"I'm afraid not," said Fitz. "The larders were quite bare as we were still recovering from the civil war."

"War can be harsh," said Leofric, "but this marriage has secured both our kingdoms from future aggression."

"Let us hope so," said the baron.

The king turned to Gerald, just as the old warrior was cutting off some meat.

"We need to discuss troop movements," said Leofric. "Now that this wedding is complete, we can move men from our joint border."

"Of course," said Gerald. "I have discussed the matter at some length with Lord Jack. We have all agreed that small garrisons should be maintained in Kingsford and Colbridge to keep the area free from bandits and such.

"Naturally," said Leofric, "and we will reduce our garrisons in Falford and Waldstock. I can use the troops in the west."

"Trouble with the Clans again?" asked Gerald.

"It is a constant problem," said the king.

"I thought you had their High King as insurance?"

"We do have King Dathen," said Leofric, "but the Twelve Clans are a fractious people. With his influence removed, I'm afraid they have fallen back into old habits."

"In that case," said Gerald, "I shall see if I can speed the process along. Do you need us to send you aid?"

"I think we can manage for now," said Leofric, "though I thank you for the offer. Things will be much easier on us now that we don't have to worry about our eastern border."

"Remember," said Gerald, "we have a defensive pact. Should they invade, you have only to inform us. Now that some of your mages can use the magic circle, we can maintain much closer ties."

King Leofric took a sip of wine, a smile creasing his face. "So we can!" he exclaimed. "I'd forgotten about the mages."

"And," interrupted Queen Igraine, "it means we can meet in person more often. I should very much like to see my grandchildren."

"Malin's tears," said Leofric, "give them some time, my dear, they haven't even been married a day."

"Don't you already have grandchildren?" asked Gerald. "I thought Alstan had been married for some time."

"He has been," said Igraine, "but Erylor has not seen fit to bless their union."

"It's not for lack of trying," said Leofric, "those two are as tight as-"

"Leofric!" said Igraine. "This is not the place to talk about such things."

Leofric looked chagrined. "My dear wife is quite right, of course. I apologize."

Igraine turned to look at the head of the table, where Alric and Anna were chatting with Lady Aubrey.

"They make such a handsome couple, don't you think?"

"They do," agreed Gerald.

"I'm curious," said Leofric, "when do you think they came to realize they were in love."

"It was pretty obvious when we left Weldwyn," said Gerald, "but I think they truly discovered each other in Loranguard. That whole business with Princess Brida seemed to push them together."

Leofric snorted. "Brida was no princess," he said, "and her father was no king!"

"He was High King of the Clans," Igraine reminded him.

"Yes, but only because they couldn't agree on anyone else. Have you met the man?"

"I can't say that I have," said Gerald.

"He's not the most original thinker," declared Leofric. "There's no way that he organized the invasion."

"Are you saying he's incompetent?" asked Gerald.

"He's certainly brave, I'll give him that, but I can't help but feel someone else did all the planning."

Gerald felt a sense of foreboding. "Someone else? Like who?"

"I don't know," said Leofric, "though I think his court mage might have had something to do with it. Unfortunately, he died in battle, so we may never know."

"And now you feel the Clans are getting anxious again?" asked Gerald.

"I could describe them no other way."

"You should move your troops as soon as possible," said Gerald. "It sounds like something's brewing."

"With the losses they took in the war," said Leofric, "I doubt they'd try that again anytime soon. Quite frankly, I'm more concerned about raiding than invasion."

"I think I have another way to free up your troops," offered Gerald.

"Oh?" said Leofric. "Do tell."

"I was thinking that you could move them away from your northern border."

"I can't," said the king, "we need to protect ourselves from the Orcs of the Greatwood."

"The Orcs are our allies," said Gerald, "as is Weldwyn now. They are also capable of communicating over great distances. I'm sure we can convince them to leave you alone if you recognize their right to the Netherwood."

"Netherwood?" said Leofric. "Where's that?"

"It's their name for the Greatwood," said Gerald.

"But what of our hunters?" said the king.

"We can help you work something out with the Orcs. I'd be happy to act as an intermediary if you wish."

"I'll take you up on that offer," said Leofric. "It'll also give us a bit more time in your wonderful city. Igraine does love seeing Alric again."

"I shouldn't wish to make you late to return," said Gerald.

"I've already decided to let the mages take us back."

"Through the magic circle?" said Gerald. "I thought you didn't approve of such things."

"I am learning to change my ways," said Leofric. "And Igraine likes the idea of being only a short trip away from Alric. He's always been her favourite."

"That's not true," said Igraine. "It's just that I don't see him much anymore."

"See what I mean?" said the king.

"Well, there would certainly be no objection here to more visits," said Gerald.

"You realize," said Igraine, "that using those mages means that Wincaster is now more accessible than any city in Weldwyn."

"It does," said Gerald, "though I hope you wouldn't travel unannounced. I'd hate for you to arrive without someone to welcome you."

"Fear not," said Leofric, "we'll give you plenty of notice."

"Can I convince you to inspect the troops while you're here?"

"Certainly," said the king. "I'm curious to see what actual Mercerian troops look like. The last time you visited us, you used our soldiers."

"Don't worry," said Gerald, "they're not much different than yours."

"Aside from the Orcs," said Igraine.

"Yes," said Gerald, "and the Elves, and Dwarves, and...come to think of it, they're quite a bit different."

SEVEN

The Delegates

Summer 964 MC

Beverly trotted Lightning through the gates of the Palace, coming to a halt just past the building's main entrance. Behind her, the carriage carrying the Norland delegation rolled to a stop.

She dismounted, passing the reins to a servant. Ordinarily, she would have seen to the massive horse herself, but presenting a foreign diplomat to the queen must take priority.

She watched the stable hand lead Lightning away, then turned to meet the Norland diplomat who was climbing down from the carriage.

"Lord Wilfrid," she said, "if you'll follow me, I'll take you to your quarters. We've arranged for you to stay at the Palace during your visit."

"That would be most wonderful. Thank you," the man replied, "though I am most eager to meet your queen."

"All in good time," said the knight. "Queen Anna wishes to allow you time to refresh yourself before I present you and your people at court."

"Very well," the man replied, "please lead on."

Beverly led him into the Palace where guards stood watch in the larger hallways, each wearing heavy armour, a fact that was not lost on the Norland delegates.

"Tell me," said Lord Wilfrid, "do you always have so many guards?"

"Only when we have important visitors," said Beverly. "Is it not so in Norland?"

"Hah!" he replied. "Norland has never had important visitors, at least not foreign ones."

"You have never welcomed your neighbours?"

"Merceria is our only neighbour," said Lord Wilfrid. "We are bordered on the north and east by mountains, and to the west lies nothing but wilderness and inhospitable terrain."

"I'm afraid I'm not familiar with the area," said Beverly, "though I'm sure the queen has learned as much as she can from our own sources."

"Sources which are, I'm sure, woefully inadequate to the task. Fear not, I meant no disrespect, for even our own scholars are in disagreement over what lies there."

"Has no one ever explored the region?" she asked.

"Many have tried," he said, "but few have returned, and those that did, talked of Trolls and Giants."

"Stories, I think, that Queen Anna will take great pleasure in hearing."

"We shall see," said Lord Wilfrid. "After all, I'm here at the behest of my king. I shouldn't like to detract from that duty."

Beverly led them upstairs. "We are now at the second-floor guest suites. This entire section has been allocated to you and your people. These guards will be here night and day, and can summon servants when needed."

The knight opened the door, revealing the opulent room beyond. "I hope you find the rooms to your satisfaction, my lord," said Beverly. "I shall send word when the queen is ready to receive you."

"Most generous of you," said Lord Wilfrid. "In the meantime, do you think some food might be arranged?"

"I shall have the kitchen send something up," she replied.

The Norlanders entered the room, closing the door behind them.

Beverly turned to the guards. "Sir Preston is the official point of contact," she said. "Send word to him of any requests they make. The only other people you are to answer to are me, Marshal Matheson or the queen. Is that clear?"

"Yes, Commander," replied the guards.

"Now, I'm off to see the queen. I'll send Sir Preston when she's ready."

Anna sat behind her desk, poring over reports from her couriers while Gerald sat in a sturdy, well-padded chair, looking over a ledger of some sort. She looked up from her work to see Gerald squinting at the pages before him.

"Something wrong?"

"I seem to be having trouble reading this," he said. "I'm afraid my eyes aren't what they used to be."

"Time for another treatment," she said. "I'll have to get Aubrey to cast regeneration on you. How have your legs been? I noticed you had trouble at the wedding."

"I'm just old, Anna," he stated.

"So you are," she agreed, "but there's no reason you have to put up with all these troubles. Aubrey's magic can cure you, remember?"

"I feel so guilty," said Gerald. "Surely there are others that need it more?"

"I'm the one that should feel guilty," said Anna. "I want you around for years to come."

"You have other things to worry about than me," said Gerald, "like your new husband. Where is he, by the way?"

"He's visiting with his father," said Anna.

"I still think you and he should get away for a few days. Why don't you go to Uxley?"

"We will," she replied, "but I have to meet with the Norland delegation first. Once I've dealt with them, we'll take a nice trip to Uxley, I promise."

"Good," he said, "then I can get some work done instead of spending all my time with you."

"You won't get out of it that easily," she said.

"What do you mean?"

"You're coming with us to Uxley."

"Why would I go there?" he said. "I'm the marshal, and I have duties here."

"First of all, you're my family, and I know how much you like Mrs. Brown's cooking."

"Well," he admitted, "she does make a very nice Mercerian Pudding."

"Then it's settled," she said. "Don't worry, we'll take one of the mages with us so we can return to Wincaster quickly once we're done. Eventually, I'd like to put a magic circle there, but I'm afraid other cities must take priority."

"Remind me, how many circles do we have at present?" asked Gerald.

"Four, if we include the two in the Whitewood. The Hawksburg circle is quite old. Aubrey thinks it was made in the time of her great grandmother, though it may be even older."

"So which circle is to be built next?"

"I was thinking Kingsford," she replied. "It would allow lesser mages to make the trip to Summersgate in two stages."

"Lesser mages?"

"Yes," said Anna, "those with less power."

"We only have four mages, Anna."

"For now, but we must plan for the future."

"Speaking of the future, what's happening in the search for Revi?"

"Albreda has returned from Summersgate," she replied.

"And?"

"She brought back a Weldwyn mage, an Enchantress named Gretchen Harwell. She has some ideas on how we might proceed."

"Interesting," said Gerald.

"Yes, by allowing the Weldwyn mages to have access, we've more than doubled the number we can call upon for assistance. I've given them permission to learn the circle in Wincaster."

"It only makes sense," said Gerald, "but I'm worried that now too many people might have access."

"I've already considered that," said Anna. "King Leofric and I met only this morning concerning that very thing. He and I agreed that we should both have approval on who is allowed time to study each circle. In that way, we can limit who has access to them."

"I see you've been busy," he said.

"Yes," she replied, "in fact, I've already granted permission for two of them."

"Anyone I might know?"

"You remember Roxanne Fortuna," she said, "she was the Life Mage that healed me when I was attacked."

"I remember," said Gerald. "I think I lost ten years that day, worrying over you. Who's the other?"

"Aegryth Malthunen, she's an Earth Mage. Albreda said she was instrumental in researching how to create the magic circle in Wincaster."

"I suppose we'll also have to add this Enchantress to the list," he said.

"Yes," she said, "assuming she's willing to abide by our rules, of course. Oh, did I mention that Kraloch can now use the spell of recall?"

"That makes three," said Gerald. "What about Kiren-Jool and Aldus Hearn?"

"They're on the list, but they've been kept busy trying to find Revi."

"Let's hope this Weldwyn Enchantress can be of help," said Gerald.

He set his ledger down, then reached across to the edge of the desk where a tankard sat. He lifted it, only to find it empty.

"Shall I send for some more?" said Anna.

"No, that's all right," he said, "I'll go and get some. How about you, do you want some more cider?"

"I have plenty," she said, "though maybe Tempus might like to stretch his legs."

Gerald looked at the great mastiff. "What do you think?"

In answer, Tempus let out a bark and wagged his tail.

Anna laughed, "There's your answer."

Gerald rose, letting out a grunt as his muscles complained.

"And while you're at it," she said, "find Aubrey and get her to cast a regeneration spell, that's an order! I can't have my marshal grunting and groaning all over the Palace."

With an exaggerated bow, he acquiesced, "Your wish is my command, Your Majesty."

Gerald wandered into the Palace kitchen, where the staff were hard at work.

"Can I get you something, Your Grace?" asked one of the cooks.

"Some cider, if you'd be so kind, Linette."

She refilled his tankard as Gerald took in the view. Food was cooking in preparation for a great feast to welcome the Norlanders, and the smell made his stomach growl. He looked down at Tempus, who was licking his lips in appreciation.

Linette returned the tankard. "Here you are, Your Grace," she said.

"Thank you," he replied. "Tell me, is all this for the feast?"

She looked across the kitchen to where dozens of people were preparing food. "Yes," she replied, "would you like a sampling?"

"I'd be lying if I said no, but I don't want to detract from the preparations."

"It's no bother," she replied. "Hold on, and I'll scrounge you up something."

Gerald turned his attention back to Tempus, petting the gentle creature's head. In reply, the mastiff turned to him, licking his hand. Moments later, Linette presented him with a plate full of tasty morsels.

"All this for me?" he said in surprise.

She briefly looked at Tempus, who wagged his tail. "Well, for the both of you," she said, "unless you want some more for the queen?"

"I don't think she's hungry just yet," he said. "She had a late breakfast. Has anyone seen Lady Aubrey of late?"

He looked around, but everyone was shaking their heads.

"Well," said Gerald, "I'd best be off then, thank you for the food."

"You're quite welcome, Your Grace," said Linette.

Gerald wandered back into the hallway, tankard in one hand, plate in the other. He was looking for a room to sit and eat when he spotted a familiar face.

"*Kraloch,*" he called out, using the Orcish tongue.

"*Marshal,*" replied the Orc, "*I didn't expect to see you wandering about the place.*"

In answer, Gerald looked at his plate. "Care for some food?" he asked, switching back to the common tongue.

The Orc slowed as he approached, looking over the plate.

"What have you there?"

"An assortment from the kitchen," Gerald explained.

Kraloch chose a piece of cheese, taking a bite.

"This is very good," said the Orc. "Nothing like the cheese that we have back home in the Artisan Hills, though."

"It's a Stilldale," said Gerald, "one of my favourites."

The Orc laughed, a low resounding rumble that Gerald recognized. "I hear every cheese is your favourite."

"True enough," said Gerald, "though I prefer sausages."

He set the plate down on a nearby table, freeing up his arm to select a piece for himself. "You haven't seen Lady Aubrey by any chance?"

"Not this morning," said Kraloch. "Why, do you need her for something?"

"I'm supposed to have her cast regeneration on me," he said.

"I can do that," said Kraloch, "or did you forget how I regenerated your teeth during the dark time?"

"Dark time?"

"Yes, when you were fugitives of the crown," said the Orc.

"Ah, yes, of course," said Gerald. "I could hardly forget that."

"Let us finish this repast," said the Orc, "and then I shall cast the spell."

"An excellent idea," said Gerald.

Two guards marched down the hall. Gerald half expected them to halt before him, so used to being the marshal was he, but they simply shifted their gait to try and get past.

"I'm sorry," said Gerald, "I suppose we're blocking the hallway."

"Not at all, Your Grace," said one of the guards.

Gerald moved to the side, allowing them to pass.

"Should we adjourn to another room?" suggested Kraloch.

"Good idea," said Gerald, searching the hallway for some sign of an empty room.

It was Tempus that found what they were looking for. He sat before a door, his tail wagging. Gerald moved closer to the mastiff while Kraloch grabbed the plate and followed. No sooner had he reached the faithful hound than the door opened, revealing a surprised Jack Marlowe.

"My lord," said the cavalier, "were you looking for me?"

"No," said Gerald, "Kraloch and I were simply looking for somewhere to eat and chat."

"Come in, Gerald," called out Prince Alric.

Gerald peered past Jack to see the young prince sitting at a table, a platter of food before him.

"I don't want to interrupt," said Gerald.

"Nonsense," said Alric. "Show them in, Jack."

The cavalier stood to the side, bidding them enter. Gerald took a seat, with Kraloch taking up the one opposite.

"Your Highness," said Gerald, "I don't think you've met Kraloch, have you?"

"No," said Alric, "though I've heard of him, of course. Welcome, Kraloch. I'm Prince Alric of Weldwyn."

"Of Merceria," corrected Jack.

"Ah, yes," the prince agreed, "I suppose I'll have to get used to that now."

"Greetings, Your Highness," said Kraloch. "It is an honour to meet you."

"You speak our language quite well," said Alric. "Much more so that I would have thought."

"Our tribe lives in the hills near Eastwood," said Kraloch. "We have traded with Humans for generations."

"Interesting," said Alric. "The Orcs in Weldwyn have little contact with us."

"There has always been some animosity between our races in the Western Realm," explained Kraloch.

"I'm sorry to hear that," said Alric.

Kraloch shrugged, a very Human habit. "It is often so between Humans and Orcs."

"And yet you get along with us in Merceria?" said Gerald.

"We do now," said the shaman, "but it was not always so. Even on the Continent, we are perceived as wild savages by most."

"People often fear what they don't understand," said Alric.

"Anna doesn't," said Gerald, "it's what sets her apart. When we first learned of the Orcs in the Greatwood, she wanted to meet them. It was the whole point of us visiting Norwatch all those years ago."

"The Greatwood?" said Kraloch.

"Yes," said Alric, "it's what you call the Netherwood."

"A much more interesting name," offered Jack, "don't you think?"

"I'd have to agree with you there," said Alric. "So tell me, Kraloch, how do you find working with the Mercerians?"

The Orc took another piece of cheese, staring at it a moment as he composed his thoughts.

"I think it has been beneficial to both our races," he said, then popped the morsel into his mouth.

Alric chuckled, "That's a very tactful answer. Are you a diplomat?"

"I am a shaman," said Kraloch, "and we represent the collective wisdom of our race."

"The Orcs can talk to their ancestors," explained Gerald.

"Surely not?" said Jack.

"It's true," said Kraloch, "we are masters of Spirit Magic."

"Spirit Magic?" said Alric. "I don't think I've ever heard of it."

"It's a specialized form of Life Magic," said Gerald, "or at least that's what Aubrey told me."

"Fascinating," said Alric. "I'd love to learn more, but I'm afraid my other duties will be keeping me busy for a few days, at least."

"What duties are those?" asked Gerald.

"I'm accompanying my father as he makes his way around all these functions. That reminds me, will the guard be ready for inspection this afternoon? I thought, with Beverly away, that we might have to put it off."

"She's back," said Gerald. "Didn't anyone tell you?"

"No," said Alric. "I take it she arrived with the Norland delegation?"

"She did."

Alric stabbed down with his fork, attempting to skewer a piece of bacon. It crumbled beneath his attempt, eliciting a sigh of frustration from the young prince.

"You're supposed to eat it with your fingers," said Gerald.

"You Mercerians, always overcooking your bacon," noted Jack.

Gerald laughed, "And in Weldwyn, you always undercook yours. I suppose that's what makes things so interesting."

"What does? Bacon?" asked Jack.

"No," said Gerald, "a lot of our culture is the same, but little things, like bacon, illustrate how different we can still be."

Alric smiled, "You're becoming quite the philosopher, Gerald."

"You know," said Gerald, "if you want your bacon undercooked, you have only to mention it to the staff."

"I'm a Prince of Merceria now," said Alric, "I should learn to appreciate your food."

"If you must, my prince," said Jack, "but I'll stick to traditional Weldwyn cooking."

"Have you no sense of adventure, Jack?" asked Alric.

"I'm always up for excitement," the cavalier responded, "just not in my food."

Alric returned his attention to their visitors. "What kind of food do you like, Master Kraloch?"

"We eat much as you do," said Kraloch, "though I find your use of metal instruments quite strange."

"Metal instruments?" said Jack.

"He means your fork," explained Gerald. "Orcs tend to use knives when eating."

"And here I thought they ate raw meat," said Jack.

"No," said Gerald, "as Kraloch said, they eat similarly to us. They even use plates, though maybe wooden platters might be a better description."

"You seem to be quite knowledgeable about the subject," said Alric.

"I led the army during the rebellion," said Gerald. "I'd often sit with my troops as they ate, including the Orcs."

"So of all the races," said Jack, "who has the strangest sense of taste?"

"I'd have to say the Elves," responded Gerald. "When they're on the march, they eat these very strange wafers."

"Wafers?" said Jack. "I'm not sure I understand."

"They're like very dry biscuits. They're filling, but they always leave me thirsty."

"And the best?" pressed the cavalier.

"The Orcs," Gerald replied, "on account of the generous helpings."

"We are physically larger," added Kraloch, "and thus need to consume more than Humans."

Alric put down his fork and emptied his tankard, tipping the golden-hued wine down his throat.

"Well," he said at last, "as much as I'd like to sit and chat, I have to meet with my father."

He rose, leading Jack to do the same.

Gerald stood, bowing slightly, "Your Highness."

"Please," said Alric, "call me Alric in private. After all, we're family now."

"Of course, Your Majesty," said Gerald with a grin.

The throne of Merceria most often resided within the great hall, but with a banquet being prepared, it had been moved to one of the smaller rooms. Here Anna sat, waiting for the arrival of the Norland visitors.

She looked at Beverly, who stood nearby. "Did you learn anything of use during the trip?"

"I'm afraid not," replied the knight. "Lord Wilfrid was not the most verbose individual."

"He's being careful," said Anna, "and doesn't want to give anything away. I shall have to watch him closely."

"You really think they want peace?" asked Beverly.

"Even if the chances are slim, it's still worth pursuing."

"Sir Preston should have them here shortly," said Beverly, "he's very punctual."

"He's made an excellent addition to the Knights of the Hound," said Anna. "We need more like him."

"I'll keep my eyes open," said Beverly, "but men like that are few and far between."

"I think my knights must be the smallest order in the known world," said the queen.

"For now," said Beverly, "but their quality makes up for the quantity, and we still have the Knights of the Sword."

The door opened, and Gerald peered in. "Are they here yet?"

"No," said Anna. "Come in, Gerald. They should be here any time now."

"I have Kraloch with me," he advised her.

"Good, I'd like to watch the Norlanders' reactions when they see him. I haven't forgotten the Orc's concerns."

Gerald opened the door wider and entered, the Orc shaman following.

"Your Majesty," said Kraloch, bowing. "It is so good of you to invite me to this meeting."

"Nonsense," said Anna. "We value our allies, and the Orcs have been staunch supporters of the crown. We welcome your opinion."

Gerald moved to stand to Anna's right, while the Orc took up a position beside Beverly.

"Where's Tempus?" asked Anna.

"I thought it best to leave him with Sophie for now," said Gerald. "I didn't want to frighten the delegates on their first official visit."

"Probably for the best," noted Anna, "but I want him there for the feast."

"Of course," said Gerald, "I wouldn't be able to keep him away even if I wanted, he has a nose for food."

"Just like you, Gerald," she said, breaking out into a smile.

"Married life seems to suit you," said Gerald.

"I'd have to agree," said Anna, "though if truth be told, I haven't seen much of my husband of late. I think I saw more of him before we were married."

"Surely not," said Gerald. "I should think that, after the wedding night, there wasn't much more to see?"

Anna blushed, and Gerald chuckled.

"I meant no offense," he said.

"And none was taken," she replied. Anna turned to Beverly. "Tell me, did you have the same feeling when you married Aldwin?"

"We had time together in Bodden, Your Majesty," said Beverly, "and have rarely been separated since. In fact, this trip to the border is the longest I've been away from him since we were married."

"Let's hope I won't have to send you on any more long journeys in the near future," said Anna.

The door opened, revealing one of the guards. "They're coming down the hall now, Your Majesty."

"Very well," the queen replied, "show them in as soon as they arrive."

She turned to Gerald, then looked at Beverly and Kraloch. "Ready?"

They all nodded their assent, then waited as the doors opened, revealing the Norland delegation.

"Your Majesty," said Lord Wilfrid, bowing deeply. "I am Lord Wilfrid of Hansley, envoy from King Halfan of Norland."

"Greetings, Lord Wilfrid," said Anna, "and to what do I owe this visit?"

The Norland lord moved closer, his companions remaining by the door.

"As you are no doubt aware," the man continued, "our two kingdoms have been at war for centuries. King Halfan wishes to end this war and bring peace to both our realms."

"We have been at war for more than four hundred years," said Anna. "It makes me wonder why, after all that time, he would seek peace now?"

"He is dying," admitted Lord Wilfrid, "and wishes to leave behind a peaceful kingdom."

"And so you are here to negotiate such a peace?"

"No," the man replied, "though I am humbled by the thought that you would perceive me as worthy."

Anna leaned forward, "If you are not meant to negotiate this peace, then what is your reason for being here?"

"I have come at the behest of the king to invite you to Norland," said Lord Wilfrid.

"You must be joking," said Gerald.

If Lord Wilfrid were insulted, he certainly didn't show any sign of it. "I understand that this is a lot to digest," the Norlander continued, "but I come bearing a letter from King Halfan."

He held out his hand, and one of his companions moved up to place a scroll in it. Lord Wilfrid unrolled the missive and then turned it to face the queen. Beverly stepped forward, taking the scroll and passing it to Anna, who examined it carefully, then gave it to Gerald.

"You have given me much to think about," she said. "I shall consider your king's offer and consult with my advisors."

Lord Wilfrid bowed deeply. "I thank you on behalf of my king," he said, "and look forward to moving forward, to peace."

"As do I," said Anna. "Sir Preston?"

The knight, who had been waiting outside, stepped into the room. "Your Majesty?"

"Please take Lord Wilfrid and his entourage back to their rooms, and make sure they are shown to the banquet this evening."

Sir Preston gave a slight nod of his head. "Of course, Your Majesty." He turned to the Norland delegation, "Gentlemen, if you'll follow me, I'll show you back to your rooms."

Gerald waited until the door shut, then turned his attention once more to the letter. "Is this real?"

"It certainly looks so," said Anna. "Still, I'll have the Master of Herald's examine it, just to be sure."

"You can't seriously be thinking of travelling to Norland?" he asked. "It's far too dangerous."

"People said the same thing about Weldwyn," said Anna, "and yet we are now allies."

"This is different," countered Gerald. "We've been in a constant war with these people since the five hundred's."

"Since 520, to be exact," said Anna, "and it's time we put an end to it."

"I suppose it wouldn't hurt to send a delegation," said Gerald. "Who did you have in mind?"

"I'm going myself," declared Anna. "I can trust no one else."

She recognized the look of shock on his face. "Let me rephrase that," she said. "It's not that I don't trust people, but I need to conduct these negotiations myself. It's the only way to ensure a lasting peace."

"You'll have to pass this on to the Council of Nobles," said Gerald. "They won't like it, it's too dangerous."

"I'm well aware of that," she said, "but sometimes great risk brings great rewards."

EIGHT

The Council of Nobles

Summer 964 MC

Lord Alexander Stanton, Earl of Tewsbury, looked across the table at his companion, Lord Horace Spencer, the Earl of Eastwood.

"What do you suppose this is all about?" Stanton asked.

"I haven't the foggiest," said Spencer, "and on such short notice, too. I suspect it must be something big."

"Like what? War, perhaps?"

"If it is, there's been no hint of it."

The door opened, and Baron Richard Fitzwilliam entered.

"Fitz," said Spencer, "have you any news? What's this all about?"

"The queen has called this meeting," said the baron. "It is for her to reveal the reason."

"Are you trying to tell us you know nothing?" pressed Stanton.

The baron smiled, "I said no such thing, but it is not my place to speak of it. Where are the others?"

"They're not here yet," said Stanton.

"I believe Anglesley won't be present," said Spencer, "as he's back in Colbridge."

"And Somerset?" asked Fitz.

"He's here, somewhere," said Spencer. "I saw him in the Queen's Arms only yesterday."

Baron Fitzwilliam broke out in laughter, and Lord Spencer blushed. "Oh, for Saxnor's sake, I was talking about the tavern."

"Sorry," said Fitz, "it was just so funny."

"I doubt the queen would think so," warned Stanton.

"I disagree," countered Fitz, "I think she'd find it quite amusing."

The sound of the door opening drew his attention.

"And this, if I don't miss my guess," said the baron, "is the Duke of Wincaster. Good to see you, Gerald."

"Thank you," replied the marshal, shaking the baron's hand.

"I trust things are well in Bodden?"

"More or less," said the baron.

"Meaning?" asked Gerald.

"We've still got Norlanders fleeing their own country. Not that we mind, it's given us a lot more farmers to work the land."

"Will the queen be joining us shortly?" asked Lord Stanton.

"Yes," said Gerald, "she'll be arriving along with Lady Hayley and Lady Aubrey.

"Any word on Arnim?" enquired Fitz.

Gerald took a quick look around the room. "I thought he was already here. Don't worry, he's still got time. Oh, Lord Chesterton sends his regards, but he won't be able to make it."

"Why is that?" asked Stanton.

"He is indisposed," said Gerald.

"What in the Gods' name does that mean?" asked the earl.

"It means," explained Gerald, "that he is unable to attend due to an injury."

"I hope it's nothing serious," said Fitz.

"Lady Aubrey assures us that he will make a full recovery," said Gerald, "but he lost a lot of blood. He fell from his horse, then the damn thing almost trampled him to death."

"A horse, you say?" said Spencer.

"Yes," said Gerald. "He's been trying to breed Mercerian Chargers."

"I thought that was done at the Brandon estate?" said Stanton.

"It is," said Gerald, "but we need to increase their numbers. Unfortunately, it takes a lot of skill to care for them."

"I daresay," said Stanton, "and with Baron Robert Brandon dead and buried, I suppose there's no other to take over?"

"Not so," said Gerald. "Lady Aubrey has a gift for that sort of thing, and the Orcs in Hawksburg have proven quite adept at assisting."

"Orcs?" said Stanton. "What utter rubbish."

"I might remind you," said Fitz, "that they are our allies."

"Nonsense," said Stanton. "The war is over. Send them back to the hills, I say."

"They are still quite useful to us," said Fitz.

Lord Stanton glared at the baron. "Stick to what you know, Baron, it's not your place to run this kingdom."

"Nor is it yours," said Fitz. "That is for the queen alone."

"What utter nonsense," said Stanton, "everybody knows you have great influence." He glared at Gerald, "The pair of you ought to be ashamed for the way you have manipulated her."

Gerald was about to argue the point, but the door opened, drawing the attention of the room. A large group had arrived, led by Arnim Caster.

"Lord Caster," said Fitz, "good to see you again. I trust the children are well?"

"They are, Baron," said Arnim. "I thank you for the kind words."

Gerald chuckled, "I see you're still lacking in sleep."

Arnim flushed. "They won't sleep through the night unless I tell them a story," he said, "and even then it has to be a long one."

"They're not even half a year old yet," said Gerald. "They don't understand what you're saying."

"Still," said Arnim, "they like to hear my voice. Tell me, Baron, was Beverly ever this much work?"

Fitz smiled. "That much and more," he said. "Wouldn't you agree, Gerald?"

"Hey, now," came a voice from the door, "I wasn't that bad, surely?"

Beverly had followed Arnim into the room and took up her place behind the queen's chair. Next came Hayley and Aubrey, both of whom took their customary seats.

As was typical, their arrival presaged that of the queen. Anna stepped through the doorway, Tempus at her heels. The nobles all stood as she made her way to her chair.

"Please," she said, "be seated."

They all sat, looking at their queen for answers.

"I have gathered you all here," she started, "because an opportunity has presented itself, and I need your counsel on the matter."

"Why?" said Stanton. "What has happened?"

"We have, this day, met with a Norland ambassador," she explained.

"Is this war?" asked Lord Spencer.

"No," said Anna, "in fact, it is an offer of peace."

"Peace?" said Stanton. "But we've been at war for centuries."

"Precisely why I sought your advice," said Anna.

"I don't understand," said Stanton. "You don't need us to sign a peace treaty."

"That's true," said Anna, "but the ambassador has proposed that I travel to Norland to meet directly with King Halfan."

"I think not," said Stanton, "it's obviously a trap."

"The queen would travel with a heavy escort," added Gerald, "and any attack on her would bring immediate war. They know that."

"I still don't like it," said Stanton.

"You don't like anything," said Fitz.

Stanton glared at the baron.

"What is it that you need us for?" asked Lord Spencer.

"I shall have to leave someone behind to rule while I am away," the queen explained, "and I want to make sure everyone here understands that."

"But you have no heir," said Stanton. "Who would rule in your stead?"

"I would appoint a Royal Steward," said Anna.

"And the army?" asked Arnim.

"Would fall to Baron Fitzwilliam," said Anna, "since the Duke of Wincaster would be with me, along with Beverly."

"I see no problem with that," offered Spencer.

"I do," said Stanton. "Baron Fitzwilliam is ill-suited to command an entire army. It should be placed in the hands of someone more senior."

"Baron Fitzwilliam is a general," said Gerald.

"But I am an earl," said Stanton, "and, as such, I should be given the responsibility."

"I might remind you," said Anna, "that command of the Royal Army is the sole prerogative of the Crown. The baron's qualifications to command are not in question, nor is his loyalty."

"She's got you there," said Lord Spencer.

"Very well," said Stanton, though to Gerald's mind, he looked like he was pouting.

"Might I ask," said Arnim, "who is to be the Royal Steward in your absence?"

"I am appointing Lady Hayley to that position," the queen replied.

"Me?" said the ranger. "Surely Aubrey would be better suited?"

"Aubrey will be travelling with me," said Anna, "and you have experience commanding the rangers. Prince Alric will also be here to assist you."

"You cannot be serious," burst out Lord Stanton. "He is a foreign prince. He cannot command in Merceria!"

"Nor will he," said Anna, "he will act only in an advisory capacity."

"If you're not going to listen to our advice," said Stanton, "then why did you summon us?"

"I am willing to listen to your points of view, gentlemen, providing that you mind your manners. Now, does anyone have any reasonable questions?"

She looked around the room, meeting each person's gaze. When her eyes fell on Lord Spencer, he spoke up.

"Might I ask how long this trip would take?"

In answer, Anna looked at Beverly, who moved forward to explain. "As far as we can tell, their capital, Galburn's Ridge, is somewhere between three hundred fifty and four hundred miles away."

"As far as you can tell?" stammered Stanton. "What's that supposed to mean?"

"It means," said Beverly, "that we possess no accurate maps of Norland, beyond the border regions."

"That's a very long journey," said Baron Fitzwilliam.

"It is," admitted the queen, "but we shall not be travelling unprotected. King Halfan has given us permission to bring a small force to protect me."

"What does that mean, exactly?" pressed Arnim.

"We shall be taking about fifty men," said Anna. "we'll bring the Guard Cavalry, of course, but we'll also need footmen to guard us while we're at their capital."

"Plus, you'll need servants," advised Fitz.

"Yes, and supplies," said Gerald. "The actual supply wagons will likely outnumber the footmen."

"When would you leave?" asked Lord Spencer.

"At the end of summer or early autumn," said Anna.

"To return when?" asked Lord Spencer.

"Likely not till spring," said Anna. "The trip there alone will take weeks, and then we don't know how long the negotiations will take."

"Yes," agreed Fitz, "and you can't really march in wintertime."

"I don't like this," said Stanton.

"For once, I agree with you," said Gerald, "but it's an opportunity we cannot resist."

"Gerald is right," said Anna. "We have been enemies with Norland for far too long. It's time we swallow our pride and brought real peace to the kingdom."

"Well said," agreed Arnim, "but the question remains, what is at risk?"

"Our queen, for one," said Stanton.

"The queen will be protected," said Gerald.

"How can you guarantee that?" demanded Stanton.

"He can't," said Aubrey, "but I can."

"You?" said Stanton.

"Yes," she replied, "if things go badly, I shall use my magic to bring the queen back to Wincaster."

Stanton let out a sigh of relief. "In that case, I remove my objections."

"That surprises me," said Fitz.

"Why," said Stanton, "because we actually agree for once? We just fought a devastating civil war. I don't want the kingdom descending into chaos again."

"Baron Fitzwilliam has been informed of our current status," said Anna, "and I have faith that he will conduct his duties with the utmost professionalism. I shall have some weeks yet to prepare Lady Hayley for her stewardship, and of course, I have seen to the contingencies, should I be lost."

"Meaning?" said Stanton.

"Meaning that I have made arrangements for the future ruler of the realm, should I die."

"What arrangements?" pressed Lord Spencer.

"These shall remain secret," the queen replied. "Have no fear, Lady Hayley will have access to the documents should it prove necessary."

The room fell silent.

Anna rose. "I think we are done now," she said. "Lady Hayley, if you would accompany me, we have things to discuss."

Everybody stood as the queen and Hayley left, then filtered out slowly, leaving Gerald and Fitz alone.

The old warrior looked at the baron. "Why is it that you and Lord Stanton are always at odds?"

"It goes back many years," said Fitz. "He always felt that Lady Evelyn should have married him instead of me."

"That's outrageous," said Gerald. "She loved you, that much was obvious."

"It wasn't about love," said Fitz, "not to Stanton. No, for him, it was about power. He always had his way, you see, and once he set eyes on her, he wouldn't take no for an answer."

"And yet she married you," said Gerald.

"She did," said the baron, "and she gave me Beverly. She looks so much like her mother, don't you think?"

"She does," said Gerald, "though I believe your daughter is now older than Evelyn ever was."

"I believe you're right," said Fitz, "though I never really thought about it before. You know, I promised Evelyn on her deathbed I'd look after Beverly."

"And you've done a fine job of it," said Gerald. "Anyone would be proud to have her for a daughter."

"Thank you, my friend. Now, what say we go down to the Queen's Arms and get some of that stinky cheese?"

"And sausages!" added Gerald.

The baron smiled, "You read my mind!"

Alric stretched out his legs, setting them onto the footstool.

"I feel like I've been walking all day," he said.

Anna laughed, "You're getting old."

"I'm serious," he said. "I'm exhausted."

"We have kept you quite busy of late," mused Anna. "Between visiting with your family and meeting the Norland delegates, I'm surprised you've held up so well. I half expected you to fall asleep."

A gentle knock on the door caught her attention. "Come in, Gerald," she called out.

The door opened, revealing a very surprised marshal.

"How did you know it was me?"

"You have a rather distinctive knock, Gerald," said Anna. "Is this a social call or business?"

"A bit of both, to be honest," said Gerald.

"Come and sit down then, and tell me all about it."

"I don't want to interrupt anything," he said, looking at Alric.

"You're not," said Alric, "we're just relaxing. It's been a long day."

"I'm afraid tomorrow promises to be no better," said Gerald. "The Norlanders would like to meet King Leofric. Do you think you could arrange such a thing?"

"By Malin's tears, why would they want that?" asked Alric.

"I think they got wind of our alliance," explained Gerald. "They're likely seeking support for their endeavour."

"But we've already decided to go," said Anna.

"Yes," Gerald agreed, "but we haven't told them yet, at least not officially."

"A fair point," said Anna.

"Don't worry, Gerald," said Alric, "I'll take care of it first thing tomorrow morning. Do you think they'd be up to an afternoon meeting?"

"I'll get Sir Preston to speak with them," said Gerald, "but I think they'll be amenable to it."

"Amenable?" said Anna. "What's happened to you, Gerald, you're using fancy words?"

"I'm afraid it's Alric's influence," said Gerald. "All that Royal Breeding is starting to rub off on me."

Alric chuckled. "Well, it suits you, Gerald. We'll make a duke of you yet."

"He's already a duke," said Anna, "and I quite like him the way he is. Ignore what he says, Gerald, you just be yourself."

"I didn't mean to start an argument," said Gerald, blushing slightly.

"You're not," said Alric, "just some good-natured ribbing. I hope I haven't caused offense?"

"Not at all," said Gerald, though if truth be told, he wasn't entirely sure.

"How are you doing, Gerald?" asked Anna.

"Quite well," the old warrior replied. "The training is going well, and we've been working hard to integrate the Orcs into the army."

"No," said Anna, "I've read your reports about the army. I want to know how YOU are doing."

"Me?" said Gerald. "I'm fine, why?"

"I think you're working too much," she said. "Did you manage to see Aubrey the other day?"

"No," said Gerald, eliciting a frown from Anna, "but I did run into Kraloch, and he used a regeneration on me."

"Good," said Anna.

"A regeneration?" said Alric. "Are you injured, Gerald?"

"No, merely suffering from a lifelong malady."

"Which is?" asked the prince.

"Old age," declared Gerald.

"Really?" said Alric. "I would have said you look quite spry for your age."

"And there you have it," said Gerald. "'For my age'. It's always the same with you young folk."

"You were young once, weren't you?" asked Alric.

"Of course," said Gerald, breaking into a grin, "and I was just like you."

"Really?" said Alric. "You were a prince of a foreign realm?"

"Well, no, of course not. But I was full of life and ready to take on the world."

"Whatever happened to change that?" asked Alric.

Gerald fell silent, leaving Anna to explain.

"His parents were killed by Norland raiders," she said, "and then he was taken back to Bodden to serve Baron Fitzwilliam."

"Lord Richard?" said Alric. "I knew the baron was old, but I had no idea he was that ancient."

"His father was the baron at the time, Alric," said Anna. "But it was a young Richard Fitzwilliam that found Gerald wandering in the woods."

"I'm sorry," said Alric, "had I known, I wouldn't have teased you."

"That was many years ago," said Gerald, "and a past I left behind long ago."

"So you have reason to hate the Norlanders," said Alric.

"That's not the half of it," said Gerald. "You see, years later, they killed my wife and daughter."

"I don't know what to say," remarked Alric. "I can't imagine something so heinous."

"I swore to make them pay," said Gerald, "and dedicated my life to becoming a warrior for that sole purpose."

"And yet somehow, I don't see that in you," noted Alric.

"I came to realize that not all Norlanders are raiders," said Gerald. "A Norland farmer taught me that if you can believe it."

"A farmer? Really?"

"Oh, yes," said Gerald, "but it's a long story, better told another day. As for me, I'm off to bed. I have a full day tomorrow."

He rose, eliciting a word from Anna.

"Gerald," she said, "why don't you take some time off? Maybe you need a rest? It sounds like you've been run off your feet. You can always delegate some of your responsibilities to others, it's not like you don't have people you can trust."

"I can still do my job as marshal," defended Gerald.

"I'm not saying you can't," said Anna, "but we all need a break from time to time, Saxnor knows I'd like one."

"I'll think about it," said Gerald, "but there likely won't be an opportunity until this Norland business is over with. That reminds me, I'd like Prince Alric to take on some more responsibility within the army if you have no objections?"

"I think it a marvellous idea," said Anna, "don't you, Alric?"

"I do," said the prince. "What did you have in mind, Gerald?"

"I thought," said Gerald, "that he might serve as my aide so he can learn how we do things. Unless, of course, you think that beneath him? He would, in fact, be a prince reporting to a commoner."

"No," said Anna, "he'd be reporting to the Duke of Wincaster. What do you think, Alric?"

"I think it a terrific idea."

"Good," said Gerald, "but I'll need a few days to work out responsibilities and such."

"That works well for me," said Alric. "Father will be leaving in a few days, and that should free up my time by a considerable degree."

"Very well," said Gerald, "we'll start once your parents leave."

Anna rose, giving him a hug. "Good night, Gerald."

"Good night, Anna," he said, "and to you also, Your Highness."

"Please," said the prince, "you must call me Alric in private. We can't be formal all the time."

"Very well, Alric," said Gerald. "Pleasant dreams to you both." He left, closing the door behind him.

"I'm worried about him," said Anna.

"He'll be all right," said Alric, "he's just feeling his age."

"But he had a regeneration spell, he should feel better."

"It's not only his body that's ageing, Anna, his mind is as well."

"I shall have to talk to Aubrey," said Anna. "Hopefully, she has a way of making him feel better."

"I know a way that would help," said Alric.

"You do?"

"Yes, let's give him some grandchildren!"

Anna flushed slightly, holding out her hand to him. "Let's go then," she said. "You know it takes a lot of practice to get it right."

The morning mist rolled across the lawn as Alric looked out the window. When a servant announced the arrival of the Norland delegation, he turned to see them being ushered in.

"Lord Wilfrid," said Alric, "so glad you could make it."

"Thank you," the Norlander replied. "I don't think I've formally introduced my entourage. Allow me to present Commander Frederick Cole, my military advisor."

"How do you do?" said Alric, shaking the man's hand.

"Glad to make your acquaintance, Your Highness," Cole replied.

"And this is Edmund Taffington," Lord Wilfrid continued. "He's my personal bodyguard."

"Greetings," said Alric.

Taffington nodded, "Highness."

"And lastly," said Lord Wilfrid, "we have Lord Rupert of Chilmsford. He's here to advise on matters pertaining to Merceria."

"Glad to make your acquaintance, Highness," said Lord Rupert. "I fear we have little knowledge of Westland."

"We prefer the name Weldwyn," advised Alric.

"Of course," said Lord Rupert, "forgive me if I've given offense."

"That's quite all right," said Alric, "there are still many Mercerians who use their old name for us."

"Something we must all learn to overcome if we are to see a peaceful way forward," said Lord Wilfrid.

"I have arranged a carriage," said Alric, "though the embassy is but a short distance."

"Do you think we could walk?" asked Lord Rupert. "The weather promises to be fair this day."

"An excellent idea," added Lord Wilfrid. "That is if Your Highness has no objection?"

"None at all," said Alric.

"Shall you summon your bodyguard?" asked Lord Wilfrid.

"Jack?" said Alric. "I hardly need him to walk me the few blocks to the embassy."

"Do all the lords of Merceria travel without protection?" asked Lord Rupert.

"Of course," said Alric. "Is it not so in Norland?"

"I'm afraid we have a much more...volatile society," explained Lord Wilfrid. "It has become commonplace for nobles to always be accompanied."

"I have soldiers that always follow at a discreet distance whenever I leave the Palace," said Alric, "but I've never had any problems here in Wincaster."

"Very well," said Lord Wilfrid, "shall we begin then?"

Alric led them out of the Palace and through the courtyard, where three soldiers fell into place a few paces behind.

"It is quite the city these Mercerians have built," noted Lord Wilfrid.

"Was it not here when your people fled north?" asked Alric.

"Oh, no," said Lord Rupert. "Wincaster was founded shortly before the war that saw the split, but it was little more than a military camp at the time. It was built to fight the Elves, you know."

"Was it now?" said Alric. "I suppose that explains the cool relations they've always had with the Elder race."

"I was surprised to see an Orc at our meeting with the queen," noted Lord Wilfrid.

"The Orcs were instrumental in the recent war," said Alric. "Why? Is that a problem?"

"We have had our own issues with the greenskins over the years," said Lord Wilfrid, "but it is not something that would jeopardize our quest for peace."

"I have to tell you," said Alric, "that the queen will insist that the Orcs are included in any peace talks."

"Surely not!" declared Lord Rupert. "They are nothing but vagabonds and thieves."

"They are an ancient race," said Alric, "and have been a great ally to Merceria. Do not expect the queen to abandon them."

"You have given me food for thought," noted Lord Wilfrid. "I shall have to give it my attention."

"You think that might be a problem?" asked the prince.

"I think that King Halfan will see reason on this matter," said Lord Wilfrid, "though it may take him by surprise. I shouldn't worry too much about it, we'll have months to prepare him."

"You will?" said Alric.

"Oh, yes," said Lord Wilfrid, "we shall be returning to Norland soon."

"I thought you'd be riding with the queen," said Alric.

"No, we have much to do to prepare for her arrival. We shall, however, rendezvous with Her Majesty's group once they enter Norland territory, to provide a fitting escort."

They were halfway down the block when the mist that had lingered for so long began to burn off with the heat of the rising sun.

"That's the embassy, just up on the left," said Alric.

"Interesting," said Lord Rupert. "Tell me, Highness, how is it that you came to possess such a building in the first place?"

"It was a gift from the crown," said Alric. "It was owned by the Duke of Wincaster, but he gave it to Weldwyn to use as an embassy."

"Then, where does the duke live?" asked Lord Wilfrid.

"At the Palace," said Alric.

"The Palace?" said Lord Rupert. "That's unusual, isn't it?"

"Not as strange as you might think," said Alric. "The duke is like a second father to the queen."

They drew closer to the Weldwyn embassy and Alric noted the presence of a trader of some sort, arguing with one of the guards.

"What's going on here?" the prince called out.

"This man claims to have a delivery, Highness," the guard responded.

"Let me see," said Alric. He stepped closer as the Norlanders watched, their interest sparked. The trader held forth a heavily weighted sack.

"It's one of my best hams," the man said.

"There's a trades entrance around back," said Alric.

"The note said to deliver it to the front door," the man insisted.

Alric, suddenly alert, stepped back. "Arrest this man," he commanded, "and search him for weapons."

The guards seized the tradesman by the arms, taking the sack from his hands. One of them opened it, then turned to show Prince Alric the ham that lay within.

"I don't understand," said Alric.

A piercing cry erupted from the Norland delegation, and Alric turned to see Edmund Taffington bleeding from a knife wound. Alric's own guards were rushing down the street in pursuit of a man dressed in everyday clothes.

"What happened?" said Alric, crouching by the wounded bodyguard.

"He came out of nowhere," said Lord Rupert. "He tried to stab Lord Wilfrid."

"Yes," the other lord agreed, "if Edmund hadn't moved quickly, it would be me lying there."

"We need a Life Mage," announced Alric, turning to one of the embassy guards. "Is Roxanne Fortuna still here?"

"She is, Your Highness," the guard responded.

"Then get her immediately," ordered Alric as he pressed his hand to the wound, desperate to stem the flow of blood.

"That's a gut wound," said Lord Rupert, "he'll not survive."

"You've obviously never heard of Life Magic," said Alric.

"We believe in the real, not the mystical," said Lord Rupert.

"Surely, you have mages in Norland?" said Alric.

"Very few," said Lord Wilfrid, "and those we do have only deal with the four base elements."

Alric held the wounded man, a pool of blood growing beneath him as his associates looked on in dismay. Alric's own guards soon arrived, but their news was not helpful.

"I'm afraid he eluded us, Highness," one of them reported.

The door to the embassy opened, and a group of people issued forth. Chief among them was an elderly woman, her greying hair worked into braids.

"Mistress Roxanne," said Alric, "this man has been stabbed. Can you help him?"

She came closer, crouching by the injured Edmund.

"We shall see," she said, closing her eyes as she held her arms before her, palms upward. She began chanting. The air around her filled with an electrical charge, causing the hairs on Alric's arms to stand on end, and then her hands began to glow. The moment Mistress Roxanne touched Edmund Taffington, the colour transferred from her fingers to his body, lingering where the wound existed. Moments later, his eyes fluttered open.

"My lord?" said Edmund.

Lord Wilfrid knelt, tears coming to his eyes. "By the Gods, man, we thought we'd lost you."

"He will have to rest," said Roxanne, "but he will make a full recovery."

"That was incredible," said Lord Rupert.

"She is one of our most gifted healers," said Alric. "It's lucky she came with the king, else your man would have died."

"Do the Mercerians have such magic?" asked Lord Wilfrid.

"They do," said Alric. "Lady Aubrey is a Life Mage, but judging from his injury, there would have been scant time to summon her from the Palace."

NINE

Repercussions

Summer 964 MC

Lord Alexander Stanton, Earl of Tewsbury, paced the floor while his visitor, Roland Valmar, watched from an oversized, padded chair.

"Oh, do sit down, Alexander," said Valmar. "You won't solve anything by pacing."

In answer, Stanton wheeled around, looking his companion in the eyes. "Was this your doing?" he demanded.

Valmar held up his hands. "I had nothing to do with the attack on the Norlanders," he said, "and why would I? What could I possibly gain from such an act?"

"War with Norland!"

"I may disagree with the rulership of this kingdom," said Valmar, "but the last thing I want is a foreign invasion."

"I wish I could believe you," said Stanton, "but I know you have your own agenda."

"We both do," said Valmar. "Let's not deceive ourselves. In any case, it is to our advantage for the visit to Norland to proceed."

"It is?

"Think about it for a moment," said Valmar, "all the principal people will be away from Wincaster. There'll never be an opportunity like this again."

"I might remind you that the queen is leaving people behind to look after things."

"Yes," said Valmar, "a mewling prince and an ex-poacher."

"What of Fitz?" asked Stanton.

"What of him?" countered Valmar.

"He is not a man I would discount so quickly."

"I might remind you," said Valmar, "he spends most of his time in Bodden, and that is quite some distance away."

"What of his witch?"

"His witch? You mean the druid?"

"Yes," said Stanton, "she has some powerful magic. She's a wild mage, you know. They say those are the most dangerous."

"Mages are powerful," said Valmar, "I'll give you that, but only against individuals. When we strike, we shall have numbers on our side. By the time the queen realizes what we've done, it'll be too late."

"I hope you're right," said Stanton, "for if we fail in this, it'll mean both our heads."

Anna leaned forward, grasping the hand of Edmund Taffington as he lay in his bed.

"Lady Aubrey tells me you'll soon be well enough to travel. How are you feeling?"

"I am doing much better. Thank you, Your Majesty."

"You make sure you rest properly," she commanded as she patted his hand, then straightened.

"We must thank you again," said Lord Wilfrid. "If it hadn't been for the timely intervention of your mage, we would have lost him."

"It was a Weldwyn mage that healed him," said Anna, "not ours."

"Even so, we are thankful for the effort you've gone through on our behalf."

"When will you leave for Norland?" asked Anna.

"At the end of the week, Your Majesty. We have much to discuss with our king before your arrival."

"Did they capture the man responsible for this attack?" asked Lord Rupert.

"Not yet," said Anna, "but we've made some progress, and the merchant is still a prisoner."

"What will happen to him?"

"He will be executed if he is found guilty of conspiring to kill you," said Anna.

"If?" said Lord Wilfrid. "Isn't his role plain enough for all to see?"

"We don't make judgements on appearances alone," said Anna. "We have enquiries to make yet, and it may turn out that the merchant was duped and used unwittingly."

"And you would have the man set free?" asked Rupert.

"Only if he is innocent," said Anna.

"I must insist he is punished," demanded Lord Rupert.

Anna turned to him, her face a mask. "We follow the rule of law in Merceria," she said. "It may not be perfect, but we assume innocence until guilt is proven."

"That's a very noble sentiment," said Lord Rupert, "but the real world doesn't work that way."

"It does here," asserted Anna, "and our courts will render no penalties without a fair trial."

"A trial?" said Lord Wilfrid. "You mean to make this attack public knowledge?"

"I could hardly prevent it," said Anna. "By now, talk of the attack will have already spread throughout Wincaster. It won't take long for it to reach the border regions."

"Have you any ideas who might be behind it?" asked Lord Rupert.

"There are many in Merceria with cause to hate your people," said Anna.

"The death toll has been equally as egregious on our side," Lord Wilfrid responded.

"Let us not let this sabotage our plans," said Anna. "With your permission, we would still like to make the trip to Norland."

"I am sure King Halfan would agree," said Lord Wilfrid.

"Good," said Anna. "We shall arrange for extra protection until you reach the border. I'd hate to see a recurrence of this attack."

Lord Wilfrid bowed his head respectfully, "Thank you, Your Majesty."

"Now," said Anna, "I've had two guards posted on his door, and all visitors will have to go through Sir Preston. I would suggest we let the patient rest peacefully."

"As you wish, Your Majesty," said Lord Rupert.

They exited the room, the queen pausing as the door was closed.

"I'm sorry you never got the chance to talk to King Leofric," she said.

"We can try again tomorrow," said Lord Wilfrid.

"I'm afraid that won't be possible," said Anna, "his entourage left this morning."

"Then I shall look forward to meeting him at some time in the future," said Lord Wilfrid, bowing yet again.

Arnim Caster looked over the table at the man sitting across from him.

"Is that all you have to say for yourself?" he demanded.

"It's true, I swear it," the man responded. "He was most insistent that I deliver it to the front door."

"Did you not think that strange?" asked Arnim.

"Of course," the merchant agreed, "but the fellow paid in advance, including a hefty bonus!"

"And you say this individual was of average height?"

"Yes," the merchant replied. "As I said earlier, with dark hair and a rough beard."

"You've just described half the population of Wincaster," said Arnim. "That's of no help to us."

"Perhaps if I took you to the store, it might help?" offered the merchant.

"I don't see how," said Arnim.

"He paid in fresh coins," the man said.

"What do you mean, fresh?"

"Newly minted ones. I've never seen their like before."

"Go on," urged Arnim.

"I'm not one to forego payment just because of a few foreign coins. Saxnor knows we get enough Weldwyn shillings in our purses, but these were different."

"Different how?" said Arnim.

"I figured some new King of Weldwyn must have had them made. His head was on the coins, you see."

"King Leofric?"

"No," said the man, "I would have remembered that. It were something else, started with an H."

"Halfan?" said Arnim.

"Aye, that was it." The man sat back, a look of relief flooding his face.

"Why didn't you mention this earlier?" pressed Arnim.

"I'm but a simple merchant, a butcher by trade. I didn't know it was important."

"I'd like to see those coins," said Arnim. "I shall take you to your shop and exchange them for Mercerian ones."

"And after that?" the butcher asked.

"After that, you're free to go," said Arnim, "but if I discover you were involved, it won't go well."

"I can assure you I'm innocent," the man professed.

"We shall see," said Arnim, "we shall see."

"Are you sure about this?" asked Anna, examining a coin.

"Positive, Your Majesty," said Arnim. "I had Nikki reach out to some of her contacts. Apparently, someone's been passing coins like these all around the city. I suspect the would-be murderer was a local hire. Nikki's been trying to track the man down, but we have little to go on."

Anna passed the coin to Gerald. "What do you think?"

"It's a Norland coin all right," he said. "I'm afraid there can be no doubt."

"It changes nothing," said Anna.

"On the contrary," noted Alric, "it changes everything, don't you see? If Norland coins were behind the attempt on Lord Wilfrid, they likely have their own problems at court. Someone wants this attempt at peace to fail. They've already tried to kill one person, who's to say they might not try again?"

"I have to agree with him," said Gerald. "This whole trip could turn disastrous."

"Even so," said Anna, "I have to take the risk, even if there is the slightest chance of ending this war."

"Then let us at least take extra precautions," said Alric. "Let me go with you."

"You can't," said Anna. "I need you here, in Wincaster, to keep an eye on things while I'm away."

"But now your life's in danger," he pleaded.

"I shall have Gerald and Beverly with me," said Anna, "not to mention Tempus."

"Don't worry," said Gerald, "at the first sign of trouble, I'll have Aubrey bring her directly back here."

"Very well," said Alric, "but I'm not happy about it."

"Nor am I," added Gerald, "but you know how Anna can be once she makes up her mind."

"You know I'm still in the room," interjected the queen.

"They're just worried for your safety, Majesty," said Arnim.

"When will we leave?" asked Gerald.

"We'll stick to our original schedule," Anna replied. "Once the delegation departs, we'll travel to Uxley for a week or two. I think I need to get out of the city for a bit."

"Fair enough," said Alric. "I've been looking forward to seeing the place of your birth."

"I wasn't born there," said Anna, "but it is where I spent my youth."

"It's also where she first met Tempus," added Gerald.

"He's not the only person I first met there," corrected Anna. She smiled, "Gerald came to Uxley to work as the groundskeeper."

"We'll have to take you to the Old Oak," said Gerald.

"What's that," asked Alric, "a giant tree?"

"It's a tavern," said Gerald, "though there is a large tree outside that gave the place its name. I think you'll find the ale there quite to your taste."

"Ale?" said Alric. "I usually favour wine."

"That's all right," said Gerald, "you'll learn to appreciate a good ale once you settle in as my aide."

"Is that mandatory?"

"No," said Gerald, "but it does endear one to the troops."

Alric sighed, "Very well, I shall try this ale you speak of. If it's half as good as you say, it might turn out to be quite passable."

"There," said Anna, "then it's all settled."

Lightning shifted his feet, causing Beverly to take note.

"I know," she soothed, "you're eager to be on the way. I can't say I blame you. These Norlanders are taking forever to get moving."

She looked up to where the carriage was just beginning to roll forward. The Guard Cavalry led the way, twelve strong, while another dozen followed along behind. She tried to urge her mount forward, but Lightning refused.

"What is the matter with you?" she said. "It's not like you to be so stubborn."

In answer, Lightning turned his head, looking towards the Palace. A lone horseman was approaching, and Beverly broke out into a grin.

"Aldwin," she said. "Did you come to see me off?"

"No," her husband replied, "I came to join you."

"I can't take you to the border," said Beverly, "it's far too dangerous. There's already been one attempt on Lord Wilfrid."

"I thought I might accompany you as far as Hawksburg," he said. "I have to spend some more time studying the circle there."

"That's an excellent idea," said Beverly. "Then, I can meet you back there after we've dropped this lot off at the border."

"There, you see," said Aldwin, "I found a way for us to spend more time together."

"Are you sure you'll be comfortable riding all day?"

"I'll get used to it. I did ride all the way from Bodden to Hawksburg once, don't you remember?"

She smiled. "Of course I do," she replied. "Now, let's get going, shall we?"

She urged her mount forward into a slow walk as Aldwin brought his own horse alongside hers.

"Lightning knew you'd be showing up," said Beverly.

"He did?"

"Yes, he wouldn't let me start moving until you arrived."

Aldwin smiled, "Lightning's a smart horse, he was probably picking up on your emotions."

"Emotions?" said Beverly.

"Weren't you just a little bit sad that you wouldn't see me for weeks?"

"Of course," she replied.

"Well then, there you have it."

"Lightning doesn't read minds," said Beverly. "He's a horse, remember?"

"I wouldn't be so sure," said Aldwin.

She stared at him, watching as a smile crept across his face, a smile he was desperately trying to suppress.

"Come on," she said, "out with it. What did you do?"

He looked at her, finally breaking out into a grin. "I might have talked to him early this morning."

"You can't talk to horses," declared Beverly.

"No, that's true, I can't," he said, "but Albreda can."

"So you had Albreda tell him to wait?"

"I did," he admitted. "I hope you're not upset with me."

"Not at all," she said, "I think it's very romantic."

Gerald made his way through the Palace, Tempus trotting along at his side. He paused for a moment at the door to the Royal Suite, then knocked respectfully.

"Come," came the answer.

He pushed open the door to see Prince Alric pulling his tunic over his head.

"Sorry to interrupt, Highness," he said.

"Nonsense, Gerald," the prince replied, "we were just dressing for breakfast."

"I take it Anna's in the bedroom?"

"She is," said Alric, "I'm sure she'll be out any moment now."

"Is that Gerald?" came a familiar voice.

"It is," said Alric.

"Just a moment," Anna called back.

She came out of the bedroom, her blonde hair looking scraggly. Tempus barked and ran over to his mistress, who crouched to give the great dog a pet.

"Shall I send for Sophie?" asked Gerald.

"Please do," said Anna, "I can't go down to eat with my hair like this."

"Oh, I don't know," said Alric, grinning, "I think it suits you."

"You'll have to excuse my husband," said Anna, "these Weldwyners have a strange sense of decorum."

Gerald smiled, pleased to see Anna in such a good mood.

"Married life seems to agree with you," he said.

"So it does," she said, "but you didn't come here to tell me that."

"No," Gerald agreed, "I came to tell you that the Norland delegation is on the way back home. They left early this morning."

"Good," said Anna, "that means we can start planning our trip to Uxley."

"You're a little late for that," said Alric.

Anna turned to the prince in surprise. "What's that supposed to mean?"

"It means," said Gerald, "that Alric and I have already made all the necessary arrangements."

"Oh, you have, have you?" said Anna. "I can see how this is going to work, the two of you conspiring against me." She grinned, lessening the blow. "Very well, when do we leave?"

"Right after breakfast," said Gerald, "or even later, if you wish, but we do have to make The Gryphon's Rest before nightfall."

"In that case," said Anna, "fetch Sophie, and have my food brought here. I shall dine in my room. Have you eaten yet?"

"No," admitted Gerald, "I was busy making preparations."

"Well, we can't have you going hungry," said Anna. "Have them send up lots of food, and you can join us."

"I don't want to impose," said Gerald.

"Nonsense," said Alric, "the company would be welcome."

"Very well," said Gerald, "I shall return promptly."

He left the room, leaving Tempus with his mistress.

"I've been looking forward to this," said Alric.

"Breakfast?" said Anna.

"No, surprising you," he said.

"Well, you succeeded," said Anna. "How long have you been planning this?"

"Close to a week," he replied.

"A week? Why so long?"

"We sent word to Uxley that we'd be arriving, and then we had to arrange rooms at the Gryphon's Rest."

"And what's so difficult about that?" Anna asked.

"You're the queen now. We can't just rent a regular room."

"Why not?"

"Well, for one thing, your entourage is too large. You can't travel without guards. You're the queen, for Saxnor's sake."

"Why, Alric, you just invoked Saxnor. There's hope for you yet!"

"I'm taking my role as Prince of Merceria seriously," he said, though his grin told a different story.

"And how did you solve this problem?"

"Gerald and I discussed it at length before we came to a solution. We looked at how many people were to be in the column and then calculated how many rooms we'd need."

"Column?" said Anna. "Are we to be a military convoy now?"

Alric blushed, "In a manner of speaking, yes. You are, after all, a warrior queen."

Anna smiled. "I like that, Anna of Merceria, the Warrior Queen."

"It suits you."

"As do you," said Anna. "So tell me, what was your solution?"

"We simply booked the entire inn."

"I'm sure that made Master Draymon happy."

Alric looked at her in surprise. "How do you know the innkeeper's name?"

"I've stayed there before," said Anna, "when I was younger. Of course, he didn't know who I was back then, we travelled incognito."

"I should like to have met you back then," said Alric.

"Really?" said Anna. "I don't think I would have impressed you. I hadn't travelled outside of Uxley at that point in time."

"I assume you were travelling to Wincaster?"

"We were," said Anna. "Gerald and Sophie were with me, along with Tempus, of course. It was an exciting time."

"And now you're bored?" asked Alric.

"Hardly," she replied. "I'm far too busy to become bored."

"The whole point of this visit is to relax," Alric reminded her.

"And so I shall," said Anna, "but that doesn't mean sitting around and doing nothing. I intend to visit my friends in the village. I've got a new husband to introduce, don't I! Did I ever tell you about Mrs. Brown?"

"The cook?" said Alric. "Yes, I believe you've mentioned her once or twice."

"Wait until you taste her scones!" said Anna.

Albreda stepped through the door, calling out as she went. "Is anyone there?"

"Up here," came the voice of Aldus Hearn. "We're in the casting room."

Albreda ascended the stairs, finally arriving to see Kiren-Jool, Gretchen Harwell, and Aldus Hearn.

"Found anything of interest yet?" she asked.

"Not yet," said Gretchen, "but we have several more combinations to try."

Albreda walked around the mirror, admiring its construction as the others discussed the runes surrounding the glass.

"Don't let me interrupt," she said.

"We're trying to identify this rune," said Gretchen. "Are you familiar with it?"

Albreda came around the front of the mirror to examine the carved border in more detail.

"I can't say that I am, but didn't Master Bloom discover some additional runes at one of the temples?"

"He did," said Aldus Hearn, who had sat down at a small table they had set up and was flicking through the pages of a book. "Aubrey left us some notes, but I see nothing that matches this one."

"Couldn't it be a maker's mark?" suggested Albreda. "All the other runes we can identify."

"Of course," said Kiren-Jool, "I should have realized. No mage in his right mind would make an item of such power and not identify themselves."

"I don't recognize the mark," said Hearn.

"None of us do, apparently," said Albreda, "but that shouldn't prevent us from activating it. What have you tried so far?"

Aldus Hearn waved her over to the table, indicating a loose piece of parchment on which he had made annotations.

"These are the combinations we've attempted so far," he said, "but none of them have had any effect."

She looked down at the list, a flicker of annoyance passing across her face.

"I would have thought you'd be further along by now. Need I remind you that Revi Bloom is missing and may need our help."

"It's not as easy as you might think," said Aldus Hearn. "Each attempt drains some of our power, and then we have to wait for the mirror to reset."

"Reset?" questioned Albreda. "What in Saxnor's name are you talking about?"

"When you invoke runes," said Gretchen, "there is a period of time when they remain activated. This allows multiple runes to be used in combinations."

"I understand that," said Albreda. "The circles of stone in the Whitewood work in a similar matter, but they don't take that long to cool down, or reset as you call it."

They all looked at her in surprise.

"You could have mentioned that before," said Aldus Hearn.

"Why would it even cross my mind?" said Albreda. "I had no idea you were contemplating such a thing."

"I suppose that's true," said Kiren-Jool, "but we are working in the dark here. None of us has ever used something like this mirror before."

"And yet," said Albreda, "both our Enchanters are versed in such magic."

Kiren-Jool looked at his feet as Gretchen blushed.

"Sorry," the Weldwyn mage said, "but this is new to all of us."

"Then let us continue with all haste," said Albreda. "Have you written down the rest of the sequences?"

"We have," said Aldus Hearn, producing another paper. "They're right here." He handed the page to Albreda, who scanned the sheet briefly, then stood before the mirror.

"Very well," she said, "let us proceed."

She invoked her magic, reading the magic letters from the page as she did. As the last syllable fell from her lips, she looked at the mirror, but there was no effect.

"I think we can safely cross that one off the list," she said. "Let us try again."

"Surely you should wait?" advised Aldus Hearn.

"Why?" she asked. "I'm not tired, and the words of power obviously had no effect. No, I shall continue right on to the next sequence." She gazed back down at her notes, then closed her eyes a moment.

"I have them," she said, passing the parchment to Kiren-Jool.

She began uttering the words once more, this time using the new sequence. Almost immediately, she felt a sense of power surging through her and then one of the runes on the mirror's border began to glow.

"That's it," said Gretchen, "it's working!"

Albreda continued, letting the words of power pour forth from her mouth. Soon, six of the runes were glowing, and then a ripple effect took hold on the mirror as the image shifted. Now, instead of her reflection, the druid was looking through the mirror into a room of some sort. The other mages all drew closer.

"Where is it?" asked Kiren-Jool.

"I have no idea," said Aldus Hearn.

"Somewhere in the mountains," said Albreda.

"How can you possibly know that?" asked Hearn.

"There's a window to the right through which I can see a peak. Wherever this is, I suspect it's quite high up."

"Do we just step through?" asked Hearn.

"No," said Gretchen, "we have only activated the viewing function, but another command would be necessary to step through."

"Like the Saurian gates," suggested Hearn.

"Yes," Albreda agreed.

"So we've failed," said Kiren-Jool.

"On the contrary," said Gretchen, "we have solved the first part of the puzzle."

"Agreed," said Albreda, "and the rest will be easier to determine, as a rune that is already lit cannot be reused. That leaves us with a significantly smaller number of combinations."

"Do you know how to use the Saurian gates?" asked Aldus Hearn.

"I do," said Albreda, "though I've never personally activated them, why?"

"The magic must be similar as they both transport people over long distances. Could the combinations be the same?"

"An excellent thought," said Albreda, "but the gates require you to identify the other end's location, and for that, we'd need to know where this room is that we are viewing."

"Maybe not," said Gretchen Harwell. "These gates you describe exist at many destinations, don't they?"

"They do," said Albreda, "what of it?"

"Mirrors always work in pairs," the Enchantress continued. "Therefore, there is only one destination."

"I hadn't considered that," said Albreda, "but it's an excellent point." She waved her hand, dismissing her magic, and the runes light faded away.

"Why did you do that?" asked Aldus Hearn.

"We must find Revi's notes regarding the Saurian temples," she said, "and hope they are detailed enough to give us the answers we require. I shouldn't like to use up all my power trying random combinations."

"I thought you said you remembered how to use the temple flames?" said Kiren-Jool.

"I only witnessed the one that took us to Queenston," said Albreda, "and I'm certain it wouldn't work here. Now, let us find his notes on the Saurian temples and see if we can unravel the rest of this mystery."

TEN

Galburn's Ridge

Fall 964 MC

K ing Halfan shifted uncomfortably, then winced, an action noted by Lord Hollis, the Earl of Beaconsgate.

"Are you in pain, Your Majesty?" he asked.

"No more so than usual," the king replied. He looked around the room, taking in the assembled nobles. It had required a lot of effort to gather all his earls, an effort, he hoped, that would prove beneficial.

"Everyone is here, Your Majesty," noted Lord Rutherford. "You may begin at your leisure."

Halfan looked at the man in irritation. "I might have some ailments," the king said, "but I'm fully aware of my surroundings."

Lord Rutherford diverted his gaze, but the king knew his thoughts. Like all the other earls, he was waiting for King Halfan to die. They had already started flexing their political muscles in anticipation of the coming conflict. The Norland court had never been as fractious as it was now, and Halfan hoped he could at least secure peace with Merceria before his passing.

"Send in Lord Wilfrid," commanded the king.

Guards opened the door, admitting the elderly lord. He moved to stand in the centre of the room, facing the king. The earls, all seven of them, sat to one side of the room on high-backed, padded wooden chairs, eager to see what this business was about.

"Lord Wilfrid has returned from a diplomatic mission to Merceria," declared King Halfan

The announcement had an immediate effect. Halfan watched as Lord Hollis leaned forward in his chair, replacing his bored countenance with that of keen interest. The other earls, not to be outdone, locked their eyes on the elderly diplomat.

Lord Wilfrid bowed deeply. "It is with the greatest joy that I announce my mission was a success, Your Majesty."

"What mission is this?" called out Lord Rutherford.

The king turned his eyes on the Earl of Hammersfield. Rutherford was generally a cautious man, but the look of irritation on his face betrayed his casual concern.

"I sent him to open negotiations with the Queen of Merceria," said Halfan.

"Surely you jest, my king," said Rutherford. "We cannot trust the Mercerians to negotiate in good faith!"

"We have been at war for centuries," countered the king, "and it has drained our resources. We can no longer afford to spend all our energies preparing for an invasion."

Lord Calder, the Earl of Greendale, stood, looking at the king. Halfan nodded, granting his permission to address the court.

"My lords," said Calder, "the king speaks the truth. For hundreds of years, we have had to maintain troops on the border. It is time we made peace."

"Easy for you to say," said the Earl of Beaconsgate, "you're not on their border. I know these Mercerians, they raid our lands on a regular basis. We must show them strength. Negotiating peace will be seen as an act of weakness."

"I would agree," added Lord Rutherford. "Hollis and I are dedicated to protecting our southern border. We cannot let them think we are unprepared."

"Nor shall we," said the king, returning his gaze to his recently returned diplomat. "Tell me, Lord Wilfrid, what was the Mercerian Queen's response?"

Lord Wilfrid straightened. "She has agreed to come to Galburn's Ridge in person."

The room exploded with raised voices. King Halfan let them talk amongst themselves, then called all in the room to silence.

"Lord Hollis," began the king, "you have voiced your disapproval, have you anything to add?"

"Only that we must be cautious, Your Majesty," the Earl of Beaconsgate replied.

"Very well," said the king. "Lord Rutherford, your opinion?"

"It is well known that I dislike the Mercerians," the Earl of Hammersfield replied, "and yet I commend you on luring the Mercerian Monarch to our lands."

"It is not a trap," said the king, "but an earnest attempt to negotiate a lasting peace."

"I am all in favour of negotiating," said Lord Rutherford, "providing we are not giving away anything of value."

"You fear them demanding land?" said the king.

"I do," Rutherford replied.

"Then you may rest assured," Halfan continued, "I have no intention of giving up anything."

Lord Rutherford bowed respectfully.

The king turned to Lord Thurlowe. "You have been quiet of late, my lord, I would have you speak."

"I am cautiously optimistic," said the Earl of Ravensguard, "and hope that this new Mercerian Ruler proves amenable to your proposal. She is young, is she not?"

"She is," replied Lord Wilfrid.

"How young?" asked Calder.

"She is but seventeen years of age," replied Lord Wilfrid.

"This is ridiculous!" noted Lord Marley, the elderly Earl of Walthorne. "Surely they are not ruled by a child? Who controls her? Who is the power behind the throne?"

Lord Wilfrid smiled. "I can assure you that Queen Anna is very much in control. She has surrounded herself with trusted advisors. I saw no signs of undue influence over her."

"And when she marries," asked Lord Waverly, "who will then rule their land?"

"She is already married," said Lord Wilfrid, "to a prince of Weldwyn, the land we call Westland."

"Are you saying that Westland controls the throne of Merceria?" asked Lord Hollis.

"No," Lord Wilfrid answered. "The queen still rules. After the recent civil war, she took steps to change their laws of succession. Her husband remains a prince and has no kingly powers."

"This is preposterous," said Hollis. "She has clearly lost her mind."

"It is not our place to rule Merceria," King Halfan reminded him.

"I beg to differ," said Hollis. "Our kingdom was founded by a Royal Heir to the Warrior's Crown. Have you so soon forgotten?"

King Halfan rose to his feet, "I have forgotten nothing, Lord Hollis, but the fact remains that in the last four hundred years, it has proven impossible to recover the throne. It is time we set aside that dream to build a better kingdom for ourselves."

"I must object," asserted Lord Hollis. "We have honed our armies taming this land, surely it is time we struck back at the Mercerians?"

King Halfan winced as he shifted his feet. "Are you suggesting that we throw away this opportunity for peace?"

"Think of it," said Hollis, "we would finally have a Ruler of Merceria in our grasp. We could force them to accept our claim to the throne!"

"I will not betray a guest," declared Halfan, "and neither will you!"

Lord Hollis lowered his head. "As you wish, my king, I only offer suggestions."

King Halfan sat, resting his hands on the arms of the throne. "Lord Waverly, have you anything to add?"

"No, Your Majesty," replied the Earl of Marston.

"Creighton?"

The Earl of Riverhurst looked at Lord Wilfrid. "These Mercerians," he said, "what is your opinion of them?"

"I think they are to be trusted," the old man replied. "They were gracious hosts during our visit and extended us every courtesy."

"That's not what I heard," piped up Lord Thurlowe.

"What does that mean?" asked Hollis.

"It means," continued Thurlowe, "that someone tried to kill Lord Wilfrid. If it hadn't been for his bodyguard, he wouldn't have survived."

"Is this true?" asked the king.

"Alas, yes," said Lord Wilfrid, "though they were unable to capture the culprit."

"That's convenient," said Hollis.

"While that is true," said Lord Wilfrid, "it did reveal another interesting fact. They have mages that can heal the injured."

"Surely you jest," said Rutherford. "There haven't been healers in generations."

"It's true," declared Wilfrid, "I witnessed it with my own eyes. A Westland mage healed my bodyguard, and I'm led to believe the Mercerians have them as well."

"It changes nothing," noted Creighton. "The queen would be welcome whether she has mages or not."

"True," said Hollis, "but if they have mages in their employ, we must take steps to secure ourselves."

"Meaning?" asked Rutherford.

"We know so little about Life Magic," said Hollis. "Who knows what they are capable of?"

"Don't be absurd," said Creighton, "they heal the wounded, nothing more."

"Are you sure?" asked Hollis. "Our Fire Mages can do more than just start a fire."

"You forget," said Creighton, "Fire Magic only deals with fire AND heat. Outside of that, there is little they can do."

"Enough of this discussion," said the king. "You can argue the finer points of magic on your own time. Right now, we must decide how best to welcome them."

"Allow me to escort them," offered Lord Hollis.

"You?" questioned King Halfan. "I'm surprised to hear you volunteer for such a task with the animosity you hold for our southern neighbour."

"They will be traversing my land," said Hollis. "I shouldn't like anything happening to them on route."

"Very well," said the king, "but Lord Wilfrid will accompany you. He was, in the end, the man that invited them."

The Earl of Beaconsgate bowed his head, "Of course, Your Majesty. I shall meet with him this evening to make preparations."

"Good," said King Halfan, "then I think our business here is finished. I will announce a grand feast to welcome the Queen of Merceria upon her arrival. I need confirmation when she has crossed the border, Lord Hollis."

"Of course, my king."

"Very well, then I officially dissolve this meeting. Be off with you, I have things to consider."

The earls all rose, bowing to their monarch as they left the room. Halfan watched them go, then beckoned Lord Wilfrid closer.

"Yes, Your Majesty?"

The king rose to his feet, but a spasm of pain ebbed through him, causing him to stagger. He caught the edge of the throne to steady himself and took a moment to breathe through it.

"Your Majesty?" said Lord Wilfrid.

"I will be fine momentarily," said the king. "Now tell me, what did you really think of this young Queen of Merceria?"

"I believe she is earnest in her wish for peace."

"And her courtiers? Are they as fractious as ours?"

"While there is some opposition to her, her grip on power is strong, Your Majesty, and I believe she is well-liked by the general populace."

"Good," said King Halfan, "then perhaps peace can finally be achieved."

"You must be wary of Lord Hollis," warned Wilfrid.

"I am well aware of his intentions," said the king, "but I'm not dead yet."

"He would be king," advised Wilfrid.

"It has come to my attention," said Halfan as he sat back down, trying desperately to get comfortable. "I will not last much longer," he admitted, "of that, I have no doubt, but I will see our border secured before this realm falls into internal conflict."

"You think a civil war inevitable?" asked Lord Wilfrid.

"I do," said the king. "There is too much desire for power, and I am without an heir."

"Then why bother with this peace?"

"To prevent the Mercerians from taking advantage of our weakness. I fear they would make short work of us if we're busy fighting amongst ourselves."

"Couldn't they do that anyway?"

"They could," said the king, "but during their visit, I intend to make a show of force. We have to convince them that we have a strong military, fully capable of retaliation if needed. We must negotiate from a position of strength."

The Earl of Beaconsgate moved down the corridor, deep in thought. He had just reached the corner when the familiar voice of Lord Rutherford caught his attention.

"Hollis," the man said, "might I have a word?"

"Of course, what is it?"

Lord Rutherford looked up and down the hallway before speaking, "Perhaps this is not the best place to discuss such things. Might I suggest my quarters?"

"An excellent idea," said Hollis, "providing, of course, that you have some of that Oaksvale White left?"

"I do indeed," said Rutherford. "I just received a new shipment this morning, in fact."

"Then lead on, my friend, and we shall converse at length."

Rutherford led him through the Royal Castle, an immense structure built into the side of the hills, bristling with towers, each earl claiming one for their own. The castle formed the end of the ridge that gave Norland's capital city of Galburn's Ridge its name.

Hollis followed the Earl of Hammersfield into his tower, noting the guards wearing Rutherford's livery. Ordinarily, he would have insisted on bringing some of his own men, for to enter another earl's domain was considered dangerous, but Rutherford had been an ally for years, and so he simply nodded at the guards, following his friend into a well-decorated room.

Rutherford sat, indicating a nearby chair for Hollis. Before they could begin their conversation, the door opened quietly to admit a couple of servants bearing wine. They quickly poured each earl a drink, then left as quietly as they had entered.

"There," said Rutherford, "now we're free to talk."

"Very well," said Hollis, "what in particular is it you wanted to discuss?"

"You know damned well," said Rutherford. "The king won't last much longer. We must prepare ourselves for the inevitable."

"Seizing power," said Hollis.

"Precisely," said Rutherford, "and I would be willing to support your claim once the fighting commences."

Hollis shook his head. "I'm afraid it's not the crown of Norland I'm working to gain," he said, "but that of Merceria!"

"How in Saxnor's name would you accomplish that?" asked Rutherford.

Hollis leaned forward, talking in a lower voice, "If we can get Thurlowe on our side, I think it can be accomplished."

"But how?"

"We bring this Mercerian Queen here, then finish off the king. It shouldn't be too hard to pin his death on these southerners."

"Uniting everyone against them," said Rutherford. "That's very clever."

"Oh, there's more," said Hollis. "With their queen here, among us, we can take her hostage. The confusion at their court alone should paralyze them, then, when they're leaderless, we send our armies flooding across the border."

"That won't work," said Rutherford. "They have fortified cities along the border."

"Then we bypass them," said Hollis, "drive straight for Wincaster. One siege and it'll all be over."

"You make it sound so easy," said Rutherford. "Are you forgetting that their capital is heavily fortified?"

"It is, but we have battle mages to help."

"Don't they have mages as well?"

"They do," agreed Hollis, "but I'm led to believe there are very few of them. Numbers are on our side, Rutherford. It's what we've been building up to for years."

Lord Rutherford sat back, letting the idea sink in. "It's achievable, but the cost would be high."

"Naturally," said Hollis. "What war doesn't have its price, but think of it, we would finally have the throne of Merceria in our grasp!"

"And all we have to do is capture the queen?"

"I'm not saying it'll be easy," said Hollis, "but she'll be here with little more than a small bodyguard. Surely not enough to withstand the troops we can call upon in the capital!"

"I'm in," said Rutherford, "provided, of course, that you can convince Thurlowe to join us."

Hollis smiled, "Good, for I've already ascertained his feelings in this matter. Rest assured, we can now begin to move forward on this."

ELEVEN

The Border

Fall 964 MC

Beverly reined in Lightning, coming to a halt before the queen. "We've spotted them, Your Majesty," she said. "They're approaching from the north."

"How many?" asked Gerald.

"A sizable force," said Beverly, "likely a hundred or more."

"That many?" said Aubrey.

"We ARE a rather large force ourselves," said Anna. "And they can't have us marching through their territory without an escort."

"I wish Revi were here with us," said Aubrey. "He could use Shellbreaker to spy them out."

"Speaking of Revi," said Anna, "is there any news?"

"The last I heard," said Aubrey, "they'd managed to activate the mirror for viewing purposes, but they're still trying to determine how to travel through it."

"Interesting," said Anna. "What did they see?"

"Our initial conjecture seems to be correct. It looks like a tower, likely that of Andronicus."

"I wonder what secrets it might hold," mused Anna.

"Let them worry about it," said Gerald. "We need to concentrate on the task at hand."

"Shall I ride out to meet them?" asked Beverly.

"Yes," said the queen, "and let them know we'll rendezvous with them at the ford."

"Very well, Your Majesty," said Beverly. She wheeled Lightning around and then galloped off to the north.

"Nervous?" asked Gerald.

"Of course," said Anna, "there's so much that could go wrong."

"Don't worry," said Aubrey, "that's why I'm here. I can have you back in Wincaster in no time, should it prove necessary."

"Let's hope it doesn't come to that," said Anna. "The whole point of this meeting with the Norland King is to negotiate a permanent peace. It's a little hard to do that if I'm not present."

Gerald glanced back at the camp behind them. In addition to their escort of cavalry, they also had a half company of footmen who would be delegated to act as guards for whatever place they would be staying while visiting Norland. Yet, their numbers paled in comparison to the multitude of others present, for there were supply wagons, food for the trip, black-smiths to help look after horseshoes and nails, not to mention the various servants necessary for the queen's entourage.

He thought back to his earlier life with Anna. It had been so much easier to make a trip in those days. Now, however, it seemed even short trips required an entire army to accompany them.

They all sat in relative silence, watching as Beverly slowed her pace. When the knight brought her horse to a halt, two riders detached them-selves from the Norland group, riding towards her. There was the briefest exchange of words, then Beverly turned, riding back towards the Royal Party with the two Norlanders.

"This looks interesting," noted Anna.

"That's Lord Wilfrid," said Gerald, as they drew closer, "but I don't know who the other man is."

"We'll find out soon enough," said Anna.

The trio was soon splashing across the ford, close enough for even Gerald to make out their faces quite clearly.

"Judging by his clothes, he's someone important," he noted.

Beverly led them directly to the Royal Party. "Your Majesty," she said, "may I introduce Lord Hollis, Earl of Beaconsgate, and I believe you remember Lord Wilfrid of Hansley."

Gerald was taken aback. The Earl of Beaconsgate had long been a thorn in the side of Bodden, his troops had even tried to siege the Keep multiple times. He looked at Beverly, but the knight sat, stone-faced, unwilling to reveal her loathing.

"Lord Hollis," said Anna, "we are well met this day. I take it you have come to escort us to Galburn's Ridge?"

Hollis bowed. "Indeed, Your Majesty. My men are waiting to the north. We may proceed at your leisure."

"Very well," said Anna, "then let us be on our way for I would be in your capital before the snow comes."

"Of course, Majesty," said Hollis. The earl turned his horse around, then sat waiting as Gerald gave the order to march.

The column started moving slowly, Anna and her immediate entourage at its head. Gerald rode to one side of the queen, Aubrey to the other while Arnim Caster rode up and down the column, keeping a close eye on it as it entered the ford.

On the far side of the river, a group of Norland horsemen had trotted down to the bank and were watching with interest as the first of the Guard Cavalry reached Norland soil.

Beverly looked at Gerald, "With your permission, Marshal, I shall rejoin the advance guard."

Gerald nodded, watching her splash across the river.

Lord Hollis was watching her as well, and Gerald wondered what thoughts might be crossing the earl's mind. Was he even aware that Beverly was heir to Bodden?

"An interesting horse your knight has," the earl said. "Have you many of them?"

"I'm afraid I'm not at liberty to discuss that," said Gerald, "just as I'm sure you wouldn't tell me the strength of your army."

Hollis smiled, "An astute observation. You are quite right, of course, we should not be discussing such things. Let us move onto safer topics. Tell me, do they still serve Mercerian Pudding in Wincaster?"

Gerald smiled, "Of course, it's one of my favourites."

"I think you'll find everything is my marshal's favourite," added Anna.

"You are the Duke of Wincaster, are you not?" asked Lord Hollis.

"I am," said Gerald.

"Tell me, Lord, are these all your troops?"

Gerald looked to Anna, confusion on his face.

"He is the Marshal of the Royal Army," said Anna. "In Merceria, the army falls under the command of the monarch."

"Ah," said Lord Hollis. "In Norland, the armies are controlled by the earls."

"Surely the king has his own troops?" said Gerald.

"He is permitted a small retinue," said Hollis, "principally to protect him in the capital."

"That must make things difficult in times of war," said Anna.

"We have no neighbours save for Merceria," said the earl, "and so the issue has seldom come up."

"I can see we have much to learn from each other," said Anna.

Lord Hollis turned to Aubrey. "I assume this is your lady-in-waiting?"

"No," said Anna, "this is Lady Aubrey Brandon, Baroness of Hawksburg."

"Pleased to make your acquaintance," said the earl.

"Lady Aubrey is also one of our mages," said Anna.

The earl looked at the queen in surprise. "A mage?"

"Indeed," said Anna, "a Life Mage to be precise."

Aubrey smiled at the man's sudden discomfort. "I can assure you, my lord, my magic is dedicated solely to healing the sick and injured."

The earl seemed to relax a little, though he was still gripping his reins tightly.

"Will you ride with us, Lord Hollis?" asked Anna.

"I would be delighted, Your Majesty," the earl replied. "Lord Wilfrid?"

The older lord bowed. "I regret I must ride ahead. There are preparations to be made for this evening, but I look forward to seeing you again, Your Majesty."

He rode off, climbing up the far bank. Anna urged her horse forward, Gerald keeping pace with her. Lady Aubrey fell in behind, alongside Lord Hollis.

"I hear you have Orcs in Norland," she said.

Hollis looked at the young mage. "You seem remarkably well informed."

"It's my duty," said Aubrey.

"As a Life Mage?"

"No," she replied, "as an advisor to the queen."

"You surprise me, Lady Aubrey. I had no idea the court of Wincaster had women in such high positions."

"And why wouldn't we?" she asked. "It's what's on the inside that's important, not our exterior."

"Wise words from one so young," said Lord Hollis. "I mean no offense, it's just that we do things differently here in Norland."

"Perhaps the exchange of knowledge will benefit us both," said Aubrey. "Have you no women at court at all?"

"We do," said Hollis, "but they are not what you would refer to as advisors. Instead, they are playthings for the wealthy and powerful."

"We are familiar with the custom," said Aubrey. "Our previous king had a mistress."

"Yes, precisely what I meant," said Hollis. "You see? We are not so different, after all."

"It makes sense," noted Aubrey, "we do share a common ancestry."

"True," the earl replied, "and yet four centuries have left their mark on both our cultures in some ways. Tell me, do they still have the games in Merceria?"

"What games would those be?" asked Aubrey.

"In the old days," said the earl, "prisoners would fight to the death for entertainment."

"You know as well as I do that the practise ceased long before the founding of Norland."

The earl smiled, "So it did, but I'm surprised you would know of such things."

"Why? Because I'm a woman?" she said.

"No, because you are so young. How old are you, just out of curiosity?"

"Old enough to not answer that question," said Aubrey. "And in any case, what has my age to do with anything?"

"I can see our cultures look on age much differently," said the earl. "In Norland, we value age and experience."

"That is valuable for us as well," said Aubrey, "but intelligence and education are also highly prized."

"Surely you were trained by your mother?" said the earl.

"Naturally," said Aubrey, "but what, do you suppose, she taught me?"

"The finer points of womanhood, no doubt," answered Lord Hollis.

"Which would be?"

"Needlecraft, music, and literature, I would surmise."

"I hate to disabuse you of that belief, my lord, but my mother ran the barony in my father's absence. I can assure you I have learned much more than what you describe. I AM a Life Mage."

"What does that entail, precisely?" asked the earl.

"A good knowledge of anatomy, for a start, not to mention the non-magical methods of treating the injured. On top of that, I've had to learn how to channel magical energies to heal flesh and bone."

"Remarkable," said Lord Hollis, "I never would have thought it."

"Why," asked Aubrey, "because of my gender?"

"No," said the earl, "as I said earlier, because of your youth. Tell me, are you promised?"

"I beg your pardon?"

"Are you yet promised in marriage?" explained Lord Hollis. "I only ask because an arrangement might be made to marry you off to a Norland lord. Think how beneficial that would be to both our realms."

"I am not a piece of property to be bartered away," asserted Aubrey.

"Of course you are," said Hollis, "we all are. We may be earls or, in your case, a baroness, but ultimately, we all serve the crown."

"Are you married yourself?" asked Aubrey.

"I am," Hollis confirmed, "for some years, as a matter of fact. It was an arranged marriage. The Earl of Hammersfield is, truth be told, my brother-in-law. What of you? You must have relatives in various places. Any I might have heard of?"

"My uncle is the Baron of Bodden," she said, watching him closely.

The earl's eyes went wide. "Well, that is something I hadn't expected."

"And that's not all," said Aubrey, relishing the effect. "My cousin, Beverly, is his daughter. She's the knight that escorted you across the river."

Lord Hollis swivelled his gaze to where Beverly led the Guard Cavalry.

"It seems you Mercerians are full of surprises," he noted, smiling slightly. "I shall have to keep a closer eye on you, but for now, I think it time I rejoined my people. I hope we have time to chat in the future, it's been quite enlightening."

"Of course," said Aubrey, nodding her head slightly, "I look forward to it."

Lord Hollis spurred on his horse, riding around Anna and Gerald and then galloping off towards the Norland troops that led them. Aubrey urged her mount forward, coming up beside Anna.

Ahead of them, possibly alerted by the activity, Tempus barked, causing more than one look of concern from the Norland troops. Anna laughed.

"He's enjoying himself," said Gerald.

"And why wouldn't he be," said Anna. "We don't get out into the country-side much these days, and he's always liked being outdoors." She turned her attention to Aubrey. "What did you make of Lord Hollis?"

"He seems rather...how should I put this?"

"Old fashioned?" offered Gerald.

"Yes," said Aubrey, "and he doesn't have much of an opinion about the usefulness of women."

"I imagine that will be common in Norland," said Gerald.

"But surely they have the same traditions as us?" asked Aubrey.

"They do," said Anna, "but when Prince Talburn tried to usurp the throne, he had no female warriors in his entourage."

"And how do we know this?" pressed Aubrey.

"Need you ask?" said Gerald. "Anna has read every book on Norland that she can find."

"Prince Talburn was the founder of Norland, wasn't he?" said Aubrey.

"Indeed, he was," said Anna. "After his defeat at the Battle of the Hills, he fled north with his followers. Back in those days, our nobles controlled the bulk of the army, but after Talburn's defeat, the crown created the Royal Army."

"That explains a few things," said Aubrey. "Do we know which followers fled with him?"

"We do," said Anna, "though you likely wouldn't recognize the names. I suspect that their descendants became the earls of Norland, though we won't know for sure until they're introduced to us."

"I heard you mention the Orcs earlier," said Gerald, "what was the earl's response?"

"He evaded the topic," explained Aubrey.

"We shall have to keep a close eye on him," warned Gerald.

"On that, we are in agreement," said Anna.

"What do you expect in Galburn's Ridge, Your Majesty?" asked Aubrey.

"I imagine they'll be quite polite," said Anna, "but I doubt we'll make much headway. I have a feeling the earls are not all in agreement with peace."

"And why would they be?" said Gerald.

"I'm afraid I don't follow," said Aubrey. "Surely they would all desire peace?"

"A state of perpetual war gives the earls a reason to maintain strong personal armies," said Gerald. "Peace would end all of that."

"Yes," agreed Anna, "so peace would be good for Norland, but not, it appears, good for the nobles."

"It hardly seems fair," noted Aubrey. "All we want is for our people to live in peace, surely they are the same?"

Anna smiled, "You would think so, wouldn't you, but the truth is that Merceria has been in an almost constant warlike state since its founding."

"We haven't fought that many wars, have we?" said Aubrey.

"When we're not at war, we're often fighting each other," said Anna. "I frequently wonder if mercenaries founding a kingdom was a bad idea."

"What else could they do?" asked Gerald.

"I don't know," mused Anna, "surrender to Weldwyn, perhaps?"

"And what good would that have done?" asked Gerald.

"The land might be more peaceful, for one."

"You're forgetting the history of Weldwyn," Gerald replied. "Without our ancestors as a threat, the tribes would never have formed Weldwyn."

"I suppose that's true," said Anna, "but in any event, it doesn't matter, we're here now because of our ancestors. Nothing we do can ever change that."

"True," said Aubrey, "but we can influence what comes after us."

"Wise words," noted Gerald. "Of course, first we have to meet the Norland king. What was his name again?"

"Halfan," said Anna.

"Strange name, that," said Gerald.

"It's actually quite a common name," noted Anna, "or at least it used to be. A lot of the Mercerians that supported the uprising were of Vikovian descent."

"Vikovian?" said Gerald. "Never heard of it."

"They were a powerful kingdom back on the Continent. Some of our original ancestors were of Vikovian descent."

"Interesting," noted Gerald, "I had no idea. Maybe we'll see more of them in Norland."

"Now that," said Anna, "would be interesting indeed."

By mid-morning, they were approaching Brookesholde, a small village that lay north of Wickfield. They didn't stop, contenting themselves with riding around the perimeter of the place rather than moving through it. Gerald noted the farmers out in their fields, but he could have just as easily been looking on Wickfield or Mattingly, so similar were the views.

They camped that night on the open plain, some distance from their Norland escort. Once guards were posted, Gerald made sure they were alert, for the last thing they needed was an attempt on Anna's life.

As it turned out, their precautions were not needed, and the next day they resumed their march. The road led them directly from Brookesholde to Oaksvale, the next village on their route, which they reached two days later.

Here, they were informed that they were almost halfway to Galburn's Ridge, a fact that surprised Anna. Aubrey, for her part, had taken to making notations in her sketchbook, along with a working map, but the relatively short distance to the Norland capital surprised everyone.

Early the next morning, they marched out of Oaksvale, the Norland warriors once again in the lead. Gerald rode up to Beverly, who led the Guard Cavalry. He nodded to her as he drew alongside.

"You look wide awake this morning," she noted.

"It reminds me of the old days, back in Bodden," he said, "though I can't say I feel comfortable with all these Norlanders before us."

"At least they're not behind us," she said.

"Tell me, Beverly, what do you make of our hosts?"

"Do you mean the earl or his troops?"

"Both," said Gerald, "but let's start with his soldiers."

Beverly thought for a moment before answering. "They're better equipped than those he sent against Bodden," she said, "and they seem more disciplined. I suspect these are the cream of his troops."

"That would make sense," said Gerald. "After all, he's escorting a queen, he likely wants to make a favourable impression. Anything else you've noticed about them?"

"Yes," said Beverly, "they have quite a few warriors wearing chainmail. I was under the impression they were poor in iron, but the state of the earl's forces tells me otherwise."

"Perhaps they've found a new source?" said Gerald.

"Possibly," said Beverly. "They have had a lot of time to explore this land."

"And their earl?"

"Lord Hollis seems to know his way around a horse, and he certainly displays his wealth, but I have no clue as to his competency."

"Even after all the raids against Bodden?" said Gerald.

Beverly turned to him. "We don't know how long he's been the earl," she said, "or if he's even aware of the attacks on Bodden. Maybe he has followers that carry out the raids?"

"I hadn't considered that," said Gerald. "I just assumed Hollis was the earl all along."

"Aubrey was telling me that she chatted with him earlier. He indicated that the earls hold all the military power in Norland. If that's the case, we should mind our manners. Even this small escort could cause us problems if they became hostile, and we have no idea how many other troops might be in the area."

"I'll keep that in mind," said Gerald, "and we'll make sure Lady Aubrey is close to the queen at all times. How long does it take her to cast her spell of recall?"

"Long enough," said Beverly, "but don't worry, the guards could buy her the time needed if it becomes necessary."

"Let's hope it doesn't come to that," said Gerald. "In the meantime, let's not mention this to the queen. She's got enough on her plate to worry about at present."

"Agreed," said Beverly. "Anything else?"

"Yes," he continued, "keep the sentries alert tonight. I'll check them myself just before dusk, and then you check them some time after darkness falls."

"I always do," she replied, "why? Are you expecting trouble?"

"It occurs to me that a diplomatic incident at this point in time could easily ignite a war."

"You think someone might try to kill the queen?"

"I wouldn't put it past our host," said Gerald. "From what I heard from those Norland refugees, the earl is not a pleasant man."

"He seems polite enough," said Beverly.

"That's because we're still of use to him. I can't help but feel he's got some ulterior motive."

"Good, I was beginning to think I was the only person that thought that," said Beverly.

"You know what they say," said Gerald, "never trust a Norlander that's out of sword reach."

TWELVE

In the City

Fall 964 MC

Harry Hathaway looked once more at the address he had written down. It was odd to be in this part of the town, among the well-to-do, but he was confident his information would be of value. A soldier, one of the local Wincaster garrison, ambled down the street, and Harry instinctively moved into an alleyway, waiting until the man had passed. He chided himself for his overly-cautious demeanour, reminding himself that he was on legitimate business for once in his life.

As his target drew closer, he stepped from the shadows, striding purposefully towards the front door. It was a modest house for the area, but compared to the slums that Harry called home, it was a palace. Knocking on the door, he waited nervously.

Moments later, a dour-looking servant answered the door. "Can I help you?" she said.

"Good afternoon to you," said Harry. "I am here to speak with Lady Nicole Caster. Might she be available?"

"That depends," she said, "on who you might be?"

"I am Harry Hathaway, and I would be forever in your debt if you would tell your mistress that I am here to see her on a matter of...shall we say, business?"

The woman was about to reply when the cry of a baby echoed from behind her, to be joined, moments later, by that of a second.

"Now look what you've done," she said, "you've gone and woken the twins. You'd better come in. You can wait in the foyer."

Harry crossed the threshold as the woman ran up the stairs. It was a pleasantly furnished house with an entranceway that was larger than his own rooms back in the slums. He swept his gaze over the furnishings with appreciation, for not so long ago he would have loved the opportunity to purloin many of these belongings, but he quickly shook the feeling, for this was the house of one of his oldest acquaintances, and he would never betray that friendship with theft.

The sound of mewling babies soon died down and then he heard footsteps at the top of the stairs. He looked up to see Lady Nicole, dressed in a stylish outfit, her hair neatly arranged, but the old Nikki was still there, as evidenced by the smile that broke out upon seeing him.

"Harry!" she called out as she ran down the stairs and hugged him, then held him out at arm's length. "For Saxnor's sake, Harry, you look so thin."

He shrugged, "What can I say, Nik, the pickings aren't so good these days."

"Well, we must feed you, Harry. Come in, and I'll get Marrianne to prepare something."

She led him into a small side room where seats waited.

"You've done well for yourself," said Harry.

"I'm a lady now," she said, "as well you know."

"How's Arnim doing?"

"He's in the north, travelling with the queen," said Nikki, reverting to her old pattern of speech. She moved to a side table, "Something to drink, Harry?"

"Certainly," he replied, taking a seat.

She poured him a goblet, handing it to him before taking a chair opposite.

"It's good to see you, Harry. Tell me, what have you been up to?"

"You know, the usual," he said. "I had a fair run at a visiting lady from Shrewesdale, but her father showed up and ruined everything."

Nikki laughed. Harry was a notorious rogue, an expert at charming the jewellery off a woman, but the laughter died when she suddenly realized that she was now one of the very women he would target. The thought sobered her.

"So what brings you here?" she asked.

"Information."

"I take it you're selling?"

"I am," he replied, "assuming the price is right."

"That depends on the information, Harry. I assume this is something of interest to the crown?"

"It is."

"All right," said Nikki, "tell me what you know, and I'll see what I can do. That's all I can promise for now."

"Fair enough," said Harry. He took a sip of his wine, a smile creeping over his face. "This is quite good," he said, "is this local?"

"Get on with it, Harry."

"There's been a lot of talk in the slums."

"What kind of talk?"

"Someone's been sowing discontent," said Harry, "bad-mouthing the queen and the nobility."

"What of it?" she said. "You and I did the same thing all those years ago."

"Yes," he admitted, "but this time it's different. Someone's spreading around a lot of coins to encourage it."

Nikki leaned forward. "You have my attention. Are they foreign coins, perchance?"

"No," said Harry, "good old fashioned Mercerian crowns. I get the impression someone's trying to organize something. Whoever is behind it has contacted several of the gangs. I thought at first it might have been you, but then again, you benefit more from your new position at court."

"It wasn't me, I can guarantee you that," said Nikki. "What else can you tell me?"

"Not much at this point in time," said Harry, "but I know the Hawtrey gang is involved, and I shouldn't have to tell you what that means."

"The Hawtreys? Are you sure?"

"Positive," said Harry. "I witnessed Igran Hawtrey recruiting down at the Three Rings, passing out shillings quite freely."

Nikki knitted her brow. The Hawtreys were notorious strong-arms, willing to beat anyone for the right price. If they were recruiting, it could only mean one thing, something big was brewing.

"You think it might be riots?" she asked.

"I don't know," Harry replied. "There's no shortage of food, and the local town watch hasn't been particularly brutal of late."

"That's due to the queen's reforms," said Nikki. "The town watch now falls under the rangers' jurisdiction. Have you noticed anything else?"

"The slums have been peaceful of late," continued Harry, "but you know how it is, there's always some new gang trying to gain dominance."

"Are there any new players I should know about?"

"In terms of gangs, no," said Harry. "The territories have shifted a bit since you were there, but it's still the same players."

"And yet someone has an influx of funds," mused Nikki.

"Precisely," he said, getting to his feet and setting down the empty goblet. "I should get going, I just wanted you to know. It's up to you if you want to pass things on."

"Wait a moment, Harry," said Nikki, "I have an idea."

"Go on then," he said.

"How would you feel about a quick trip to the Palace?"

"I thought the queen was up north?"

"She is," said Nikki, "but Lady Hayley is the Queen's Steward while she's away. I'd like you to tell her what you told me."

"And you think that might help?" he said. "She's the high ranger, isn't she?"

"She is," said Nikki, "but she's well aware of the assistance you provided during the war. I'll guarantee your safety, providing you don't pinch anything from the Palace."

"You have my word," said Harry, "though I'm hardly dressed for a visit."

"Don't worry about it," said Nikki, "we'll go in the back entrance. It's probably better, for your own sake, if people don't see you there."

"Very well," said Harry, "when do you want to do this?"

"Right away," said Nikki, "just give me some time to change. I don't want to draw unwanted attention."

Harry sat back down. "Very well, though I may need some more of that wine to fortify myself. It's not every day that a man of my standing goes to meet the high ranger."

Nikki chuckled, "Help yourself, Harry, and I'll get some food into you before we leave. I can't have you passing out from hunger."

"Now, there's the Nikki I used to know," said Harry, "always looking after yourself."

She turned on him in surprise, stung by his words. "I'm not that person anymore," she said. "I've got a family now, and friends, including you."

He looked down at his goblet in shame. "Sorry, Nik. I suppose I'm just a little bitter. The war didn't work out for all of us."

"We'll rectify that, Harry," she said, "I promise you."

Lady Hayley Chambers, the High Ranger of Merceria, sat at her desk, staring at the mass of papers before her.

"Are you sure I need to read all of these?" she asked.

Prince Alric nodded. "Anna routinely reads these reports."

"How often?"

"Every day," he responded. "She generally pores over them as she eats breakfast. Usually, Gerald is here with her, so she can pass on anything to the army if needed."

"I think I'll need your help with these," Hayley said. "Do you think you can read through them and pass on anything that needs my immediate attention? I still have to deal with all my ranger duties."

"Of course," said Alric as he gathered up the papers. "I'll have Jack give me a hand, and then provide a summary for you."

"Thank you, Your Highness," said Hayley.

"None of that," said Alric. "While you're in this office, I think we can be less formal. Now, where's that aide of yours?"

The door opened. "You called?" came the deep baritone of Gorath.

"Were you listening?" asked Alric.

"Of course," said the Orc, "how else would I anticipate your requests?"

"I keep Gorath informed of everything," said Hayley, "in case he's needed to take over."

"Shall I summon a servant to help you with those?" asked Gorath.

"It's fine," said Alric, "I have them." The prince turned back to Hayley, "I'll have a summary for you by noon. Until then, I shall leave you to your duties."

Gorath stepped aside, letting Alric through the door. His footsteps echoed down the hall, then the Orc stepped in, closing the door quietly behind him.

"Something up?" asked Hayley.

"You have visitors," said Gorath.

"Oh?" said Hayley.

"Yes, Lady Nicole Caster and another one I'm not familiar with. Lady Nicole says it's important."

"Then send them in," said Hayley, glancing down at her now-empty desk. "It appears I've freed up some time."

The Orc ushered them in, then took up a position by the door. Nikki sat, indicating that Harry should do likewise.

"Lady Nicole," said Hayley, "this is a bit of a surprise. How are the twins?"

"They are well," replied Nikki, "thank you for asking."

"I take it that's not why you're here."

"Indeed not," said Nikki. "This is Harry Hathaway, no doubt you've heard his name before?"

"So this is the infamous Handsome Harry," said Hayley. "I'm told he was very helpful during your escape from Wincaster, before the war."

"He was," said Nikki, "but now he brings news from the slums. I was hoping you'd hear him out."

"By all means," said Hayley, turning her attention to the man. "What is it you've discovered, Harry?"

Harry leaned forward slightly, talking in a quiet tone. "Someone has been hiring muscle in the poorer sections of Wincaster," he began. "There's a lot of coins flowing and someone's seeding discontent with the crown."

"What, precisely, are they saying?" asked Hayley.

"People are accusing the queen of wasting away the kingdom's treasury, holding lavish parties, and giving out huge sums to her friends and allies."

"I can assure you she's not," said Hayley, "I've seen the accounts."

"That's not the point," said Nikki. "Someone wants people to believe it and coins are a strong incentive to those that have little."

"I'm familiar with the concept," said Hayley. "After all, my father spent years trying to earn a living as a poacher."

"Your father was a poacher?" said Harry. "And now you're the high ranger?"

"Yes," said Hayley, "strange, isn't it? Whoever would have thought that such a thing was possible."

"What of the slums?" interrupted Nikki. "Surely we can't let this go unchallenged?"

"We need more information," said Hayley, "and I can't just send in the town watch to arrest people. Our jails would never be able to handle the overcrowding."

"Then what do we do?" asked Harry.

"That depends on you," said Hayley.

"I'm not sure I follow," said Harry.

"Tell me, Harry," Hayley continued, "would you be willing to investigate this further?"

"I don't know," he said. "I'd be putting my life in danger, and besides, no one likes a snitch."

"You wouldn't be a snitch," said Hayley, "you'd simply be working for a new gang boss."

"And who would that be?"

"Nikki," Hayley replied, "provided she's interested, of course."

"You can't be serious," said Nikki. "I'm a new mother, not to mention the wife of a viscount."

"What if you operated from the shadows? You keep Harry here as your sole contact, but pull the strings, so to speak?"

"It would take a lot of work," said Nikki, "but I suppose it could be done."

"Good," said Hayley. "I'll find the necessary funds to finance the whole operation. You only have to establish enough of a presence to look legitimate. Do you think you could do that, Harry?"

"I know enough freelancers that would be interested, for the right price," he said, "but what's the goal here?"

"I want you to recruit as many people as you can," Hayley continued, "and I want them out listening. We need to identify who's behind this and what they're up to. Maybe we can even get someone on the inside."

"Then what?" asked Harry.

"That depends on what you find," said Hayley. "I can always arrange raids on some of the local gangs if it'll give you leverage. We can make it look like you've got a wealthy sponsor, but we'll keep Nikki's involvement a secret."

"The gangs won't like losing territory," said Harry, "and without holding some ground, we won't get far."

"You know the lay of the land better than I," said Hayley. "You find the area you think best, and I'll arrange for the watch to make some arrests. That should buy you some time to set things up. Do you think you're up to it?"

"Providing the funds are made available," said Harry.

"Good," said Hayley. "Believe it or not, this is likely cheaper than hiring more watchmen. I'll authorize payment through the crown."

"Won't that raise suspicions amongst the nobles?" warned Nikki.

"Good point," said Hayley, "I hadn't thought of that."

"Suppose you listed it as extra training expenses," said Nikki. "You could hide the funds by allocating them to the rangers, couldn't you?"

"I could," Hayley replied, "but I'd have to inform the queen."

"Are you sure the queen would approve?" asked Harry. "After all, you'd be funding criminals."

"Yes, ironic, isn't it," said Hayley. "Still, I think the queen would see the reasoning behind it, provided your gang doesn't go around murdering innocent people. I tell you what, you two come up with a plan and bring it back to me. In the meantime, I'll arrange some funds for Harry here."

"How long will that take?" he asked.

"You'll have it by the end of the day," promised Hayley. "How long do you think you'll need to plan this out? We may not have much time."

"Why do you say that?" asked Harry.

"The timing here strikes me as suspicious," said Hayley. "This news comes just as the queen is out of the kingdom. It's the perfect time for her political enemies to make a move."

"In that case," said Nikki, "we'll have a plan worked out by tomorrow."

"Excellent," said Hayley. "When you're done, send word to me, then we'll meet back at your estate. I don't want anyone at the Palace overhearing any of this. If something crops up and you can't reach me, let Gorath know."

"What of the prince?" asked Nikki. "Will you tell him about this?"

"No," said Hayley, "the fewer people that know about this the better. I'm not sure how Prince Alric would take the idea of funding criminals, and I have no idea how good his people are at keeping secrets. Best we leave him out of it for now."

"And when the queen returns?" said Nikki.

"Then I'll fill her in on the details. At that point, it will be up to her if she wants to continue."

"Very well," said Nikki, rising to her feet. "Come along, Harry, it sounds like we have quite a bit of work ahead of us."

Hayley rose as did Harry. The high ranger extended her hand towards the man. "Thank you for bringing this to my attention," she said, "I know it couldn't have been easy."

Harry shook her hand, a smile creeping across his face.

"Something amusing?" asked Nikki.

"I was just wondering what my mother would have said," explained Harry, "me, shaking hands with the high ranger herself!"

THIRTEEN

Arrival

Fall 964 MC

The Royal Party continued their trek north, following the road to Galburn's Ridge. The terrain grew rougher here, with hills and patches of trees that broke up the countryside. Two more days passed, and then a large body of water appeared in the distance.

Lord Hollis, pleased with the progress they were making, had ridden back to speak to the queen. He deftly pulled up to her left while Aubrey rode to the right.

"Your Majesty," he said in greeting, "'tis a fine day today."

"Indeed it is, Lord Hollis," said Anna. "What is that body of water to our east?"

"It is the Lake of Kings," said the earl.

"An interesting name. Is there a story that goes with it?"

"There is, indeed," said Hollis. "You see, when Prince Talburn came north with his followers, they settled on the shore of this lake, near an ancient ruin."

"But your capital lies some distance north, does it not?"

"It does," said Lord Hollis, "but Prince Talburn never saw it, for he died of the wounds he had received at the final battle. His son, Galburn, claimed kingship on his father's death, and the capital is named for him. Of course, it was little more than a defensive position in those days. King Galburn was always worried that you Mercerians would come seeking his demise, so the first order of business was to fortify the area. I think you'll find the Royal Castle to be quite impressive when you see it."

"I look forward to it," said Anna. "Tell me, will Lord Rutherford, the Earl of Hammersfield, be in the capital?"

Lord Hollis smiled, "I see Lady Aubrey's been talking to you."

"She IS a trusted advisor," said Anna.

"In answer to your question," he said, "yes, I believe Lord Rutherford will be present, as will the rest of the Earls of Norland. In our country, you see, a majority of earls would be needed to ratify this proposed peace treaty. Is it not so in Merceria?"

"I seek the advice of my nobles," said Anna, "but I, alone, reserve the right to declare peace, or war, for that matter."

"I see," said Hollis. "A most interesting development. We had assumed things were much the same in Merceria as in Norland."

"Is there a great deal of opposition to the proposal at court?" asked Anna.

"No more so than any other item of interest," said Hollis. "I rather suspect it will mostly rest on what kind of impression you make."

"Her Majesty is used to that," added Aubrey. "It's how she won over the Court of Weldwyn."

"A most impressive achievement," noted Lord Hollis, "but I fear our court will not be so easily swayed. Most of the earls are hardened in their opinions concerning Merceria. You are, after all, our traditional enemy."

"As was Weldwyn," said Anna, "and yet we now count them as friends."

"The court at Galburn's Ridge is far more...what's the word I'm looking for?"

"Treacherous?" suggested Aubrey.

Hollis laughed, "I was going to say fractious, but I suppose either term could be applied."

"And where do you stand on peace, Lord Hollis?" asked Aubrey.

"I am willing to admit the possibility is intriguing," he replied. "I shall be watching my colleagues closely to see what their reactions are to the proposal."

"Was it not their idea?" said Anna. "If the council holds so much power, then how is it they are not for it? Surely one of them must have proposed it?"

"It was King Halfan's idea," admitted Hollis, "and he is ailing of late. To be perfectly honest, I think it all depends on how the concept is presented to the council. Many of the earls are concerned with their own individual power. Anyone who sees a personal advantage to peace will likely support it. It will be your job, Your Majesty, to make the offer palatable to as many as you can."

"You've given us much to think on," said Anna. "I shall have to discuss this at greater length with my advisors."

"I am only sorry," said Hollis, "that you have but one here."

"Aubrey is not the only advisor I travel with," said Anna. "Some of my most trusted friends are here with me."

Hollis looked around in surprise. "I see no nobles," he said.

A loud bark to their left drew their attention. Tempus was running across the field, chasing a small animal of some sort. Lord Hollis winced at the sight, an act noticed by Aubrey.

"Do you not have dogs in Norland?" the mage asked.

He snapped his attention away from the distant sight. "Of course," he said, "though none the size of that beast. What in Saxnor's name is it?"

"It's a Kurathian Mastiff," said Anna, watching the man's face for any sign of reaction.

"If you'd wanted hounds for hunting, I would have been glad to lend you mine," he said.

"Tempus is not a hunting dog," said Anna. "He's trained to bring down warhorses." She watched Lord Hollis pale at the thought.

"Indeed," the earl replied, for once at a loss for words.

"Oh, yes," said Anna, "and he's my companion." When she gave an ear-piercing whistle, the great mastiff halted, raising his head to look in their direction. No sooner had he spotted them, then he came charging across the field, eliciting cries of alarm from some of their Norland guides.

Lord Hollis bowed his head. "With your permission, Your Majesty, I shall resume my duties at the head of the column."

"Very well, my lord," said Anna, "you are dismissed."

The earl rode off, and the queen turned to Aubrey. "What did you make of that?"

"It seems the earl doesn't like Tempus," said Aubrey. "Good thing you didn't mention how he can rip someone's throat out."

Anna smiled, "I'll save that for the future. In the meantime, let Gerald, Beverly, and Arnim know that I'm calling a meeting this evening. We have much to discuss."

Gerald made his way across the field of tents to the queen's pavilion. The guards stationed outside nodded as he drew closer, allowing him entry, where inside, the rest of the group stood waiting.

"We're all here now, Your Majesty," Beverly announced.

"Good," said the queen, "then we can begin." She took a drink, considering her words before starting. "As you know, we shall be arriving in

Galburn's Ridge shortly, and that means we'll be surrounded by Norlanders."

"Aren't we already?" asked Arnim.

"Yes," said Anna, "but here, at least, we're in the outdoors. Once we reach the Norland capital, we'll be inside a castle, and that complicates matters greatly. I should like to hear everyone's opinions and suggestions."

"I think the first priority must be your safety, Majesty," said Beverly. "To that end, I'd suggest you're always accompanied by at least two bodyguards."

"That's an excellent idea," noted the queen, "though I don't know what the Norlanders might allow. After all, we'll be in the presence of King Halfan during the negotiations."

"Still," said Beverly, "I think it a wise precaution, just the same. No doubt, the Norlander's will inform us if they think it too much."

"I doubt they would even notice," suggested Aubrey. "They're in the habit of not going anywhere without their own bodyguards, you saw the group that accompanied Lord Wilfrid."

"Aubrey has a point," noted Anna.

"We cannot overlook you as a target," said Arnim. "If someone were to kill you, it would do irreparable harm to Merceria. To that end, I would suggest that Lady Aubrey always be in your presence, at least when you're not in your quarters."

"Agreed," said Gerald, "and I think Tempus should be with you at all times as well."

"I can agree to that," said Anna, "though I think taking Tempus to see the king might be pushing a little too hard. I gather, from Lord Hollis's words, that the sight of Tempus might be seen as intimidating, so I shall leave him in Sophie's care when I meet with the king."

"I should very much like a chance to look over their defences," added Arnim.

Anna chuckled, "I'm sure you would, Lord Arnim, but I doubt that's something they would allow. I must remind everyone that we are guests of the king here, and so we must be gracious and polite."

"Have we any idea of what will transpire once we arrive?" asked Aubrey.

"From what I understand of their culture," said Anna, "we shall be settled into our rooms first. The king will likely have a big dinner for us where we will meet the members of their Nobles Council. I'm told the earls will all be there."

"How many earls are there?" asked Arnim.

"Seven, all told," said Anna, "though outside of Lord Hollis, we know little of them or their political leanings. It's also quite likely that some of them are against the idea of peace with Merceria. We must give them no further reason to distrust us."

"I would suggest," said Arnim, "that we learn as much about all these earls as possible. At least some of them may be sympathetic to our cause."

"Agreed," said Anna, "but we must use caution. Those that are against us may try to lull us into their confidence."

"I don't trust Hollis," said Gerald. "The man's been organizing raids against Bodden for years."

"Are you sure of that?" asked Aubrey. "We know so little of regional politics here."

"I have no doubt," said Gerald. "We've taken prisoners before, and there is little question, among the Norlanders at least, as to who ordered the attacks."

"I would agree," said Beverly, "the man can't be trusted."

"He's been gracious to us so far," said Arnim. "If he truly is opposed to us, he might be setting us up for something."

"Like what?" asked Aubrey. "He's had ample time to try to kill us if that's what he truly wanted."

"Could it be something more sinister?" offered Arnim.

"Like what?" repeated Aubrey.

"What if he's using us to seize the throne of Norland?"

"How would he accomplish that?" said Gerald.

"Suppose King Halfan died," said Arnim. "What would be the result?"

"The next king would be crowned?" suggested Aubrey.

"Yes," Lord Arnim continued, "but who would that be? I don't think the king has a living heir, does he?"

"Not that I'm aware of," admitted Anna. "But, that being the case, would he not have chosen someone as his successor?"

"Possibly," continued Arnim, "but that doesn't mean the earls would support his choice. We know the earls hold all the power here. With the king dead, they'd likely fight amongst themselves over who would rule."

"Are you suggesting a civil war?" asked Gerald.

"I think it likely," said Arnim. "We already know that someone attacked Lord Wilfrid. What if one of these earls was responsible?"

"It's not beyond reason," said Anna. "After all, what better method of defeating the peace than having someone attack the messenger. We're lucky Mistress Fortuna was available to save him."

"And what better way to start a war than to blame the Queen of Merceria in the killing of their king," suggested Arnim.

"Or the poisoning of our queen," warned Aubrey. "It might not be Lord Hollis that wants you dead, Majesty. It's something we must consider."

"That being the case," said Anna, "what's the most likely form that such an attempt would take?"

"An assassin?" suggested Aubrey.

"No, they'd be hard-pressed to get past our guards," said Beverly. "But poison is a possibility as they're supplying all our food while we're guests here."

"How do we protect ourselves from that?" asked Arnim. "Have a taster for everyone's meal?"

"No," said Aubrey, "I can use magic to protect us."

"Neutralize toxins?" suggested Anna.

"Yes," the mage replied, "though I fear it could have unfortunate side effects."

"Such as?" asked Gerald.

Aubrey grinned, "It would also neutralize alcohol. I'm afraid the wine just won't taste the same."

"I'd prefer to have bland alcohol than be dead," said Anna. "But it also means everyone, including the servants, will have to be extra careful."

"This is all starting to sound very difficult," said Gerald. "Maybe we would have all been better off staying in Wincaster?"

"Too late for that now, Gerald," said Beverly, "and in any event, someone could poison you in the Palace just as easily."

"I prefer not to think of that," said Gerald. "At least at the Palace, we know what we're dealing with. What are your thoughts, Sophie?"

Anna's maid was taken aback. "Me, Your Grace? Why in Saxnor's name would you want my opinion?"

"You work with the staff," said Anna, "do you trust them all?"

"To be honest, no," said Sophie. "Most of the staff is left over from your brother's reign. I'd feel safer if you moved Mrs. Brown to the Palace."

"Now that would be an excellent idea," said Gerald. "She makes those delicious scones."

"I wouldn't want to take her from Uxley," said Anna, "it's her home. Eventually, we'll get a magic circle put in, then we can spend more time there."

"We'd need more mages, Majesty," said Aubrey. "As it is, we've only a handful."

"I wish we had a way of communicating with Wincaster," said Anna. "I feel so isolated up here."

"We should have brought Kraloch," said Aubrey.

"No," said Anna, "the presence of an Orc would be pushing our luck, and in any event, he's needed in Hawksburg."

"There is, perchance, another way," said Aubrey.

"Go on," said Anna.

"We know that the Elves of the Darkwood have mages. Perhaps they might be convinced to lend some to us."

"I'm not sure we could trust them," offered Arnim, "especially now that we know Penelope was one of them."

"Just because Penelope was evil, it doesn't mean that all Elves are," said Aubrey.

"What about the Dwarves," said Gerald, "do they have mages?"

"That's a good question," said Anna, "but all of this will have to wait until our return. Right now, we must deal with the situation before us. Has anyone got anything they wish to add?"

She looked around the room, but nothing was forthcoming.

"Very well," she continued, "then for now, whenever I meet with King Halfan, I shall have Gerald and Aubrey with me, along with Tempus, if they have no objection. Where permitted, I'll add Beverly to my retinue. Lord Arnim will oversee the guards to our rooms, and any servants our hosts provide will fall under Sophie's watchful eye. There is little else we can do until we arrive and learn where we will be housed. Now, I suggest you all get some rest, we still have some distance to travel before we reach the capital."

They all started making their way from the tent, but Gerald lingered. "Aubrey," he said, "stay a moment, won't you?"

He waited until the others had left before continuing.

"Something wrong, Gerald?" asked Anna.

"Just a thought," he replied. "I would suggest that Aubrey sleep in the same room as you. I'm sure they can move another bed in, space permitting, of course."

"Isn't that being a little extreme?" said Aubrey.

"No," said Gerald. "We can't predict what the Norlanders might get up to, and with Aubrey present, you could be recalled to safety at a moment's notice."

"Speaking of using recall," said Aubrey, "in an emergency, how many people would I be taking with me? Aside from the queen, of course."

"Sophie and Tempus," said Gerald.

"I could take more," offered Aubrey.

"I'm sure you could," said Gerald, "but you also have to travel a great distance. Better to conserve your strength where possible."

"A good point," said Anna. "In fact, you should use your magic to take us to Hawksburg, it's even closer. We can always use a second spell to get to Wincaster."

"True," said Aubrey, "and Kraloch could take over if necessary."

"But what of you, Gerald?" asked Anna, concern written on her face.

"Beverly and I will lead the others back," he said, "fighting all the way if it comes to that."

"I can't lose you, Gerald," said Anna.

"Let's hope all this planning is for nothing," the old warrior replied, "then we can all look forward to a nice leisurely ride home."

The next day they continued the march north, along the western shore of the lake. By the end of the day, the hills surrounding the capital came into view, and by the time they halted, the Royal Fortress at Galburn's Ridge looked down upon them. They camped that night within sight of its walls, the interior lit by distant candlelight.

The next morning, as they were preparing to move, Lord Wilfrid arrived. He rode up to Anna, who had not yet mounted.

"Your Majesty," he said, dismounting and bowing deeply. "I come bearing you welcome from King Halfan."

"Are you to accompany us the rest of the way?" asked Anna.

"With your permission, Your Majesty," the lord replied. "We are but a short distance away, though we must traverse the road."

"The road?" said Gerald as he cinched his saddle.

"Yes," said Lord Wilfrid. "The hills here are steep, making the approach to the Royal Castle difficult to navigate. As a result, the road runs back and forth, cutting into the rock itself. It's why we didn't have you attempt the trip in the dark last evening."

"Is it dangerous, then?" asked Gerald.

"Not unless one is under attack," noted Lord Wilfrid. "It is made that way by design."

Gerald turned, staring at the distant castle. It protruded from the rock as though an extension of the cliff face upon which it was built.

"An impressive structure," he noted. "How long will it take to navigate?"

"We shall have you inside the castle by mid-morning," said Lord Wilfrid, "though I fear your horses may be tired from the effort."

"Then let us begin," said Anna, pulling herself into the saddle. She called out for Tempus, and the great dog appeared from behind her, wagging his tail. Gerald, having completed his preparations, climbed into the saddle as well.

They set off at a slow trot, allowing the rest of their party to organize the wagons. To their front rode a dozen Guard Cavalry, while to their rear came twelve more. The footmen, under the command of Arnim, would soon follow, keeping the wagons under their constant eye.

They trotted through the city itself, which lay at the foot of the cliff. Someone had organized soldiers to keep the commoners at bay, but it seemed unnecessary to Gerald's eyes. The people that lived here took little interest in the newcomers, though Tempus garnered some attention.

The city itself was not walled, for, with the castle within bow range, an army would be hard-pressed to occupy such a location. They were soon making their way uphill, the road cutting north and south in a zig-zag pattern to make it less steep. The Dwarves called it a switchback, a road formed in a series of hairpin curves. It was a solid design, for anyone on the path above them had a commanding view of those below. Gerald wondered how such a road might be assaulted, his military mind occupied with a host of details.

Halfway up, the column halted as the horses rested. Only Lightning seemed unaffected, though Gerald doubted that even the mighty charger could make the ascent in one go. Tempus flopped down to the ground, looking thoroughly exhausted, and even Gerald felt saddle sore.

They were by the side of the road, staring down at the city below. Tempus was lying down, Anna resting her lower back against the faithful beast while Gerald sat beside her.

"It's quite a view," he noted.

"It is," she agreed, "though I'd hate to have to attack the place."

"Oh, I don't know," he said, "every design has its flaws."

She cast her eyes upward, at the castle that loomed in the distance. "Apparently, you've given this some thought."

"I have," he replied, "but here is not the place to address such things."

"Agreed," said Anna, "but think on it some more. If things do go badly, you'll have to plan an escape, or at least hold out until help comes."

"I think I can manage that," he said. He took a drink of some wine, then chewed on a sausage he'd been saving.

"I'm looking forward to a rest," said Anna. "This whole trip has been exhausting, don't you think?"

"Oh, I don't know," said Gerald, "it's no worse than travelling in Weldwyn. Of course, back then, you had a young prince to keep you company."

Anna smiled, "Yes, and now he's my husband. How far we've come!"

"Do you regret any of it?"

"Some days, when we get very busy, I miss the time we used to have at Uxley," she admitted. "But then again, if none of that had happened, I'd have never met Alric. I know everything didn't go as planned, but we can't change the past, and quite frankly, I wouldn't want to. We have to take the bad as well as the good. You?"

"No regrets," he said. "I've come to accept that we can't control the past, only the future."

They were interrupted by Beverly bellowing out orders.

"Sounds like it's time to move on," said Anna. "Are you rested enough?"

Gerald looked back in surprise. "I'm not dead, you know, I can still ride a horse."

She was about to apologize then saw the smile on his face.

"Come along then, Marshal," she said, "let's get into that castle."

The road curved back on itself several more times, then finally led into a gatehouse where two immense towers flanked the entrance with a multitude of arrow slits. Several archers manned the tops, their bows clearly visible.

"Longbows," noted Gerald. "I didn't even know they had them."

Anna looked up. "They never used them against Bodden?"

"No," he replied, "then again, most of the raiders had been mounted. It's a little hard to use them from a horse. We shall have to be careful, those things can penetrate our armour."

"Yet one more thing to consider," said Anna.

The gates had been swung open in preparation, and so they rode straight through the outer keep into another set of doors. These, too, Changed to - stood open, and several soldiers could be seen beyond, formed up as a welcome.

Lord Hollis, who had left early that morning, was waiting for them, accompanied by another noble. The Earl of Beaconsgate trotted forward to meet them as they passed through the second gate.

The Guard Cavalry had peeled away to either side, allowing Anna and Gerald entry into the inner courtyard. Tempus, trotting along just behind them, barked, the sound carrying across the yard and echoing off the high walls.

Lord Hollis came closer. "Welcome, Your Majesty, to Galburn's Ridge."

FOURTEEN

The Tower

Fall 964 MC

Aldus Hearn looked up from his notes, "Ready for the next one?"

"Just a moment," said Kiren-Jool, "we've been at this all day. I need a drink."

The Enchanter made his way to the table, pouring himself some cider.

"You know we have wine," said Hearn.

"I'm fully aware," said Kiren Jool, "but it would dampen my senses. I like to feel the magic as it flows."

"I might remind you we have yet to get any magic to flow through the mirror, aside from viewing, that is."

Kiren-Jool took a sip, then moved, cup in hand, to stand once more before the mirror. He activated the runes that allowed viewing, then stood there, transfixed by the image before him.

"We've been staring at that image for days now," said Hearn. "Don't tell me you've noticed something new?"

"It helps me think," said the Kurathian. "You know, mirrors that allow viewing like this one are quite common where I come from. An Enchanter would use one to scry distant objects, but this one is paired."

"Meaning?" said Hearn.

"Meaning that maybe we're approaching this all wrong."

"I'm not sure I follow?"

Kiren-Jool turned to face his companion. "We thought that the other mirror would have coordinates, much like the gates, but it occurs to me that we may be incorrect in our assumptions."

"Surely, there has to be a destination to connect to?" said Hearn.

"Yes, but it's a mirror, it can't have a set of coordinates."

"Why ever not?" asked Hearn. "A mirror must exist in a specific location."

"No, it doesn't, don't you see? If the mirror is anything like this one, it can be moved, changing its coordinates."

Aldus Hearn looked at the mirror, taking in its view. "I see what you mean. There must be a single destination that links to the other end."

"Precisely," said Kiren-Jool, "but I cannot fathom how it would work."

"Wait," said Hearn, "what if it uses Spirit Magic?"

"You're forgetting, Spirit Magic is a type of Life Magic, but mirrors are Enchantments."

"You know as well as I do that the schools are simply there to allow us to understand magic. We really don't know how it works outside of casting spells."

"So, you're postulating that the magic of the spirit realm connects the mirrors?"

"Yes," said Hearn. "Think about it for a moment. We know the Orcs can communicate over long distances."

"Using a spell called spirit talk, if I'm not mistaken," said the Kurathian.

"Precisely. According to them, the spirit realm has no concept of distance. That's how they can talk to each other, despite being in different lands."

"An interesting concept," said Kiren-Jool, "but we don't really know how that works."

"No, WE don't," agreed Hearn, "but Kraloch does. Suppose I were to bring him here?"

"You can use the recall now?"

"I can," said Hearn, "I learned it just before the Royal Party left for Norland."

"That sounds like an excellent idea, my friend, the Saints smile upon us. How long will it take to get him?"

"That depends on how busy he is," said Hearn. "I can be in Hawksburg in no time, but I shall probably have to rest before my return."

"Nonsense, Kraloch can bring you back. He's been able to use the circle for weeks."

"Has he now?" said Hearn. "Nobody told me."

"That's because you've been too busy poring over Revi's notes. You need to get out more."

The druid frowned, "Not me, I became a druid for a reason, you know. I really don't like being around people."

"You've been fine here," noted Kiren-Jool.

"That's different," said Hearn, "we're colleagues."

"In any event," said the Enchanter, "you should be leaving if you're going to find Kraloch before nightfall."

"Good point," said Hearn. "I'll head to the Palace and recall from there."

"You know you could travel directly from here."

"I know," the druid retorted, "but using the circle will expend less energy. I must conserve my strength if I am to return."

"Once again," said the Kurathian, "Kraloch can bring you back."

Hearn straightened his back. "I am quite capable of doing it myself," he said.

"Very well," said Kiren-Jool, "have it your way."

"What will you do in the meantime?"

"I shall find Albreda. I'm sure she'd like to be present once Kraloch arrives."

"You're assuming he'll have the solution," warned Hearn.

"He may not," confessed the Enchanter, "but he may be able to contact those that do."

Aldus Hearn broke into a grin. "Very clever, my Kurathian friend. I never would have thought of that."

"Precisely why I am here," said Kiren-Jool. "Now, you'd best be on your way. We have work to do."

Kraloch watched as the Orcs lifted the beam, settling it onto the frame. The rebuilding of Hawksburg was taking a great deal of effort, but the Orcs had grown accustomed to the Human way of building. He admired the timber frame as the workers fell to the ground in exhaustion.

Approaching feet drew his attention, and he turned to see an Orc hunter rushing across the road.

"Great Shaman," he was calling, "the circle has been activated."

"Then let us see who has come visiting this day," said Kraloch.

He followed the hunter back towards the old manor house as a new group of workers hauled wood to the construction site. They arrived in time to see the familiar figure of Aldus Hearn emerging from the circle.

"Ah, Kraloch," said Hearn, "the very person I was looking for."

"What can I do for you today, Master Hearn?" asked the Orc.

"I come seeking your wisdom," said Hearn, "and your presence in Wincaster."

"I take it this has to do with the missing Master Bloom?"

"It does," admitted Hearn. "Kiren-Jool and I are of the opinion that your knowledge of Spirit Magic may be of some use to us."

"I was led to understand you were working with a mirror," said Kraloch, "not something we Orcs generally empower."

"My colleague has postulated that the mirrors use Spirit Magic to find each other. Does that sound reasonable?"

"What makes you think that?" asked the Orc.

"Mirrors that are paired can connect regardless of location or distance. It occurred to us that your spirit talk works in a similar fashion."

"That is true," said Kraloch. "The ability to connect to a remote person is based on familiarity rather than distance."

"That being the case," continued Hearn, "wouldn't it make sense that two mirrors, bound to each other, would be the equivalent of a close familiarity?"

"I suppose that is one way of looking at it," said Kraloch, "but I would have to examine this mirror in more detail. If what you say is true, I would likely recognize patterns in the arrangement of the runes."

"I was hoping you'd say that," said Hearn. "Would you be available to return with me to Wincaster? We have the mirror in Master Bloom's house."

"Very well," said Kraloch. "Give me a little time to delegate my responsibilities here, and then I shall return with you to the capital."

"Excellent," said Hearn. "That will give me some time to rest."

"Rest?" said Kraloch. "Are you fatigued?"

"I've been spending a lot of time studying the mirror and trying to read Revi's ramblings. He's not the best person for taking notes, and his handwriting is atrocious! It simply wears me out."

"You can find refreshment at the main hall," said Kraloch. "I shall meet you there in due course."

"Would you pass me the salt, Richard?"

"Of course," the baron replied. He lifted the bowl, passing the finely ground salt across the table. "Will you have some more wine, Albreda?"

"I have sufficient," she replied. "I must say, your manor here in Wincaster is quite nice. Have you redecorated recently?"

"I have," said the baron. "I thought since I'm spending more time here, I should spruce the place up a bit. What do you think?"

She looked around the dining hall, taking in the weapons mounted on the wall. "It needs a woman's touch," she admitted. "It's a bit too martial for my taste."

"Really?" said the baron. "You surprise me."

"How so?"

"I just assumed you would like the decor."

"I'm a druid, Richard, I like the outdoors and nature, as you well know. I've never been one to fancy weapons and armour."

"Oh, yes, I see what you mean." He stared down at his food, suddenly quiet.

"Something on your mind, Richard?"

"You have given me pause to think," replied the baron. "I wonder if you might consider taking up residence here, at my Wincaster estate?"

Albreda smiled, "I should like that very much."

Baron Fitzwilliam looked up in surprise. "Really?"

"Of course," said Albreda, "and why wouldn't I? We are, after all, close friends, are we not?"

"I should like to think so," said the baron.

"Of course, I would need to make some changes."

"Such as?"

"Well," Albreda began, "for one, you can remove some of those weapons from the wall."

"Done," he replied. "Anything else?"

"I think it's high time we do away with separate bedrooms, don't you?"

Baron Fitzwilliam cleared his throat. "What would they say at court?"

"Likely that we are lovers," said Albreda, taking a bite of food. She chewed it, then swallowed, all the while watching the crimson cheeks of the baron.

"Come now, Richard," she soothed, "surely rumours at court are of no concern to you. After all, we have been intimate with each other."

"Well, I..." he stammered.

"Are you ashamed of our relationship?"

"No," he blurted out, "not at all, but I wouldn't want Beverly to hear spiteful gossip."

"Beverly is a grown woman," said Albreda, "and has no concern for idle gossip. Now stop making excuses, will you accept my conditions or not?"

He reached across the table, placing his hand over hers. "I will," he said. "It would, in truth, make me very happy to do so."

"Good," said Albreda, breaking into a smile. "Then we can start right after we eat."

"I beg your pardon?" said the baron.

Albreda laughed, "Taking down those decorations, I mean. Did you think I was talking of bed?"

"Well, I..."

"That," she said, "is for later tonight!"

A quiet knock announced the arrival of the servants. They cleared away the plates, refilling the goblets as well. They were just exiting when the baron's head servant entered.

"Something wrong, Lucas?" asked the baron.

"There is a foreigner here to see Mistress Albreda, my lord."

"A foreigner, you say?

"Yes, one of the Kurathians, I believe," replied Lucas.

"That would likely be Kiren-Jool," said Albreda, "the Enchanter."

"Very well," said the baron, "send him in."

"As you wish, my lord," the man replied. He bowed deeply, then left the room.

Baron Fitzwilliam took a sip of wine. "I wonder what he wants?" he mused.

"Likely, he has some news about the mirror," said Albreda.

"You think they might have cracked its secrets?"

"Perhaps," she replied, "either that or they need my help with something." The door opened to admit Kiren-Jool.

"Greetings, my lord," said the Enchanter, bowing to Richard, "and to you, Mistress Albreda."

"Never mind the formalities, Kiren. Have you something to report?"

"I have," the Kurathian answered. "I think we might have determined how the mirror works. Aldus has gone to Hawksburg to fetch Kraloch."

"When is he due back?" she asked.

"Shortly," the Enchanter replied. "We thought you might want to be present when he examines the mirror."

"I think that a splendid idea." Albreda turned to the baron, "What about you, Richard? Have you anything on your schedule?"

"I was thinking of redecorating," he said with a smile.

"Would you care to accompany us?"

"I would be delighted. Shall I summon some soldiers to help in case of trouble?"

"I doubt that will be necessary," she said, "but you might want to bring your sword, just in case."

"I shall fetch it immediately," he said, "then we can make our way to Master Bloom's house."

. . .

They arrived in time to see Gretchen Harwell standing at Revi's front door. The Enchantress had been summoned from the Weldwyn embassy where she had been staying and looked like she had just woken up. She smiled as she recognized Albreda, and the two embraced like old friends.

"Gretchen," said Albreda, "might I introduce Lord Richard Fitzwilliam, Baron of Bodden? I don't think you two have met. He's Dame Beverly's father."

"Well met," the mage replied. "I am Gretchen Harwell, Enchantress to the court of Weldwyn."

The baron bowed respectfully. "Good evening," he said, "it is a pleasure to finally meet, I've heard so much about you."

Kiren-Jool opened the door, beckoning them in.

"It's up this way," said Albreda, leading the others to the stairs. They ascended quickly, the sound of voices growing closer as they did. Through the open door at the top of the stairs, they could see Kraloch standing before the mirror, examining its frame while Aldus Hearn sat at a small table, carefully making notes.

"How are we doing?" asked Albreda as she entered.

Kraloch turned to face her. "These runes have much in common with ancient stone circles," he said. "I believe I can decipher them."

"Stone circles?" said Albreda. "What do you know of such things? Have you such constructs in the Artisan Hills?"

"No," said Kraloch, "but the Ancestors tell us that long ago, the Meghara built many, scattered across this land."

"Your Ancestors?" said Fitz.

"Yes," explained Aldus Hearn, "the Orcs can communicate with their Ancestors using magic."

"Does that help us?" asked the baron.

"We shall see," said Kraloch. "If you would stand to the side, I shall attempt to activate the mirror."

"Should we draw weapons?" asked Fitz.

"I doubt that will be necessary," said Hearn. "We've been able to view the other end of the mirror for a while, and there's nothing dangerous visible."

Kraloch waited until everyone was in place then started casting. He called forth the magic words, glancing from time to time at a paper he held. The surface of the mirror began to ripple, and then the image shifted to reveal a distant room.

"It worked," said the baron.

"That is only the first step," warned Albreda. "It's what comes next that's important."

Kraloch halted his spell, glancing at the image in the mirror. "I shall attempt the next step," he said, "but I don't know how it will manifest. I might disappear, only to reappear in the mirror, or I might have to step through it. Regardless, Master Hearn will write down the sequence." He turned to his companion, "Are you ready, Aldus?"

"I am," said Hearn. "You may proceed when ready."

Kraloch turned his attention back to the mirror and its glowing runes. He closed his eyes, summoning forth words of power. As they trickled from his lips, more runes began to glow, and then the entire frame lit up as if a thousand fireflies had landed upon it.

The Orc opened his eyes in time to see the light shift in the distant room, the magic bathing it in a soft glow.

"I think we are ready," he said.

"Wait," said the baron, "how do we come back?"

"By using the same words," said Kraloch. "I shall go first."

He stepped forward, touching the mirrored surface with a finger. The Orc appeared to dissolve into dust and then reappeared on the other side of the mirror, in the distant room, his pose turned around by one hundred and eighty degrees.

"Remarkable," he said, though his voice sounded distant, as though he were talking through a door.

"Come along," said Albreda, grasping Richard's hand. She touched the surface, and the baron felt a surge of energy as if his whole body was enveloped in pins and needles. Moments later, he was looking out from the mirror, though to his view, it was Revi's room that looked back at him.

"That was remarkable," he said, "and, I must admit, somewhat unsettling."

Kraloch stepped to the side, examining the frame. The mirror was identical to that at their point of origin, as was the stand that held it, allowing it to rotate.

Baron Fitzwilliam moved to the window, still grasping Albreda's hand, and pushed it open. He peered out, feeling the cold blast of air on his face.

"We're high up," he said, "but I see nothing that might indicate our position."

Albreda took in the view. "I would surmise we are somewhere northeast of Wincaster," she said. "Likely somewhere in the Artisan Hills."

"Surely not," said the baron, pointing at a distant peak, "that is definitely a mountain, not a hill."

"The window faces east," explained Albreda, "you can tell from the sun. Those peaks you see are the edge of the mountains, so we are likely close to Eastwood."

"How can you be so sure?" he asked.

"Revi's notes on the Saurian gates were quite detailed, though difficult to read."

Aldus Hearn, who had just stepped through the mirror, looked at her in surprise. "You read them?"

"Of course," she replied. "After all, I can't rely on others to keep me informed of such things."

"That's a little harsh, isn't it?" said Hearn. "We have been quite occupied trying to figure out the mirror."

"I'm not saying you didn't do a good job of it, Aldus, merely that things often get missed in explanations. When Aubrey told me you were reading through Revi's notes, I knew I must also do so myself."

"But they were in his house," said Hearn.

"His older notes, perhaps, but Aubrey had been digging through his more recent scribblings."

"Tell me, Albreda," said the baron, "what leads you to conclude that we're in the Artisan Hills?"

"I believe we're on a confluence of ley lines," she said.

"I'm afraid I don't understand," said Fitz.

"Nor would I expect you to, Richard, you're not a mage. There are lines of power that run all across the land."

"I've heard of those," said the baron, "but don't they run north and south?"

"Yes," Albreda replied, "but there have been theories that there are secondary lines that run roughly east and west. Where these lines meet, there is a powerful node where great magical forces can be tapped. I believe this is just such a location."

"How can you be sure?" he asked.

"I can feel the magic of this place," she said, "and this is no ordinary tower."

Kraloch had moved to the wall and was examining the stone as Kiren-Jool stepped through the mirror. Moments later, there was a flash and then the glow of the mirror ebbed, leaving them in a room lit only by the open window.

"It appears," said the Kurathian, "that I made it just in time." He waved his hands in the air, uttering words of power and then a glowing orb of light materialized before him, bathing the room in a yellow glow. "That's better."

"This room could use a good cleaning," noted Albreda. "It doesn't look like anyone's been here for some time."

"That makes sense," noted Hearn. "Andronicus did die years ago, and this place has been empty ever since."

"Uninhabited certainly," said Albreda, "but likely not empty."

"What are you suggesting?" said Fitz. "Do you think something is alive here?"

"Hopefully, Revi," noted Albreda, "but I was referring to artifacts."

"Artifacts?" asked the baron.

"Yes, notes, books, all sorts of things. Andronicus must have hidden his greatest secrets here. I met him once, you know, many years ago."

"You met Andronicus?" said Fitz. "Astounding. Where?"

"He helped save my life in Shrewesdale," said Albreda, "but that's an entirely different story."

"You must tell me all about it some time," the baron replied.

She smiled at him, "I would be delighted to, but we should continue our investigation here first."

"I see markings on the floor," interrupted Kiren-Jool.

The baron looked down at the stone bricks beneath their feet. "I think you're correct," he said, "but they somehow look familiar."

"They should," noted Albreda, "they form a magic circle, much like the one in the Palace."

"A Life Circle?" asked Fitz.

"Of course," said Albreda, "that was his chosen realm of magic, after all."

"How powerful is it?" the baron asked.

"Not as powerful as the one at the Palace," said Albreda.

"Wouldn't it have been easier for Revi to use it to travel back and forth?" asked the baron.

"He hasn't yet learned the spell of recall," Albreda explained.

"It might be a good idea to commit this one to memory," suggested the baron.

Albreda smiled, "An excellent suggestion, Richard. Would you mind guarding me while I begin the examination? It will take some time, and I would value the company."

"Of course," he said, "I would be delighted."

"Good," she said. "The rest of you should begin examining the rest of this place.

"There are stairs over here," said Hearn, "leading down."

"A good place to start, then," she replied.

"Won't you need some light?" asked Kiren-Jool.

In answer, Albreda moved to the middle of the casting circle then began an incantation. The air started to tingle with energy, and then small vines crept through the window and crawled along the wall. Albreda's words continued to flow, and the baron watched in fascination as the vines began to sprout flowers with glowing petals, illuminating the room with a pale green light.

"Astounding," said Fitz. "You never cease to amaze me with your magic."

"Where did the vines come from?" asked Hearn. "You can't just conjure them from nothing!"

Fitz moved to the window, poking his head outside to peer downward.

"Here's your answer, Master Hearn, she's had the vines climb up the outside of the tower. Your theories of magic are still intact."

"How high up are we?" asked Hearn.

"At least a hundred feet, if I'm any judge of distance," said Fitz, "but it looks like the tower's made from solid rock. How is that even possible?"

"Earth Magic," said Hearn, "though manipulating stone is not my specialty. I suspect the influence of a Dwarven mage."

Albreda had lowered herself to the floor and was now crawling about on her hands and knees, examining the magic circle in greater detail.

"You lot had best get a move on," said Fitz, "and let Albreda continue committing this circle to memory."

Kraloch began descending the steps which were curved to match the tower. The inside wall of the stairwell was made of wood, and he soon found himself facing an interior door at the base of the stairs. This he opened, then waited as Kiren-Jool and Aldus Hearn joined him, the magical globe of light illuminating their way.

"What have we here?" said Hearn.

"It looks like a bedroom," said Kraloch, peering into the shadows.

"I can't see a thing," muttered Hearn.

"I have to get the light through the door," said Kiren-Jool. He motioned with his hand, waving the orb into the room, revealing the interior.

"It appears you are correct," said Hearn, "your eyesight is obviously better than mine."

"Orcs see better in dim light," explained Kraloch.

The room was circular, matching the outside perimeter of the tower. A large bed, complete with curtained posts, sat against the northern wall with a small shuttered window visible against the south. The stairs opened up on the west while a similar portal was visible to the east.

The Orc shaman made straight for the bed. "This has been slept in," he noted, "the blankets are disturbed, though I suppose that could have been ages ago."

Kiren-Jool remained by the door while Hearn made his way to the shutters, unlatching them and throwing them open. Daylight flooded the room, along with a welcome breath of fresh air.

"There's something here, on the floor," said Kraloch, crouching low. "It looks like a book."

The news caught Kiren-Jool's attention. The Kurathian Enchanter made his way to Kraloch's side to watch as the Orc lifted the object of his attention.

"It looks like a journal of some sort," said Kraloch, flipping through the pages.

"That's not Master Bloom's hand," noted the Kurathian, "we've been reading through his notes for days."

"Were they made by Andronicus?" suggested the Orc.

"I'm not familiar with the man's work," said Kiren-Jool, "but it's as good a guess as any."

"Would you like to peruse it?" asked Kraloch.

"You should probably be the one to read it. It likely concerns Life Magic, and that's your specialty."

"Very well," said Kraloch, "but I shan't read it in depth just yet, we still have a mage to find."

Aldus Hearn opened the other door, revealing another set of descending stairs. "It occurs to me," he said, "that this layout is very similar to his house, you know, casting room on top, bedroom below."

"If that's the case," said Kiren-Jool, "I would think the next level will be the library, followed by the kitchen and storage areas."

"We shall likely have to make our way to the lowest level to find Revi," said Kraloch.

"What makes you say that?" asked Hearn.

"Revi was always infatuated with the Saurian gates," Kraloch continued. "Lady Aubrey would often talk of it. I believe that he was consumed by the flame."

"You fear he was burnt alive?" asked Hearn.

"No," said Kraloch, "rather, I suspect his mind was consumed by his quest for knowledge. My people have known of the flames for generations, though we never harnessed them. Even our ancient shamans warned that pale skins can become obsessed with the green flame."

"But your people weren't?" asked Hearn.

"No," said Kraloch, "and I would suspect the Saurians were unaffected as well."

"Very interesting," said Kiren-Jool. "Perhaps whatever it is that gives you green skin protects you from its effects?"

"That is a possibility," said Kraloch, "for the ancient Saurians were also green in colour."

"I'm getting a very uncomfortable feeling," said Hearn. "I doubt I shall ever step through a Saurian portal again."

"You have no need now," said Kraloch, "for Albreda has taught us how to recall. A remarkable achievement."

"If what you say is true," said Hearn, "then Revi, wherever he is, might be dangerous, his mind acting irrationally. Should we fetch the baron and his sword?"

"All three of us are mages," said Kiren-Jool. "Surely one Revi Bloom will not be beyond our ability to cope."

"Let us hurry," said Hearn, "for the longer we wait, the more nervous I become."

He led them down the stairs, emerging into a room that was jam-packed with shelves of books. In the centre was a cleared space with a pair of well-padded chairs between which sat a small table holding an oil lamp. Hearn stepped forward quickly, lifting it, only to find it empty.

Kiren-Jool manoeuvered his orb of light across the room, the shelves casting sinister-looking shadows.

"No sign of a window," he said, "but more stairs leading down, this time with no door."

Aldus Hearn stood a moment, letting the sheer number of volumes sink in. "We'll have to come back to this later," he said, "our first priority must be to find Revi."

Down they went, each floor slightly larger than the one above as the tower widened at its base.

Albreda stood, groaning as she did, and wiped the dust from her hands. "I'm getting old."

"Aren't we all," the baron replied. "All done?"

"Let's see, shall we?" she said, moving to the window. She held out her hands and closed her eyes, calling forth the magic of the earth. A wind whipped up from nowhere, whirling around her and then she vanished only to re-appear, a moment later, in the centre of the circle.

"There," she said, "I have now committed this Life Circle to memory. We may return whenever we wish."

"How many of these circles can you memorize?"

"There is a limit, I'm sure, but I haven't yet reached it. I guess that one day I'll have to forget one to make more room."

"You can do that?" Fitz said. "Selectively forget one?"

"I don't see why not."

"I wish I could selectively forget things," he said. "I've witnessed far too many deaths on the battlefield."

"And yet, it made you who you are today. We cannot undo the past, Richard, only make better decisions for the future."

"Well said," he agreed, "but shouldn't we be finding the others? They're likely wondering what happened to us."

Albreda plucked a flower from the vines, handing it to the baron. "Take this, Richard, it should glow for some time before its magic fades."

She also took one for herself, then led him down the stairs. "Now, let's find out what the others have been up to."

Aldus Hearn paused. They were deep in the cellars where stacks of barrels, boxes, and sacks lined the shelves. A dim light shone out from the bottom of a doorway.

"More stairs?" mused Kiren-Jool.

"No," said Hearn, "I believe we are far below the base of the tower, likely in the very rock itself."

"Another store-room then?" said the Kurathian.

"No," said Kraloch, "the light is green. I think we've found an eternal flame, the same magic that powers the Saurian gates."

Hearn grasped the handle. "Here goes," he said, giving it a pull.

It swung open towards him, revealing a rough-looking room hewn from the very rock itself. There was a fissure halfway across from which green flames climbed upward, sometimes short, other times leaping high to the ceiling.

Hearn, letting his eyes adjust to the light, noticed a figure lying near the fissure's edge.

"Revi!" he called out.

FIFTEEN

The Norland Court

Fall 964 MC

Gerald knocked on the door as the two guards watched in silent witness.

"Come," Anna replied.

He pushed open the door, revealing the guest chambers beyond. Anna was seated before a large mirror while Sophie combed through her hair. The trip up the ridge had played havoc with her blonde locks, and it was taking all her maid's efforts just to clear the tangled strands.

"Are you all settled in?" he asked.

She turned her head to look at him. "You look nice," she said, "I see you found that tunic I left for you."

"Well," he replied, "I can't very well go and meet the king in my battered old chainmail, can I?"

"She'll be with you in a moment," said Sophie, "I just have to remove this last knot."

She pulled on the brush, eliciting a cry from the queen.

"Ow," said Anna.

"Sorry, Majesty," said Sophie.

"It's all right," said Anna, "I know how hard my hair can be to keep straight."

Sophie tugged again, and the strands came free. "There," she said, "all done. Would you like it braided?"

"Not for today," said Anna, "we haven't the time. I don't want to keep King Halfan waiting any longer." She turned to Gerald, "Is my guard ready?"

"Beverly has six men waiting down the hall," he replied.

"Good, then it's time we met the King of Norland."

She rose, holding out her hand for Gerald's arm, "Lead on, Marshal."

When Sophie opened the door, Anna and Gerald passed through into the hallway. The two guards there stood straighter as the Mercerians passed by but maintained their positions. Farther down, Beverly stood chatting with Aubrey, along with half a dozen guards. The knight bowed her head briefly as the queen approached.

"We are ready, Majesty," she said.

"Lead the way, Beverly," said Anna.

The knight turned, leading the group through the castle, the guards falling in behind. Gerald felt nervous treading the halls of their enemy and had to remind himself that it wasn't so long ago that they would have seen Weldwyn the same way.

The route to the great hall was not difficult to find for King Halfan had been eager to make the visitors feel at home and so had roomed them nearby. Beverly led them down a side corridor that stopped at a large wooden door where a Norland guard stood. At their approach, he turned and opened it, the sounds of talking drifting towards them, along with the smell of tallow candles.

Beverly stepped in first, pausing a moment to take her bearings. She had entered by a side door, and to her left, she could see people standing around, their gaze directed to her right. Looking over, she saw the nobles of Norland gathered around an oblong table, one long side empty where Anna would be seated, along with her advisors. The knight turned, bowing to those assembled. "Your Majesty and noble lords," she said, "I present Anna, Queen of Merceria."

Anna stepped forward, eliciting a gasp from the crowd. Beverly, looking to see what the commotion was about, overheard someone utter, "She's so young!"

Lord Hollis, who was sitting at the table, rose. "Your Majesty," he said to his king, "it has been my honour to escort these Mercerians to our halls. May I have the privilege of introducing them to our esteemed council?"

He looked at an elderly man who, despite his frailty, watched with keen eyes. "You may," the man said.

Hollis seemed to grow in stature, his back straightening as he cleared his throat. He then turned to Anna and bowed slightly. "This," he said, indicating the old man with a sweep of his hand, "is his most regal Majesty, King Halfan of Norland."

The king nodded slightly.

"Pleased to meet you, Your Majesty," said Anna. "I look forward to forging a lasting relationship with your people."

"As do I," said Halfan.

"You already know me," said Hollis, "so let me introduce Lord Rutherford, Earl of Hammersfield."

The man sitting to Hollis's right nodded his head in greeting.

"And to his right," the earl continued, "is Lord Thurlowe of Ravensguard."

Thurlowe, a thin man with a cadaverous face that seemed pale and sickly, stood, bowing at the waist. "I am pleased to make your acquaintance," said Thurlowe, "and look forward to meeting with you in the future."

Hollis waited as Thurlowe sat, then indicated a fairly rotund individual. "This is Lord Calder, Earl of Greendale."

Hollis waited, but as Calder failed to make any acknowledgement of the meeting, he continued on.

"To the other side of our king is Lord Creighton of Riverhurst."

Creighton, the youngest of the earls, nodded his head, his sandy coloured hair catching the light as he moved.

"Greetings," he said, "I trust your journey here was pleasant?"

"It was," said Anna, "thank you."

"To the other side of him," said Hollis, "sits Lord Waverly, Earl of Marston."

Marston stood, revealing an impressive height. Beverly was immediately reminded of Sir Heward, but where the Mercerian knight smiled from time to time, she had the impression that Lord Waverly would never deign to show any emotion whatsoever. His lordship bowed, quickly sitting, allowing the man at the end of the table to stand.

"And finally," said Hollis, "Lord Witcombe, Earl of Walthorne."

Witcombe smiled, showing his teeth. On anyone else, it would have been comforting, but the Earl of Walthorne was missing many of his teeth, and the ones that remained were an unhealthy colour. The man merely nodded his head in greeting but said nothing.

"Thank you, Lord Hollis," said Anna. "Allow me to name Lord Gerald Matheson, Duke of Wincaster and Marshal of Merceria."

Gerald bowed slightly, keeping his eyes on the king.

"He is accompanied by Lady Aubrey Brandon," she continued, "Baroness of Hawksburg."

The mention of her title raised some eyebrows, but the Norlanders kept silent.

"And this," continued Anna, "is Dame Beverly Fitzwilliam, Knight of the Hound."

Beverly nodded her head in greeting. Like Gerald, she was on alert, but her attention was riveted on Lord Hollis. King Halfan waved a hand at Hollis, prompting the earl to sit. The king leaned forward, resting his forearms on the table.

"Come," he said, "sit and eat with us. It is our custom to welcome strangers with a meal before we get to business."

Servants came forward, placing chairs on the empty side of the table. Anna chose to sit in the middle, with Gerald to one side, Beverly and Aubrey to the other.

Wine was poured, but before Anna could drink, Beverly took her goblet, sniffing it, then took a sip. She waited a moment, then handed it to her queen with a nod.

"I see you are cautious," said Halfan, "a trait I admire, though I promise you it is entirely unnecessary. We have not brought you here to kill you. That would only start a war, the very thing we seek to prevent."

"Some of us, anyway," added Lord Creighton.

Beverly noted a twitch of irritation on the king's face and immediately started wondering which earls favoured peace.

Servants began carrying in their meal, laying it before them to display a feast of epic proportions. Most of the food was easily recognizable, but Beverly could see at least two meats that she couldn't identify. She chose, instead, to stick with more familiar fare. To the queen's other side, Gerald sliced off some beef, laying in onto Anna's platter. He had stood to reach it, and when he sat back down, he looked confused, as if searching for something.

Beverly held up her knife, mouthing the words, 'No forks'.

A look of realization dawned on the old warrior's face, and then he speared a small hen that dripped with some type of sauce.

Beverly looked to her hosts, only to see them ripping off wings and drumsticks with their hands. A large dog pushed past her, and she watched as Lord Marley wiped his hands on the beast's fur. The queen seemed unsure of how to behave and looked at her for guidance. The knight cut off a thin slice of chicken, holding it between thumb and knife and pecked away at it gingerly, the queen soon following suit. Aubrey, not one to miss a hint, did likewise, though somehow she managed to make the action look refined.

The meat was tender if a tad overcooked to Beverly's liking. Everything seemed to be smeared in sauces of various descriptions, leading to a very messy meal. She looked at the Norland nobles, but they appeared to care little for the niceties of society, digging in with gusto. Lord Marley, perhaps incapable of eating such fare, had settled in with a thin soup which he slurped noisily from a bowl.

Lord Creighton, the neatest of the earls, held a drumstick, picking away at it in small bites.

"Have you such fare back in Merceria?" he asked, looking at Beverly.

"We have," the knight replied, "though we seldom have so many choices at one meal. At the court in Wincaster, the meal is usually only one or two meats."

"Only two?" burst out Lord Calder. "That would never do here." He stuffed a piece of bread into his mouth, chewing it noisily, an action that Beverly found distasteful.

She turned her attention to a plate of buns that had been placed before her, selecting one at random. It was still warm to the touch, and she broke it open with her hands, enjoying the delicious aroma of the freshly baked interior. Using her knife to smear butter on it, she then placed some of her meat within.

Suddenly, those on the Norland side of the table fell silent, and Beverly looked around to see everyone staring at her.

"What are you doing?" asked Lord Marley.

"Eating," said Beverly.

"You should use your hands," said Lord Calder.

"And so I shall," she replied, "but the bread allows me to hold it without getting my hands messy."

"What a strange notion," said Calder.

Beverly placed the other half of the bun on top and took a bite, a bit of grease dribbling down her chin.

"Hah," said Calder. "It didn't work, you'll have to get messy now."

Anna turned to Beverly. "I shall give it a try," she said, "it looks interesting."

"That's an old trick," said Gerald, "we used to do it when we were on patrol up by Bodden."

His words brought a frown to Hollis's face. "Bodden, you say?"

"That's right," said Gerald, "do you know it?"

"I understood that Lady Beverly was from there," Lord Hollis replied, "but I had no idea you were familiar with it."

"Oh, yes," said Gerald, "I was born there, in fact."

"Lord Matheson served my father years ago," added Beverly.

"Ah, yes," said Hollis, "the Baron of Bodden. Lord Richard Fitzwilliam, isn't it?"

"It is," said Beverly.

"Tell me," continued Hollis, "have you a brother?"

"No, why?"

"I was wondering who would inherit Bodden when your father passed to the Afterlife."

"That would be Dame Beverly," said Anna.

"Surely her husband would be baron," said Rutherford between chews.

"Beverly will inherit the barony," said Anna. "Our laws are now clear on that."

"And are you married?" asked Rutherford.

"I am," Beverly replied, "and my husband will eventually become Lord of Bodden, though not the baron."

"How does your husband feel about that?" asked Marley.

"He has no objection," she replied.

"Astounding," said Rutherford, "the things these Mercerians get up to. Tell us of your husband, does he have lands of his own?"

"He is a smith," said Beverly, enjoying the looks of shock that passed down the line of Norland nobles.

"You mean he's a commoner?" said Rutherford.

"Not anymore," said Anna. "He's a lord by marriage. Surely you have people that have been elevated to the nobility?"

"Not in Norland," said Hollis. "The earls you see here all trace their lineage back to the supporters of King Talburn, our founder."

"I thought his son, Galburn, was your first king," said Gerald.

"He was," said Rutherford, "but Talburn was the rightful ruler of Merceria, and so earns the title of king."

"I suppose that makes sense," said Gerald.

"Tell me," said Rutherford, "is your family ancient?"

"My family?" said Gerald.

"Yes," Rutherford continued, "you're the Duke of Wincaster, from what line do you hail?"

"I was born a farmer," said Gerald.

Rutherford stopped chewing. He leaned forward, spitting his food onto the table.

"And by what right do you sit among us now?" he asked.

"Easy, Lord Rutherford," said King Halfan, "their customs are different from ours. We must learn to accept them."

"This is outrageous," Rutherford fumed, "to force us to sit in such company is beyond all reason."

"Do you wish to give offense so easily?" said Anna. "Lord Matheson is a seasoned veteran and Marshal of my Army. I will not sit idly by and allow you to insult him."

"Tell me," said Lord Creighton, "how did you rise to such prominence, Lord Matheson."

"I was Sergeant-at-Arms to Lord Fitzwilliam," said Gerald. "When I was wounded by..." he bit back his words, choosing instead to be more diplomatic, "by raiders, I was sent away to recuperate from my wounds. I ended up at the estate where the queen was being raised."

"I was only a little girl at the time," said Anna, "and Gerald became my friend."

"A royal can have no friends," mused King Halfan. "Isn't that what you're always saying, Hollis?"

"It is sad but true," Lord Hollis replied. "For a king must be wary of any who would claim friendship, lest they seek power."

"There," said Halfan, "you see?"

"I disagree," said Anna. "I have many I can trust, none of whom seek power."

"Then they are weak," said Rutherford. "It is the way of men to seek power, it has always been so."

Anna smiled knowingly, "It may surprise you to know that I have elevated several women to positions of power, including Lady Aubrey."

"I presume through marriage?" said Rutherford.

"No," said Aubrey, "by inheritance. My father was the previous baron."

"But surely that title will fall to your husband once you marry?" Rutherford huffed.

"No," she continued, "much like Lady Beverly, the barony will remain mine."

"Ridiculous," muttered Lord Thurlowe.

"There you have it," noted Lord Marley, "the Mercerians have become weak. Your women wouldn't last a day in Norland."

"I beg to differ," said Anna, "even my champion is a woman, and I'd lay odds that she could defeat any Norland warrior, one-on-one."

"I doubt that," said Marley.

Anna looked at Beverly, who simply nodded.

"Shall we see?" the queen asked.

"What are you proposing?" countered the king.

"A fight between my champion and a warrior of your choosing," said Anna.

"Very well," said the king, "though not to death, of course."

"I would only ask that Lady Aubrey be allowed to intervene if needed," said Anna. "As a Life Mage, she would be able to attend to any wounds, should it prove necessary."

"Very well," said the king, "we shall test your champion's mettle. Who is this champion whose prowess you speak of?"

"Dame Beverly Fitzwilliam," said Anna.

Beverly stood, bowing to the queen.

"But she is a noble," said Rutherford, "you said so yourself."

"What of it?" asked Anna. "Do nobles not fight in Norland?"

"Not in a duel," said Rutherford, "we have champions for such things."

"Nevertheless," said Beverly, "I stand ready to defend the queen's honour. Choose your champion."

The earls all looked at each other.

"Hollis, use yours," said Marley, "you're always bragging about the man."

"Very well," said Hollis, "with the king's permission, of course."

King Halfan nodded his approval.

"Send word for Marik," the earl barked out, "and we shall give this 'Knight of the Hound' a true lesson in combat. Tell me, Dame Beverly, what weapon would you prefer? A lady's sword, perhaps?"

"Sword, axe, hammer, you decide," said Beverly. "I am familiar with them all."

"Let your champion choose that which is most familiar to him," said Anna, "though Beverly, I think, will use her sword."

"Blades it is then," said Hollis.

"Clear away the food," the king ordered, "but leave the wine. We shall have splendid entertainment this day, and I would not have the view obstructed by this meal, delicious though it is."

A few servants rushed forth, clearing plates while others carried a cloth from noble to noble, allowing them to wipe their hands and mouths.

"Lady Aubrey will stand by with her magic," said Anna.

"Your warrior shall need it," said Marley, as the Life Mage rose from her seat.

"It is not Dame Beverly that will need it," said Anna, "but her opponent."

"You seem awfully sure of her abilities," said Waverly.

"As you seem to dismiss them so readily," countered the queen.

"There's no need to stand, Lady Aubrey," said the king, "come and sit."

"I will be able to attend to healing quicker on foot," said the mage. "Fighting can still be dangerous, even with a healer, and I take my duties very seriously."

Anna caught Beverly's arm as she stood, drawing her close for a moment. "Make it as quick as you can, Beverly," she said.

"Understood, Your Majesty," the knight replied.

"Good thing she left her hammer in our quarters," whispered Gerald, "I'd hate to think what kind of damage that thing would do to the floor. Do you remember the tower at Redridge?"

"I could hardly forget it," said Anna, "she managed to cave in the entire floor."

The attention of those in the room was all on the red-headed knight as she began a warm-up, moving around the area, her sword in constant motion.

"Impressive," said the king. "Tell me, are there many women knights in Merceria?"

"There used to be a lot more," said Anna, "but the war saw an end to many of them."

Gerald wanted to explain how they had been murdered by King Henry, but something held him back.

"And Dame Beverly here," continued King Halfan, "you say her father is a baron?"

"Of Bodden, yes," said Anna.

"Are you sure the baron has no son?" the king said in surprise.

"Yes," said Anna, "Beverly is his only child."

"Did he not think to produce a son to inherit?"

Gerald could see Anna biting back her words.

"Beverly's mother died in childbirth," he quickly explained, "and the baron never remarried."

"A fascinating tale," said the king. "She has certainly piqued my interest. How did she come to be a knight?"

"She was knighted on the battlefield," said Gerald, "as a reward for saving King Andred's life."

"Truly?" said King Halfan.

"Yes, the king was swarmed by raiders," said Anna, wisely choosing to neglect to share that they were Norland raiders. "Beverly had to fight off the lot of them to keep him safe."

"Remarkable."

"Here comes Marik," announced Lord Hollis, as the door opened.

The warrior that stepped through was impressive, armoured, head to foot, in chainmail, with a dark blue surcoat displaying the coat of arms of the Earl of Beaconsgate. The man was almost the same height as Beverly, but his broad shoulders hefted a one-handed battle axe with ease. In his other hand, he held a rounded shield, typical of the Norland people.

"Place your bets, gentlemen," announced Hollis.

Gerald looked on in disgust as the earls of Norland bet on the outcome of the fight. "I don't like this," he whispered. "Betting on a fight just doesn't seem right."

"I agree," Anna replied quietly, "but it is not our way to change their culture."

"Will you place a bet?" asked Hollis, looking at Gerald.

"I think not," said Gerald.

Hollis returned his attention once more to his fellow nobles as coins were tossed on the table. King Halfan watched, a slight look of irritation to his face.

"The combat shall be to first blood only," he commanded.

He waited as the nobles settled their bets then turned to the rest of the court, who had been watching with keen interest.

"You may begin when ready," he announced.

Marik stepped to the middle of the room, keeping his distance from Beverly as he swung his axe a few times, loosening up his muscles. Finished, he took a ready stance, his shield held before him.

Beverly watched him with interest, holding her sword two-handed, the point towards her Norland opponent.

Marik struck first, stepping forward and swinging his axe from right to left. Beverly easily dodged the blow then stabbed forward, hitting her opponent's shield.

Their audience reacted with cheers, urging them to continue the fight. Beverly stepped back, parrying a blow, then struck low at the Norlander's legs, but Marik, in anticipation, brought his shield down, and the blade scraped along its surface.

When the knight attacked again, swinging from left to right, Marik leaped backwards, the blade passing harmlessly before him. Just as it did, he struck out again, this time driving the head of his axe towards Beverly's face, forcing her back unexpectedly. She knew the axe was a slow weapon and so she moved to the left while watching his footwork, preparing herself to take advantage of his next attack.

Her chance came soon enough when the Norlander stepped forward, thrusting out with his axe. This time, however, as she moved her sword to parry, he pushed forward with his shield, taking her off guard. It pressed against her sword, knocking it aside and then he was within reach, striking down with a solid hit to her leg. The axe's edge scraped across the metal thigh guard and angled downward, clanking as it struck the stone floor.

Beverly drove forward, using her elbows to push him back. Marik staggered but kept his wits about him and planted his feet, sweeping the battle axe low in an attempt to trip her up. The weapon contacted again, the solid thunk echoing through the air as blade met metal armour.

They were in close now, far too close for the reach of her sword and she was tempted to drop it in favour of her dagger, but the axeman needed space as much as her, and so she struck out with the hilt, hearing a grunt as it hit the Norlander's forearm.

Marik pulled back, catching his breath. He shook his weapon arm, sore from Beverly's hit, then struck out once more, the axe coming down, impacting heavily with Beverly's sword. She felt the man's raw strength pushing down on her, and she bent her knees slightly, absorbing the blow, then quickly turned her sword, causing the axe to glance off and slide to the side. Seeing an opening, she jabbed straight out, striking the Norlander's hip, but once again, his chainmail did its job, and the blade slid off, failing to penetrate.

The thrust had thrown her off balance, and this was precisely the moment Marik was waiting to take advantage of it. Somehow, he brought his weapon in close, and then Beverly felt the axe dig into her glove, pain lancing through her hand. Next, the Norlander hooked the cross guard of her sword with his axe, pulling it from her grasp as she sprawled forward. The man stood over her, his battle axe raised, ready to strike.

"Enough!" roared the king.

Marik paused as indecision wracked his face. He looked over at Lord Hollis, who shook his head, and then the champion backed up, lowering his axe.

"You have fought well," said King Halfan, "there is no dishonour in being bettered by Lord Hollis's champion."

Aubrey moved over to her cousin, who cradled her hand, blood flowing, her gauntlet cut and mangled by the blow.

"Straighten your hand if you can," Aubrey said. "We must get this glove off of you before I cast my spell." She tugged the gauntlet gently, feeling resistance and then it came free, followed by a rush of blood.

Beverly grimaced in pain as Aubrey examined the wound. "It looks clean," she said, then started uttering words of power. Those in the room fell silent as the mage's fingers began to glow and then she placed them onto Beverly's hand, the energy flowing through her and absorbing into the knight.

"How does that feel?" Aubrey asked.

"Much better," said Beverly, "though I'm now down one gauntlet."

"It could have been much worse, cousin," said Aubrey. "You might have lost a finger, and that takes much longer to repair."

Beverly rose to her feet, nodding at Marik.

"I concede the fight," she said, "you have bested me."

Marik grunted, though whether or not he returned the compliment was anyone's guess.

King Halfan watched his nobles passing coins, then swivelled his gaze to

Anna.

"Your knight is an impressive fighter," he said, "but she cannot match the might of a Norland champion."

Anna returned his stare. "Are all your champions so skilled?"

"Marik is among our best," said the king, "though others have claimed that title from time to time, he always wins the games."

"Games?" said Anna.

"Our champions compete with their peers," added Hollis.

"Against the champions of other earls?" asked Gerald.

"Saxnor, no," he said, "that would incite a war. No, they compete within their own earldom."

"When you say compete," said Gerald, "I assume you mean they train?"

"No," said Lord Hollis, "they fight, sometimes to the death."

"Don't you lose a lot of good fighters that way?"

"We do," said Hollis, "but the winners emerge even more powerful. A man can only elevate his skills so far with training. There comes a time when only killing others will further his martial prowess. We call it the Blood Price." He turned to his champion. "Tell me, how many men have you killed in the games, Marik?"

"Twenty-one, Lord," said the warrior.

"There, you see?" said Hollis. "I have lost twenty-one warriors of my own to advance him to this level of ability. Can you say the same of yours?"

"Lady Beverly has killed many in combat," said Gerald.

Unexpectedly, Halfan grimaced slightly, and Gerald wondered if his words had upset him, but then the king rose slowly, as if in pain.

"It is time for me to withdraw," he said. "I shall meet with you on the morrow, Queen Anna. Until then, you may stay and enjoy yourselves."

Anna stood, as did Gerald, both bowing as the king made his withdrawal.

After he left, she turned to Lord Hollis. "Tell me, Lord, is the king ill?"

"No," said Hollis, "he suffers only from the ravages of time."

"How old is the king?" she pressed.

"This year marks his sixty-ninth year among us," said Hollis, "though I fear he will not see seventy."

"Might I offer the services of my Life Mage?" she asked.

The Earl of Beaconsgate paused for a moment, looking like he was considering it. "No," he said at last, "we must let nature take its course. Now, if you will excuse me, I have much to do, as do the other earls."

"Of course," said Anna, "I shall leave you to your work."

"It has been an honour, Your Majesty," said Hollis, bowing, "and I look forward to speaking with you in future."

SIXTEEN

The Capital

Fall 964 MC

Harry Hathaway sat back, nursing his drink. The Serpent's Coil was packed, a not altogether unusual occurrence, but what set this day apart were the coins that were flowing freely. He looked across the room at Igran Hawtrey as the man made his way through the crowd, stopping at each table in turn.

Hawtrey was a big man, topping off at more than six feet and known for being boisterous and crude, but today he was reserved, chatting with people in an amiable tone as he moved from table to table.

He finally made his way to where Harry sat, pausing to look down at the confidence man.

"Well, well, well, if it isn't old Handsome Harry."

"Igran Hawtrey," said Harry, "it's been a long time."

"What are you doing here, Harry?"

"I heard a rumour you were hiring, and I thought I'd give it a try."

"This is muscle work, Harry, not your typical thing."

"Times are tough, and I need the coins."

Igran stared at him, and Harry felt a nervous sweat building between his shoulder blades. He fought down the urge to flee and then finally, Igran nodded his head.

"All right," said the big man, "I'll let you in on it. I've been hired to assemble a large group."

"This isn't a break-in, then?" said Harry.

Igran smiled, showing his yellowed teeth. "You're damned right," he said, "this is much bigger."

"How much bigger?"

Igran sat down, lowering his voice. "Listen, Harry, you're smarter than the rest of this crowd, so I'll give it to you straight, we're forming a mob."

"You can't be serious," said Harry. "The last time a mob assembled, it didn't end well."

"If you're talking about the riots back in '53," said Igran, "believe me, I know, I was there."

"The army slaughtered us."

"This is different," said Igran.

"Different, how?"

"Let's just say that my employer has made certain arrangements."

"Your employer?"

Hawtrey smiled, "Someone with lots of spare coins, but I can't say more."

"And this mob is expected to fight?"

"It wouldn't be much use otherwise. Look, I know this isn't your thing, Harry, but I need people that can take direction. A lot is riding on this."

"Such as?" said Harry.

"This will put the Hawtrey gang at the top of the food chain, and we'll remember who put us there."

"How does your father feel about that?"

"He's too old to participate," said Igran, "but he relishes the thought of uniting the gangs."

"Uniting the gangs?" said Harry. "How many people have tried that over the years?"

"Many," Igran replied, "but they didn't have the funds to back them up." He reached into his belt pouch, pulling forth a golden crown. "This is what it's all about, Harry, and there's plenty more where that came from." He dropped the coin onto the table, drawing Harry's attention.

"So what's the deal?"

"I need to assemble two large groups," said Igran. "One will act as a diversion while the other strikes."

"Strikes at what?"

"Never you mind. Are you in or out?"

"I don't know, Igran," said Harry, "it sounds dangerous. Any sign of a mob and the soldiers will be sent in."

Hawtrey grinned, "That's precisely what we want them to do."

"People will die."

"Not necessarily. The main purpose of the first group is to lure the troops in. Once that's done, they can disperse. No one need get hurt."

"You're drawing them away from their barracks."

"You're a smart man, Harry, but you should keep that to yourself. Now, are you in or not?"

"I'm in."

"Good, I need someone to draw off the guards. What do you say to leading the diversion? I can make it worth your while."

Harry sat back, eyeing the man suspiciously. "What's in it for me?"

In answer, Igran Hawtrey tossed two more coins onto the table. "Consider that a down payment. I'll double it when we've assembled everyone we need."

"And when will that be?"

"I have a few more stops to make," Igran continued, "but word should come down by the end of the week."

"Very well," said Harry, "I'm your man."

"Good. Keep an eye on this place. I'll pass the word when we've settled on a date."

He got up to leave, leaving Harry to scoop up the coins.

"Wait," said Harry, "how will you send word without alerting the watch?"

"Keep your ears open," said Igran. "You'll hear of a special card game, here at the Serpent's Coil. That's the signal to assemble."

"That's a lot of people to fit in here."

"Don't be a fool, Harry. This is only one group, we don't want to raise any suspicion. We'll march down the street and pick up others along the way. Now take care, I'm counting on you."

"I'll be there," said Harry.

"Are you sure of this?" asked Hayley as she paced.

"As sure as I can be," said Nikki. "Harry tells me the Hawtrey gang is definitely being funded by a wealthy benefactor. Igran Hawtrey was spending quite freely."

"That can't be good."

"There's more," said Nikki. "There's to be two mobs. One to draw away soldiers and the other to strike."

"Yes, but strike where?"

"Harry said that Igran slipped up and said 'guards.'"

"What type of guards, I wonder?" said Hayley. "Do you think he wants to take a city gate?"

"That seems unlikely," said Nikki. "They already have soldiers in their pockets, smuggling things in and out is relatively easy."

"It is?" said Hayley. "That surprises me, I thought the gates were secure."

"They are, at least against foreign attack," said Nikki, "but you know how it is, soldiers are woefully underpaid, and they're not averse to making a little on the side."

"I suppose that's true," said Hayley. "So then, what is the object of this plot? The Palace?"

"I can't see how they could attack here," said Nikki, "wouldn't the Royal Guards defeat them?"

Hayley halted her pacing. "The Royal Guard is largely in the north with the queen."

"How many are left here?" asked Nikki.

"Fewer than a dozen," said Hayley.

"That must be it," said Nikki. "They intend to attack the Palace!"

"To what end?" said Hayley. "Surely they can't seize power?"

"They could if they had troops on their side," said Nikki.

"The Palace Guard is loyal to the queen."

"What about the Knights of the Sword?"

"Saxnor's beard," said Hayley, "I hadn't considered that possibility."

"We know Shrewesdale had co-conspirators. Were they ever unmasked?"

"No," said Hayley, "though we had our suspicions."

"The Earl of Tewsbury was involved," said Nikki. "Couldn't you at least arrest the man?"

"We know nothing of the sort," said Hayley, "and we have a system of laws in place. We don't just arrest people for no reason."

"But he spoke out against Gerald," said Nikki, "or have you forgotten the court case so quickly?"

"No, but speaking his mind in court is not the same thing as treason. We have to tread carefully here, he's a powerful man."

"So what can we do?" asked Nikki. "Beef up the town watch?"

"That will only give us away," said Hayley, "and I can't trust the watch. They're too susceptible to bribery."

"We have to do something!" Nikki urged.

"And so we shall. I will bring some rangers to the Palace."

"Won't that raise suspicions? We can't just increase the number of guards, that will tip our hands as surely as increasing the watch."

"Not if we do it surreptitiously," said Hayley.

"You're starting to sound like Revi."

"I'll take that as a compliment," said the ranger.

"By the way," said Nikki, "how is the search for him going?"

"The last I heard, they were still trying to decipher that magical mirror of his. I haven't heard from them for some time."

"You should keep our mages close," said Nikki. "We may have need of them soon if this plot goes any further."

"A valid point," said Hayley, "but that gives me an idea. I shall have to speak with Kraloch."

"He's in Hawksburg, isn't he?" asked Nikki.

"No, he was brought here to help in the search for Revi."

"Shall I find him for you?"

"No, I'll send Gorath. I need you to get back in touch with Harry. Have him notify you as soon as he hears they're assembling."

"And if riots break out?"

"Then we'll respond as the crown always has," said Hayley, "and let them think we're unprepared."

Runes began to illuminate as distant magic called, and then the entire circle began to glow brightly. A wall of light shot towards the ceiling, obscuring the centre and then it dissipated, revealing a group of mages.

Kraloch carried Revi's thin form as Albreda strode before him. Aldus Hearn, Kiren-Jool and the Weldwyn Enchanter, Gretchen Harwell, all fell in behind as the druid opened the door, drawing the attention of two surprised guards.

"Mistress Albreda, we weren't expecting you!"

"Nevertheless, here I am," she said in response. "We have recovered Master Revi Bloom."

The guard looked at the sickly form of Revi. "Is he alive?"

"For the time being," snapped Albreda, "but he is very weak."

The guard moved to the bell that hung beside the door. It was designed to give warning that someone was attempting to gain entry to the circle, but he thought it best to alert the other guards in the vicinity of the mages' unexpected arrival.

Aldus Hearn turned to the limp form of Revi. "He doesn't look good, are you sure there is nothing further you can do?"

"I have healed him," said Kraloch, "and his physical form is restored, but he is malnourished. He has likely not eaten or drunk anything for days."

"Can't you regenerate him?" asked Hearn.

Albreda turned on her fellow druid. "For Saxnor's sake, Aldus, he can mend damaged flesh, not cure hunger. Do you see any physical injury on Revi?"

"Well...no," said Hearn.

"Then you must trust that Master Kraloch knows what he is about."

Sir Preston arrived with half a dozen soldiers. "Mistress Albreda," said the knight, "you've found Master Bloom!"

"We have," said the Mistress of the Woods. "Now, will you escort us to his quarters? He needs rest and send someone to the kitchen, for he shall need sustenance."

"Food?" asked Sir Preston.

"Yes," said Albreda, "a broth would be best. He shouldn't have anything solid for a while."

Sir Preston dispatched a man, then turned his attention to Kraloch. "Can we help carry him?"

"He is no burden," said Kraloch, "and I can manage well enough. Where shall we take him?"

"This way," said Sir Preston. He turned, barking out an order, "Brenton, send word to Baroness Hayley."

"Aye, sir," the soldier replied.

Evard Brenton had served the Royal House of Merceria for years, first in service to King Andred, and then his son, Henry. He prided himself on his devotion to duty, a duty that had resulted in him being injured last year as he helped search for one of the shapeshifters. Knowing the Palace intimately, he ran off, determined to reach the office of the high ranger as quickly as possible.

Gorath sat at his desk, examining the wooden construction. As an Orc, he thought it unusual that these Humans relied so heavily on paper. So much so that they constructed these strange tables to be able to deal with it. Suddenly, the door burst open, revealing an out of breath guardsman.

"Is something wrong?" asked Gorath.

"It's Revi Bloom," stammered out Evard Brenton, "they've found him."

Gorath stood, crossing to the door to the high ranger's office. He knocked politely, waiting for the call to enter, then opened the door.

"What is it?" called out Hayley.

"A messenger has just arrived," said Gorath. "It seems they found Master Bloom."

"Revi?" said Hayley, rising from her chair. "Where is he?"

"They've taken him to some rooms in the guest wing," offered Brenton.

Hayley pushed her way past Gorath. "Take me there immediately," she said, turning to her aide. "Come along, Gorath, you're with me."

"Right this way, my lady," said Brenton.

"Who found him?" asked Hayley, following closely.

"He was brought in by Mistress Albreda," Evard explained. "They used the Palace circle."

"Was there anyone else with her?"

"I saw the Orc shaman, and three others," he replied. "One of them was the old druid."

"You mean Aldus Hearn?" said Hayley.

"That's him," he replied, "but I don't know the other two. One was a foreign-looking man, and the other was an older woman."

"I take it you don't regularly guard the circle," said Hayley.

"No, ma'am, I serve under Sir Preston. Our duty is to react to any emergency."

"I thought that was Beverly's responsibility?" said Hayley.

"It is, normally, but she's in the north, with the queen."

They rounded a corner and began making their way up a set of stairs.

"How did he look?" she asked.

"Sickly," said Brenton, "but he was alive. Very thin, I thought, as if he'd been starved."

"Oh, Revi," said Hayley, "what have you gotten yourself into?"

"Pardon?" said the guard.

"Nothing," snapped Hayley, "I was just thinking out loud."

Finally, they reached the top of the stairs and passed down another hallway. They were close by now, a fact that was soon obvious from the discussion drifting down the hall. They turned the corner to see Kiren-Jool and Aldus Hearn standing in front of an open door, deep in conversation.

"Aldus," said Hayley, "what news have you?"

"He is alive," said Hearn, "and in the care of Kraloch."

"Where was he?" asked the ranger.

"We found him in the tower of Andronicus," explained Hearn. "He was in the very bottom, collapsed near a fissure."

"A fissure?"

"Yes, one that was emitting magical flames."

"Like those of the Saurian temples?" asked Hayley.

"Yes, he had likely been there for some time."

"Can I see him?"

"I wouldn't suggest that until Kraloch says he's ready," said Aldus. "Revi's been through an ordeal, and is very weak."

A noise erupted from the room, followed by the sound of someone falling onto the floor. Hayley pushed past Hearn to see Gretchen Harwell lying prone, while on the bed lay Revi, mouthing words of power. Hayley could feel the air buzzing with magical energy.

Kraloch was casting a spell as well, calling forth his power even as Revi cast again. Hayley staggered as an invisible wall of energy hit her and then felt fatigued as if she had been active all day.

When the Orc released his magic, Revi fell eerily quiet. Albreda, standing to one side, moved forward to kneel by the unconscious form of Gretchen Harwell.

"It's all right," she said, "she's been put to sleep, nothing more. Luckily, she didn't hit her head when she fell."

"What happened?" said Hayley, staggering into the room.

Kraloch placed his hand upon her forearm. "Easy now," he soothed, "you must sit, you are weak."

The Orc led her to a chair, and she sat, thankful to be off her feet.

"I don't understand," said Hayley, "are you saying he attacked us?"

"He's not in his right mind," said Albreda. "I fear he is loosing uncontrolled magic."

"I have slept him for now," said Kraloch, "but further measures must be taken."

"Such as?" asked Hayley.

"Magebane," said Albreda.

"Will that hurt him?" asked Hayley.

"No, but it will make it impossible for him to cast magic. Fear not, it is only a temporary measure."

"How long will he need it?" the ranger asked.

"Until he is once again in control of his mind," said Albreda, "but I'm afraid we have no idea how long that might be."

"Indeed," said Hearn, "or, in fact, if he'll ever recover at all."

Albreda shot the Earth Mage a nasty glare. "We know nothing of his condition at present," she said. "Let us leave it to the healer to make that assessment."

"I have never known a man to regain his mind after losing it," added Hearn.

"Nor have I ever heard of someone collapsing by a fissure while staring into a magical flame," snapped Albreda. "We are treading new ground here, Aldus, let us not jump to conclusions."

Gretchen Harwell staggered to her feet with the help of Albreda. "That was...intense," she said.

"I fear Master Bloom is not in control of his faculties," admitted Albreda.

"Luckily, he is not operating at full power," said the Enchanter, "or else I'd be out for much longer."

Albreda looked at Kraloch. "Have you any idea how this might be rectified, Master Shaman?"

"It is beyond my skill," admitted Kraloch, "but once he is dosed with magebane, I shall consult the Ancestors. Hopefully, they can give us some guidance."

"What about Roxanne?" asked Gretchen. "She's the most gifted Life Mage in Weldwyn, maybe she might have some ideas of how to proceed."

"It's worth a try," said Hayley. "Can you fetch her?"

"I will recall to Summersgate tomorrow morning," said Albreda, "but we need to ensure that Revi is safe first."

"And the magebane?" Hayley added.

"I believe I can help with that," said Hearn. "It is, after all, brewed from plants, a particular specialty of mine."

Hayley rose, moving to sit on the end of Revi's bed to look down at him. His face was gaunt, his skin sickly pale, and tears came unbidden to her eyes. She caressed his cheek, feeling the coldness of it.

"What have you done?" she whispered.

"He was lying prone when he was found," said Kraloch. "We have no idea how long he was there before we discovered him."

"This flame," said Hayley, "you say it was coming out of a crack in the ground?"

"Yes," said Kraloch. "It was a green flame, much the same as that in the temple, though perhaps more powerful."

"Gorath tells me the Orcs can talk to spirits," she said.

"That's true," said Kraloch, "but I doubt that would work on someone who is unconscious."

"We must send word to all temple locations," insisted Hayley. "All further use of them will be put on hold until we can determine the cause of Revi's condition."

"That will mean cutting off direct communication with Queenston," warned Aldus Hearn, "not to mention the Orcs in the Artisan Hills."

"Our Ancestors tell us we are unaffected by the flame," offered Kraloch, "as were the Saurians. We have spent years examining the one in our home with no signs of illness, but until you Humans arrived, we had not unlocked its secrets."

"Then, as we have no Saurians here in Wincaster," said Hayley, "I shall decree that for the foreseeable future, only Orcs are permitted to use the temples."

"Are you sure you wish to do that?" asked Hearn. "It would mean placing a heavy burden on the Orcs."

"A burden we can well bear," offered Kraloch. "We shall keep the lines of communication open for you."

"How long will he remain unconscious?" asked Hayley.

"At least till noon," said Kraloch, "though I can administer the spell again, should the need arise."

"Good," said Hayley. "In the meantime, Master Hearn, seek out what herbs you may and prepare the magebane while Albreda travels to Summersgate."

SEVENTEEN

King Halfan

Fall 964 MC

A ubrey stood in the doorway. "Are you sure, Your Majesty?"

"Quite," said Anna. "King Halfan insisted on meeting privately. I'm sure you and Gerald will be more than sufficient to keep me safe."

"But surely Beverly would be better suited," Aubrey protested.

"Beverly is an excellent warrior," said Anna, "but Gerald is more than capable of protecting me. I also need someone to help with diplomacy, and you're better suited to that."

"Me? Whatever gave you that idea?"

"I'm well aware of your efforts in Hawksburg," Anna explained, "and you've worked with the Orcs, not only that but with the rangers as well. You're quite adept at dealing with people, and that's why you're one of my advisors."

"If you say so," the mage replied.

"I do," said Anna, "and so I'll brook no more argument. Where's Gerald?"

"He'll be along shortly," answered Sophie. "He was just going over a few things with Beverly."

Tempus sat up quite unexpectedly, his tail wagging.

"I think that's him now," said Anna.

Aubrey turned to see the old marshal walking towards her.

"Everything set?" he asked.

Aubrey moved out into the hallway. "We're ready. The queen was just waiting for you."

Gerald halted, waiting as Anna exited. "You look quite regal," he noted.

"Thank you, Gerald," said Anna. "Now, shall we go and see King Halfan?"

"By all means."

Anna took his proffered arm, and they moved down the corridor while Aubrey followed.

Gerald had spent the morning familiarizing himself with the castle, at least as much of it that he was allowed to see. He led them through a series of confusing corridors and across an open courtyard to an inner keep. Along the way, they were observed by Norland guards, but none blocked their path.

They went up a grand set of stairs to a larger, more palatial room, where King Halfan sat waiting.

"Greetings, Your Majesty," said Anna, bowing.

"Queen Anna," the man replied, "so good of you to visit. Will you come and sit with me?"

"Certainly," said Anna, moving to a solid wooden chair with pillows opposite him. Gerald stood behind her while Aubrey moved to her side.

"Come now," said the king, "we can't have your advisors standing while we sit. We have plenty of chairs. Please, make yourselves comfortable."

Gerald sat, though he certainly didn't look comfortable. Aubrey, on the other hand, was a vision of grace and elegance as she took a seat to Anna's left.

"Some wine?" asked the king.

"No, thank you," said Anna, "but feel free to have some, if you wish."

King Halfan held out a goblet while a servant moved up to fill his cup. "Tell me," said the king, "what did you make of our nobles?"

"They seem a dedicated lot," said Anna.

The king laughed, almost spilling his wine. "A very diplomatic answer. Dedicated they are, if only to enriching their own pockets. Tell me, is it the same way in Merceria?"

Anna smiled, "There are some with that attitude, though thankfully, not many."

"You are a young queen," said Halfan, "with many years ahead of you, Saxnor willing. Make sure you pick advisors you can trust, for they are few and far between."

"I have already surrounded myself with those I can trust," said Anna. "It is a lesson I learned very early."

"Good, then I propose that we talk more openly if we are to make progress."

"I would agree with you," said Anna, looking around the room, "and yet there are many ears here, perhaps a smaller venue might be more appropriate for a frank discussion?"

Halfan smiled, though he grimaced afterward, as if in pain.

"Is something wrong, Your Majesty?

"Nothing but age," said the king.

"Something my marshal is well acquainted with," said Anna, bringing another smile to the old king's face.

"Let us retire to the reading room," suggested the king, as he leaned forward, struggling to stand. Aubrey stepped forward, offering her hand.

"May I help, Your Majesty?" she asked.

He took her arm. "Yes, thank you. Lady Aubrey, isn't it?"

"Yes, Your Majesty."

"You were quite impressive with your magic yesterday. Might I ask how long you have been studying it?"

"I apprenticed under the Royal Life Mage, Revi Bloom," said Aubrey.

"The baroness began her studies only four years ago," added Anna.

"Four years?" said the king. "Most impressive. I was led to understand that mages needed years to master even the basics of the arcane arts."

"It runs in my family," said Aubrey.

"So your mother was a mage?"

"No, but my great grandmother was, and she left substantial notes on the subject."

"You must have a sharp mind," said Halfan. "Do you read?"

"Extensively," said Aubrey, "though not as much as the queen."

Halfan turned to Anna in surprise. "Well then, let me show you my library, we can talk there." He pointed to a side door. "It's this way. Will you be my cane, Lady Aubrey?"

"I would be delighted, Your Majesty," she replied.

He led them across the room as a servant, anticipating their destination, opened the door. The king paused, looking at one of his servants, a fairly short, balding man. "Bring the wine, Harcourt, then leave us in peace."

"Yes, Your Majesty," the servant replied.

They passed through the doorway into a smaller room where one wall was full of bookshelves, though they were sparsely populated. The king selected a wide-backed stuffed chair before the fire, which was burning low. He looked over at Gerald, "Be a good fellow and put another log on the fire, will you?"

Gerald did as he was bid, picking through the stack of wood to select a suitable log, which he then tossed onto the fire, watching as the flames caught.

"There," said King Halfan. "Now, where is my wine?"

As if in answer, the door opened, and Harcourt strode in bearing a tray with four cups and a bottle. He set it down on a small table by the bookshelves.

"Would anyone else care to partake?" the man offered.

"No, thank you," said Anna.

"Come then," said Halfan, "fill up my goblet, man, and leave us in peace."

Harcourt did as he was told, filling a goblet, then carrying it carefully over and placing it in the hands of his king.

Halfan took a sniff, then smiled. "Ah," he said, "the Burnford Red, an excellent choice. Is it fresh?"

"It just came in last week," said Harcourt, retreating to the door. "If there is anything else, please don't hesitate to call."

"Get out with you," grumbled the king, though the smile on his face betrayed his affection.

The door closed, leaving them in solitude.

"He's a bloody nuisance sometimes," said the king, "though he means well."

"Has he served you long?" asked Anna.

"Harcourt has been with me far longer than I care to admit," Halfan said, "and that's saying something, these days."

"I take it you have few people you can trust," said Anna.

"I seem to have outlived all the servants I grew up with," he admitted. "Such is the fate of those that live to my age."

"Tell me, sire," said Aubrey, "have you ever been treated by a Life Mage?"

"No," said the king, "and even if we had them here in Norland, I wouldn't trust them."

"Why is that?" asked Aubrey.

"The mages are all pawns of the earls," explained the king, "and as such, have their own motives. It is no secret that I am old and without heirs. When my time comes to pass to the Afterlife, I shall leave behind no legacy."

"Except for peace with Merceria," added Anna.

"I see you understand me now," said Halfan. "I have done little enough during my reign, but I wish to see my kingdom better off than the way I found it."

"How long have you been king?" asked Gerald.

"Let's see, it would be close to forty years now. You, on the other hand, I understand, have only been queen for a short time."

"Yes," said Anna, "my coronation was just over a year ago, though I reigned for a few months as a princess."

"I envy you," said Halfan, "for you are at the beginning of your reign, while I am at the end of mine. Live the best life you can, Anna of Merceria, for one day you will look back and judge your actions from a new perspective."

"I shall endeavour to do just that," she promised.

King Halfan sat forward in his chair. "See that you do," he said. "Now, shall we get down to business?"

"There is little business to conduct," said Anna. "The proposal you sent us was very straight forward. You wish each of us to acknowledge the river as the boundary of our respective realms."

"Yes," said Halfan, "and in addition, we shall renounce our claim against your throne."

"And your nobles are in agreement?" asked Gerald.

King Halfan winced, though the action was subtle. "Most," he said, "but I think the rest can be convinced."

"There is another matter I'd like to address," said Anna.

"By all means," said the king. "It is, after all, what we're here for."

"It concerns the Orcs," she began. "I'm led to understand that you have been at war with them for some time."

"War? With the greenskins?" said the king. "I'd hardly call that a military campaign."

"Nevertheless," said Anna, "it is something that must be addressed. You see, the Orcs are our allies."

"Surely not! Such creatures cannot be trusted, they are nothing but savages."

"I admit they are a unique culture," said Anna, "but they fought beside us to put me on the throne of Merceria. I shall not abandon them now."

"And so you would expect us to what? Retreat before their raids?"

"I understand that they were driven from their home in Ravensguard," continued Anna.

"Ravensguard is a fortress," said Halfan, "and the earl has fought hard to tame the territory."

"The Orcs were defending their homes!" declared Anna.

"What are you proposing?" asked the king. "That we simply give away our castles?"

"No, but a general cease-fire would help, and hopefully a resolution to this conflict? I'd be happy to act as an intermediary."

"Fascinating," said the king, "but tell me, how did you become aware of this problem?

"We learned about it through our allies," said Anna. "They have a well-developed communication system."

"They would have to, to bring word to Merceria," said Halfan.

"Will this be a problem?"

King Halfan sat a moment, staring at his goblet as he thought. He took a deep drink then savoured the taste, swirling it about his mouth before swallowing.

"No," he said at last. "I will have to talk to the Earl of Ravensguard, no doubt, but I think I can convince him it's in his best interest to fall into line."

"And the other earls?"

"That may be a bigger problem," said Halfan. "The truth is, I need four earls to sign off on this treaty, and five would be even better."

"I thought a simple majority would be sufficient," said Anna.

"You don't know Norland politics," said the king. "I could sign the treaty now, but then my successor might just repudiate it."

"Who's your successor?" asked Gerald.

"That's just it," said the king. "I haven't named one, nor do I intend to any time in the immediate future."

"Is that wise?" asked Anna.

"It is necessary! As a king without heirs, I must select an earl to rule after me. Once I name one, the others will become unmanageable, making it impossible to get anything done."

"And so you keep them guessing," said Anna.

"Yes," admitted Halfan. "You must see my dilemma."

"I do," said the queen, "but surely there's also a risk. If you were to die before naming an heir, what would happen?"

"Norland would fall into civil war, I shouldn't wonder. I'm afraid at this point, it's almost inevitable."

He sat back, leaning his head against his chair and looked upward. "Saxnor, give me strength," he said, then started to shake.

Aubrey immediately moved towards him. "Something's wrong."

"What is it?" Anna asked as the king began frothing at the mouth, spittle falling onto his chest.

Aubrey had already started casting, the words of power pouring from her mouth at a rapid pace. Moments later, her hands glowed with a pale blue light. She placed them to either side of the king's head and watched as the magic flooded into him. It dissipated rapidly, restoring the king to a more healthy hue.

Halfan opened his eyes to see Aubrey standing over him.

"What happened?" he asked.

"Someone tried to poison you," said Aubrey.

"It was fortunate that she was here," added Gerald.

"Fortunate indeed," said the king.

"Have you any idea who might have attempted such a thing?" asked Anna.

"Too many to single out just one!" said Halfan. "It seems that one of my earls wishes to expedite my demise, and that can mean only one thing, war!"

Anna looked across at Gerald, who was fidgeting nervously. They had returned to the queen's quarters and now sat, waiting for their next meeting.

"What is it, Gerald?" she asked.

"I don't like this," he replied. "Someone tried to kill the king, and they chose the exact moment we were with him to do it."

"You think someone's trying to blame us?" said Anna. "I thought the same thing."

"They won't fail a second time," he warned.

"I doubt they'd try poison a second time," said the queen. "The king will be looking for it."

"That means they'll likely have to take a more direct approach."

"Agreed," she said. "Is that what's bothering you?"

"To a certain extent," said Gerald. "We're trapped here, Anna. If we're blamed for this, there won't be an easy way out. We can get you to safety, certainly, but we brought a lot of people with us, and I have to think of them as well."

"Time to draw up a contingency plan," said Anna. "If things do go badly, you'll need a way out."

"I've already been giving it some consideration," he said, "and I think I have an idea, but it hinges on some unknowns."

"Anything I can help with?"

"I'm afraid not unless you can provide me with detailed maps of the castle?"

"I wish I could," said Anna, "but I'm reasonably certain that's a request that King Halfan would refuse. Perhaps we can figure out who tried to kill him?"

"A difficult task, I should think," he said, "and we know very little about the earls, other than their names."

"Then it's time we changed that," she said.

"What are you suggesting?"

"We are here to negotiate a treaty of peace. I think it only proper that we should meet with each of the earls to gather their thoughts and opinions, don't you?"

Gerald smiled, "That's very clever, Anna, but not something I can really assist with."

"That's all right, I'll have Aubrey's help. You and Beverly find out as much as you can about the defences here, and we'll worry about the earls."

"I can do that, but where will you start?"

"We already know Lord Hollis," said Anna, "so we'll start by sending out requests to the others and see who responds first."

Lord Waverly, the Earl of Marston, waited as his guests were shown in. Sitting in a massive high backed chair, his giant frame dwarfed by its immense size, the earl prided himself on showing no emotion, and so remained still, stone-faced, as his guests were let in.

"Your Grace," said Queen Anna, "so good of you to see us."

He merely nodded his head in greeting, trying to look as imperious as he could.

"Please sit," he said, indicating the additional seats that were arranged so that he could look down on them, increasing his towering presence even more.

Queen Anna sat first, giving no sign of being intimidated. "I thought," she began, "that given the importance of our mission here, I might seek your counsel, Your Grace."

Waverly raised an eyebrow in genuine surprise. "You wish my counsel?"

"Indeed," she continued, "for I understand that you are a man of influence."

He leaned forward, intrigued by what this young monarch wanted. "Go on," he urged.

"If you were to support the cause of peace, it would go a long way towards convincing the others."

"What makes you think I would support it?" he asked.

"Marston is a fair distance from the Mercerian border," said Anna, "and therefore, we are certainly no threat to your earldom."

"Agreed," said Waverly, "and yet you seem to think that automatically makes peace desirable."

"There are many economic benefits to peace, including goods flowing across the border between our two lands."

"An interesting idea," he replied, "but what has that to do with me?"

"Might I ask where your lands lie, Your Grace? We are familiar with those earldoms on our borders, but the rest of your kingdom is unknown to us."

"Marston lies to the northwest of here," said the earl. "It is mostly flat land, but the northern plains stretch into the mountains. Tell me, have you ever heard of Dragon's Peak?"

"I have not," said the queen, "but it sounds quite fascinating. Are there actual dragons there?"

The earl laughed, a sound that came out as a snort. "No," he said, "it is so named for the ridge that looks like a dragon, at least from a distance."

"I would imagine the land there must be fertile," added Aubrey.

"Why would you say that?" he asked.

Aubrey straightened her back. "I would suspect the runoff from the mountains would bring fertile soil to the area. Would crops be your primary source of wealth?"

"Farming is certainly important to us," he replied, "but no, horses are our major export."

"How very interesting," said Aubrey. "My family has been raising horses for generations. Tell me, do you train warhorses?"

He sat back, intrigued by this well-spoken woman. "We do, as a matter of fact."

"So you must be familiar with the Eldred method."

He found himself smiling, despite his pledge to remain emotionless. "Yes, I am quite familiar with the writings of King Eldred. He laid down the concepts of training horses hundreds of years ago, long before Norland was founded, but things have changed substantially since then."

"I'm afraid I'm not following," said the queen.

Aubrey turned to face her monarch. "King Eldred was a man who was very forward-thinking," she explained. "He organized a system of breeding to improve the horses that our ancestors brought to this land. It was his foresight that brought cavalry to the forefront in later years."

"Yes," agreed the earl, "and he laid out the instructions for training war horses."

"And all this was done by a king?" asked Anna.

"I'm sure he consulted others," said Aubrey, "but he was the one that insisted it be recorded and made available to all."

"Thus improving all breeds," added Waverly.

"Do you sell your horses to all the other earls?" asked the queen.

"I do, though not in great numbers. I have also developed my own breed of warhorses, one that I use exclusively, due to the great cost."

"Fascinating," said Aubrey, "for I find myself in the same situation. My family helped develop a very large breed. You may have seen Dame Beverly's horse?"

"Mine are bred for speed," said Waverly, "something that took many generations."

"They must be worth a fair amount," said the queen. "Have the other earls shown no interest at all?"

"They have," he declared, "but they lack the funds necessary. After all, I cannot just give them away."

"Merceria is wealthy," said the queen, "and always looking to expand its herds. It's a pity that our two nations are at war."

Waverly grinned, "Oh, I see what you've done there. Well played."

Queen Anna continued, "I think we both see how peace could be mutually beneficial."

"We do," he agreed, "and I see now why you are a queen. I will support your push for peace, though I daresay the others will not be so easily persuaded."

"What can you tell us of them?" asked Aubrey.

"Hollis looks on the treaty as no kindness," said Waverly, "for he, alone, of all the earls, traces his ancestry back to King Galburn."

"Wait," said the queen, "are you telling us that King Halfan has no claim?"

"It's true," continued the earl, "for you see the line of kings was broken back in the late six hundreds, while Hollis traces his lineage through the king's sister."

"That's why he's not king," said Anna.

"Precisely," said Waverly. "Agreeing to the peace would mean forever surrendering his claim to the throne of Merceria."

"Has he support for his claim?" asked Aubrey.

"Rutherford is certainly on his side," noted the earl, "though I cannot speak for the others."

"Thank you for your candour," said the queen.

"You're welcome," replied Waverly, "though I will, of course, deny it should anyone ask."

"As is only fitting," Anna agreed. She turned to her companion, "Have you any other questions, Lady Aubrey?"

"None that I can think of," the Life Mage replied, "though if peace comes, I would certainly welcome the chance to visit your herd."

"If peace comes," he said, then corrected himself. "No, WHEN peace comes, I shall be delighted to host you."

Queen Anna rose, followed by her advisor. "You have given us much to think on, Lord Waverly. I thank you for seeing us."

"Not at all," he said, rising from his own seat, "it is I that should thank you."

EIGHTEEN

Return to the Tower

Fall 964 MC

Aldus Hearn pulled another volume from the bookshelf. "This looks interesting," he muttered.

"What does?" asked Albreda.

"Notes from Andronicus, in his own hand from what I can tell."

Albreda stepped closer, bringing the lantern to bear. "It's a large library, Aldus, far larger than the one in Wincaster. I'm sure there are lots of books in his hand."

"This looks a little different," he said, flipping through the pages, "and it mentions quite a few dates."

"Interesting to historians, but we're looking for clues as to Revi's condition."

"Still," said Hearn, "I'll put this aside. I have a feeling it's important, it must be the scholar in me."

"This would be easier if there were some sort of system to the organization of the books."

"You mean like at the Library of Kendros?"

"Yes," she agreed, "at least there you could find what you were looking for."

"Only if we understood their system," he said. "Perhaps this tower has its own way of categorizing books?"

"The tower has no such thing. It is people that organized them, not a building."

"You know what I mean," he grumbled.

Albreda looked up. "That's it!"

"What is?" he asked.

"There is a system, I should have seen it sooner."

"There is?"

"Yes," she said, closing the book in his hands. "Look at the cover of this volume."

Hearn looked down, examining the leather binding. "I don't see anything of interest."

"It looks new," she said, "or at least reasonably so."

"I still don't understand what bearing that has on how it's organized."

"Don't you see? Every book on this shelf is in a similar state. I'm willing to bet that the books are organized by date."

"That's a rather silly way to arrange things," said Hearn.

"Not necessarily. It depends on the purpose of this library."

"I don't follow," he complained.

"What is the primary purpose of a library?" Albreda asked.

"That's obvious," said Hearn, "to store books."

"Yes, but to what purpose?"

"For future reference, of course."

"What if that's not true. What if this library represents history?"

Hearn looked around the room, taking in the sheer volume of books. "That's a lot of history. That being the case, wouldn't there be multiple books for the same time period?"

"Likely there is," she said, "and so there is another sub-category within each grouping."

"I see what you're getting at," said Hearn. "Each shelf might represent a decade, let's say. And within each shelf, books might cover different topics."

"Precisely."

"But how does that help us?"

"I'm not sure it does," said Albreda, "since we don't know when the fissure was discovered."

"I do," announced Hearn.

"You do?"

"Of course, at least in relation to the construction of the tower," he said. "I can manipulate stone using magic, remember?"

"Then how old is it?"

"The cavern below predates this tower, of that I am sure."

"Then we need to find the oldest books in the library," said Albreda. "They will, I'm sure, have some reference to it."

"You think it of interest to whoever built this place?"

"Of course," she said, "don't you? After all, what's the likelihood that the tower just happened to be built here?"

"A good point," he said, placing his book back on the shelf. "You start over there," he said, pointing, "and I'll start here. Between us, we should be able to narrow down the search for the oldest books."

Albreda descended the steps once more, carrying a tray. "Time to eat, Aldus," she said, pausing when she saw the old druid sitting at the table, a candle held high to illuminate some text. "Something interesting?"

"Indeed," he said, "though not, I fear, related to Revi's condition."

She moved closer, placing the tray carefully on the table. "What is it?"

"It's a hidden history," he said.

"What do you mean, 'hidden'?"

"It references events that are not mentioned elsewhere."

"How do you know?" Albreda asked.

"I was a scholar before I was a mage, remember? I'm fully conversant with Mercerian history."

"If you say so," she said. "But tell me, what are these hidden events you speak of?"

"Something called the Shadow War," said Hearn.

"That sounds ominous."

"It gets worse," he continued. "According to these notes, there was a war between a group of dark mages and the forces of light."

"Forces of light? Really? Who might they have been?"

"I don't know, it doesn't say, but the dark mages were definitely Necromancers."

"I take it, from the name, that this was all hidden away from the common folk?"

"And the crown, from the sounds of it," added Hearn.

"That sounds a little like the Dark Queen."

"It may, in fact, be related. According to whoever wrote this, the group of Necromancers was led by a Dark Council."

"Can't they come up with something more original than that?" Albreda asked.

"I suppose we could call them the Council of Evil if that makes it more palatable," said Hearn.

"It doesn't matter," she replied, "get on with it. What happened?"

"The war lasted for several years, with each side scoring victories and suffering defeats, until they finally destroyed the Necromancers' power base."

"When was this?"

He scanned the page, looking for dates. "The first mention of them is in the year 753. It appears that's when the court mages of Merceria first became aware of them. They were destroyed in 913, the same year that King Haran was crowned."

"That's just over fifty years ago," she said.

"Too old for us," said Hearn, "but not too long ago for Andronicus."

"Agreed, or the Elves. Lady Penelope was one, remember?"

He looked up at her, the realization dawning on his face. "You think she was one of them?"

"It would make sense," said Albreda. "We know she was a Necromancer, after all."

"And if she survived," said Hearn, "then others might have as well."

"Forming a Council of Shadows," said Albreda. "It all makes sense now."

"What does?"

"Years ago I had a vision," she said.

"What type of vision?"

"A shadow growing across the land. I remember telling Dame Beverly."

"I thought that shadow was Lady Penelope?"

"So did I, but what if I was wrong? What if that shadow was the return of this Dark Council?"

"That would be particularly bad," said Hearn. "It took all the mages Merceria could assemble to defeat them."

"How many?"

"More than twenty, from what I could tell, and we have, what? Four?"

"Five if you include Revi," said Albreda, "and that's with Kraloch, who isn't technically one of ours."

"A far cry from twenty," said Hearn. "What do we do?"

"Do? What can we do?" she said. "We are only speculating here. We don't know if our premise is even possible."

"Still, we must do something. What about our Weldwyn allies?"

"They have maybe a dozen mages and some untrained apprentices," said Albreda, "but only five or six of any real power. If the Dark Council has been reconstituted, it could well be the end of us all."

"We must keep digging," said Hearn, "and hope more will be revealed."

Kiren-Jool examined the page. "And you say this was in the tower?"

"It was," said Aldus Hearn. "Albreda and I feel this Dark Council may still exist."

"This text gives us very little to go on. Are you sure it's accurate?"

"I would hardly think it worth keeping if it wasn't," noted Hearn. "Remember, it was hidden away from normal folk, including the Kings of Merceria."

"Do you think they suspected the influence of these Necromancers at court?"

"I can't say," said Hearn, "but the notes make it clear that only the court mages knew of this Shadow War."

"We must inform the queen!" urged Kiren.

"Do you think that wise?" asked Hearn. "The original mages thought it best to keep it secret."

"Yes," the Kurathian agreed, "but they failed, didn't they?"

"Failed, how?"

"At least one Necromancer escaped them, possibly more, and Queen Anna already knows about Lady Penelope and her affinity for Death Magic."

"I suppose that's true," noted the druid, "but there is little we can do until her return from Norland. The real question here is what we do in the meantime?"

"What does Albreda think?"

"She feels it is best to inform the mages of Weldwyn," said Hearn. "At least then, we shall have more eyes watching for the return of these people."

"We need to begin training apprentices," said Kiren-Jool.

"Isn't it a little late for that?"

"We don't know how long they're willing to wait. We know Penelope, as an Elf, is more likely to think in longer terms. If you remember, she spent years building up her power base behind King Andred."

"You're suggesting we start training other mages, but how do we find them?"

"And interesting conundrum," noted Kiren-Jool. "Lady Aubrey had some ideas on the matter, but we were all so busy with our lives that we never investigated further."

"Then we shall have to make it a priority," said Hearn.

"And we will, but we still have to deal with the problem of Revi's illness."

"Illness?" said Hearn. "More like a curse."

"Nonsense," noted the Enchanter. "He has an illness, nothing more."

"But he went mad!"

"Not of his own accord," said Kiren-Jool. "He spent too much time staring at the flames. I would gather his mind was afflicted, but I must admit I'm no expert in such things. It will fall to Lady Aubrey to determine the cause. What of Kraloch, he's a healer? Has he any ideas on the matter?"

"I'm afraid not. He's used healing and regeneration on the poor soul but to little effect. I'm afraid with Revi's mind gone, we have to keep him dosed with magebane."

"Magebane? Surely he's not attempting to cast?"

"He was," noted Hearn, "though he had little control."

"Then his mind isn't completely gone," noted Kiren-Jool. "If it was, he'd be unable to recall the words of power."

"I can't see that as being any help," said Hearn. "He's still not in control of himself."

"Maybe not, but at least he's still capable of thought, even if his mind is jumbled."

"Kraloch is going to consult the Ancestors. Perhaps they will have some idea of a cure."

"Let us hope so," said Kiren-Jool, "for I fear it might prove to be our last chance to help him."

Kraloch advanced to the centre of the magic circle, then sat, cross-legged, placing his satchel before him and rummaged around inside.

Off to the side, yet still within the circle, sat Hayley and her aide, Gorath. The Orc was explaining Kraloch's movements as the old shaman prepared himself for the ritual.

"He will conduct a ritualistic cleansing before he begins the spell," Gorath explained. "I have seen him do so before."

"Is that something we should do?" asked Hayley.

"No. Kraloch's ministrations should more than suffice. Cleansing is only used when the matter is of great importance. By doing this, he is showing himself to be worthy of the Ancestor's attention. We, on the other hand, will be nothing but passive observers."

The Orc shaman withdrew a small bowl from his bag, placing it before him.

"The bowl is made of clay," continued Gorath, "and signifies the earth. In a moment, he will withdraw some dried river grass, representing the element of water.

Hayley watched as Kraloch removed a straw-like plant tied in a small bundle from his satchel. He tore some off, no more than a thumb's worth, which he then added into the bowl before him. Placing a stick in, he stood it up and held it between his two palms, rotating it quickly, using a back and forth motion to rub the end into the bowl. Soon, a wisp of smoke appeared and he redoubled his efforts until the grass caught fire, glowing, and then smoke began to issue forth from the bowl.

"The burning plant represents fire," said Gorath, "while the smoke represents air. He will breathe in deeply, to purify his mind and protect his spirit."

"What is he protecting himself from?" asked Hayley.

"There are many creatures of the spirit realm that could do him harm," explained Gorath. "This ritual will call on those of a good nature to protect him."

They watched as the plume of smoke before him grew, and then Kraloch leaned forward, placing his head directly above the bowl, inhaling deeply. Moments later, he sat back, a contented look upon his face.

"He is now ready to cast," said Gorath.

Kraloch straightened his back, his eyes closing as he began the ritual. Sounds tumbled from his mouth in an endless stream. Hayley struggled to make out distinct words, but it was impossible. She knew that magic words were universal, forming a language all on their own, but none of the words coming from Kraloch sounded anything like those used by Revi.

They sat for some time until her legs began to cramp. She was ready to move, eager to stretch, but then Kraloch's chanting ceased, his words echoing briefly in the large chamber before it grew quiet.

"I call upon the Ancestors," he said, using the common tongue. "Heed my words and come before me this day."

The shaman's head turned slightly, and though his eyes were still closed, Hayley could tell he was facing some one, or some THING!

"I am Kraloch," the shaman continued in answer to an unheard question, "of the Black Arrows."

He waved his hands briefly, uttering some more words, and then suddenly, Hayley felt light-headed. She closed her eyes and the feeling soon passed. When she returned her attention to the centre of the circle, she gasped, for before them stood an ancient-looking Orc, with animal skulls hanging from his neck. The Ancestor stared back at Kraloch with an intensity Hayley found disturbing.

"Why have you summoned me?" he demanded.

"I seek your wisdom," said Kraloch.

"Then speak so that I would know your desire."

"An ally of my people has fallen ill," the shaman continued.

"What is the nature of his illness?" asked the spirit.

"The green fire," said Kraloch. "He has spent days staring into it, and now his mind is gone. Is there any there who can offer a cure?"

"There is one," offered the spirit, "but I fear their mere presence could put you in great danger. Are you sure you wish to continue?"

"Though the risk be great, I must," said the shaman.

"Very well, but I warn you, Khurlig is dangerous. Most powerful of all shamans was she, but her journey since death has been fraught with peril."

"And she can be of assistance?" asked Kraloch.

"While she was among the living, she held power over life and death, but such power is not used without cost."

"I will consider your words carefully," said Kraloch.

"Then prepare yourself," said the spirit, "for she is on her way."

The image faded, leaving the room once again in silence.

"How did I understand that?" asked Hayley. "Were they speaking in Orcish?"

"They were," said Gorath. "Were you not paying attention?"

"I could have sworn they were speaking the common tongue."

"Spirits work in mysterious ways," said Gorath, "and I am no expert, but they seem to have permitted you to understand."

"What happens now?"

"We wait for this Khurlig to appear."

"And who is she?" asked Hayley.

"I have no idea," said Gorath, "but I would surmise a great healer, judging from the description."

"What did he mean by cost?"

"This is also unknown to me," replied her aide. "I suppose we shall just have to wait and see."

Hayley sat, her eyes glued to the form of Kraloch, who remained in place, unmoving, his eyes still closed.

Motion off to the side drew her attention. The hairs on her arms stood on end when an Orc came into view, a bent figure shuffling forward on wilted legs.

"I am Khurlig," the Orc intoned, "Mistress of Life and Shamaness of the Red Hand."

"The Red Hand?" whispered Hayley.

"A tribe on the Continent," replied Gorath. "It is they that gave us the secret of the warbows."

"You seek information about the green flame?" asked Khurlig.

"We do," said Kraloch, "for one of our allies has been afflicted, and he has lost his mind. Can you help him?"

The ghostly figure smiled. "I can," she said, "but to do so, I must inhabit a body. Such things do not work from the spirit realm."

"No!" interrupted a new voice. Hayley turned to where the sound was coming from. Someone outside of the circle was speaking, but to her mind, it sounded as if they were close by.

The figure of Khurlig wheeled about, turning her back on Kraloch. "You!" she sputtered, "you have dogged my steps for far too long, Uhdrig."

"And you have overstepped yours," replied the newcomer, entering the circle. The visitor was bent with age, yet her eyes looked keen and observant.

"Do not lecture me," said Khurlig. "I shall return to the world of mortals and tread upon the ground once more."

"You cannot," said the newcomer, "I forbid it."

Khurlig laughed, a high screeching sound that echoed through the chamber, "You cannot stop me this time." She turned to face Kraloch and then stepped forward, her body passing through that of the shaman.

"He is mine!" came Khurlig's voice, then a scream of anguish.

"You have failed," said Uhdrig.

"I do not understand," said Khurlig. "Long have I waited for this opportunity, practising my arts by day and night."

"And yet Kraloch has stayed your hand," said Uhdrig. "You have gambled and now lost. Never again will the Ancestors allow you to communicate with our living descendants."

Khurlig gave a shrill cry and then began to fade.

"I don't understand," said Hayley. "What happened?"

Kraloch turned to face the high ranger. "I cleansed myself as a protection from vile forces," he said, "and it saved me from Khurlig's malevolence."

"But now we'll never learn how to cure Revi," said Hayley.

"The answer lies in your ally's past," said Uhdrig.

"You speak in riddles," said Kraloch. "Master Revi cannot recall his past."

"No, he can not," agreed Uhdrig, "but his apprentice can recall hers. She has only to seek that which is buried."

Kraloch nodded his head. "Wise words, Uhdrig of the Red Hand, I shall heed them well."

"Fare thee well, Kraloch, and may your tribe prosper."

"As should yours," said the shaman.

The old spirit faded from view, and Hayley was left feeling somehow lighter.

"I don't understand," she said. "What just happened? Did we get a cure for Revi?"

"Hopefully," noted Kraloch, "but it now depends on Aubrey."

NINETEEN

Valmar

Fall 964 MC

R oland Valmar looked up from his notes, "You have news?"

Sir Warren nodded, "Aye, sir. Everything is proceeding according to plan."

Valmar rubbed his hands together. "This is it," he said, "what I've been working towards for years. This will be a historic day, Warren, you mark my words. The legitimate royal line shall be restored and usher in a new era."

"Yes, my lord," said Warren, though he knew full well that Valmar was far from a legitimate heir. "Would you like to address the men?"

Valmar considered it, closing his eyes and seeing himself on a balcony, speaking to a large, adoring crowd. Then, they all fell silent, and he just stood there, like a fool, at a loss for words.

"My lord?" said Warren, interrupting his thoughts.

"Sorry?" said Valmar.

"Do you wish to say anything to the men, my lord?"

"Oh, very well," said Valmar, "I'll come and say something."

He rose from his seat, taking a moment to arrange his notes into a tidy pile. Valmar was a stickler for details and always insisted on things being kept neat and orderly. Content with the surface of his desk, he stepped around.

"Lead on, Warren."

The Knight of the Sword led him out of the room and down the stairs, emerging into the courtyard of the barracks. The men of the Wincaster Foot stood formed up and ready, eager to start what would likely be the most momentous day of their lives.

Valmar saw their eyes lock onto him expectantly. He was nervous, feeling the weight of history upon him. Sir Warren nodded to Captain Fielding, who called out to his men, causing them to straighten their backs and look straight forward.

The captain, a seasoned veteran, turned to the former marshal-general, "The men are ready for you, Lord."

"Very well, Captain, I shall begin the inspection."

Sir Warren fell in behind as Valmar and Fielding made their way down the line. He was struck by the sheer disinterest displayed by his commander, for Valmar ignored the men, walking past them quickly and giving them little notice.

Valmar, finished with his inspection, turned to Fielding, "Good turnout, Captain. Are they ready to fight?"

"Fight and die, if necessary."

Valmar looked skyward, trying to judge the time of day. It was nearly noon, and he fretted that his other men were not yet in place. When a distant bell tolled, marking the midday, he returned his attention to his officer.

"That's your signal, Captain. You may begin!"

Fielding barked out orders, and then the men all turned in unison. A moment later, they were filing out the gates of the barracks, intent on their destination.

Valmar watched as they left the courtyard, turning onto the street heading towards the Palace. Their boots echoed on the cobblestones as they made their way eastward, the sound only fading from his ears as they disappeared from sight.

A lone messenger rushed across the courtyard, handing a note to Sir Warren. Valmar turned to his aide with interest, "News?"

The knight of the Sword smiled, "The third and fifth companies are with us, my lord."

Valmar returned the smile. "It's working," he said. "The crown will soon be ours."

"Was there ever any doubt, my lord?"

Valmar ignored the comment. "Bring the carriage around," He ordered.

In answer, Warren nodded to a nearby aide. The man ran off, eager to perform his duty. Valmar was nervous, for much was at stake this day.

"We are making history today," he finally said, more to himself than anyone else.

The knight looked at his commander, sensing his unease. "What will your first official act as king be, my lord? Or should I say, Your Highness?"

Valmar turned to the knight in surprise. "That's an excellent question. I suppose I should order the death of the rabble that took the crown from us. What do you think, Warren?"

"I think you would do well to first reward your allies, my lord. They will be the ones that give longevity to your reign."

"An excellent idea," he replied, his words trailing off as if deep in thought.

"Something wrong, Sire?"

"Tell me," said Valmar, "who commands the cavalry?"

"Sir Gavin, a fellow Knight of the Sword," said Warren, "from Shrewesdale?"

"Ah, yes," said Valmar, "one of the Shrewesdale Five."

"I'm afraid that's a term I'm not familiar with, my lord."

"I'm not surprised," said Valmar. "Most of Shrewesdale's knights were lost at the Battle of Eastwood during the first uprising."

"Killed by Orcs, were they not?" asked Warren.

"They were," admitted Valmar, "all due to that Fitzwilliam woman. I won't deign to call her a knight."

"Isn't she the one that saved King Andred?"

"She was an opportunist," said Valmar, "nothing more. It was I that saved the king that day. I was, after all, commanding His Majesty's Bodyguard. It seems everyone is intent on robbing me of my due in that regard."

"Where do the Shrewesdale Five fit into this?"

"Ah, well," said Valmar, "only five of Shrewesdale's knights came back that day, you see, and we have four of them on our side."

"Who's the fifth?"

"A man named Sir Heward. He saw fit to go over to the other side during the civil war, an act I'll not soon forget."

"Ah, yes," said Warren, "now I remember. They all testified against the earl during his trial, didn't they?"

"They did," said Valmar, "though it couldn't be helped. Knights are sworn to tell the truth, as you well know. One could hardly expect them to lie under oath. I blame the whole thing on Montrose, the man was a fool."

"Lord Shrewesdale?" said Warren. "Surely not?"

"Oh, yes," continued Valmar. "He should have acted with more determination and rid us of that Fitzwilliam woman once and for all when he had the chance."

"Are you suggesting he should have executed her, my lord?"

"It would have made things so much simpler," said Valmar. "It was his undoing, in the end."

"But she is the daughter of a baron, my lord. Such things cannot go unanswered."

"I'm not suggesting he should have killed her with his own hands," said Valmar, "but an accidental death could have been arranged, I'm sure. As it was, he put all his cards on the table, thinking he was immune from prosecution, and it cost him his life in the end."

"And the Shrewesdale Five?"

"I've kept my eye on them ever since the trial. When Montrose was executed for treason, I reached out to them, well, four of them that is. They've been secretly in my employ ever since."

"A shrewd move, my lord," said Warren.

The carriage appeared, coming to a halt while a soldier ran forward, placing a small step on the ground before he opened the door for Valmar. The former marshal-general climbed up, pausing for a moment to look back at the barracks.

"This shall be the last time I'm forced to live here," he declared. "Now come along, Warren, we've work to do!"

～

Harry Hathaway watched as the mob advanced down Walpole Street. A line of soldiers was strung across the road, ready to meet them, a scene reminiscent of the slaughter that took place over ten years ago, back in '53.

The warriors stood shoulder to shoulder, their shields interlocked and their weapons held at the ready. The crowd hesitated, coming to a halt before the armed soldiers of the queen, jeering at their demonstration of might.

Harry noticed a distinct lack of enthusiasm on the side of the mob. Coins had bought this scene, but now, faced with cold, hard steel, many were starting to reconsider their decision. The insults continued, but they grew less and less frequent until he saw the crowd begin to thin as the reality of their situation started to sink in.

Suddenly, in a macabre re-enactment of the past, a bottle flew through the air, striking a shield to shatter into a thousand tiny fragments. Next came a brick, creating a loud thud as it, likewise, struck a wooden shield.

The royal troops held their position, their discipline intact, staring down the mob from behind an unwavering wall of shields while a mounted officer sat behind them, surveying the crowd.

Slowly, the mass of people began to back up, women now urging their children to safety. Harry wondered why a mother would even think to bring a child to such a place, but he knew in his heart that desperate poverty had driven them to it. The horde steadily put more distance between themselves and the soldiers while Harry made his way to the side of the street, hoping to avoid being swept up in the panic he feared was yet to come.

The officer called out a command, and the line of troops moved forward. It was only three steps, followed by a halt, but it was enough. With the tips of their spears protruding from between the shields, they presented such a vision of violence that panic erupted.

The commoners, the dregs of the slums, broke, stampeding down the street in a hurry to get away, all caution thrown to the wind. Harry saw people trampled in their mad rush to safety, while others cast their makeshift weapons aside to avoid the ferocity of the expected counter-attack.

Harry watched as the crowd thinned, thankful there would be no wholesale slaughter this day. The queen's troops, their discipline intact, refused to advance any farther, holding their position as their opposition trickled away.

Giving a silent thanks to Saxnor, he ducked down an alleyway, intent on the next part of the plan.

～

Igran Hawtrey moved farther down the street, a large mass of people following in his wake. From a side street came more, swelling his numbers with the finest men that coins could buy. Ahead of him, he spotted the iron gates of the Palace and the Royal Guards beyond. Having taken notice of his people, they were scrambling to shut the gates, but Hawtrey simply smiled. Let them close them, he thought, for this was only a diversion.

"Death to the queen!" he called out. At first, the cry was taken up only by a few, but then, as they were emboldened by their numbers, more and more joined in.

Igran broke into a run, and soon, others were rushing past him, intent on venting their rage. While he slowed, content to let others do the dirty work, he noticed a merchant ducking into a nearby doorway and absently wondered what had brought them outside this day. Would they live to regret their actions, or were they destined to die along with a slew of nobles?

The mob, HIS mob, rushed the gate. It was an iron gate, consisting of vertical iron bars, made more for display than a practical defence, and his men started grabbing the bars, shaking the gate itself. The guards backed up, trying to remain out of reach.

Igran Hawtrey merely laughed, for soon he would be a wealthy man.

~

Captain Harlon Eldritch halted his men. The rear of the Palace was only one block away, and he wanted to give his troops a short rest before the last stretch. He hoped there would be no resistance, but there was always the possibility that the Royal Guards might prove stubborn and put up a fight, so he let his men gather their strength.

This, he thought, was his chance at redemption. Under the current regime, he had been forced to resign his commission as the Captain of the Wincaster Light Horse, but now, under Valmar, he had been promised a reinstatement. Nay, better than that, a promotion!

Harlon had been placed in charge of the fifth company of the Wincaster Foot, hardened soldiers each and every one! He was determined to use them to the best of his ability.

He glanced around at the men, HIS men, and thought of what he was about to do. Attacking the rear gates of the Palace was a dangerous move and he knew that failure would result in that which he feared most, dishonour and death.

Initially, Eldridge had been ordered to accompany the mob that was, even now, forming out front, but that company's captain, a man named Saunders, had refused to participate in this act of treason. As a result, Saunders now sat under guard, detained at the very barracks Harlon had just marched from.

As the men rested, he moved to the corner to peer down the street. The Palace gates stood waiting, the guards lounging at their post, unaware of the storm of steel that was about to be unleashed.

He turned, calling to his sergeants and moments later, the men were forming back up, each one nervously drawing their weapon. Captain Eldridge stepped out in front of them, turning to face the distant gates.

"Onward men!" he commanded, then started the advance. He feared for a moment that they might not follow, but the sound of echoing feet behind him calmed his nerves. His confidence grew with every step, and then he drew his sword, marvelling as the sun caught its blade.

The Palace guards looked on in bored fascination as they drew closer. It wasn't unusual for troops to march down this road, for several barracks were housed north of the Royal Estate, but as Eldridge's men drew closer, he watched real fear settle in.

Someone shouted an alarm, and then two of the guards started closing the iron gate that would bar their entry.

"Attack!" screamed Eldridge as he broke into a sprint. His boots echoed on the stones and his scabbard jangled as he pushed himself onward. He felt his heart beating in his chest, his blood pumping through his veins, and then suddenly he was at the gate, stabbing out with his sword, the blade scraping across his opponent's mail, then sinking into the man's armpit. The guard fell, and Eldridge stared down in disbelief as his own men rushed past him, carrying their fury into the courtyard beyond. The guard at his feet dropped his weapon, holding up his hands in supplication, but Eldridge stabbed down with his sword, driving it into the man's jaw. It scraped across bone then slid into the man's neck, eliciting a cry of anguish as the metal found its mark. The body twitched for only a moment, then lay still.

Eldridge looked around, only to witness his men flooding into the area. A few guards rushed out from the barracks, but the attackers made short work of them. Eldridge cast his eyes about, finally settling on a sergeant.

"Find Valmar," he commanded, "and tell him the rear gate is ours!"

TWENTY

Death of a Ruler

Fall 964 MC

"Now tell me," asked Anna, "who's next on our list of earls?"

"Lord Marley," said Aubrey.

"Ah, yes, the Earl of Walthorne. What do we know of him?"

"Not much, I'm afraid," said Aubrey. "We think he's a moderate, but we don't know for sure."

She was about to continue when a knock at the door forestalled her.

"Yes?" called out Anna.

"It's Gerald," came the familiar voice.

"Well, for Saxnor's sake," said Anna, "don't knock, just come right in."

The door opened, revealing the aged face of her marshal.

"I'm afraid our plans have changed," he said.

"How so?" asked Anna.

"It seems the king wishes to see us again."

"That's good news," said Anna. "When?"

"Right now," said Gerald.

"Now? But we're supposed to go and see Lord Marley."

"I should think this would take precedence," offered Aubrey.

"And so it does," agreed the queen, "but we'll need to send word to Lord Marley to reschedule. Where's Beverly?"

"In her room," said Gerald. "Shall I fetch her?"

"In her room?" said Anna. "That's a tad unusual for this time of day, isn't it?"

"She's a little under the weather," said Aubrey.

"Then heal her," said the queen.

"It's not that simple," said Gerald.

Anna turned to her oldest friend with a stern look. "What aren't you telling me, Gerald? Surely she's not homesick?"

"No," said Gerald, "but she's lost some of her confidence. Her defeat at the hand of Marik has shaken her."

"That was dumb luck on his part," said Anna. "Doesn't she realize that?"

"Still," said Gerald, "a warrior relies on luck as well as skill. An unlucky break can be seen as an omen of ill-fortune."

"I never took you for someone who believes in such things, Gerald. Don't tell me you believe in curses?"

"I suppose not, but there's something to be said for confidence. Beverly's been defeated, and it'll take time for her to regain her confidence."

"Go and fetch her," commanded Anna. "Shaken or not, I still want her with me when we meet the king."

"As you wish," replied Gerald, disappearing from sight.

"Well, I must say," said Anna, "I did not see that coming."

"Warriors are generally superstitious people," noted Aubrey.

"And what of mages?" asked Anna.

"We're far too practical to be so," said Aubrey. "Though there are likely exceptions."

"I can't quite see Albreda as being superstitious," noted the queen. "Though for the life of me, I'm not sure what she believes in. Does she worship Saxnor?"

"I've never asked," said Aubrey, "though as a druid, I suspect she worships nature."

"I don't see her worshipping anything," noted Sophie.

"What makes you say that?" asked Anna.

"She seems so...what's the word I'm looking for?"

"Practical?" suggested Aubrey.

"Yes," the maid agreed, "that's it, exactly."

Anna stood, examining herself in the mirror.

"You look very nice, Your Majesty," offered Aubrey.

"Thank you," Anna replied, "though I'm missing one thing, my sword."

"I have it here," said Sophie as she moved to the queen's front and buckled the scabbard in place. "There, you are now the very model of a warrior queen."

The door opened. "I found her," said Gerald, stepping into the room. Beverly followed him, standing to the side of the door.

"Beverly," said Anna, "I'd like you to take Nature's Fury with you, I think a display of power might go over well."

"Yes, Your Majesty," said the knight.

"You can leave your sword here if you like, and I'll have Sophie fetch your hammer."

"I can do that myself," said Beverly.

"So you can," said Anna, "but I must insist, there's something I need to talk to you about."

Beverly nodded, surrendering to the inevitable. "Yes, Your Majesty."

"I'll be right back," said Sophie.

"Take Gerald with you," said Anna.

"Me?" said Gerald. "To fetch her hammer?"

"Yes," said Anna. "Why, do you think yourself above such things?"

He stared at her a moment, and then recognition of her intent dawned on his face. "Come along, Sophie, I'll give you a hand."

Anna waited until the door had closed behind them before speaking again. Aubrey had moved to the other side of the room and sat, examining a kerchief in some detail to give them a bit of privacy.

"I understand you are suffering a crisis of confidence," the queen stated bluntly.

Beverly bristled, "Who told you that?" Her eyes swivelled to the mage, who kept examining the stitching.

"Not Aubrey, if that's what you're thinking," said Anna. "I know you suffered a defeat at the hands of Hollis's champion, but that's hardly a reason to feel you're not worthy."

Beverly stared at her queen. "I..." words failed her.

"You are Dame Beverly Fitzwilliam," said Anna, "the Rose of Bodden, or have you forgotten?"

"No, Your Majesty."

"You may have all the time you need to sulk back in Wincaster, but here, in Norland, I need you at your finest. Is that clear?"

"Yes, Your Majesty."

"Good, then I'll have no more of this maudlin state. Tell me, how was it that he defeated you?"

"I'm not sure," said the knight.

"Yes, you are," said Anna. "I know how your mind works. You've gone over that fight many times, am I right?"

"I have," said Beverly with a slight nod.

"And what is your opinion?"

"He caught me by surprise," said Beverly. "I hadn't expected him to use his axe in that manner."

"Do you not use your hammer in a similar tactic?" asked Anna.

"I do, but I underestimated my opponent. It's not a mistake I will make again."

"Good," said Anna. "Now that we have that out of the way, I want you with us when we meet King Halfan. This is likely to be the best chance we get to negotiate a lasting peace, and I promise you there will be no distractions this time."

"Very well," said Beverly.

"And you," said Anna, turning to Aubrey, "have you finished examining my kerchief?"

"Yes," replied the mage, "the embroidery is exquisite."

"That's Sophie's handiwork," said Anna, holding out her hand. Aubrey deposited the finely crafted cloth into the queen's palm.

"Now, where are they?" pondered the queen. She tucked the kerchief into her sleeve, then rested her hand on the hilt of her Dwarven blade.

Aubrey looked at Anna. "You should name that blade," she said, "and perhaps you could get it empowered?"

"Empowered?" said Anna. "Whatever for? I'm a queen, not a warrior."

"Still," added Beverly, "it's proved useful on more than one occasion."

Anna smiled. "I'll consider it," she said, "but we've more important things to deal with at the moment."

A light tap at the door announced the return of Sophie and Gerald. They both entered, and the young maid held out the hammer for Beverly.

"Thank you," said the knight, grasping Nature's Fury with a firm grip.

"Now you are complete," noted Anna, "the Queen's Champion."

"Time to go," urged Gerald. "The king won't be happy if we keep him waiting."

They filed out into the hallway, Beverly and Gerald taking the lead while Anna and Aubrey followed.

"This is very short notice," said Anna. "I hope the king isn't ill."

"I hadn't thought of that," replied the mage, "but then again, we did save him from being poisoned. Do you think he wishes to thank us?"

"I'd be happy just to sign this peace treaty and get home," the queen replied. "I know we haven't been here long, but it seems like ages."

"It's all this enforced idleness," noted Aubrey. "Back in Wincaster, there's always something to do. Here, it feels like all we do is wait."

They made their way through the castle, the King's Hall finally coming into view.

"All set?" asked Anna.

Beverly halted quite suddenly, bringing the group to a sudden stop. "Something's wrong," she said, "the guards are missing."

Gerald drew his sword as Beverly readied her hammer.

"I don't like this," said the old warrior. "We should get you to safety, Anna."

"Nonsense," said the queen. "We have to find out what happened. Open the door, Beverly, but be ready for trouble."

The knight stepped forward, pushing the door open with her left hand, her right gripping Nature's Fury tightly. The sight that greeted them was like a scene from the Underworld.

King Halfan sat, slumped in his chair, ripped open from neck to belly, his tunic bathed in blood, with the contents of his stomach laying pooled on his lap.

Beverly, mesmerized by the grisly tableau, stepped through the doorway, her foot slipping sideways as she entered the room. Looking down, she saw blood everywhere, and then the enormity of the scene shook her to her core. Scattered about the room were the mutilated bodies of half a dozen servants, their blood fresh upon the cold, stone floor.

"Saxnor protect us," she prayed.

Gerald moved past her, taking care to avoid the pooling blood. "Footprints," he noted, pointing, "and fresh ones at that."

Anna stood in the doorway, too overcome to speak. Aubrey moved about the room, checking the bodies, but it was soon apparent that none had survived.

"Whoever did this is nearby," warned Gerald. "The blood leads there," he said, pointing to a side door.

"We must find whoever is responsible," said Anna.

Gerald moved to the door, grasping the handle with his left hand, then he looked at Beverly, who nodded. The old warrior heaved on the door, his eyes down, expecting to follow a trail of blood, but as it swung open, he instead saw armoured legs. He raised his head to stare into the grim face of Marik, Champion of Lord Hollis. Behind him were four men, each wearing a bloodied countenance.

Gerald stepped back in surprise. "The king," he announced, "he's been murdered."

"So he has," sneered Marik, "and now we have caught the murderers, red-handed."

"This was not our doing," argued Anna, stepping into the room.

"So say you," said Marik, "and yet the evidence would seem to contradict that. Surrender yourselves!"

"You're the ones covered in blood," accused Gerald.

Footsteps echoed behind them, and Gerald turned to see Lord Thurlowe, who had just entered through the front door with two men in tow.

"What is this?" the earl demanded.

"These assassins killed King Halfan," announced Marik.

Thurlowe looked at the blood-soaked champion, then back to the Mercerians.

"So it would seem," the earl said. "Surrender yourselves, and justice will be done."

Anna drew her Dwarf sword. "Never!" she shouted. "I would rather die!"

Thurlowe smiled. "Then so be it," he declared. "Kill them!"

The Norlanders rushed forward, Marik making a direct line for the queen. Gerald tried to intervene but was soon overwhelmed by three opponents, slashing and stabbing at him.

"Your puny blade will not protect you," called out the champion, his axe rising high for a killing blow.

He stepped forward to complete his strike, but Beverly interceded, swinging Nature's Fury up to meet the heavier weapon as it was raised high. The clash of metal rang out as the hammer hit the head of the axe, causing sparks to fly.

Thurlowe ordered his men forward, but as they drew their swords, one of them let out a yawn, falling to the floor amongst the blood. His companion rushed forward, his sword thrusting out towards the queen.

Anna stepped to the side, slicing down with the Dwarf blade and cutting into the man's forearm. He fell, clutching his wound and screaming in pain.

Gerald, backing up, attempted to break out of the press of attackers. Then he swung low, feeling his sword dig into a thigh, while a second Norlander struck out with his mace, catching the old warrior in the upper arm. Gerald saw it coming and managed to roll, taking some of the force out of the blow, coming to his feet just in time to parry an attack from his first foe. Luckily, the third man held back, waiting for an opportunity.

Beverly struck out, thrusting the hammer into Marik's stomach. It was a weak attack, but it at least forced him back slightly, while beyond him, another guard stepped forward, taking his place.

She pulled back the hammer and swung it wide, stepping to the right and smashing it down onto the guard's foot. Nature's Fury sank deep, and she felt the head strike stone. A scream of agony erupted, and the man fell to the floor, his foot now a bloody mess.

Lord Thurlowe, both his guards down, turned and fled, leaving Marik and his men to finish the job.

Another thrust of a sword drove Gerald back yet again, but he was beginning to anticipate the attacks now, watching the footwork of his opponents out of the corner of his eyes. The maceman stamped forward, raising his weapon high, and then Gerald struck, thrusting into the man's stomach. As the sword penetrated the Norland mail, he felt the iron links scraping across his blade as it sank deep into flesh.

His second opponent, now sensing an opportunity, lashed out, a wild, uncontrolled blow that glanced off Gerald's cloak, tearing the cloth. He reacted with another thrust, temporarily forcing his opponent back. Not content with merely buying time, Gerald stomped forward, driving his booted foot down onto his assailant's toes. The Norlander screamed out in pain and Gerald followed up with a finishing swing that struck his opponent in the neck. Blood gushed forth as the man fell, and Gerald turned to face his last opponent.

Marik struck again, putting all his strength into the blow, but Beverly dodged, and the axe struck stone, the sound echoing throughout the room. The great Norland champion had fought many battles, however, and reacted quickly, leaping out of the way as Nature's Fury swung over his head. Once more, he stepped forward, thrusting with the head of his axe, but Beverly countered, using the haft of her hammer to knock his weapon aside.

Hollis's champion backed up, and the two of them stood there, watching each other warily, each looking for an opening. The sound of distant footsteps approaching informed Beverly that Marik had reinforcements on the way.

"We have to get out of here!" she shouted.

"Back the way we came," called out Anna, moving towards the main entrance.

Gerald's last opponent rushed forward, but the floor, slick with blood, proved his undoing. The guard lost his footing and crashed to the floor, a sickening crunch heard throughout the room as his knee hit the stone floor. Gerald turned, taking the opportunity to run for the entrance.

They rushed through the doorway with Anna in the lead. Aubrey had followed, but halted in the hallway, turning to watch her cousin, still fighting the Norland champion.

"Beverly," she called out.

Marik swung, a side blow meant to sink into Beverly's side, but the knight dodged back, the tip of the axe merely scraping along her breastplate. As soon as it was past, she pushed forward, thrusting at her opponent's face with the head of the hammer. When the great champion stepped back, Beverly turned and ran.

"You'll not escape me!" he called out.

Gerald was in the hallway now, watching as Beverly rushed towards them. "Look out!" he shouted as Marik struck out at her.

It was aimed high, a shot to decapitate the knight, but Beverly, in a moment of sheer desperation, went to her knees, skidding across the blood-soaked floor as she swung the hammer with both hands.

Nature's Fury struck the door frame, unleashing its full power as bits of stone exploded from the impact. A great rumbling echoed through the room, causing Marik to halt his advance. Moments later, a loud cracking could be heard as the entire doorway collapsed, sending dust billowing into the air.

Gerald held out his hand, lifting Beverly to her feet. Aubrey stared at the doorway, overcome with the sheer force of the magic.

"Come," said Anna, "we must save our people!"

Sophie tied off the knot, then used her slim knife to cut the thread. She held up the hem of the dress, examining it with a critical eye. Behind her, as if sensing her interest, Tempus wagged his tail.

"There," she said, holding it out for him to see. "What do you think?"

The great mastiff wagged his tail some more, then lowered his head back to a sleeping position.

"I suppose that's as good an agreement as I'm likely to get," she mused, rising from her chair and crossing the room to lay the dress out on the bed.

A loud thump outside her door drew her attention. Moments later, the door rattled as someone tried to open it. She halted, listening carefully for the knock that would identify the visitor.

Tempus growled, and she hushed him with her fingers, moving closer to the door to double-check that the bolt was thrown. Someone was talking outside, and she placed an ear to the door to listen.

"They're bound to come this way," said a deep baritone. "Block this door, and we'll wait in the next room to spring out when they arrive."

There was a shuffling of feet and then another voice, this one slightly higher, "You two stay here, the rest of you bring those bodies."

She heard feet scraping along the floor, and her heart jumped a beat. What has happened, she thought, and where was the queen?

A number of footsteps receded, but someone was still there, their feet shuffling occasionally. Sophie, now alert, cast her eyes about the room, searching for anything that might be of use. She spotted Beverly's sword lying nearby but knew she had little skill with such a weapon, then her eyes were drawn to the table and her slim knife. She picked it up, feeling the reassuring weight of the handle in her hands. It had been a gift from the princess, to protect herself from unwanted attention, but now she wondered if she might have to use it, not in defence, but to rescue the queen.

She moved back to the door, once more placing her ear to the wood. It felt like forever before she heard anything new. She was just about to give up when she caught the sound of a distant footfall.

"Someone's coming," called out one of the guards, "make ready."

"Halt!" called the other guard.

"Stand clear!" came the distinctive voice of Dame Beverly.

Tempus let out a growl and Sophie threw back the latch, opening the door a crack to reveal a pair of Norland guards. They were looking down the hall towards the approach of the queen's party, unaware of the maid's observation.

She took a deep breath, clutching the dagger tightly, and then threw open the door. Tempus rushed past, his teeth sinking into a guard's leg and bearing him to the floor. The great mastiff bit deeply, tearing the flesh as he shook his head, eliciting cries of anguish from his target.

Sophie struck out with her dagger, driving it into the second guard's back. His mail softened the blow, letting the slim blade inflict only a surface wound, but he bellowed in surprise. He turned on her, just as another door opened, flooding the corridor with more Norland warriors.

Beverly's voice echoed along the hall, "Mercerians, to me! Save the Queen!"

Sophie's opponent raised his sword to strike her, but as he did so, words of power echoed from down the hallway, and then the man yawned, slowing his movement.

Sophie quickly jabbed at the warrior's face, the only part of his body that wasn't covered in armour, cutting into his cheek to expose raw flesh. She felt the blade scrape along teeth and bone, and then he leaned backward, trying to avoid further damage and lost his balance, falling to the floor.

Tempus, his first victim now motionless, turned his attention to Sophie's assailant. The hound jumped forward, his massive jaws digging into the man's throat. Sophie heard a scream, then the sound of the metal coif giving way to unrelenting teeth. The Norlander gurgled, then his eyes glazed over, and he slumped to the floor.

She wheeled about as footsteps approached from the other direction, but it was only Arnim, leading a half a dozen of the queen's guards. He paused as his men ran past, "Are you all right?"

She merely nodded, at a loss for words, and then watched as he joined his compatriots in battle farther down the hallway.

Sophie started shaking uncontrollably, for she was only a maid, not used to such things. The horror of the scene before her struck her deeply, but the death and destruction all around her captured her attention, and she was unable to look away until a hand on her shoulder startled her. She looked up to see the reassuring face of Lady Aubrey.

"It's all right, Sophie," the mage said. "It's all over now."

The maid shook her head, refusing to look back down at the carnage. Instead, she focused her attention on Aubrey, "The queen?"

"Is safe," said Aubrey, "along with the rest of us."

Gerald appeared out of nowhere. It was like time was standing still, so addled was Sophie's mind.

"Have you energy left?" he asked.

"Yes," said Aubrey, "though not as much as I'd like."

"Good, then get the queen to safety."

Aubrey guided Sophie back into the room, Tempus following.

"How many can you take?" asked Gerald.

"Only a few," said Aubrey, "and I shall have to recall to Hawksburg."

"That will prove fortuitous," said Anna, "for it will allow me to get word to Heward on the frontier. Then they can send a relief column to your aid."

"No," said Gerald, "it's too dangerous. We'll find our own way back to Mercerian soil. The army will have their hands full."

"Why do you say that?" asked Aubrey.

"They killed the king and blamed us," said Gerald. "They obviously intended to start a war. Troops could be crossing the border even as we speak."

"Then we must leave immediately," said Anna.

Gerald surveyed the room. Arnim was just outside, along with his guards, but Beverly was there, her hammer slick with blood.

"Take the queen, Sophie and Tempus," he commanded, "and get them to safety. Beverly and I will lead the others home."

Aubrey moved to the centre of the room, leading Sophie by the hand. Tempus sat at her feet, but Anna moved to embrace Gerald.

"I can't leave you here," she sobbed.

"You must," he replied, his voice hoarse with emotion. "You must protect the realm."

She nodded, her eyes filled with tears, then took her place beside Aubrey. The mage lifted her hands, closing her eyes to concentrate on her magic. Words began to pour forth and then the air crackled with energy. A cylinder of light engulfed the tiny group, illuminating the room with a brilliant glare. Moments later, it vanished, along with Aubrey and her charges.

Arnim poked his head in the doorway, "Is the queen safe?"

"She is safely back in Merceria," said Gerald. "Now, we must gather our people and escape to freedom."

TWENTY-ONE

Rebellion

Fall 964 MC

Roland Valmar rapped the top of the carriage with his cane, and it came to a stop behind the crowd that was growing in size and volume. People were massed before the gate, their angry jeers and catcalls echoing down the street.

Sir Warren pointed, "Looks like a messenger, my lord."

Valmar watched as a man pushed his way through the mob, his partial chainmail armour easy to spot in amongst the commoners. Clutching a scroll case tightly in his fist, he fought his way past everyone to come to a halt at the side of the carriage.

"My lord," he said, handing over the scroll case, "a message from Captain Eldridge."

Warren took the tube, opening it to reveal the parchment within. After scanning its contents, he tried to hand it over, but Valmar just waved it away.

"Out with it, man!" the former marshal-general urged.

"They've secured the back gate," said Warren. "It appears your plan has succeeded."

Valmar sat back, letting out a deep breath of air. "As I always knew it would," he said with more confidence than he felt.

"Shall we proceed, my lord?"

Valmar stared at the knight as he thought things through. It had been an immense gamble, he knew, to try and seize the crown, particularly when he had no legitimate claim to it, yet the Gods seem to have rewarded him this day.

"Very well," he finally said. "Let us proceed to the gate and demand the surrender of the Palace."

Sir Warren called for the guards, then waited as ten men-at-arms formed up to provide the soon to be king with protection.

Valmar stepped down from the carriage, stumbling slightly as he dropped to the ground, so used was he to having a step provided. He began moving towards the front gate of the Palace grounds, his men clearing the way for him. The crowd, now taking notice of his arrival, stepped aside, allowing him unfettered access to the gate, where a small group of Royal Guards waited.

Valmar halted. "In the name of the crown, I call on you to surrender," he demanded.

The guard captain, whoever he was, appeared unimpressed with the declaration. "By whose authority?" he called back.

"I am Marshal-General Roland Valmar, Duke of Eastwood, and I demand you allow us entrance to the Palace."

The crowd started calling out for them to surrender, and then a different call emerged, "Let him in!"

Valmar raised his hands in the air, turning to quiet those assembled. When the noise subsided, he turned once more to face the gate. Just as he was deciding on his next words, a distant sound came to him, echoing off buildings and down the street. At first, the words were indistinct, but as the noise drew closer, it became clearer, "Long live the queen!"

Valmar looked at Sir Warren, but the knight was as perplexed as he. "What is the meaning of this?" he demanded.

"I have no idea," said the knight.

One of his guards pulled himself partially up on the gate in an attempt to see over the crowd. A Royal Guard stepped forward, ready to reach out with his spear, but one of his companions held him back.

"What is it?" shouted Valmar.

"A horde of people," said Valmar's man, "and they're heading this way!"

Valmar turned in annoyance, pushing his way back through the crowd. He had paid for these commoners to be here, and he was not about to have them scattered by Royal Troops.

He cleared the edge of the mob to see the approaching group, led by a woman. Something about her looked familiar, but he couldn't quite place her face. Beside her, strode a man in the clothes of a vagrant, but it was the crowd itself that drew his attention, for they dwarfed his small group.

Armed as they were with clubs and other makeshift weapons, they looked like they meant business. Even as he watched, his own group of people became agitated. Many of them had been spoiling for a fight and now, unable to vent their thirst for violence on the Palace Guards, they refocused their hatred on these newcomers.

Valmar pointed. "Kill them!" he bellowed.

Baroness Hayley Chambers looked out the window at the courtyard below. Enemy soldiers were swarming the back door of the very Palace itself, flush with the victory of taking the rear gate.

"Now," she ordered.

The second-floor shutters flew open, and the Orcs stepped forward, their great warbows at the ready.

She turned to Albreda, who was waiting beside her. "If you'd be so kind?" she said.

"Of course," said the druid, stepping forward. She pointed at the gate, words of power flowing from her mouth. The air began to buzz with magical energy, and then dozens of tiny lights began glowing before her as if fireflies had appeared out of nowhere. She spoke the final word of command, and the lights flew across the courtyard, over the heads of the invaders to land by the back gate, sinking silently into the ground.

The invaders, their attention momentarily caught by the display, jeered as the lights faded from sight, and then redoubled their efforts to take down the back door to the Palace.

A low rumbling sound interrupted their plans. All around the courtyard, the treasonous soldiers paused in their efforts, trying to ascertain the source of the noise. A loud crack, like that of lightning, echoed off the Palace and then thick vines erupted from the ground, pushing cobblestones aside to reach up to the iron gate. They grabbed the metal construction like hands, pulling them closed and then curling around them, sealing the attackers in the courtyard.

"Let fly!" called out Hayley.

All along the windows, the mighty Orcs loosed their arrows. The range was short, and arrows thudded into their targets, taking down men despite their armour.

Hayley aimed her own bow, taking time to pick out an officer. She let loose and had a second arrow nocked almost before the first hit its target. Her quarry fell, disappearing amongst the mass of invaders trapped below.

Someone tried to scale the vines and was halfway up before Albreda spotted him. She uttered a word of command, then snapped her fingers. The vines grew strong tendrils that grabbed the man's arms, tearing them from his body. He dropped to the ground, a dripping, pulpy mess.

∾

Captain Eldridge looked up to see the windows opening.

"It's a trap!" he yelled, but his voice was lost in the pandemonium that erupted. He tried to get to cover, but the press of men prevented him from moving quickly. Eldridge stared up at the Palace, not quite believing his own eyes. Somehow greenskins were in every window. How was this even possible?

A man to his front went down, an arrow protruding from his chest. Backing up, Eldridge was desperate to avoid a similar fate when an arrow caught him in the left shoulder, spinning him around in surprise. He grasped the shaft in a vain attempt to remove it, but as he did so, another found its mark, driving deep into his skull, killing him instantly.

All around his dead body, men dropped their weapons and raised their hands in surrender, but arrows continued to rain down on them.

∾

Harry felt a hand grab his arm.

"This way," said Nikki, dragging him clear of the crowd. The fighting was growing more vicious, and Harry looked on in horror. This was no common battle, fought by soldiers, but that of desperate men, struggling to survive. He saw one, his eyes gouged out, stagger to the side of the road, a woman on his back, driving a knife into his skull. Harry felt the bile rise in his throat and bent over to empty the contents of his stomach.

Nikki pulled him forward just as one of Valmar's men staggered past, bleeding from the scalp, his helmet missing. Even as Harry watched, a shop-keeper struck with a stone, cracking the man's head open like an overripe melon, dropping him to the ground.

"We need to find whoever's in charge," yelled Nikki.

Harry cast his eyes about, looking for a vantage point. "There," he said, pointing over at the Queen's Arms, where a sign hung out from the second storey. Shoving his way through the crowd, he stopped beneath it and cupped his hands to boost Nikki up. She grabbed the overhanging bar and pulled herself onto the wall, then held out her hand and Harry pulled himself up out of harm's way. The street had become one giant brawl, with little to distinguish the two sides. Harry watched in fascination as knives and clubs rose and fell.

"There's Valmar," shouted Nikki. "I'd know that face anywhere."

Harry strained to pick out the well-dressed individual, but he was being overrun by the mob, his own men already swamped by opponents.

The former marshal-general tried desperately to reach his carriage, but suddenly the mob turned on him. Harry watched as Valmar went down beneath a flurry of arms, his screams of terror cutting through even the roar of the crowd. Axes and knives rose and fell, blood flying everywhere. Nikki turned, no longer able to witness the savagery, but Harry stared, somehow unable to tear his eyes away as a limb went flying, and then something that looked like entrails.

Suddenly, the fight seemed to go out of everyone, almost as if that grue-some act had marked the final straw. The people in the street backed up, perhaps finally overwhelmed by the violence before them.

"Come on," called Nikki, climbing down from her perch.

Harry followed as they weaved their way through the stunned mob to come upon the body of Roland Valmar, the former marshal-general of Merceria, lying in a large pool of blood. His right arm had been completely ripped off, along with his left hand, while his stomach had been cut open and his innards pulled out. Dozens of cuts to the face had rendered the man almost unrecognizable.

"What a horrible way to die," said Harry.

"From what Arnim tells me," said Nikki, looking around, "he got what he deserved. The crown is safe, and it's all due to these folk."

TWENTY-TWO

The Border

Fall 964 MC

The mist drifted across the land, settling into the lower pockets, while a wolf, tearing the meat from a hare, looked up, his attention caught by something in the distance. The noise drew steadily closer, and then the creature smelled horses in the air. Many, many horses. Suddenly, hundreds of horsemen emerged from the fog, their trappings jangling as they trotted. The wolf rose, then ran off, leaving its carcass unattended.

Lord Hollis halted, letting his men carry onward while his aide, a dour man named Finlad, rode up beside him.

"Trouble, my lord?"

"How far to the border?"

"We'd see it now if it weren't for this cursed fog," his aide replied.

"And you're certain Wickfield is just beyond?"

"I've ridden this part of the country many times, Lord. I can assure you we are in the right place."

"Excellent," said Hollis, "then let us hope that Lord Rutherford has been as well guided. By nightfall, both Wickfield and Mattingly shall be ours."

"And Hawksburg in two days?" asked Finlad.

Hollis smiled, a rare enough display these days. "No," he simply said.

"But surely we must capture it, my lord?"

"Quite the reverse, actually. The plan is to bypass Hawksburg, as well as

Tewsbury and march directly on Wincaster. We have it on good authority that their defences are weak."

"But doesn't that place an enemy force to our rear, Lord?"

"Yes, it does, but you forget, we carry all our supplies with us. This is a war of speed, Finlad, one which we will execute with precision. Remember, we have their queen safely bottled up in Galburn's Ridge. By the time these Mercerians can react to our invasion, we shall be at their capital, and they will be helpless."

"Then why two armies?"

"The better to split their defences," said Hollis. "As we march on Wincaster, so, too, does Rutherford. We, from the west, and he, from the north."

"And is he to bypass Eastwood, as we do with Tewsbury?"

"Alas, no," said Hollis, "though I tried to convince him of the wisdom of it. No, I'm afraid our ally is determined to capture the city. A rich prize you understand, even though it isn't walled."

Finlad smiled, "You seem to have thought of everything, my lord."

"I certainly hope so," said Hollis. "I've spent years preparing for this."

"And when it's all over?"

"I shall be the ruler of both Norland and Merceria," declared the earl. "And you, as my aide, will never lack for anything ever again."

"I look forward to that day," said Finlad.

"As do I, my good friend. As do I."

The lone horseman galloped into Wickfield, his mount lathered. Pulling up in front of the church, he dropped from the saddle and handed the reins to a surprised looking guard. Throwing the door open, he sent a cold gust of wind into the room.

Sir Heward looked up to see one of his scouts, his breath frosting in the early morning air. "News?" he asked.

"Horsemen," said the rider, "hundreds of them."

The knight stood, instantly on the alert. "Are you sure?"

"I saw them with my own eyes, sir. At least three companies worth, and that was only those I could spot before I left. The sound of their horses' hooves was like the denizens of the Underworld come to claim souls, so it was."

Heward looked around the room. "Call out all the officers," he commanded, then turned his attention back to the scout. "How much time before they arrive?"

"They should be here by mid-morning, sir."

"Damn," said Heward, "they've caught us at a bad time."

"Your orders, sir?"

"Get a fresh horse and ride for Hawksburg. Tell them we're facing an invasion. I shall begin evacuating Wickfield and fall back."

"You won't fight them, sir?"

"That would be madness," said Heward. "We'd be slaughtered, leaving the north vulnerable. No, we shall stick with the plan, fall back to Hawksburg, and from there, we can counter-attack. Now be on your way, time is of the essence."

The messenger ran out to his waiting horse and immediately set off for Hawksburg.

Inside, Heward looked over at Captain Wainwright of the Wincaster Bowmen. "Harold, are your men ready?"

"As ready as they'll ever be," Wainwright replied.

"You know what to do," the knight continued, "begin the evacuation. I want your men bringing up the rear of the evacuees while I remain here with the light horse."

"Is that wise, sir?" said the captain. "You'll be vastly outnumbered."

"Don't worry, I have no intention of engaging with the Norlanders. My mission will be to draw them off and buy you some time."

"And how will you do that?"

"I'll make it look like we're guarding an evacuation into the Wickfield Hills. That should give you a good head start."

"Won't that leave you stranded?"

"We have allies in those hills," said Heward, "Orcs to be exact. They'll guide us to the Tewsbury-Bodden road, and we'll meet up in Hawksburg. You'll simply get there before us."

"Any sign of help from the Kurathians?" asked Wainwright.

"I'm afraid not, and that concerns me. Commander Lanaka has a large detachment at Mattingly, almost two hundred men. His orders would be to regroup at Hawksburg at the first sign of trouble."

"He could be cut off, sir, or completely unaware we are under attack."

"Lanaka is experienced on the frontier," said Heward. "I'll trust him to use his best judgement. In the meantime, we must follow through with our plans to the best of our ability. Give the order, Captain. We need to get the townsfolk to safety as quickly as possible."

"Aye, sir, I'm on my way."

Commander Lanaka pulled back on the reins, slowing his mount. He was on the north side of the river, technically Norland territory, but knew the border counted for little. He looked to either side, ensuring his men were spread out in a skirmish line. They were well-trained horsemen, perhaps the finest this side of the Sea of Storms, and their new home, here in Merceria, had been welcoming. Many only spoke their native language, Kurathian, but his officers were all learning the common tongue of Merceria, an act that was starting to influence the lower ranks as they struggled to adapt.

"Listen, my friend," Lanaka said, soothing his horse with one hand. "Do you hear them? Horsemen, many of them, enough to shake the very ground."

He looked left, and circled his hand in the air, signalling his men to form up to the rear. He repeated the move, looking right, then turned his horse around, trotting back to where the rest of his men stood waiting.

"The fog is lifting," said Caluman, "then we shall see these invaders."

Lanaka laughed, "They are not invaders yet, my friend, not until they cross the border."

"Are we to leave them alone, then?"

"When they come to the border in such large numbers? Of course not. By the Saints, Caluman, what do you take me for, a fool?"

His captain smiled, for he was used to such words. "Your orders, Commander?"

"We wait until they appear, then I will warn them off."

"And if they don't turn around?"

"Then we fight. We are Kurathians, after all. We must earn our keep!"

"What if they have knights?" asked Caluman. "You remember what happened to us at the Battle of the Crossroads?"

"Relax, my friend, the Norlanders have no such warriors. They have armour, that's true, but not the heavy metal plates that our Mercerian friends seem to be so fond of. They are much like us, but less well trained." He grinned, showing his teeth.

It was pure bravado, for inside he was worried. He had led this patrol north, as was his custom, but earlier this morning, they had heard reports of distant thunder. The clear day and his own experience told him it was horses, and so he had brought his men north, in force, to investigate. Now, he sat waiting amongst his men, the finest warriors he had ever served with, but he was nervous.

"There!" pointed Caluman.

A slight rise had hidden the approaching horses, but now they emerged, showing their strength for all to see.

"Saint Mathew protect us," said Caluman.

Lanaka watched as more and more horsemen joined the enemy line, swelling their numbers until he estimated there were more than two hundred such warriors.

"It appears they have the advantage over us," he said, "so we shall have to be swift."

Raising his sword, he held it briefly in the air.

"For the Saints!" he called out.

"For the Saints," came the echo. The line started moving as he swept his sword down.

It began as a trot, closing the distance at what felt like an agonizingly slow pace. He knew he must preserve their horses' strength, for their tactics demanded it. Charging in at the last moment, they would engage the enemy in quick combat, then withdraw, hoping to lure them out. An unformed enemy was a gift to the experienced horsemen of the Kurathian Isles, and Lanaka couldn't help but smile in pride.

The enemy, seeing the Mercerians for the first time, halted their advance. A few riders raced back and forth along their line, presumably making reports. Lanaka could make out an enemy standard, though he was unfamiliar with Norland heraldry.

Here, the ground inclined, forcing the Kurathians to ride uphill. It was a disadvantage, of course, but it would give them a much needed boost when they feigned their withdrawal.

They drew closer to the enemy until Lanaka could make out distinct faces. When he saw the Norlanders lowering their visors, intent on battle, he raised his sword high into the air. Now was the moment, he thought, now was the time to give it their all. Behind him, a horn sounded, drawing his men's eyes to him. Lowering his sword, he aimed the tip directly at the enemy standard.

The Kurathian horses, released from their enforced trot, galloped forth, rapidly increasing their gait. He watched the enemy as their faces revealed surprise at the disciplined charge.

Lanaka could tell the Norlanders were inexperienced in such warfare, for their horses were spaced out too unevenly. He aimed for a gap, then forced his way through, slicing out with his sword as he rode past, allowing his mount's mass to add power to his attack. His sword struck true, scraping along a Norlander's arm, and then the Kurathian flicked his wrist, lest the blade sink too deeply.

Sweeping past his target, he reached the second line, thrusting the tip of his blade into an opponent's face, striking bone. Lanaka withdrew and quickly repeated the action, his new foe falling backward and toppling from the saddle.

Once again, Lanaka ignored him, pushing farther in and seeking out a fresh target. All along the line, his men were doing the same, shredding the first line, sending the Norlanders into confusion.

When their horn sounded a second time, Lanaka turned, galloping back through the now decimated front ranks, swinging as he went. Spotting a riderless horse running about, he angled towards it. As he drew closer, he scabbarded his sword, and then reached out, hanging low in the saddle to grasp the creature's reins. Sitting back up, pleased with his prize, he turned south, back to where the rest of his men waited. The Saints had smiled on him this day, though he knew it was only a minor wound to the enemy.

Slowing to a trot as he regained his lines, Lanaka passed off the captured horse to an aide, then swept his sword up and down, signalling the second line to begin its charge.

Finally, he halted, turning to watch the carnage as he took a sip from his waterskin. The second rank eventually fell back, then a third surged forward, but Lanaka noticed their efforts were less effective. The enemy had learned to adapt, and such a tactic would not work again.

When the third wave returned, he ordered them to turn around. A few Norlanders rushed down the hill intent on repaying the damage, but the Kurathians were used to such challenges. A dozen of them turned, then charged forth, easily cutting down the invaders. Their duty complete, they wheeled around in perfect unison, riding south to rejoin their compatriots.

"It is a fine day," said Caluman. "The Saints have blessed us."

"So they have," agreed Lanaka, "but let us not take it for granted. The Saints help those that help themselves. We have bloodied the enemy, but our tactics will not work a second time. Let us return to Mattingly. We have an evacuation to see to."

"Surely not," said Caluman, "we must fight them the whole way."

"We are mercenaries no longer," said Lanaka, "but members of this new realm of ours. As such, we must protect our countrymen. Their safety is now our concern."

Caluman grinned, "As you wish, Commander."

Kargil yawned. Guarding the Hawksburg Circle was not the most exciting thing for an Orc, and yet he was determined to represent his tribe to the best of his ability. He walked down the ramp, eager to wake himself from his weariness. As a young hunter, he had come to this Human city only three months ago, unsure of what to expect. For centuries his people had been at odds with the Humans and yet here, in Hawksburg, they had found common ground. He smiled as he thought of Humans and Orcs working together to rebuild this city. What would his Ancestors think?

The room lit up with a soft glow as one of the magic runes was activated. Kargil's pulse quickened, for this meant that someone was arriving, the first such time this had happened while he was on duty. Another rune glowed, then two more. He stepped back, waiting for the spell to complete.

When a cylinder of bright light shot upward, it forced him to shield his eyes. For a brief moment, he felt as if the air was alive with a thousand bees, and then it abruptly halted. Kargil lowered his hands to see a small group of people within the circle. He immediately recognized Lady Aubrey Brandon, but the others were not known to him

"My lady," he said, using the greeting he had been taught.

"This is Queen Anna of Merceria," the mage responded, "along with her maid, Sophie, and Tempus, the hound."

Kargil's eyes widened. So this was the famous warrior queen! "Your Majesty," he said, bowing clumsily.

"Where is Kraloch?" asked the queen.

"He is not here, Majesty," said Kargil. "He has gone to Wincaster with most of the hunters."

"Why?" asked Anna, a worried look on her face. "What has happened?"

"I do not know," said the Orc, "for I am but a humble hunter."

"Who commands in his absence?"

"Sir Preston," said Kargil. "He arrived late last night."

"Take us to him," she commanded.

Kargil bowed, then led them up the ramp. It was only a short distance to the new manor house, and before long, they were within its walls, warmed against the chill of the day.

"I shall get him," announced Kargil, leaving them alone.

Anna looked around the room. "I should have spent more time in Hawksburg," she mused. "Tell me, how has the city been recovering?"

"The rebuilding has been proceeding quickly," said Aubrey, "though the winter snow will soon be upon us, slowing our progress."

"Have the people enough shelter?"

"They have," the mage replied. "It was our first priority. Many of the townsfolk are living in temporary quarters, but we expect to have housing for them by next summer. The real challenge will be getting crops in the ground next spring."

"How can the crown help?" asked the queen.

"We will be short of seed, Your Majesty. Most of what we had was carted away by the king's army during the war."

"I shall call upon our mages to travel the land," said Anna. "We can buy seed elsewhere, then use your magic to bring it here."

The door opened, revealing Sir Preston. The knight bowed gracefully.

"Your Majesty," he said, "we weren't expecting your return for some time. I take it all is well?"

"No," said the queen, "all is not well. We were attacked in the Norland capital. I'm afraid many of our people are still there."

"I am sorry to hear that," the knight replied, "for we have had problems here in Merceria as well."

"Kargil told us that many of the Orcs went to Wincaster," said the queen.

"Yes," Sir Preston agreed, "to suppress a rebellion, but we had advance warning of it."

"I take it we were successful?"

"I haven't heard back," said the knight. "They only left early this morning."

She turned to Aubrey. "How soon can you return us to Wincaster?"

"I'm afraid I used most of my energy bringing us here," said Aubrey. "It will be some time yet."

"We could have horses made ready," offered Sir Preston.

"No," said the queen, "it would take days to ride there. We'd be better served to let Lady Aubrey rest. Would you be ready to recall by this evening, Aubrey?"

"I should think so, Majesty," replied the mage.

"Good, then let us rest and replenish our strength, for I fear the next few days are going to be taxing."

They were eating dinner when the messenger arrived, a horseman covered in dust and looking exhausted.

"Sit," commanded the queen.

Before sitting, he handed her a letter. Anna opened it carefully, reading it over twice before passing it to Aubrey.

"News, Majesty?" asked Sir Preston.

"Sir Heward reports a large invasion at Wickfield. They are falling back to our present position."

"An invasion?" said Sir Preston. "Surely not?"

"You forget, Sir Preston, the Norlanders are unaware of Lady Aubrey's recall spell. They think they have me, prisoner, in Galburn's Ridge. I rather suspect they wish to use me as a hostage."

"Along with our marshal," said the knight. "But we must have other military commanders?"

"We do," said the queen. "We are blessed in that way, but still, this invasion is ill-timed from our perspective. It has caught us unprepared."

"What are your orders, Majesty?" asked Sir Preston.

"It will take some time for Heward to withdraw to Hawksburg. In the meanwhile, Sir Preston, you will have to organize our defences as best you can."

"Is there any indication of how large the Norland army is, precisely?"

"Sir Heward cannot tell for sure, but he estimates there may be as many as two thousand, most of them mounted."

"Two thousand riders?" said Sir Preston. "I didn't even know they had that many horses."

"Yes," said Anna, "they seem to have been preparing this for some time, but that may work to our advantage."

"How so?" asked the knight.

"Cavalry is not particularly effective against prepared defences," said the queen, "which means we should remain safe here in Hawksburg."

"Does this change our plans?" asked Aubrey.

"No, we must still return to Wincaster, even more so now that we know what's coming. First, we must secure the capital, then find Baron Fitzwilliam. I will need his counsel."

"In that case," said Aubrey, rising from the table, "I shall retire to rest and restore my energy."

"Very well," said the queen. "In the meantime, I will inspect our defences." She turned to her maid, noting the look of shock still on Sophie's face. The young woman was pale and trembling, sure signs of what she had just been through. "What about you, Sophie? Would you care to accompany us, or would you like to rest?"

Her maid appeared wracked with indecision. It was Sir Preston that finally brought her out of her state by stepping forward and holding out his arm for her.

"I would be delighted if you should decide to accompany us," he said.

She looked up at him, her face softening. "Very well," she said, a smile creeping in.

The queen rose, turning to the messenger. "Thank you for your prompt delivery. Stay and rest yourself. I'll have the servants prepare you something to eat." She looked around the room, then under the table. "Come along, Tempus, we've work to do."

The great dog let out a bark that echoed off the walls.

TWENTY-THREE

Escape

Fall 964 MC

"We can't hold out much longer," said Arnim. "The next assault will overrun us. We'll have to try to fight our way out."

They had barricaded the corridors and were holding out in the guest quarters of King Halfan's castle. Three times the Norlanders had tried to overrun their position, and each time they had been beaten back. Now, their enemy appeared content to wait, hoping to starve them out.

"I will not abandon our people," said Gerald, "and we've few enough fighters amongst us."

"Then arm them," Arnim persisted. "Better to die fighting than starve to death."

"We have no spare weapons," Gerald reminded him. "I don't like it any more than you do, but we are at an impasse."

A crack of thunder echoed in the distance.

"More rain," said Arnim. "At least we'll have plenty of water."

"It could be worse," offered Beverly.

"Worse?" grumbled Arnim. "How could it possibly be worse?"

"It could be snowing," she suggested.

He stared at her, preparing a reply but then changed his mind. Instead, he whirled around and marched off, muttering, "I've men to see to."

"You seem in remarkably good spirits considering our predicament," said Gerald.

"I'm just following your example," she replied.

"Mine?"

She laughed, "I'm just pulling your leg, Gerald. We've been in tougher spots than this."

He looked at her in surprise. "We have?"

"Certainly, remember the drake we fought in Tivilton?"

"That was different," he said. "We didn't have civilians to look after."

"Civilians," she repeated, "an interesting term."

"It refers to people that are not warriors," he explained.

"I'm fully aware of what it means," she responded, "but when you say it, you sound just like my father."

"I could do worse," he said.

She smiled, "So you could. Now tell me, what's the plan?"

"What makes you think I have a plan?"

"I know you, Gerald. You're not one to give up so easily. You've got something going on inside that head of yours. Are you going to share it with me, or do I have to wheedle it out of you?"

He looked around the hallway, taking in the men holding the barricade. "Not here," he said, "let's talk privately."

He led her into one of the bedrooms that lay empty, then sat on the bed.

"We are faced with a number of problems," he explained. "Care to guess what those are?"

"Well," said Beverly, "the most obvious one is that we're hemmed in here with no food."

"Correct," said Gerald.

"Arnim obviously thinks we should fight our way out."

Gerald paused a moment. "Let's say that we manage to fight our way out of this hallway, then what?"

"Then we make our way cross country, back to Merceria."

"And how do we do that? Think carefully, Beverly."

"We head south," she replied, "that's where the border lies."

"And what is the terrain like?"

"Mostly flat," she paused, the problems falling into place. "We'd be easy to pick off."

"Precisely," Gerald said, "but that's not all. How do we get our horses back? We don't even know where they are."

"They're somewhere in the castle," said Beverly.

"I doubt that's true at this point. They likely moved them out of our reach when they attacked. We honestly have no idea at all where they might be, and without them to scout terrain or watch for Norland soldiers, we'd be sitting ducks."

Beverly frowned, "So what you're really saying is that you don't have a plan?"

He smiled, "Don't look so glum. I have the beginnings of a plan, I just need more time to piece it together."

"Tell me what you have so far."

"Galburn's Ridge sits at the west end of a line of hills," Gerald said. "We came here up that steep incline."

"I remember, it was a switchback path. We'd be easy to pick off going back down."

"Yes, but there are hills to the east."

"And a large lake to the south, if you remember," said Beverly. "How does that help us?"

Gerald leaned forward, warming to the task. "We came up the western shore of that lake. I'm proposing that we travel east, across the hills and then come down the eastern shore of that same lake."

"We don't know the terrain," she warned.

"True, but as long as that body of water was in sight, we'd be able to navigate our way."

"Through unknown hills?"

"I'm not saying it wouldn't be dangerous," Gerald continued, "but the hills would at least give us some protection from the Norlanders."

"Fair enough," said Beverly, "but how do we get out of the castle to begin the journey?"

He sat back, letting out a deep breath of air. "That's the part I haven't figured out yet. Do you have any ideas?"

"Can't say that I do," she admitted, "but neither can I stand the thought of leaving our horses behind."

A soldier interrupted them from the doorway, "My lord?"

"Yes?" said Gerald.

"Someone is calling for a parley," the man said.

"Thank you, Conner, we'll be there directly."

Conner nodded his head. "Yes, my lord."

Gerald winced as the man disappeared from sight.

"Something wrong?" asked Beverly.

"I don't think I'm ever going to get used to this 'Lord' business."

Beverly laughed, "Don't worry, Gerald, I'll make sure your head doesn't swell."

"It's good to know I have someone I can count on."

"Everyone here feels the same way," she said. "They trust you to see us through this."

"I wish I had their confidence," Gerald replied.

"We'd best be seeing to that parley before they change their minds."

"I suppose you're right," he said, rising to his feet.

They stepped from the room, back into the corridor. Down at the northern end, they had piled chairs and tables to form their makeshift defence. Six of the queen's foot guards stood watch, crouched behind cover while occasionally peeking out over its top. Beverly led the way, her youthful steps far quicker than Gerald's. Conner was crouched by an upturned table.

"He's just over there," the man said, pointing.

"Here goes nothing," said Gerald. He straightened his back, exposing his head to potential enemy arrows.

"Speak," he commanded.

"I would speak in private," came back a familiar voice.

He looked down to Beverly, who was still crouching.

"Do you recognize him?"

"Sounds like Lord Creighton, the Earl of Riverhurst," she replied.

"What do we know of him?"

"Not much, I'm afraid. We never got around to talking with him at any length."

Gerald returned his attention to the enemy line. "Show yourself."

The scraping of wood on stone announced that the Norlanders were moving part of their own barricade, making room for the earl to advance. With this done, Creighton stepped out into the neutral area between the two lines, his hands held to the side.

"It is I, Lord Creighton," the man said, "and I am unarmed."

"Step forward," said Gerald.

The Norland earl took three steps, drawing closer to the Mercerian barricade.

"Say what you want," said Gerald.

In answer, Creighton glanced briefly back at his own line of troops. "It would be better, I think, to discuss things in private."

"So you said earlier," said Gerald, "but you must understand our hesitation to let you enter our lines."

"It would be in your best interest to do so," the earl said. "There are things we must discuss that are not meant for the ears of others." He glanced back at his own troops one more time.

"Very well," said Gerald, "let him through."

Beverly shifted the table slightly, opening a small gap. Lord Creighton advanced, slowing to navigate through the small opening.

"Lord Matheson," he said, "I thank you for hearing me out."

"Come with me," said Gerald, "and we shall talk." He turned to the men at the barricade. "Conner, see that table returned to its previous position. Beverly, you're with me."

He led Lord Creighton into the same room he had so recently vacated, offering the bed for the earl to sit upon.

Lord Creighton declined the offer. "You are surrounded," he began, "and we have men blocking both exits."

Gerald thought briefly of the second barricade to the south, but then shrugged it off. Arnim was more than capable of holding his position.

"And?" the marshal said.

"Surely you must realize by now that there is little chance of escape."

"Did you come here to talk or lecture?" asked Gerald.

"Do you know the history of Galburn's Ridge?" countered the earl.

Gerald was thrown off guard. "Norland History is not my strong suit," he admitted.

"Think about it a moment. Of all the places to build a castle, why here?"

"It's very defensible," said Gerald.

"Yes," agreed the earl, "but also very difficult to construct. Every single stone had to be lugged up here, a monumental effort."

"I have a feeling you're about to explain why," said Gerald.

"Indeed. You see, when Galburn became king, he selected this area as his capital. He was tired of being on the run, and felt this was a safe place."

"Are you saying there was already a castle here?" asked Gerald.

"No, but there was a series of caves. Still is, in fact, right below this very castle."

"So he settled into these caves and then built the castle overtop?"

"Precisely," said the earl.

"An interesting tale," said Gerald, "but why are you telling me this? I have to wonder at your motives."

"The politics of Norland are convoluted," said Lord Creighton. "Let us suffice to say that Lord Hollis and I have opposing views on many subjects."

"You don't agree with the war?" said Beverly.

Creighton looked at her in surprise. "I didn't say anything about a war."

"Come now," she continued, "you wouldn't have gone to all this trouble if you didn't have an army ready to march."

"I see we have underestimated you," the earl continued. "Be that as it may, if you agree to hand over the queen, I can assure you she'll be treated with the courtesy and respect due her station."

"Let you hold her as a hostage?" said Gerald. "That will never happen!"

"You'll never get out of here," said Creighton, "not without your horses, and they have been removed from the castle to a place not far from here. I'm afraid they're out of your reach, for the present."

"You're wasting your breath," said Gerald. "Our minds are made up. If you want the queen, you'll have to cross a line of Mercerian steel to get her."

"Very well," said the earl, "then I shall leave you now. Don't get down on yourself, Marshal, it's not the end of the world."

He stepped from the room and Gerald hurried to catch up to him.

"I'm sorry we didn't see eye to eye," said the earl, "but believe me when I say that you have earned our respect."

Conner pulled the table aside once more, allowing Lord Creighton to step through. He turned one last time, locking eyes with Gerald.

"Remember, don't be DOWN on yourself, Lord Matheson."

The earl turned away, returning behind the safety of the Norland barricade.

"What was that all about?" asked Beverly.

Gerald smiled. "He was telling us how to escape," he said. "It seems we have an ally, after all."

Arnim shook his head. "I still don't understand. You say this Lord Creighton visited, that much I get, but I don't see how he helped us."

"I'd have to agree," added Beverly.

The three of them were sitting alone, gathered around a small table.

"What was the last thing that he said?" asked Gerald.

"Something about not getting down," offered Beverly.

"Exactly," said Gerald, "don't you see?"

Arnim grumbled something unintelligent then spoke, "Spit it out, man."

"He told us about caves that the castle is built upon."

"How does that help us?" pressed Arnim. "We still don't know where the entrance to these caves is, or where they lead."

"Oh, but we do," said Gerald. "We're on the ground floor. The caves are directly below us."

"How do you know that?" asked Beverly.

"I don't with absolute certainty, but I believe his lordship was trying to tell us, hence his reference to looking down."

"Still," said Arnim, "how do we find the entrance?"

"We don't," said Gerald, "we make our own."

"How do you propose we do that?"

Gerald looked at Beverly, then let his eyes wander to Nature's Fury. Beverly smiled, her mind grasping the concept.

"He knows what my hammer did to the doorway," she said, "and he's assuming we can go through the floor in the same way."

"And could it," said Arnim, "go through the floor, I mean?"

"I would say so," said Beverly, "though I'm not sure where we'd start."

"In the queen's chamber," said Gerald.

"Why would you say that?" asked Arnim.

"It's the largest room in this section of the castle, and likely one of the oldest."

Arnim shook his head. "I'm afraid I still don't understand.

"The castle was built by King Galburn," said Gerald, "and this room was likely his for a while."

"What makes you say that?" asked Arnim.

In answer, Gerald turned to Beverly. "Will you tell him or shall I?"

Beverly looked at Arnim. "When a lord builds a castle, it takes years, especially one as large as this. The first buildings constructed are going to be the most important in the short term, such as the king's chambers. This was likely Galburn's residence as the rest of the place was constructed."

"How do you know all this?" asked Arnim.

Gerald laughed, "She was raised by Baron Fitzwilliam. Would you expect anything less?"

"I was born a simple farmer," said Arnim, "so I understand little of such things. How do you know this, you were a farmer much like me?"

"You forget," said Gerald, "I spent years in the baron's service, and if there's one thing Fitz likes to talk about its castles and battles."

"Those are two things," said Beverly.

"So they are," said Gerald, grinning.

"All right," said Arnim, "so we know how to find the tunnels. Now, assuming we can get out, what next? We're still at the mercy of enemy cavalry."

"Ah, yes," said Gerald, "the next step would be to send a small group of soldiers to recover our horses."

"But we don't know where they are," said Arnim.

"We do now," said Gerald, "thanks to Lord Creighton."

"We do?" said Arnim.

"Yes, he said they were in a place not far from here."

"That could be anywhere," Arnim grumbled.

"No, it couldn't," said Gerald. "You see, the west is a long descent down a treacherous road. The base of that road is not a quick trip, and south of the castle is a sheer cliff."

"That still leaves north and east," said Beverly.

"It does," Gerald agreed, "but when we first arrived, I spent some time familiarizing myself with the area. I have it on good authority that the only decent grazing lies to the north."

"Why couldn't Lord Creighton have been less obtuse?" said Arnim. "Surely, he could have come out and just told us all this?"

"I think it's his sense of honour," said Gerald. "This way, he can deny that he told us how to escape."

"Are you sure it's not a trap?" asked Arnim. "After all, it would get us out of our defensive position."

"It's a distinct possibility," said Gerald, "but we have no other options, as far as I'm aware."

"Very well," said Arnim, "I'm in."

"As am I," added Beverly. "How do we proceed?"

Gerald looked out the window. "We have to wait for the rain to subside. The hills will be treacherous to navigate in such weather."

"That means holding out for another half day or so," said Arnim, "and we still don't have food."

"A good point," noted Gerald, "but we shall have to endure."

It was midnight, or at least close enough. No bells had been rung in the castle, but the moon was high, and darkness had settled in some time ago.

Beverly stood in the middle of the queen's chambers, Nature's Fury in hand. They had moved the furniture out, adding it to the barricades, and now Gerald watched as she prepared to strike.

"Are you ready?" she asked.

"As ready as we can be," said Gerald. "Once the floor collapses, we'll have to move quickly. The Guard Cavalry will man the barricades while the others make their way through the tunnels. You take the lead, and I'll bring up the rear."

He glanced at Conner, who stood by the doorway, torch in hand.

"Close the door," said Beverly. "We want to dampen the sound as much as possible."

With the door dutifully closed, Gerald moved forward, his own torch illuminating the area. Beverly raised Nature's Fury high above her, gently brushing the ceiling with the head of the hammer.

"Careful," warned Gerald. "It's the floor beneath us we want to break, not the ceiling overhead."

She crouched slightly, allowing more clearance, and then brought the hammer down with all her might, smashing it into the stone floor, sending fragments spinning as a large crack appeared.

"Again," said Gerald.

She struck a second time, and as the crack widened, small chunks of stone fell through into the darkness beneath.

"Almost there," he said.

The third time proved to be the last. Nature's Fury struck the floor and continued through as the stone collapsed into a chamber below. Gerald stepped forward to the edge, holding his torch over the opening.

"I'd say no more than six feet down," he said, "and the floor looks smooth, other than the rubble, of course."

Beverly used her hammer to lightly tap the edge of the pit, dislodging any loose stones. Satisfied nothing further would collapse, she sat, dangling her feet into the hole.

"Wish me luck," she said, then dropped down into the darkness.

Gerald held his breath as she went, then relaxed a little as he heard her feet hit the ground. He leaned forward once more, illuminating her.

"Stand back," he said, "and I'll drop the torch."

She moved aside, and he tossed it down to land on top of some rubble, where Beverly quickly retrieved it.

"This looks good," she said. "The tunnel is clear, though it smells a bit musty."

"Can you see the way out?"

As she disappeared from sight, all he could see was the light flickering off the walls. Shortly thereafter, she reappeared. "There's an old stairway, but it's been sealed up. I believe it's the old entrance to the room."

"Any other way out?"

"Yes, a path that leads roughly north, though it's far from straight. Shall I investigate?"

"Yes," said Gerald, "but don't go too far, we don't need you getting lost down there."

She moved off, and the light grew dimmer, finally disappearing as she rounded a corner. Gerald stepped back to the doorway, opening it to see Conner waiting with a torch in hand.

"Any sign of trouble?" asked Gerald.

"No, my lord. Things have been quiet."

"Good," said Gerald, "they didn't hear us, then. Give me your torch, then go and fetch the first group."

Conner trotted down the hallway, leaving Gerald alone with his thoughts. With Anna safely back in Merceria, their group had shrunk to seventy-two people. No, he corrected himself, they had lost two guards when everything went sour, and then three more as the Norlanders tried to storm the barricades. That left sixty-seven, of which five were injured, three severely. They would require help to descend into the caves, and for that very reason, a sling had been devised using bed linens.

It would likely take all night to get everyone into and through the caves, but the most treacherous time would be as the last few soldiers held the barricades. Once they withdrew, there was a very real chance that the Norlanders would swarm forward and then chase them. To compensate for this, he intended to hold on until just before light, giving the others the best chance to get away, but it all hinged on how the Norlanders might react.

Time appeared to stand still as he waited for Beverly's return. The first group of Mercerians had already arrived in the chamber, four of the queen's guards and four servants.

When a flickering light below caught Gerald's attention, he looked down to see Beverly, waving her torch.

"I think I've found the way out," she said, "though I didn't follow it to the end."

"I'm sending the first group down," said Gerald. "Take two guards with you, leave the other pair at the bottom here to help the next lot climb down."

"Aye, Marshal," she replied.

Gerald looked towards those gathered around the opening.

"You're up first, Wilson, and be quick about it. I know your father was a ranger, so now you have a chance to follow in his footsteps."

"Sir?" the man responded.

"You'll be guiding these people, lad. That's normally the work of the rangers."

"I'll do my best, sir."

"I know you will," said Gerald. "Now, let's not be wasting any more time, we've plenty to do."

Wilson dropped into the chamber below, landing in a crouch. He took a moment to orient himself, then moved aside.

"Let's move some of this rubble," said Beverly. "It will speed things up a bit."

They both set to work, soon clearing the space below the opening. The rest of the soldiers dropped down quickly, but the servants would be slower. Gerald lowered the makeshift rope. They had knotted it, making the descent easier, and the first servant, a maid named Cynthia, made her way below. When Wilson gave the thumbs up, the next in line began climbing down.

Gerald waited until half were below, then opened the door to where the next group stood ready.

Arnim peered out from behind the barricade. The Norlanders were napping, of that he was sure, but still, he didn't trust them. After all, Norland had been their enemy for years. Slowly, his eyelids began to droop, sleep trying to claim him, and then moved again, forcing himself to stay awake. It must be early morning by now, he thought, and they would soon be called upon to do their part.

A lantern moved behind the Norland barricade, and Arnim put all his energy towards focusing on it. When a tap on his shoulder broke his concentration, he turned to see Conner.

"The marshal says it's time," he whispered.

Arnim nodded. "Very well. Get to the chamber as quick as you can, and we'll start falling back."

He waited until the messenger was out of sight, then tapped the guard beside him on the shoulder. "You first, Abercromby," he whispered.

The warrior rose, creeping down the hallway in a crouch, lest he draw attention to himself. Arnim watched, tapping the next man as Abercromby withdrew from sight.

He continued down the line, waiting patiently as each made their way to safety. They had discussed rushing back, but the movement of so many men at one time was sure to be heard.

Finally, he tapped the last man, then waited as he fled. Arnim peeked over the barricade, taking in the enemy one last time, then turned, moving off as quietly as possible.

~

Gerald gazed down the corridor. Only half a dozen men remained here at the northern barricade. He wondered if everything was going well in the south, but Arnim's position was out of sight, and he had to trust in the viscount's ability to carry out his orders.

The marshal watched as another of his men headed to safety, then heard a commotion behind the Norland barricade.

"Saxnor's balls," he swore under his breath, "can nothing ever be easy?"

The shuffling noise reminded him of men preparing for battle, and now his line was held by only three men, four including himself.

"Right, men," he whispered, "it looks like it falls to us. Keep low, they'll start with a barrage of bolts. You know how they operate."

He crouched, his eyes peering over the makeshift wall. Sure enough, a flurry of bolts sailed forth, digging into the furniture they had piled in their defence, then a shout announced their attack.

Gerald stood, confident that the bolts would cease, for the Norlanders flooded across the small gap, intent on breaking the Mercerian defences.

"Back up," he commanded, "and we'll hit them as they come through the barricade."

A rush of men closed the distance quickly, eager to be among their prey. One of them jumped up on a chair but lost his footing as it shifted, falling back into the man behind him. Another slowed, climbing carefully over the stacked furniture. Gerald stepped forward, delivering a precise jab with his sword between the chair legs, sinking it into the man's leg. The Norlander let out a howl of pain and then fell backward, out of sight.

When the next one reached the top of the wall, Gerald struck out, slamming his blade into the man's foot to hear bone breaking. Then another Norlander leaped, somehow clearing the barricade to land to Gerald's left. The old warrior pivoted, slamming his shield into the soldier's face. As his foe backed up, stunned and confused, Gerald struck again, this time sending the edge of his shield into the man's stomach.

A yell to his right captured the marshal's attention, and he pivoted, swinging his sword instinctively to catch an attacker in the arm, sliding it along the mail but still hurting, nonetheless.

His target dropped his weapon, and this was his undoing for one of the Mercerians, a young guard named Reese, stepped forward, driving his sword into the man's throat. But it was a short-lived victory, for no sooner had the guardsman pulled back his blade for a second thrust, then a sword swept down, striking his head, collapsing his helmet. The Mercerian warrior fell, blood oozing from beneath his coif.

Gerald backed up, overwhelmed by the ferocity of this attack. He saw Adams, who took a wound to the arm, drop his shield. The Mercerian stepped back, parrying another blow, then attacked with a vengeance. His opponent fell to the floor with a crash, and Adams struck again, reaching out to hit the next man in line.

More shouts erupted from the Norland line. Reinforcements had arrived to bolster their assault!

A calmness settled over Gerald. He would not survive the day, this much he knew with utter certainty, but he would take as many with him to the Afterlife as he could.

He roared a challenge and then surged forward, intent only on causing mayhem. He struck with his shield, pushing someone back even as his blade dug deep into another. Adrenaline coursed through him as he kept moving. Over the barricade he went, taking the fight to the enemy. Swords reached out, spears were tossed, but he kept advancing. It all became a blur. His arms ached, his muscles overworked, but still, he hacked and thrust with his sword, over and over again, desperate to make his death a costly one.

Gerald pulled his sword free of someone's neck, and then suddenly, there were no more opponents. His eyes sought out enemies that no longer existed as his mind finally took stock of the situation. He was behind the Norland debris now, the enemy dead or fled. Glancing back at his own lines, he saw Adams, helping another man to his feet.

"Go!" he shouted, then watched as they fled to safety.

He waited, forcing himself to slowly count to twenty. He took a deep breath, glancing farther down the corridor, expecting more to appear, but all was quiet.

Gerald wiped his blade, then rammed it back into its scabbard. Pushing aside a chair that blocked his way, he wondered briefly how he came to be amongst the enemy dead? As he went back across the gap, he listened for any sign of activity behind him. He had just climbed over a table, safely returning to his own lines when the enemy returned.

Ducking low, he concentrated on the sounds that drifted towards him. There was surprise at all the bodies, and fear, fear he knew he could exploit.

"Who's next?" he called out. "Who's ready to feel the bite of Mercerian steel?"

No one answered his challenge. Instead, they began dragging away their dead. Now was the time for him to leave. He rose to a crouch and quietly moved south, towards the waiting safety of the caves.

TWENTY-FOUR

The Queen Returns

Fall 964 MC

B odies lay strewn about the courtyard, and Gorath made his way among them, checking pulses in a search for survivors.

"This one's alive," he said, waiting as a fellow Orc moved closer to lift the injured man and bear him away. "Such carnage," he remarked.

"We had little choice," called out Hayley. "And I might remind you that all these men are considered traitors. Their attack was treason, there's no denying it."

"Still, the same could be said of your queen at the start of the civil war."

The ranger paused, considering her aide's words. "You have a point there, Gorath. I suppose we could show them a little more charity. What would you propose we do?"

"For a start, we can punish their leaders, rather than these men," the Orc replied. "They were simply following orders."

"These men knew what they were up to," countered Hayley. "I'd hardly call them innocent."

"Still," insisted Gorath, "we can't arrest them all, we haven't the space to hold them."

"That's true. I suppose we'll have to give some of them parole."

"At least those that can still walk. The wounded alone are going to overwhelm us. It might be a little different if we had more Life Mages."

"Kraloch is doing the best he can," said Hayley, "but even he has his limitations. He can't cure everyone, he simply hasn't the power."

She knelt, feeling for a pulse. "This one's dead," she said. Two porters rushed forward to carry off the body.

"I think you're right," she continued. "We need to separate the officers from the men. Put the leaders into the Palace dungeons, sergeants too, come to think of it. Those that aren't wounded, that is."

"And the rest?" asked Gorath.

"Send word to the city watch. See if they have any room left in their jails."

"There's also the debtor's prison," suggested the Orc.

Hayley stood, stretching her back. It had been a long day, and her muscles were complaining. She looked skyward at the darkening sky.

"Very well," she said at last, "see what you can arrange."

"Yes, High Ranger."

"What did I tell you about calling me that?" asked Hayley.

"I have to call you something, Mistress."

"Don't call me mistress either, you make me sound old."

"Then what do I call you? I can't just call you Hayley, it's not proper."

"Oh? Since when did you learn the ways of the Mercerian court?"

"I am your aide, after all," said Gorath.

"Very well, then call me Ranger Hayley, or Dame Hayley if you must. Come to think of it, you can call me Lady Hayley. I am a baroness, after all."

"Very well, Lady Hayley."

Hayley winced at the name. "We'll work on it," she said. "Now be off with you, there's still plenty of work to do, and we're losing the light."

The Orc left, issuing orders in Orcish as he went.

"I hear you had some trouble," came a familiar voice.

Hayley spun around to see the queen standing at the back door of the Palace with Aubrey at her side, the carnage of battle arraigned before her.

"Your Majesty," said Hayley, "you surprised me."

"I'd heard there was an uprising," said the queen, "but it seems you have it under control."

"Yes, we do," agreed the ranger, "but it was led by Valmar."

"Valmar?" said the queen. "I trust you have him in custody?"

"I'm afraid not," said Hayley. "He's dead, killed by the very mob he tried to incite."

"I shall lose no sleep over his death," admitted Anna, "but I fear it leaves us in a difficult situation. Tell me, how many of our soldiers supported him?"

"Quite a few, I'm afraid. Three whole companies of foot went over to him, four if you include the cavalry. That's almost half of our current garrison."

"I take it you've secured them?"

"I have," said Hayley, "or rather, we're in the middle of it. We have a lot of wounded to deal with."

"I can help," said Aubrey, "though I won't have much energy until morning."

"Anything you can do would be most appreciated," said Hayley. "Where's Gerald?"

"He's still in Norland, along with Beverly and the rest of our delegation, struggling to get home. We must do what we can to help them. I'm afraid things didn't go well there, but I'll fill you in on it later. In the meantime, I need you to send as many warriors to Hawksburg as we can spare."

"That's not very many, I'm afraid. We still have to guard all these prisoners."

"This attack has come at the worst possible time," said the queen. "The Norlanders have crossed our border in force."

"An invasion? This can't be a coincidence."

"So it would seem. I need to call an emergency meeting of the Nobles Council."

"I'll send word immediately," said Hayley. "When would you like to see them?"

"As soon as can be arranged," said the queen. "In the meantime, I must make a visit to some old allies and pray to Saxnor that they can help."

Herdwin Steelarm stood, bowing deeply as Queen Anna entered the room.

"Your Majesty," he said, "I bring greetings from King Khazad of Stonecastle."

"Have you news for me, Herdwin?"

"I do, Majesty, though it comes with conditions."

"I thought as much," she replied. "I take it the Elves feel the same?"

"They do," the Dwarf admitted. "They will only assist if they are given seats on the Nobles Council."

"And if I can arrange it, how long will it take for the troops to arrive?"

"They are already on the way, Your Majesty. I told them you could be counted on to support our cause."

"I hope you will not think me too impertinent if I were to ask how many?"

"King Khazad is sending two hundred, half of which are arbalesters."

"And the other half?" the queen asked.

"His finest heavy foot. What you would call axemen, though, of course, they're Dwarves."

"I can't thank you enough, Herdwin. You have been of great assistance to us in our time of need."

"We still need that seat, Majesty. I am under orders not to march past Wincaster until our seat is secured."

"You shall have your seat, I promise you," said the queen. "You have spoken with Telethial?"

"I have," said Herdwin, "and she will match our numbers, though they have not yet left the Darkwood. Will it be enough?"

"I've recalled the Trolls from their position at the mouth of the river, but they have some distance to travel."

"There is another option," said Herdwin, smiling slightly. "Lily has returned."

"Lily is here?" said Anna. "Why didn't anyone tell me?"

"She has only just arrived from Uxley, Your Majesty. She has returned as the Saurian representative."

"I have to see her," said Anna. "I've missed her so much."

"She has changed," warned Herdwin. "She is no longer the inquisitive young Saurian that you found in the grotto."

"What does that mean?"

"She has been learning about the heritage of her people, and is much more self-assured now, and perhaps more demanding."

"Meaning that she wants the same thing you do," said Anna.

"The elder races have decided to act in concert in this," warned the Dwarf, "though it took some persuasion."

Anna nodded. "And whose idea was that I wonder?"

Herdwin blushed. "I only wanted what's best for my people," he said.

"As do I. Fear not, Herdwin, I will do what I can."

"Can you not just demand it?"

"I'm afraid not," replied the queen. "The composition of the Nobles Council is laid down in our laws. It would take a two-thirds majority of the members to change it."

"So you think it unlikely?"

"At this exact time, yes," the queen admitted, "but as the enemy gets closer, the nobles will see the wisdom in it."

"Let us hope so," said Herdwin, "or I shall be forced to watch as your kingdom falls. I cannot commit to helping you without a seat. To do so would be a betrayal of my king."

"I understand, Herdwin. Though I suppose I must now address you as Lord Herdwin."

The Dwarf blushed. "Please, Majesty," he said, "we are in private. You must address me as Herdwin."

"I shall not forget the aid you have given us in the past, my friend. Without your help, we would have been recaptured by my brother, King Henry."

"I did as my conscience dictated," said Herdwin, "but you have done no less as queen."

"I thank you for the kind words," said Anna, "but now I must leave you, the Nobles Council awaits."

"Good luck, Majesty, and may Saxnor see fit to grant you strength this day."

Lord Alexander Stanton shifted in his seat.

"Something wrong?" asked Lady Aubrey.

"He's nervous," suggested Lord Spencer. "He's afraid he'll be blamed for the uprising."

"I had nothing to do with it," declared Stanton, his face turning red. He looked at Baron Fitzwilliam, pleading in his eyes.

"Don't look at me for support," said Fitz. "You have a history of opposing the queen's will."

"This was all Valmar's doing," said Stanton.

"Oh, yes," said Lord Chesterton, "he's an old friend of yours, isn't he?" He paused briefly, "Don't bother denying it, we all know it's true." He turned his attention back to Aubrey. "Are we expecting the queen?"

"She should be here any moment," the Life Mage replied.

The door opened, admitting Lady Hayley, who took a seat beside Aubrey.

"Is this it?" asked Chesterton.

"I'm afraid so," replied Hayley. "Lord Somerset and Lord Anglesley are too far away to summon on such short notice."

"We need more magic circles," suggested Aubrey.

"Agreed," said Hayley, "but other things keep cropping up that need our attention."

"Like Revi?" asked Aubrey. "I heard you found him. How is he?"

"Not well, to tell you the truth," replied the ranger. "His body's on the mend, but his mind is gone."

"Kraloch couldn't help?"

"He consulted his Ancestors, but little came of it."

"They knew nothing?" asked Aubrey.

"Not quite," said Hayley, "they did indicate that you might have the answer. You were, after all, his apprentice."

"Revi never taught me how to heal madness."

"The Ancestors said you'd have to seek that which is buried. Does that mean anything to you?"

"Maybe it refers to my great grandmother's casting room, back in Hawksburg."

"Meaning?"

"Meaning that there are more secrets there to unlock?"

"Great," said Hayley, "now all we need is a day free from all these other problems. It wouldn't be so bad if we didn't have a war on our hands."

"War?" piped up Stanton. "Why wasn't I told?"

"I suspect that's the reason the queen called this meeting," said Fitz. "You must have suspected something?"

"No," said Stanton, "I thought she called it because of the uprising."

The door opened to reveal Queen Anna, wearing a rather stern expression. All those in attendance rose to their feet as she made her way across the room.

"Please sit," the queen said, taking her own seat. "I'm afraid we meet under dire circumstances, for a state of war now exists with Norland."

"Are you sure?" asked Stanton. "Couldn't this all be a misunderstanding?"

"There can be no doubt," said the queen. "They tried to blame us for the death of King Halfan. I now believe they had been planning it for some time, for we have received word that a massive army has crossed the border."

"Surely not!" said Stanton.

"It seems you doubt my word," said the queen. "Perhaps Lady Aubrey can convince you. She was by my side when things went awry."

"It's true," offered the mage. "We had already prevented a poisoning attempt, but it seems they were determined to finish the job. We were ambushed as we discovered the body of King Halfan."

"What of Beverly?" asked Fitz.

"She was alive when we left," said the queen, "though she, like the others, is now trapped behind enemy lines."

"This is disastrous," said Stanton. "What are we to do?"

"I'm afraid it gets worse," said Anna. "With the recent uprising, we can no longer count on the loyalty of our troops, save for a few companies, and that will be scarce enough to hold back an invasion."

"We need help," asserted Stanton. "Can we not call on Weldwyn? They are our allies now, aren't they?"

"We can," the queen replied, "and Prince Alric has already sent word, but they will not be able to get here in sufficient numbers for some time."

"Then we are doomed," pronounced Lord Spencer.

"We still have the Orcs," offered Hayley.

"Yes," agreed the queen, "and possibly more."

"More?" said Stanton. "What's this, now?"

"We have other allies that may be able to assist us," said the queen, "but they come at a price."

"What price?" Stanton demanded.

"Representation on the Nobles Council," said the queen.

"Impossible!" roared Stanton. "Only those of Mercerian birth can hold those seats."

"Nevertheless," continued the queen, "if we are to count them among our forces, we must give them a seat at the table."

"I think it too early to consider this," suggested Lord Spencer. "After all, our own border forces may be able to repel Norland. That's what they're there for, aren't they?"

"They are," said the queen, "but we haven't much time. In the meanwhile, I have sent word summoning the other nobles to Wincaster. Hopefully, we shall have a better idea of our enemy's intentions once they arrive. However, our army is crippled, at least here, in the capital."

"How many companies rebelled?" asked Fitz.

"Four," offered Hayley, "as far as we know."

"What does that mean?" asked Lord Spencer.

"We have yet to receive word from the other cities of the realm. There's a very real chance that the uprising was one of several aimed at seizing power across the kingdom."

"We know Hawksburg is secure," said Aubrey. "We stopped off there on the way back here."

"And I can assure you Bodden is safe," said Fitz. "Albreda brought me from there this very evening. Can you make the same claim of Tewsbury, Lord Stanton?"

"I wish I could," the earl replied, "but as you know, I have been in Wincaster for the past few months."

"Where else might we expect trouble?" asked Aubrey.

"Shrewesdale comes to mind," said Fitz. "They've been unhappy ever since we executed Lord Montrose for treason."

The queen turned her gaze to Lord Spencer, "What of Eastwood?"

"I haven't the foggiest," he replied. "To be honest, I've spent less than a week there since I inherited the title. All my time has been consumed by matters here in Wincaster."

"I think we can assume Kingsford is loyal," noted the queen, "but Colbridge fought for the king during the civil war."

"That leaves us in a difficult position, Majesty," said Hayley.

Anna turned to the Baron of Bodden. "In Gerald's absence, you now command the army. What think you, Lord Fitzwilliam?"

Fitz looked around the table. "Until we receive word from each city, we must assume the worst. I shall, of course, dispatch riders, but it will take some time to confirm their loyalty or lack thereof. Valmar had a lot of influential friends, I doubt very much he planned this all by himself."

"You suspect the Dark Queen?" asked Hayley.

"No," Fitz continued, "this does not feel like her work. I have to believe Norland gold fuelled this uprising. It seems too incredulous to believe the coincidence of an uprising just as an invasion commences, not to mention the attack on the queen."

"If it's an invasion," said the queen, "what would be their objective?"

"The logical target would be to overrun Hawksburg, then continue down the road to Tewsbury."

"Hawksburg can't put up much of a fight," advised Hayley, "they're still rebuilding."

"Yes," agreed Aubrey, "but there's a decent garrison there."

"Tewsbury is walled," offered Stanton, "it won't give in easily."

"A reasonable assumption," said Fitz, "and for once, I agree with you, Alexander, but still, we are only guessing at their objectives. We need more information."

"How do you propose we get that," asked Stanton, "simply ride up and ask them?"

"Sir Heward commands the frontier," said Fitz. "I've seen his first dispatch, and it indicates a strong force of cavalry. That doesn't seem to suggest they're out to siege a city."

"Of course they're out to capture our cities," said Stanton, "why else invade?"

"Your Majesty," said Fitz, "are the Norlanders aware that you have returned here?"

"No, we gave them no indication that Aubrey's magic could do that."

"Then I suggest the invasion is meant to topple our government," said Fitz.

"By attacking Hawksburg?" asked Stanton.

"No, I now believe they may be marching to support the uprising. Likely, they expect allies at their destination. Hawksburg would offer little in its present state, but Tewsbury would give them a strong base of operations from which to push on to Wincaster."

"Then we should attack their lines of supply, if that is the case," offered Lord Spencer.

"Not if they have a sufficiently large army," said Fitz, "and Sir Heward's preliminary report seems to indicate such. The problem, for us, is how to maximize the effectiveness of the few troops we have."

"What are you suggesting?" asked Stanton.

"I need to go to Hawksburg myself," said Fitz, "especially if I am to understand their strategy."

"An excellent idea, Baron," noted the queen. "We shall leave first thing in the morning."

"We?" said Fitz.

"Yes, Aubrey and I will accompany you, along with Albreda. We will be better equipped to repulse this invasion if we are closer to the battlefield."

"Are you sure that's wise, Majesty?" said Fitz.

"I will not be convinced otherwise," said Anna. "My people need me. I refuse to skulk here in the capital while my realm is under threat."

"Very well," said the baron. "Then I suggest we all get some rest. It will be a hectic day tomorrow."

TWENTY-FIVE

The Hills

Fall 964 MC

Beverly crouched, slowly moving forward to peer over the ridgeline. "See anything?" she asked.

"The horses are definitely here," noted Arnim, "but I'm not sure how easy they'll be to recover."

They were only three miles north of the castle, looking down into a slight depression, dotted with tufts of long, green grass. A wooden fence enclosed the area, stopping any horses from escaping their captivity.

Beverly stared down at the scene. "We'll find a way," she said. "We have to."

"Perhaps our luck will hold," suggested Arnim. "After all, we managed to make it out of the tunnels without pursuit."

"That wasn't luck, it was caution. Our foes were too afraid of encountering us in the cave system, but they'll catch up with us soon enough, just you wait and see."

"They may have already," noted Arnim, pointing. "Look."

Beverly swivelled her gaze to see a group of soldiers arriving to replace those that had been guarding their mounts.

"Oh, great," said Beverly, "as if we didn't have enough problems."

"I'd say there's twenty, at least." He shifted slightly, trying to get a better view. "No, make that thirty."

"We only brought two dozen men," said Beverly. "Do you think that'll be enough?"

"It'll have to be. We don't have time to go back and get more."

"Even if we wanted to, we couldn't," she said. "They're needed to guard the others."

"All right then," said Arnim, "how do you want to proceed?"

Beverly looked back over her shoulder to where the Guard Cavalry waited, minus their mounts, which were still in enemy hands.

"Can we make our way around to the east?" she asked.

"I don't think so. The area flattens out in that direction. This is about as close as we can get without revealing our presence."

Beverly sighed. This was starting to become too much work. "Very well then, I suppose we'll have to make a more direct approach."

"At least they don't have cavalry," noted Arnim.

"Except for that officer!"

"That's not an officer," he replied, "that's a noble."

Beverly stared some more. "So it is, but I can't make out which one."

"Let's go and talk to them, shall we? If we kill their noble, maybe the rest will flee?"

"I admire your faith," she replied, "but I doubt it'll be that easy."

She waved the guard forward, waiting until they were crouched just behind her to continue.

"We're going down that hill," she explained, "and there are Norland troops down there, guarding our horses. When we advance, make sure you keep a steady pace, and whatever you do, don't break ranks. Our very discipline is what's going to win us through today. Does everyone understand?"

They all nodded their heads.

"Good," she said at last, "then let's go."

Beverly rose, and stepped forward, confident her men were following her. The enemy troops were quite far away, and she pondered the distance as she walked. Had there been Norland cavalry present, she would have been more cautious, but years of fighting on the frontier gave her the confidence that her troops could out-fight footmen in a one-on-one melee.

Once they drew close enough for the enemy to notice them, the Norlanders drew weapons, but the horseman waved them down. He trotted towards the approaching Mercerians, his hands held high in the air.

"We mean you no harm," the voice said. "I am Lord Creighton of Riverhurst."

"My lord," said Beverly, "do you mean to stop us?"

"No," the earl replied, halting just in front of her, "quite the reverse. In fact, I'm here to help you."

"Why would you do such a thing?"

"I do not desire war with Merceria," he replied, "and I can assure you that there are others that feel the same way. I regret we were unable to stop Hollis and his allies, but we can at least make amends by helping you escape his clutches."

"Where is Hollis?" asked Beverly.

"To the south," replied Creighton, "likely in Merceria by now. He planned his war carefully."

"Merceria's been invaded?" asked Beverly.

"It has," said the earl, "or at least that was the plan. I cannot, of course, speak of what has truly transpired, for we are too far from the border to know for certain."

"Will you not suffer for helping us?"

"Lord Hollis will try, but I have my own household troops. A war is upon us, Dame Beverly, and I speak not of the invasion of Merceria, but rather a civil war that has erupted within Norland at the death of King Halfan."

"Civil war?" she said.

"Indeed," he replied. "While the king's ill health was known for some time, the earls vied with each other to become his successor. Since his death, it has erupted into all-out war, and Hollis intends to defeat Merceria once and for all. Should he succeed, there will be little to stop him from claiming the crown of Norland as well."

"And what would you ask of us in return?" asked Beverly.

She was expecting him to say peace, but instead, he reached into his cloak, producing a carefully folded letter, complete with a wax seal.

"Give this to your queen when you return," he said. "It may aid her in her fight with Norland."

"You would betray your own kingdom?"

"It is not my kingdom I am betraying, but the machinations of a power-hungry nobleman."

"We shall not forget this," said Beverly.

"Good," replied Creighton, "then my men will let you retrieve your mounts. The saddles and other accoutrements are over there," he said, pointing at a small hut. "May the Gods be with you, Dame Beverly of Bodden."

"And you as well," she responded.

Lord Creighton's men were true to his word, watching from a distance as they gathered their mounts. When Beverly called her men into formation, the Norlanders turned and headed west.

"That was quite unexpected," said Arnim.

"So it was," Beverly agreed, "but we've still a long way to go to get out of Norland. I don't imagine the other earls will be so generous.

"Gerald and the rest should be miles away by now," said Arnim.

"Yes, but we've been gone from them for some time. I only hope our pursuers haven't encountered them yet."

She urged Lightning forward, the rest of the horsemen falling into step behind her. Arnim, surprised by her sudden start, quickly caught up, taking up a position to her right.

"How long till we catch up, do you think?" he asked.

Beverly looked skyward, judging the sun's position. "I don't expect we'll catch them till mid-afternoon."

"Should we send some men ahead?"

"No, best to stick together. We can't risk losing anybody."

Arnim looked left and right, examining the countryside as they rode by. "This is very rough terrain," he said, "you could hide a whole army in these hills."

"That can work to our advantage," said Beverly, "but also against us."

"What do you mean?"

"I mean that we must be careful of who we attack. A small group on a hill might be a tempting target, but there may be others behind, out of sight."

"That's not a problem as yet," said Arnim. "We haven't spotted anyone."

"True," said Beverly, "but we must be prepared, nonetheless."

They rode on in silence.

Gerald stood on a hill, watching as his people trudged by. They were tired and hungry, he knew, and they couldn't keep up this pace much longer, but they must reach a defensible position first. Glancing westward, he searched for any sign of Beverly's men. It had been a gamble, sending them off, and he cursed himself for dispatching so many warriors, but without horses, his ragtag group of Mercerians was doomed.

He noticed a servant fall, her legs simply unable to carry on. One of the queen's foot guards bent over, lifting the woman and placing her over his shoulder, then continued marching. How much farther could they go, Gerald wondered?

A cry from the back of the group drew his attention. A warrior was pointing to the northwest, and Gerald let his eyes drift off to a distant hill where a group of horsemen appeared, the sun glinting off their armour. Was this Beverly?

He cursed the sun, for the glare made identification of the distant target impossible. When the riders started descending the hill, he scanned their numbers quickly, but there was no sign of a large black horse. Beverly was not among them!

"Norlanders," he shouted. "Everyone gather round!"

Fear energized them, and they rushed towards him, their eyes betraying their panic.

He pointed west. "Horsemen are approaching," he warned, "and we must make a stand. I want all the guardsmen facing west. Those servants who have weapons will line up behind."

"In a line?" asked a sandy-haired youth.

"Not exactly," said Gerald. "We're going to form a triangle. The guards will form the base, facing the enemy. The rest will create two lines, one facing northeast," he pointed, "the other facing southeast. Any non-combatants will remain in the centre. Be quick about it now, we don't have much time."

The Mercerians took up their positions. The westward-facing men were all battle-hardened warriors, each protected by coats of mail, but the rest were little more than an armed rabble.

Gerald glanced at the enemy as they drew closer. "Now remember," he said, "no matter what happens, hold your position. We're all in this together, if one of you fails, the rest will suffer."

He saw the look of determination on their faces and grinned. "Now stand by," he said, "this is likely to get hairy."

The horsemen, numbering two dozen, halted a spear's throw away. Two of their number rode forward, bringing them within talking distance.

"Surrender yourselves," said a well-dressed man, "and avoid unnecessary bloodshed."

"It is your blood that shall be shed," countered Gerald. "Return to your men and leave us in peace. We wish only to be rid of this land."

"Alas, I cannot," said the Norlander. "My orders were quite specific on that point, but can I offer you a deal if you're interested?"

"Go on," urged Gerald.

"Hand over the queen, and we'll allow the rest of you to go free."

Gerald smiled. "That, I cannot do," he said.

"You Mercerians can be so stubborn. Can't you see that you have no hope of survival without negotiation of some sort?"

"And doubtless, you can see the folly of your attack," said Gerald. "We are Mercerians, each and every one of us trained as a warrior. Do you seek now to break our wall of steel with just your horses?"

The Norland commander stared back at him. "Surely you jest," he said. "I see warriors, of course, but only a few, the rest are nothing more than peasants!"

"Then you know nothing of our culture!" said Gerald. "Come, stop your prattling and test your steel against us, unless you're too scared?"

"Very well," the Norlander replied, "it seems you leave us with no choice. Prepare yourselves, for you shall not live to see the sun set." He turned his mount around and trotted back to his waiting horsemen.

"Was that wise, Lord?" asked Donald Harper, a guardsman.

"We have little choice," said Gerald. "We cannot move with those riders on our tail, they'd cut us to pieces. Better to face them now and get them off our back."

"And you think we can defeat them?" asked Harper.

"We have to. We must protect the queen."

"But the queen is back in Wincaster by now, isn't she?"

"Likely," said Gerald, "but the Norlanders don't know that. If we allow them to shadow us, they'll soon know she's not among our numbers."

"Then we shall fight," said Harper, "though only the Gods will know of our bravery."

"Buck up, Harper," said Gerald, "we may survive this yet."

The marshal took his position alongside his men, facing the distant cavalry. The Norland leader appeared hesitant at first, as if trying to decide what to do.

"Damned Norlanders," said Gerald, "can't even make up their minds."

"I wish Dame Beverly were here," muttered Harper.

"Dame Beverly?" said Gerald. "Not your Captain, Lord Caster?"

"He's a tough warrior," said Harper, "no doubt about it, but Dame Beverly has that magic hammer. Now that would do some damage against these curs."

Gerald couldn't help but chuckle, "I suppose it would."

"They're turning, Lord."

"So I see."

The enemy rode off slowly, scanning the terrain to either side.

"What are they doing?" asked Harper.

"I suspect they're making room to charge," said Gerald, "not that it'll help them."

"Why is that?"

"Take a look at our line," said Gerald. "If you were a horse, would you charge it?"

Harper cast his eyes to the shields, readied to face their foes. "No, I suppose not, but what if they attack from another direction? Our weakest fighters are behind us."

"They won't," said Gerald. "I've challenged his bravery, he'll want to show he's not intimidated by us."

"Are you sure, Lord?"

"I've been doing this a long time, Harper. Trust me when I say I know Norlanders, I've fought more than a few of them on the frontier."

"If you say so, Lord."

The enemy finally came to a stop. They chatted with each other for a moment, then started spreading out into a ragged line, facing the Mercerians.

"They're getting ready," said Harper.

"You're very chatty for a guardsman," said Gerald. "How about you stop stating the obvious and get your shield up?"

"Yes, my lord."

Gerald watched as the horsemen started moving. It was a slow trot at first, the officer chiding his men to keep the line intact. When they finally fell into a proper formation, their leader barked out a command, and then the horses picked up their pace, sending clods of dirt flying from the damp ground.

"Brace yourselves!" called out Gerald. He planted his back foot while leaning forward slightly with his shield held before him, his sword peeking over the top of its rim.

Closer and closer, the enemy came, the ground shaking with their approach. Gerald remained calm, concentrating on the lead horseman, who was heading straight for him. Finally, at the last possible moment, the horsemen swerved, avoiding a direct confrontation. The riders slashed out with their swords but did little other than rattle against the defender's shields.

As they milled about in front of the Mercerians, trying to calm their mounts, Gerald struck, lunging forward and extending his arm to pierce the leg of a nearby rider. The Norlander roared out in pain, then swung his sword down in a counter-attack, but the old warrior had seen it coming. He parried the blow, knocking it to the side, then plunged the tip of his sword into the man's torso.

Gerald felt his blade scrape the man's spine, then withdrew it, covering himself in his quarry's blood. As his foe started to topple from the saddle, Gerald dropped his shield and grabbed the man by the belt, pulling him down. Moments later, he had his foot in the stirrup and was hauling himself onto the enemy's horse.

He heard his men cheering, but ignored it. The Norlanders, surprised by his actions, were ill-equipped to respond to this sudden turn of events. Gerald struck out, slicing deep into a rider's arm. A bellow of pain told him all he needed to know, and so he twisted his mount, slewing the horse sideways as a sword stabbed out at him, missing him by no more than a handsbreadth. The marshal, releasing the reins and grabbing the rider's forearm as it passed before his eyes, gave it a tug, pulling his foe off balance. The Norland warrior struggled to stay in the saddle, and just as he seemed steady, a surprised look appeared on his face as a sword took him in the lower back.

Suddenly, as if a dam burst, the guardsmen were among the Norland horsemen, attacking with wild abandon. At least six horses were now riderless, and Gerald watched a group of four Norlanders rushing westward in an attempt to escape the carnage.

The scrape of a blade across his forearm was a stern reminder that he was still in the thick of it. He stabbed out with his right hand even as he sought the reins, but the damn horse was too agitated, and he struggled to maintain control.

His helmet rattled as another sword struck, and he instinctively ducked, then counter-attacked, sending the point of his Mercerian longsword into his foe's face. Gerald fought to hold onto his weapon as the horseman began to fall away from him, but the blood-soaked blade flew from his grasp, disappearing into the confusion of battle.

Another Norlander charged towards him from the left, sword held out straight, the point aimed directly at his head. Waiting until the last moment, Gerald pulled back, letting the blade pass before his eyes just as he grabbed the man's wrist in both hands, twisting it with all the strength he could muster.

Bone snapped, and the sword fell from the Norlander's grip to balance precariously on the saddle for but a moment. Gerald reached out, grabbing it before his opponent could flee the battle.

Gripping it firmly, the marshal turned, expecting more foes, but the Norlanders had had enough. The few that remained on horseback were galloping westward as fast as they could ride.

As Gerald struggled to catch his breath, he surveyed the battlefield. At least half of the enemy was injured, along with four of their horses. Some of the Mercerians were running around the skirmish area, eager to capture the riderless horses.

"Stop! Back into formation!" he shouted as more horsemen topped the rise. For a brief moment, he thought their luck had run out. The fleeing Norlanders, thinking the same, let out a cheer, but the words soon died on their lips. Gerald smiled, for front and centre of the new arrivals was a great black stallion and its red-headed rider. Dame Beverly had returned!

TWENTY-SIX

Hawksburg

Fall 964 MC

The early morning mist was burning off as Kraloch peered over the wall, straining to see what the sun might reveal.

"I see riders," he announced. "Hundreds of them."

"I suppose we shouldn't be surprised," said Baron Fitzwilliam. "After all, they've been after our land for centuries."

"Are they attacking?" asked the queen.

"No," said Fitz, "at least not that I can see. They seem to be bypassing us."

"I wish Revi were here," said Anna. "He could send Shellbreaker to have a look."

"You forget," said the baron, "we have Albreda." He turned to the druid. "Would you be so kind, my dear?"

"Certainly," Albreda replied. Closing her eyes, she began reciting words of magic, and then the air appeared to buzz before she fell silent.

Fitz searched the skies. For a moment, the wind appeared to die, and then he spotted it, a hawk, circling overhead. Looking back to Albreda, he noticed her twisting her head back and forth as if seeking something on the ground. It was then that he realized she was seeing through the eyes of the hawk.

"There are hundreds of them," she stated, "and their column stretches for miles."

"Any sign of siege equipment?" asked Fitz.

"No," she replied. "In fact, there's no sign of footmen or archers."

"They'll be moving fast," said the queen. "I doubt we could catch up with them, even if we did have the numbers."

"I expect they're counting on that very thing," said Fitz. "It's a bold gamble they're taking."

"You think they're going to Tewsbury?" asked the queen.

"No," said Fitz, "I think they'll head directly to Wincaster."

"What makes you say that?" asked Kraloch.

"They are far to the east of us," said Fitz, "with their lightest troops to the west as a screening force. Unless I miss my guess, their more heavily armoured riders are out of our sight."

"Richard is correct," said Albreda, her eyes still closed. "I can see them quite clearly."

"How heavily are they armoured?" asked the queen.

"They are similar to the Weldwyn horse," said Albreda, "and most of them look to be wearing chainmail."

"They haven't the heavier armour our knights wear," said Fitz.

"Why is that?" asked Kraloch.

"It's their iron," came a voice from behind them.

They all turned to see Aldwin approaching.

"Norland iron is of inferior quality," noted the smith, "and they have not learned to temper it properly. As a result, they are unable to forge larger pieces like chest plates."

"Don't they have smiths?" said Kraloch.

"They do," Aldwin continued, "but they are only as good as the material they have to work with."

"They forge weapons well enough," said Fitz.

"True," replied the smith, "but even we Mercerians didn't perfect chest plates until very recently, and we had the advantage of consulting with Dwarven smiths."

"He has a point," said the queen.

"Remarkable," said Fitz. "Tell me, my boy, when did you become such an expert in history?"

"Ever since Beverly and I returned to Wincaster, shortly after our wedding. I had to do something to keep me busy while she was performing her duties."

"Aldwin," said Albreda, "you've been studying the magic circle here in Hawksburg, have you found anything of interest?"

"As a matter of fact, I have," he replied. "We may be able to reduce the cost of future circles."

"Now that," said the queen, "is welcome news. Tell me, Lord Aldwin, how might that be accomplished."

"When we poured the magic runes in Wincaster," the smith replied, "we made them of solid gold, but my studies here indicate the runes are not solid."

"Meaning?" said Fitz.

"Meaning the runes are likely cast of something else, and then only coated in gold. I would think they're made of iron beneath their expensive exterior."

"Would that be difficult to do?" asked the queen.

"It would be challenging," said Aldwin, "but I think I could manage it. It would require some exact measurements. We wouldn't be pouring directly into the circle, rather we would be forming the runes and then placing them into the stone afterwards."

"I suspect," said Albreda, "that such a method would be more than adequate for less powerful circles, but I believe pure gold runes would be required should they be imbued with more energy."

"What makes you say that?" asked Fitz.

"When I empowered Nature's Fury, I could feel the magic taking hold. I believe that the rarer the metal, the greater the magic it can contain."

"I'm not sure I understand," said the baron.

Albreda opened her eyes, releasing her control over the hawk. "It's really quite simple, Richard. In order to empower an item, it must be constructed of a material capable of containing the magic. This is typically very high quality, such as the hammer that Aldwin made."

"Sky metal," said the smith.

"Precisely," she continued, "and the rarest of all metals. A sword of high quality could be empowered, but an everyday weapon, such as the spears you equip many of your footmen with, would be unable to retain the magic within them. If I were to cast such a spell on one, it would quickly dissipate."

"As fascinating as that is," said the queen, "we must still deal with the Norland threat."

"Quite," said Fitz. "Sorry, Your Majesty."

"What would you recommend we do about them, Baron?" Anna asked.

In answer, Fitz gazed east, absently stroking his beard as he thought. "We shall send out our cavalry this afternoon. They'll likely have stragglers we can pick off. I will lead them myself."

"No," said the queen, "we cannot risk your loss."

He looked at her in surprise. "Then, who?"

"Prince Alric will lead them," she said.

"Absolutely not!" said Fitz. "You cannot risk the life of the prince."

"We have little choice, and Alric IS a skilled warrior. Who better to lead the horse?"

"I wish the Kurathians were here," said Fitz, "I'd feel a lot better about this."

"How many horse can we gather?" asked Anna.

"Only about two dozen, Majesty," said Fitz. "We are still waiting for Heward to fall back from Wickfield."

"Surely he has done so already?" asked Albreda.

"He likely has," said Fitz, "but he wouldn't have come straight south, he has villagers to protect. The last thing we want is the enemy to come across them strung out along a road. Instead, he would have led them into the Wickfield Hills. If anything, we should be looking west to his arrival, not north."

"We can transport horses from Wincaster using the circles," said Albreda.

"We only have light horse in the capital," advised Fitz.

"You're forgetting Alric's guard," said the queen. "He has two companies of Weldwyn horse that his father sent, remember?"

"Would he be willing to risk them in combat?" asked Fitz.

"I'm sure he would," said the queen. "Now, gather what mages you can, Albreda. We'll be returning to Wincaster as soon as possible so that I can talk to Alric, and you can gather the cavalry."

Albreda bowed. "As you wish, Your Majesty."

Aubrey absently waved her hand, bringing the glowing ball of light closer. The walls of the casting room were dug into the dirt, then shored up by wooden beams, giving the place a very stark look. The Ancestors had talked of something that was buried, but what did that mean, exactly?

With the floor set in stone, and the casting circle occupying almost that entire space, she thought it unlikely that it held what she sought. Could they be referring to the walls?

Feeling along where the floor met the walls, and occasionally tapping the hard-packed dirt with her hands, she hoped to hear something that might indicate a small chamber or door.

All morning she searched, and yet still, it eluded her. Finally, she moved to the table and sat down to gather her thoughts. Aldwin's sketches littered its surface, and she began collecting them, piling them neatly together. She was almost done when one such illustration caught her attention. It depicted the centre of the circle, and she was struck by the pattern. She had always assumed it was in the shape of a shield, containing a coat of arms, and yet now, seeing Aldwin's picture, upside down as it was, she saw a doorway.

Aubrey rose, moving to the centre of the circle and kneeling, calling over her glowing orb of light. When casting, she had always stood facing north, but now, as she looked south, she recognized what Aldwin's sketch had revealed. Could this be some clue?

The longer she stared at that coat of arms, the more she came to realize it hid something. From her vantage point, the top of the 'door' could represent the ground above. Beneath it, was a strange-looking rune. She turned south to see the very same shape within the circle itself. She had always assumed it to be a banner, and yet from this angle, it looked more like an archway.

She stood, thinking it over, then smiled. Something was buried here, of that she was convinced, but now she realized that the answer to finding it wasn't crawling along on her hands and knees examining the wall. No, it was to use her magic.

Knowing what she now had to do, she moved to sit cross-legged in the centre of the circle. Staring straight ahead, she concentrated on her spell, then began the incantation. The runes glowed as her power increased, then she felt the familiar snapping as she left her physical form, and her spirit floated free. She watched as her body slumped forward. Now was the tricky part, for concentration was key. She had to imagine herself falling through the stone.

Aubrey felt a moment of panic as her feet sank into the floor, but then her fascination took over. Down farther, she dropped, until her head was level with the stone. She fought the urge to close her eyes, then all went dark as she passed beneath the casting circle.

Her orb of light had remained in the room above, and so she dismissed it. Moments later, as she had cast it anew, a soft light illuminated her present position, in a small room, similar in size to the one above, yet lined with wooden shelves. There was no sign of stairs or a ladder, and yet somehow, someone had built this place. She floated across the room, examining the ceiling, desperate to find some method of entry.

It was frustrating. She was here, among all these books, and yet in her current form, she was unable to peruse them. How did someone get down here?

She lowered herself to the floor, then knelt, bringing her light closer. The answer lay before her, for in the centre of the room lay a series of stones, forming a circle no more than five feet in diameter. It showed the very same pattern that lay above, on the centre stone.

Aubrey rose, walking around the circle slowly, taking it all in, committing it to memory. She had no idea how long she studied it, but her orb of light went out once before she was finished. Finally ready, she stepped upon the circle, dismissing her spell of spirit walk.

The familiar feeling tugged at her, pulling her back through the floor. She heard the snapping noise as she joined with her physical form once more and opened her eyes, taking in the room surrounding her.

She rose from her seated position and immediately started casting. Moments later, the recall spell took hold, and her surroundings disappeared, to be replaced by the room below. Aubrey stepped out of the subterranean circle, calling forth her orb of light once more. She had done it!

Moving closer to the shelves, she began examining the books.

Albreda descended the ramp, followed closely by Kraloch and the queen.

"I have no idea where Aubrey went," the druid said. "Perhaps she returned to Wincaster?"

"Without telling us?" said Kraloch. "That isn't like her."

"Still," said the druid, "I can find no other reason for her absence, can you?"

"No," said the Orc.

"We shall have to make do without her," said the queen. "I'm sure she had a good reason for her absence."

Albreda halted suddenly.

"What is it?" asked Kraloch, almost bumping into her.

"The circle," she replied, "it's activating."

They all watched as the runes began to glow, then a cylinder of light shot upward, bathing the entire room with its brilliance.

Albreda's eyes took a moment to adjust to the change in light, then she saw Aubrey standing in the circle, books piled to either side of her.

"What's this?" asked the druid.

"Books," said Aubrey, rather unnecessarily. "I found my great grandmother's library!"

Albreda moved forward, as did the queen. Kraloch, on the other hand, remained in place, his eyes still adjusting to the change in light.

"That's quite a collection," said Anna. "Where did you find this library?"

"It's directly beneath us," said Aubrey, "in a chamber accessible only by magic."

"Astounding," said Albreda. "I must say that's an exceedingly ingenious way of securing one's valuables, but how did she manage such a thing?"

"I imagine she roofed it in after its creation," suggested the queen, "then built the circle on the floor above. The real question is, how did you find it, Aubrey?"

"Magic," said Aubrey. "I went into the spirit realm."

"And these books," said the queen, "you think they might be able to help Revi?"

"I hope so," answered Aubrey, "but there are more below. I had to start somewhere, so I picked these." She was about to say more but then looked at the others. "Wait, why are you here? Has something happened?"

"Indeed," said the queen. "We were about to recall to Wincaster to bring troops back here as quickly as possible. Have you much strength left?"

"Enough to recall at least once or twice," said Aubrey.

"Good, then let us put these books aside for the moment. We have more pressing matters to attend to."

They stacked the books to the side of the circle, then moved into position. Albreda cast, and then they all disappeared in a cylinder of light.

Fitz watched the distant horsemen.

"It's damn inconvenient of them to be out of reach," he complained. "Why couldn't they follow the obvious strategy and attack us? At least then we could thin their ranks."

"You want them to attack?" asked Aldwin.

"We have a prepared position," explained Fitz, "and we can neutralize their advantage in mobility. So yes, I want them to attack us."

"Don't they still outnumber us?" asked the smith.

"They do, but better to wear out the attack here than farther south."

"Have you sent word to warn Tewsbury?"

"I have," said Fitz, "and the garrison there should be sufficient to man the walls, assuming they're still loyal, that is. Has the prince arrived?"

"He has," said Aldwin, "though he's still waiting on more horsemen."

"How many has he?"

"Only about a dozen so far," said the smith. He leaned forward, straining his eyes. "What's that?"

The baron looked east to see a commotion among the Norland cavalry.

"Something seems to be disturbing their screening force," Fitz said. "I wonder what it might be?"

An instant later, a single rider came into sight, his horse racing towards Hawksburg, Norlanders in hot pursuit.

"That's a Kurathian," said Fitz, "I'd swear to it. He must be a dispatch rider."

"He'll never make it," said Aldwin, "his horse is labouring."

"So it is," said Fitz, "but I fear there's little we can do to help him."

They watched as the horseman slowed, his pursuer's gaining ground on him.

～

Prince Alric pulled himself into the saddle. "Come," he said. "We must do what we can to help."

A wagon had been rolled across the road to act as a defence. Men and Orcs now pulled it aside, allowing the horsemen egress. Alric trotted his mount through the opening, his men, few as they were, following along. He led them north, until the last man cleared the makeshift defences, then turned them eastward, switching from column into a line.

"For Weldwyn!" he called out, spurring his mount forward.

His horse wanted to race across the fields, but the prince kept it in check, the better to husband its energy.

The Kurathian was drawing nearer, but so were his pursuers. Even as Alric watched, the warrior's mount faltered, its front legs collapsing, sending the rider tumbling to the ground. The closest Norlander roared a challenge, striking down with his sword, but the nimble Kurathian rolled aside at the last moment, and his attacker continued past.

Alric gave the command, and his horsemen surged forward, each rider pushing his mount to the limit. Their line grew ragged as the faster horses took the lead.

The Kurathian stood, drawing his sword and facing his attackers. Four men had been chasing him, and while the first was circling back around, the next two came thundering in. He stood, waiting until they were almost upon him, then leaped to the side. Of the two enemies, the one on his left tried to adjust his trajectory, but the Kurathian had chosen his tactic carefully, for the rider's mount stumbled over the exhausted horse, sending both warrior and beast crashing to the ground. The Kurathian rushed forward, striking down with an efficient stab of his sword, forever silencing the fallen man.

Alric was almost within range of the lead Norlander now, and he roared out a challenge. His opponent, hearing the call, turned his mount and dug in his spurs.

Closer they drew until Alric stood in his stirrups, extending his arm over his horse's head, leaning forward to let the weight of his mount add to the charge.

His opponent held a similar pose, but as they met, the young prince twisted his sword slightly at the last moment, deflecting the Norlander's blade and sinking his own into the man's side. Loosening his arm up, Alric dropped the blade to yank it free and concentrate on his next target.

Heading straight ahead, he sat back in the saddle, pulling slightly to his right just before impact. This time though, his target had turned sideways and was prepared to receive his attack. The Norlander struck out, a vicious slash from left to right. Years of training at the court of Weldwyn had taught the prince well, and he deftly parried the blow, then attacked back with a stab of his own, sinking into the lightly armoured man's side. His enemy dropped his sword, clutching at the wound. The prince, hearing his men behind him, rode onward, confident that his troops would take the man into custody.

The lone Kurathian stood behind the body of his horse, his sword held above him, ready to parry the next attack. The last Norland rider, seeing the approach of the well-armoured Weldwyn horsemen, did the only thing he could. He turned and fled, riding off towards the east and the rest of the invading army.

Alric pulled back on the reins, bringing his horse to a halt before the Kurathian. He scabbarded his blade and held out his hand.

"Come," said the prince, "before they send more riders."

The Kurathian took the proffered hand, hauling himself onto the back of Alric's horse. The prince turned his mount around and began riding back towards Hawksburg.

"What is your name?" Alric asked.

"I am Caluman," the man replied, "and I bring word from Commander Lanaka."

"You are brave to race through this army of Norlanders," said Alric. "The news must be dire to attempt such a feat."

"It is, Your Highness," said Caluman, "for a second Norland Army rides for Eastwood."

Evening found them gathered in the dining hall at Hawksburg Manor. Caluman had no sooner finished his meal than the questions started.

"You say a large army was heading for Eastwood?" asked the queen.

"It was, Your Majesty," the Kurathian replied. "Commander Lanaka followed it for as long as possible with pickets, but there can be no doubt as to their intentions."

"What sort of numbers are we talking about?" asked Fitz.

"Our estimates are between eighteen hundred and two thousand," said

Caluman. "We managed to penetrate their scouts and reach their main force, but they were too numerous for us to do any real damage."

"I assume they had armoured cavalry in addition to lighter horse?" asked Fitz.

"They did, but we also encountered horse archers, my lord."

The baron leaned forward. "Horse archers, you say? That's news to me. Did you see any archers among the army facing us, Albreda?"

"No," she replied, "but then again, I wasn't looking for them."

"I don't understand how they're supplying themselves," said Aldwin. "They still need to eat, don't they?"

"They do," replied Fitz. "A very astute observation."

"I can answer that," said Caluman, "for on one of our raids, we happened upon their supply column."

"So they do have wagons," said Fitz. "Finally, something we can exploit."

"Not wagons," the Kurathian corrected, "they carry their supplies on the backs of horses. These pack animals are usually led, two or three at a time, by other riders."

"A fast-attack force carrying its own supplies," said Fitz. "That's something we hadn't counted on."

"The Kurathians have used a similar tactic for ages," noted Caluman, "though the numbers we saw far exceed anything my people have organized."

"So they've been planning this for years," said Fitz.

"I wish Gerald were here," said the queen, "I would value his judgement. What are your thoughts, Baron?"

"We are trapped between a rock and a hard place, Your Majesty. Two armies are descending upon us. Either one outnumbers our defences, let alone should they join up. They are too fast to catch and too numerous to fight with only our horsemen."

A commotion outside drew their attention.

"Sophie," said the queen, "open the door and let's see who intrudes upon our thoughts."

The maid crossed the room, pulling the door aside to reveal the startled face of Sir Heward.

"Your Majesty," the knight said, bowing. "I bring news from Wickfield."

"I take it the village has fallen," said the queen.

"It has, Your Majesty, though we managed to get the villagers to safety."

"Come and sit down, Sir Heward. We were just discussing our options, having just learned that two armies are invading. One marches past us even as we speak, while the other is heading for Eastwood."

"It seems there is little I can add," said the knight, "save that the villagers of Wickfield will be straggling in from the west over the next day or two. They are being escorted by my men, and the Wincaster bowmen, but tell me, is there not enough men here to stop the invaders?"

"Events have taken a turn for the worst," said Fitz. "While you were in the north, there was an attempt to seize the throne. We now stand unsure of the loyalty of our troops."

"My men are loyal, my lord," Heward declared.

"I'm sure they are," said Fitz, "but we cannot count on the town garrisons across the realm, and without them, we are sorely outnumbered."

"Have we a plan?"

"Not yet," said Fitz, "though I would suggest we head south, to Tewsbury."

"A wise move," said the queen, "but if the enemy should bypass that city, it would leave Wincaster dangerously exposed."

"The capital is walled," said Heward.

"Yes, but we lack the soldiers to man it properly," said Fitz.

"They won't attack Tewsbury," said Albreda, "of that, I'm certain."

"How can you be so sure?" asked Heward.

"They lack the proper siege equipment," the druid responded, "and their path is leading them directly south. I believe they're riding for the Uxley-Tewsbury Road."

"That would make sense," said Fitz, "as it would lead them directly to Wincaster."

"But they still lack the siege equipment," said Heward.

The queen smiled, "You're right, of course, but then again we're forgetting something, Valmar's uprising."

"I'm afraid I don't follow," said Heward.

"They only need someone to let them in the gates," cautioned the queen.

"But aren't all the usurper's forces locked up," said Fitz.

"No," said the queen, "for we lacked sufficient space to imprison them all. Many have been released on parole. It would only take a few to seize a gate."

"And so their strategy falls into place," said Fitz. "We must start getting troops back to Wincaster at once."

"No," said the queen, "for this invasion will not be stopped here, nor there. It is at Uxley we must make our stand."

"Uxley?" said Heward. "But how? We lack the troops for such a battle."

"That is where our allies will come in," said Anna.

TWENTY-SEVEN

Flight

Fall 964 MC

Beverly raced Lightning past the first Mercerians, heading straight for Gerald. They had been wandering the hills for days, first eastward, and now south, and then, hopefully, home. She halted before her marshal.

"Anything of interest?" he asked.

"Good news and bad, I'm afraid," she said. "We're almost out of the hills, but it looks like one final obstacle is before us."

"Go on," he urged.

"It's a bridge."

"That's not so bad," Gerald replied, "I thought you said bad news."

"It's over a ravine," she added.

"And?"

"And it's made of rope."

Gerald stared at her a moment. "A rope bridge? Tell me you're joking."

"I wish I were," she announced.

"I'd better come and take a look," he said, turning in the saddle. "Lord Arnim?"

"Yes, Marshal?"

"I'm riding ahead with Beverly to take a look at something. You have command."

"Yes, sir," Arnim replied.

"Lead on, Beverly."

Beverly quickly pivoted Lightning around, but Gerald struggled with his own mount.

"I've never known you to have a problem with a horse," she remarked.

"It's this damn Norland beast," he complained. "I swear these people don't know how to train their mounts." He managed to manoeuvre it into position, then urged it forward. "Finally," he said.

They passed by the lead Mercerians, heading farther south. Less than half a mile later, they paused before a large ravine.

"This doesn't look good," said Gerald.

Off in the distance was the bridge that Beverly had discovered. On each side of the ravine, two posts protruded from the ground, supporting a total of four ropes. The base consisted of wooden planks attached to two bottom ropes at either end, while the other two lines formed handrails. Keeping it all together were smaller, vertical ropes, each tied off at the handrails, the excess hanging loose.

"Getting our people across should be no problem," said Beverly, "but the horses might prove troublesome. We may have to leave them behind."

"You'd give up Lightning?"

"Lightning will cross," she replied, "of that, I have no doubt. He's fearless, but it's the others I'm concerned about."

"I'd hate to lose them," said Gerald. "They give us eyes and ears. What if we led them across, one at a time?"

"It would be slow going," she remarked, "and what if they spook halfway across?"

"Is there some way we could calm them?"

"We could try blindfolding them, I suppose."

"It's worth a try," said Gerald, "but let's get most of our people across first, and that includes you. Once you're there, I want you and Lightning to keep an eye to our southern flank."

"Very well," said Beverly, "and the rest of our warriors?"

"We'll send the footmen across first, followed by the servants. Once they're across, I want the Guard Cavalry to cross, one at a time. We'll have to be quick about it. I don't want to be doing this in the dark."

Beverly looked westward. "That doesn't give us much time," she said. "I suggest we wait until morning."

"I suppose you're right," said Gerald, "it would be folly to split our group. Very well, we'll set up camp here tonight, but have some men cross to the other side of the bridge. I want them to look over the ropes and make sure they're secure."

"Aye, Marshal."

"It's just the two of us, Beverly, you can call me Gerald."

She grinned, "Of course, Marshal."

"Very funny," he said. "Now, ride back to the column and let them know what's coming. I'll start picking out an area for the camp."

"You know," said Beverly, "this is not unlike the patrols we used to carry out back in Bodden."

"Other than the rope bridge and the civilians, you mean."

"Good point," said Beverly. "I'd best be off, then."

"You've been off ever since you were knighted," he said.

"Very funny, my lord." She made an exaggerated bow, then urged Lightning into a gallop, disappearing off to the north.

The sun lay low on the horizon as Gerald stood by a fire, warming his hands. The first sign of trouble was when a sentry shouted a warning.

"Saxnor's balls," said Gerald, "can we have no peace?"

Arnim ran towards him. "Our sentries have spotted horsemen," he called out.

Gerald looked around, taking in the makeshift camp. "We'll never hold them here, we're too spread out. Get six men across the bridge, then the servants will cross next. Where's Beverly?"

"Saddling her horse," said Arnim, "along with the rest of the Guard Cavalry."

"Have your men form a line north of the bridge, but make sure there's enough room to get around them. We'll have them back up once our people are across."

"I'll command the rearguard myself," said Arnim.

"It's risky, my friend. If they decide to attack in force, you might be overwhelmed."

Arnim smiled, "Then we'll die with Norland blood on our blades."

"I'd prefer you didn't die at all," said Gerald. "We still have to cross miles of enemy territory before we get home."

"In that case," said Arnim, "I'll do my best not to die."

"See that you do," said Gerald.

He waited until Arnim moved off, then turned his attention northward. His pickets had spotted the enemy, that was a good sign, but the real issue was whether or not the enemy had seen them.

Beverly soon rode out of the darkness.

"Did you hear?" said Gerald.

"Aye," said Beverly, "it seems the Norlanders found us."

"Get to the bridge, and as soon as the civilians are across, you start moving the horses. Remember, only one on the bridge at a time. We don't want to collapse the damn thing!"

"We may not have the choice," warned Beverly.

"Then I'll leave that up to you," said Gerald. As she left, he peered into the gloom, soon noticing firelight reflected off another horse, one of their pickets.

"Any sign they've seen you?" Gerald asked him.

"No, sir, but it won't take long before they hear the ruckus at the camp."

Gerald looked back to his own people, struggling to cross the bridge.

"It can't be helped," he said. "How many pickets are left out there?"

"Only three, my lord. I sent the rest back here. I assumed you'd want them across the bridge as soon as possible."

"Turnbull, isn't it?" said Gerald.

"It is, my lord."

"Well then, good thinking, Turnbull. Tell me, how long have you been in the Guard Cavalry?"

"Only four months, my lord."

"Then let's make sure you make it to five. Remember, no heroics, we withdraw in an orderly fashion."

"Aye, sir."

Gerald spotted torches being lit by the ravine, the better to guide people over the bridge. Two soldiers were already across, with a sparse stream of people following.

"This is going to take too long," he grumbled.

Moving south, to where the Queen's Guard had formed a thin line, he noticed Arnim standing out front, peering back into the now-abandoned camp.

"Should we douse the fires?" Armin asked.

"No," said Gerald. "It'll let us see how far away they are. How goes the crossing?"

"Slower than I'd like," said Arnim.

A horse neighed in the distance, followed by the clash of steel.

"That's it," said Gerald, "they've found us."

The noise had an immediate effect on the servants, for they rushed the bridge, causing it to sway. Even the soldiers looked worried.

"Beverly," said Gerald, "take your horsemen, see if you can buy us some time."

"Aye," she replied. She called out a command, and the Guard Cavalry turned in unison. Their manoeuvre complete, she drew her hammer, and led her men north, towards the sound of battle.

Gerald fretted. The press of people was causing the rope bridge to swing dangerously in the middle, and he worried that it might weaken its structure, but thankfully, it was not to be. There were twenty servants among their retinue, along with two dozen of the Guard Cavalry. The rest were Arnim's guards, bringing the total to sixty-seven individuals.

With the civilians now across, next would be the wounded. Some of Arnim's guards, almost a fifth, had been injured in the initial attack on their quarters. Most were mobile, of course, but walking was easy compared to crossing a swaying bridge. To add to the difficulty were the three who had suffered severe wounds, who had to be carried. They likely wouldn't survive the trip to Merceria, but he refused to abandon them to the enemy.

Off in the distance, more swordplay echoed. Beverly was in her element now, of that he had no doubt. He tried to picture the fight, but the darkness hid all from him.

He watched as the wounded neared the far end of the bridge. "Your men next, Arnim," he ordered.

Lord Caster gave the command, and his men started crossing in single file. "I'll go last," he declared.

"As you wish," said Gerald.

The distant clash of steel ceased, and Gerald waited, anxiously listening for any sign of what had transpired. Shapes loomed out of the darkness to be lit by the abandoned campfires, and Gerald gave a sigh of relief as he recognized the Guard Cavalry returning.

"They're right behind us," called out Beverly.

"Dismount and get your horses across," ordered Gerald.

Beverly leaped from the saddle, leading Lightning to the bridge where she calmed the beast by stroking his forehead. Gerald watched as they crossed the bridge. Lighting was a large horse, a Mercerian Charger, but even this great creature looked nervous as it stepped onto the wooden planks.

"We're running out of time," said Arnim.

"We can't wait for each one to cross," said Gerald, "we'll have to send them one right after the other."

"Will the bridge take the weight?" asked Arnim.

"You tell me," said Gerald. "I know nothing of such things."

"It will hold," said Arnim.

"How can you be so sure?"

"Because it has to," replied Lord Caster. "And anyway, do you think Saxnor would bring us here just to have us all die?"

"I doubt Saxnor really cares one way or the other," said Gerald. "We make our own destiny, Arnim. We're not the playthings of the Gods."

"This is not the time to lose your faith, Gerald. Right now, we can use all the help that the Gods can give us."

Gerald frowned, then turned to the other cavalrymen. "Go," he ordered. "Cover your horse's eyes and lead them across."

Hoofbeats called his attention northward, where a rider appeared, slumped over in his saddle. It was the last of the pickets, and as his horse halted beside a fire, the man slid from his perch, falling to the ground, unmoving. Gerald glanced at his own cavalry. How much more time did they have, he wondered?

Arnim rushed forward, crouching by the rider, but shook his head, one less Mercerian was going to make it home. He jogged back, keeping to the side so as not to impede the horsemen who were streaming across the bridge.

Gerald heard the rope groan with the strain, and he held his breath. Beverly was now at the southern end of the bridge, a torch in hand, lighting the way. The last of the Guard Cavalry stepped onto the bridge, leaving only Gerald and Arnim.

Horseshoes clattered on the timbers as they made their way across. Gerald opened his mouth to give Arnim the order to retreat when enemy riders came into view. They halted some fifty paces away, and he watched as they dismounted and drew their swords, their weapons glinting in the light of the campfires.

"I guess this is it," said Arnim.

"So it is," said Gerald, drawing his own sword.

They both backed up to the edge of the bridge. Gerald considered a sprint, but then the Norlanders would be upon them in no time, leaving their companions at the mercy of the enemy. He looked at Arnim, but the former captain was staring at the loose ends of rope dangling from the handrails.

"I have an idea," Arnim said.

"Which is?" said Gerald.

"This," said Arnim. He stepped back, grasping a section of rope and wrapped it tightly about his right arm.

"Are you suggesting what I think you are?" said Gerald.

"I am."

Gerald, following Arnim's lead, reached out and pulled over a vertical rope on his side, then grabbed the excess at its top and wrapped it in his left arm.

"Stand back," he yelled at the enemy.

In answer, the enemy rushed forward. Gerald cursed, swinging his sword, trying to cut the top rope. As he struck, he felt a few threads give way, but it withstood his onslaught. Gerald hit it once more, and then the enemy was upon him. He quickly parried, blocking his opponent's attack.

Arnim had also hacked at the railing on his side. Unfortunately, swords were not as sharp as daggers, and the rope resisted his efforts as well.

Gerald stabbed out, sinking the tip of his sword into a leg. The Norlander backed up, but another took his place, trying to drive the marshal backward. Gerald cursed his luck for his arm, wrapped as it was by the rope, was now putting him at a disadvantage. He ducked low, then head-butted his opponent. The Norlander staggered, and then his foot slipped on the planks that formed the bottom of the bridge. Gerald didn't hesitate, following up with a vicious stab to the throat.

The bridge swayed unexpectedly when Arnim cut through his top rope, and a loud snap echoed throughout the ravine. Gerald struggled to remain upright, crouching slightly to steady himself. A Norlander stepped forward in a crouch, trying to balance, and Gerald kicked out, hitting the man's kneecap, crumpling him to the ground. Using this opportunity to slash out with his sword, he chopped at the bottom rope that held the wooden planks in place.

Arnim was busy hacking away at the one rope remaining on his side. The bridge swayed again, throwing Gerald off balance, and he fell to his knees, his left hand still clutching the excess rope in a deathlike grip.

Across the bridge, Beverly called out, "The horses are all safe."

It was time for them to retreat. Arnim rose to a standing position and held his sword aloft.

"I'll see you in the Afterlife!" he shouted, then drove the blade deep into the rope.

It cut clean through the frayed fibres, and as Arnim's side of the bridge collapsed, he dropped out of sight.

Gerald felt his footing give way and then he was hanging on for dear life. The bridge shuddered as Arnim reached the end of his rope, swaying it yet further. It was now suspended by only two ropes, one frayed, the other partially cut through. Gerald heard a ripping sound as the individual strands worked themselves loose, and then he felt himself falling.

Air rushed past him as he plummeted. The rope tugged painfully at his shoulder as he swung across the ravine, then he struck some kind of bush growing from the rock wall. The impact forced the breath from his lungs and then everything went black.

. . .

Pain lanced through him as he opened his eyes to see Beverly looking down at him.

"What happened?" he asked. He tried to move, but pain shot up his arm.

"Lay still," she commanded, "you've dislocated your shoulder."

"I don't understand."

"You wrapped the rope around your arm," she said. "It saved you."

"Arnim?"

"He's alive," she said, "though in a similar condition to yourself." She held up a hand to forestall any comment. "Don't worry, we're safe. The Norlanders are on the other side of the ravine."

"Where are we?"

"I've moved us away from the bridge," she said. "Come daylight, we'll move on, but in the meantime, we need to see to your wounds."

"You mean I have more than a dislocated arm?"

"Yes," she said, "I'm afraid you hit the wall pretty hard. You may have some internal injuries."

"Where's a Life Mage when you need one?" said Gerald.

"We're doing all we can," said Beverly, "but this darkness won't shield us for much longer. What do you know of this region?"

"Not much," said Gerald, "but my understanding is that we'll pass through some woods, then its flat terrain to the border."

"Good," said Beverly, "then we've bought ourselves some time. It'll likely take days before they find another way around this ravine. We should be long gone by the time they do." She fished around her armour, pulling forth a sealed letter. "You should carry this," she said. "In all the excitement, I forgot about it."

"What is it?" said Gerald.

"A letter, from Lord Creighton. It's for the queen."

"What does it say?"

"I don't know," she replied, "I haven't opened it. He asked me to give it to her when we return."

"Then why are you giving it to me?"

"You're out of the fight," she said, "whereas I might be called upon to battle our enemies. You have a much better chance of delivering it than I."

"Very well," Gerald said. He reached out for it, forgetting his injury. The pain that lanced up his arm duly reminded him of his condition.

"Here," said Beverly, "I'll tuck it into your belt."

"Where are we?" asked Gerald. He was being carried on a makeshift litter, his brow sweating with fever.

"I see you're awake," said Beverly. "You've missed a lot. We're out of the hills, and moving through a thick forest."

"We must be near Oaksvale," said Gerald.

"It lies to our west, as near as we can gather, but we're keeping our distance."

"How's Arnim?"

"Much better than you," said Beverly. "He's up and about with little more than a broken arm and some cuts and bruises. You, on the other hand, are in bad shape."

"You should leave me," said Gerald. "I'm only slowing you down."

"That's not the Mercerian way," she replied. "You know that as well as I do, so you can put such thoughts from your mind."

"How long until we reach the plains?"

Beverly thought before answering. The land north of Wickfield was relatively flat, with only the occasional hill to mark the terrain. It was also mostly devoid of trees, making it a prime area to be spotted by Norland troops.

"I expect we'll be at its edge later this afternoon," she replied.

"And then?"

"And then we rest. There's no sense in trying to cross it at night, we'd likely lose our bearing and end up wandering off into the middle of nowhere."

"You'll need to cross it in one day," warned Gerald.

"One day? That's a long march. I'd estimate it's more than thirty miles."

"More like forty," said Gerald, "but we have little choice." He was about to say more, but a lance of pain raced through him, causing him to double up.

His bearers halted, lowering him to the ground.

"Gerald? Are you still with me?" asked Beverly.

The old warrior lay back, closing his eyes. "I'll be fine," he said. "You've more important things to worry about."

"We'll get you home," she promised as she looked down at him, expecting a reply, but he had ceased moving. "Gerald?" she said, suddenly alarmed. She leaned over him, taking his pulse, then let out a breath of relief as she realized he had just fallen back into unconsciousness.

"We'll rest," she ordered, then moved her way up to the front of their column, where Arnim rode one of the captured horses.

He turned as she approached. "The edge of the woods is within sight," he said.

"You've seen it?"

"Our riders have, and it lies less than a mile off. I'd suggest we make camp here, out of the eyesight of anyone on the plains."

"Good idea," said Beverly. "It's likely the last time we'll be able to light a fire before we cross the river into Merceria."

"That's still a long way off," warned Arnim, "and chances are the Norlanders have invaded. We could be walking into an enemy army."

"I'm well aware of the risks," she replied, "but we have little choice."

"So we cross at Wickfield?"

"I've been giving that some thought," said Beverly. "If the Norlanders HAVE attacked, they're likely holding Wickfield. We'll have to move downriver and cross into the hills there."

"Are you sure that's wise?" asked Arnim. "That area of the country is quite dangerous."

"More dangerous than an army?"

"I suppose not," he replied.

"I understand there are many dangerous creatures in those hills, but I doubt they'd bother a group with this many people."

"And where do we go from there? Surely you're not expecting this lot to march all the way to Wincaster?"

"No," said Beverly, "but I'm hoping we can make it to the Saurian gate."

"We don't have a mage to activate it," said Arnim.

"True, but the last time I was in those hills, Gort lived there."

"Gort?"

"Yes, a Saurian. I'm hoping he can communicate using the gate. Once we get word to Erssa Saka'am, they can relay a message to Wincaster."

"Assuming Wincaster hasn't fallen," said Arnim.

"Not something I'm willing to entertain at this moment," said Beverly. "Our main concern right now is making it safely across the river."

"How's Gerald?"

"Not well," said Beverly. "His internal injuries are severe, but there's little we can do for him. He'd be fine if we had a healer with us, but without magic, I doubt he'll last much longer."

"That bad?" said Arnim.

Beverly nodded, too overcome with grief to speak.

"He's been a great friend to us," he said at last.

"He's still alive," she spat out, "and we'll endeavour to keep him that way as long as we can."

"I meant no offense. I merely meant the prognosis wasn't good, you even said so yourself."

"I did," she said, wiping away a tear. "I'm sorry, Arnim, his condition has hit me hard."

"Understandable," he said, "he was your mentor, after all."

"More than that," said Beverly, "he's family."

"I didn't know you were related?"

"We're not," she replied. "What I meant to say is that he's like family. I cannot bear to think what life would be like without him in it."

"He served your father, didn't he?" asked Arnim. "He doesn't talk much about that period in his life."

"He suffered the loss of his family," said Beverly, "though that was years before I knew him."

"And yet, through all that, he survived."

"He did," she agreed.

"Well then, it's settled," said Arnim. "Gerald Matheson is too stubborn to die. It seems he'll make it home after all. He must be Saxnor's chosen one."

Beverly smiled. "Perhaps he is," she agreed, "though he's not one to believe in the blessings of the Gods."

Arnim chuckled, "I'd have to agree with you there. In any event, we should all get some rest. It will be a difficult day tomorrow."

"Yes, about that. I want you to gather the men, we'll need sticks."

"Sticks? For a fire?"

"No," said Beverly, "for makeshift spears."

"That won't do much damage to the enemy," Arnim warned.

"No," she replied, "but it just may serve to keep their horses from closing."

TWENTY-EIGHT

Wincaster

Fall 964 MC

Lord Stanton stood there, shaking. Baron Fitzwilliam had informed the other nobles of their dire circumstances, but the Earl of Tewsbury's reaction had been immediate and all-encompassing, one of absolute fear.

"What can we do?" he lamented. "Surely, we must flee!"

"Mercerians do not flee from battle," said Fitz. "Better to die fighting than to run away like a coward."

"I'm with the baron," said Lord Spencer, "though it pains me to say it."

"Have we any word from Colbridge or Kingsford?" asked Stanton.

"A fast rider from Kingsford arrived late this evening," said Fitz. "Sommerset will support whatever decision the queen makes."

"And what decision is that?" asked Stanton.

In answer, Queen Anna turned to Sophie, who was standing by the door.

"Admit them, please," said the queen.

Sophie opened the door, then stood to the side as a procession of people, all of them non-Humans, entered the room.

"Gentlemen, ladies," began the queen, "allow me to introduce you to our allies." She waited until they had all filed in, then stood and moved to the end of the line.

"This is, as some of you might know, Lord Herdwin Steelarm, representing King Khazad, Ruler of Stonecastle."

The Dwarf bowed. "It is an honour to meet such distinguished lords and ladies."

"And this," the queen continued, "is Lady Telethial, daughter to Lord Arandil Greycloak, leader of the Elves of the Darkwood. She is here today representing her father."

The Elf nodded her head in greeting.

The queen couldn't help but smile as she introduced the next visitor. "This is Lily, an old friend of mine. She also represents the rulers of Erssa-Saka'am."

"Never heard of the place," said Stanton.

"It lies in the Great Swamp," noted the queen, "and is home to the ancient race of Saurians."

Lily chirped.

"What did she say?" asked Stanton.

"She said she is pleased to meet you," said the queen.

"You speak their language?" said Lord Spencer.

"Of course she does," said Aubrey, "how else would she translate."

"May I finish, my lord?" asked the queen.

"Sorry, Your Majesty," said Lord Spencer, "please continue."

"Last, but certainly not least, we welcome the chieftain of the Black Arrow Orcs, Urgon."

The great Orc stood still, a defiant look on his face.

"They have all come to help us in our time of need," said the queen, "but there is a price. They want seats on our council."

Stanton's eyes lit up, his fear now forgotten. "But that would dilute the power of our existing nobles," he said. "Couldn't we pay them instead?"

Herdwin stepped forward, his fists balled. "We have discussed this at great length," he said, "and are united in our resolve. There shall be no hope of aid from any of us until we are permitted seats on this council."

Stanton sat back, his mind working quickly. "Four seats, I suppose we could allow that. I suggest we rank them as baronets."

"No," Queen Anna, "they shall be ranked as earls, and it will be five seats."

"Five?" said Stanton.

"Yes," said Herdwin, "for we count the Trolls among us, even though none are currently present."

"Then I hardly see why we should include them," stated Stanton.

Heward was about to speak, but Chief Urgon stepped forward, drawing everyone's attention. He moved to stand beside Lord Stanton, towering over him.

"Would you rather let your kingdom die?" he asked. "Better to share your power than be masters of nothing."

Stanton paled. "This is all well and good," he said, "but their troops still have to march here. How can they possibly arrive in time?"

Anna walked back to her seat, standing behind it and resting her hands on its back. "Oh, didn't I mention it? They're already here."

"Here?" said Stanton. "In Wincaster?"

"Just outside of it, actually," said the queen, "though Urgon's Orcs are mostly in Hawksburg at present."

"You tricked us," accused Stanton. "Well, it won't work, I shall not submit to blackmail."

"It's not blackmail," said the queen. "The threat we face is genuine, so much so, in fact, that I must force a vote tonight."

"You can't," said Stanton, "it needs a two-thirds vote to change the nature of the council, and we haven't enough nobles present."

"In fact, we do," said Anna. She held out her hand, and Sophie moved closer, handing her some folded letters.

"I have here," she continued, "a letter from Lord Somerset, the Duke of Kingsford. He agrees to support whatever I feel is necessary to save the kingdom."

"Still not enough," said Stanton.

"I also hold the proxy for Lord Matheson, Duke of Wincaster."

"And I," added Fitz, "am still acting military governor of Shrewesdale in addition to being Baron of Bodden. Who here is in favour of expanding the council?"

Everyone, save Stanton, raised their hands.

"That is, I believe, all the votes we need," said the queen.

Lord Stanton's hatred was palpable as he stared daggers at Anna.

The queen turned to face her allies. "If you would be so kind as to find a seat, we'll get down to business."

Urgon sat next to Stanton.

"You can't sit there," whined the earl, "that's Colbridge's chair."

"We shall sort out proper seating another time," said the queen. "I believe we have more important matters to discuss at the moment."

Lily sat to the queen's right, the traditional seat of the Duke of Wincaster, while Herdwin took a chair beside Lady Aubrey. Telethial cast her eyes around the room, finally settling on the spot beside Baron Fitzwilliam.

"Now, shall we get started?" asked the queen. "Perhaps you'd like to begin, Lord Herdwin."

"Thank you," said the Dwarf, rising to his feet.

"Please," said Anna, "there is no need for formality here. You may remain seated if you wish."

"Very well," he said, planting himself firmly in his chair. "My king sends his regards. He has sent two hundred Dwarven warriors, half of which are archers."

"Ah, yes," said Fitz, "the famous Dwarven arbalests. They should prove quite useful."

"And the Elves?" asked the queen.

Telethial looked around the room, staring directly at each lord seated there before replying.

"One hundred Elven archers stand ready to fight. They are camped to the southwest alongside our Dwarven allies."

The queen turned to Lily, a series of strange sounds pouring from her lips. In answer, the Saurian replied in the same language.

"The Saurians will appear at Uxley," Anna translated.

"What do you mean, they will appear?" said Stanton.

"I am not at liberty to discuss the particulars," said the queen, "but suffice it to say they shall be ready to aid us in our time of need."

"And have we some idea of numbers?" asked Stanton.

"I am assured there will be a sufficient number," said the queen.

"We must know more if we are to plan an effective defence," said Lord Spencer.

"Yes," added Stanton, "and what of Eastwood? Are we to simply surrender the city without a fight?"

"No," said Chief Urgon. "The Orcs remaining in the Artisan Hills will come to its aid."

"The plan," said Fitz, "is to slow them down and buy us time to defeat the army that crossed at Wickfield."

"That's correct," said Anna. "We will deploy our forces at Uxley and make our stand there."

"That's it?" said Stanton. "Your only plan is to fight at Uxley?"

"There's more to it," said Anna, "but I will not discuss the details here. Prince Alric will assist Baron Fitzwilliam as they move south from Tewsbury. Lady Hayley will command the Uxley defence as she is familiar with our allies' tactics and can make the best use of their troops."

"We are doomed," declared Stanton.

"No," said the queen, "but we are in a perilous position. We cannot split our forces, to do so would invite defeat. Our only option is to concentrate what we have against one opponent at a time. Once the first army is defeated, we can proceed to the second."

"IF we can defeat them," said Stanton.

"No," said Anna, "WHEN. I shall not accept anything else."

"Very well," said Fitz, "Haylcy and I will meet with our esteemed allies immediately and begin making preparations."

"Good," said the queen. "In that case, this council is dismissed. We will reconvene once we have defeated this Norland incursion. Lord Herdwin, if you would be so kind, I should like you to remain. We have things to discuss."

"Of course, Your Majesty," the Dwarf replied.

The rest of the council made their way outside, each in discussion with one or more colleagues, while Anna waited until only she and Herdwin remained before speaking again.

"I must thank you, Herdwin. That was beautifully played."

"I am pleased you think so, but are you sure such actions were necessary? You seemed to already have the votes, after all."

"I needed to stress the direness of our situation," Anna said, "and Lord Stanton has been a thorn in my side since I took the throne."

Herdwin smiled, "I would suggest you have him killed, but I understand you've passed decrees against such things."

"I have. We are a kingdom of laws now."

Herdwin looked closely at the queen, reading her face.

"You're worried," he said. "Don't worry, we'll survive this."

"No, it's Gerald I'm worried about," she confided. "He's stranded deep in Norland territory. I'm not even sure if he's still alive."

"He is," said the Dwarf, "don't you worry."

"How can you be so sure?"

Herdwin chuckled, "He's too stubborn to let something like an army of Norlanders stop him."

"I suppose that's true. Still, it would be nice to have word from him."

"You concentrate on protecting your kingdom," he said. "The last thing you want is for Gerald to return to a conquered Merceria."

"I suppose you're right," Anna said, "and there's so much work yet to be done."

"Might I make a suggestion?"

"Of course, I would welcome it."

"Chief Urgon is returning to the Artisan Hills through the Uxley gate."

"I know," Anna replied, "but only Saurians and Orcs can use it safely. I had thought to send soldiers with him, but it would take too long."

"I have another solution," said the Dwarf. "We can have him deliver a message to Lord Greycloak. If an army is marching down the Eastwood road to Wincaster, it threatens his domain as much as ours. I believe he might be willing to give further aid."

"An excellent idea."

"Good," said the Dwarf, "because I already did it."

"You did?"

"Yes, I had Telethial draft it, just in case."

Anna leaned forward, hugging the startled Dwarf.

"What was that for?" he grumbled.

"For being you, Herdwin," she replied. She patted her scabbard. "I never told you how useful this sword of yours has been to me over the years."

"Aye, well, I thought you were Gerald's daughter at the time, I couldn't let that go unrewarded."

"And so I am," Anna said, straightening her back. "Thank you, you've just restored my faith in myself."

"I did?" he said. "How did I do that?"

"You reminded me that Gerald is a father to me and that the acorn doesn't fall far from the tree."

"Acorn? What in the name of Gundar does that mean?"

She laughed. "It's an old Human expression, and it means that I sometimes think like Gerald. I'm going to need that to save us from the Norlanders."

Aubrey stared down at the page, her mind absorbed with the details.

"Any luck?" said Kraloch.

"It's hard to make sense of this," the Life Mage replied. "It uses techniques I have not yet mastered."

"Let me see what it is you're reading?"

"One of my great grandmother's books," Aubrey replied. "She was an accomplished Life Mage, that much is clear, but I never realized just how advanced she was in her studies. This is years ahead of anything I've ever imagined."

"This spell," the Orc said, looking over her shoulder, "it looks familiar to me."

"You've dealt with healing the mind?"

"No, but it is similar to another I have heard of. I learned my trade from the great healer, Shular. She was perhaps the greatest shamaness that our tribe ever produced."

"Shamaness?" said Aubrey. "I thought the Orcs didn't distinguish between genders."

"We don't generally, but we have found that our female healers tend to be more powerful. The title pays homage to that."

"So this Shular, she could heal the mind?"

"So I believe," said Kraloch. "I remember her helping a young Orc hunter once. The poor fool had been gored by a boar."

"And his mind was gone? I find that hard to believe."

"He went down during the struggle and struck his head on a rock. He was lucky to still be alive."

"I take it," said Aubrey, "that he lost his wits?"

"He was reduced to little more than grunts. Shular used magic to see into his mind."

"She could read his thoughts?"

"No, but she could see the cause of the injury. It enabled her to craft a spell to help him."

Aubrey turned to look up at the Orc. "Are you saying she invented a new spell?"

"Yes," said the Orc, "does that surprise you?"

"I didn't think such a thing was possible."

"Then, where do you think all our spells came from?" asked Kraloch. "Surely you don't believe the Gods created them?"

"I suppose I hadn't thought of that," she replied. "And now that I think of it, Albreda's a wild mage. She must have created her own spells, but I'm not sure I even understand what that means."

"The Orcs have a simple approach to magic," said Kraloch. "We believe that the effects of magic are there to discover. When one creates a spell, what they are really doing is discovering the secret of how that magic can be unlocked."

"I quite like that idea," said Aubrey.

"It has served us well in the past."

"Wait a moment," she said, returning her gaze to the book. "I seem to remember something about looking into the mind, let me see if I can find it." She flipped back through the pages, quickly scanning each as they passed by. "Here it is."

The page before her had a rough sketch that looked like a series of caves. "I think this is it."

"The mind is not a cave," said Kraloch, "it is solid, this much we know."

"Yes," said Aubrey, "but as a Life Mage, we must interpret the magic that we see. Our minds must present information to us in a way that we can understand. I think that's what this is referring to."

Kraloch leaned forward, scanning the notes. "I think you are correct, I recognize some of these phrases."

"I'd always assumed that spells were the effect of combining different magical words," said Aubrey. "Is that not true?"

"Yes and no," said Kraloch. "Most of the spells we use from day to day are quite simple, but you, yourself, have used rituals, and they are far more complicated."

"Ah, I see now. You're saying this description is a ritual?"

"Yes, it would appear so."

"Then it's time we test that theory," Aubrey said.

"And how do you propose we do that?"

"I shall attempt this spell. Hopefully, it will cure Revi."

"You cannot," said Kraloch.

"Why?" she asked. "Surely you want him healed as much as I?"

"I do," the Orc replied, "but if you go into his mind, how will you know what to look for? You must try this spell on a healthy patient first as a point of reference."

"I suppose that's true," said Aubrey.

"And you will need my help."

"I will?"

"Yes," said Kraloch, pointing at the text. "If you look here, you'll note that the spell requires the simultaneous use of words of power. The only way to do that is to use two casters."

"Is that even possible?" she asked.

"It is called a linked spell," explained Kraloch. "I have never attempted such a feat, but the Ancestors have spoken of it."

"Do you think the Ancestors can give us guidance?" asked Aubrey.

"Of course," the Orc replied, "and we might even seek the advice of Shular."

"When can we start?"

"Right now, if you wish, though it might be prudent to use the magic circle. It will increase the effectiveness of our spells."

Aubrey closed the book and rose, tucking it under her arm. "Very well," she said, "let's get to it, shall we?"

They made their way to the casting circle, halting as they approached the guards that stood watch at the door. Nodding a greeting, Aubrey led Kraloch inside, then moved to the outer perimeter of the circle where the lectern sat.

"This will prove useful," she said.

Kraloch lifted the stand, moving it to the centre of the casting area, then waited as Aubrey placed the book onto it.

"We shall not need the book just yet," said Kraloch, "but let us sit. The calling of the Ancestors can take some time, and if we do manage to contact Shular, she may have much knowledge to impart."

"Very well," said Aubrey.

They sat facing each other, crossing their legs on the cold stone floor.

"Ordinarily, I would simply cast a spell to communicate with the Ancestors," explained Kraloch, "but only I would be able to hear them. To solve that dilemma, we will both start by casting spirit walk," said Kraloch. "Once within the spirit realm, I shall attempt to summon the Ancestors."

"Attempt?" said Aubrey. "Does it not always work?"

"Much like the living, Ancestors can be a moody lot," explained the Orc. "They are not compelled to answer the call. It is entirely their choice whether they heed the summons."

He nodded at Aubrey, and they both began casting. Kraloch finished first, his body slumping forward as his spirit left his flesh. Aubrey followed a moment later, hearing the snap as she fled her mortal form.

"I am ready," she said, though her voice sounded strangely muted.

"As am I," said Kraloch.

He began chanting, a sound that reminded Aubrey of a funeral dirge. It went on and on while the world around them started to fog up until she could barely make out Kraloch's form. She moved closer until she was within an arm's length of the Orc.

The shaman opened his eyes. "It is done," he said. "Now, we must wait to see who answers the summons."

Aubrey closed her eyes, counting in her head. She had just reached fifty when the Orc spoke again.

"Someone comes," he said.

She opened her eyes and followed his gaze as a figure emerged from the fog.

"Who has summoned me?" said a voice.

"It is I, Kraloch, Shaman of the Black Arrow Tribe."

The figure drew closer, revealing the aged features of a female Orc.

"Ah, my old pupil," she said, "it is good to see you again."

"And you, great shamaness. I have missed your presence."

"I see age has not taken the flowers from your speech," she said, turning to face Aubrey, "and who is this?"

"This," said Kraloch, "is the Human, Aubrey Brandon. She is a great Life Mage."

"Greetings, Human, I am Shular. In life, I was shamaness to the Black Arrow Clan."

"I am honoured to meet you," said Aubrey. "Master Kraloch has told me much of your power."

The old Orc turned back to Kraloch, raising her eyebrow. "Has he, now?"

"Your powers are legendary, oh great one," said Kraloch.

"Are they indeed?" said Shular. "You flatter me, former pupil, but let us dispense with these unnecessary platitudes. Why have you summoned me, Kraloch?"

"We need your advice. Our tribe has new allies, and they are in need."

"I am aware of the Mercerians," said Shular, "they have done much to advance our cause, but tell me, how can I help them?"

"One of their mages has fallen ill," Kraloch continued, "with a sickness of the mind."

Shular nodded her head. "I see. So you called me to find out how to cure him?"

"I did," he replied. "Will you teach us the magic we require?"

"First, tell me of this Human caster."

"His name is Revi Bloom," said Aubrey.

"A name I know," said Shular, "the incomplete Enchanter."

"Incomplete?"

"He has not yet found his mastery," said Shular. "His power will only grow stronger."

"Then he can be cured?" asked Aubrey.

"Yes, but the effort will be taxing. Are you sure you're ready to learn such things?"

"I am," said Aubrey.

"Very well," said Shular, "then let us begin."

TWENTY-NINE

Revi

Fall 964 MC

A ubrey watched as Sir Preston lay down on the bed.

"Are you sure about this?" she asked.

"If it will help Master Revi," he replied, "I'm all in. It won't hurt, will it?"

"I can't say for sure, but I doubt it. All we'll be doing is looking inside your mind. You may not feel anything at all."

The knight took a deep breath, letting it out slowly. "You may begin when ready."

Aubrey looked at Kraloch. He was on the other side of the bed, his hands clasped before him.

"Are you ready?" asked the Orc.

"As ready as I'll ever be."

They both began casting, Kraloch in his deep baritone and the Life Mage in her higher register.

Aubrey felt the power build within her as the words flowed forth. Closing her eyes, she also felt the power emanating from the shaman, combining with her own to create an even greater harmonic.

The ritual continued for some time until her arms ached, and her knees weakened. Then, as she felt a light-headedness, brilliant colours exploded in her mind. Behind her eyes, there was a sharp pain, like someone was driving needles into them, but just as quick, it disappeared.

She found herself standing in a small cavern. Above her, the ceiling was smooth as if wind and sand had worn the rock down over the years. Kraloch appeared beside her, his hand upon his forehead.

"Are you well?" she asked, her voice echoing like she was in a vast chamber.

"I felt a great pain," replied the Orc, "then it disappeared. Where are we?"

"We must be in Sir Preston's mind."

Kraloch staggered forward, his feet unsteady. "I feel odd," he said, "though I cannot truly explain it."

Aubrey took a tentative step. "I'm slightly dizzy," she said.

"Likely a result of the magic that brought us here."

She took a deep breath, steadying her own thoughts. "This is what a healthy mind looks like?" she said. "Somehow, I was expecting more."

"Your mind is struggling to understand," explained Kraloch. "Tell me, what do you see? Be as exact as you can."

"We're in a small cave, though perhaps subterranean chamber might be more precise. I see no exits."

"And the walls?"

"Smooth," Aubrey continued, "as if worn down by age."

"And yet, Sir Preston is still relatively young by Human standards, is he not?"

"He is. Why?"

"This cave looks..." Kraloch paused for a moment, "unravaged."

"What does that mean?"

"Sir Preston is a warrior, a Knight of the Hound. I would have expected to see scars from battle."

"In his mind?" said Aubrey.

"Battle is very traumatic," replied the Orc. "To see this mind in such pristine condition is somewhat unexpected."

"Do you think we are not concentrating enough? Let us move to one of the walls and examine it in more detail."

"An excellent idea," said Kraloch, "but I suggest we do so slowly."

"I'm in agreement with you there."

As they drew closer, the wall came sharply into focus.

"The surface is rough," Aubrey said, "with what looks like scrapes and cuts on it."

"So it does. I wonder if a child's mind would still be smooth?"

"You think these marks are memories?" she asked.

"It's as good a conclusion as any. In any case, I see nothing here that would require healing, do you?"

"No," Aubrey agreed, "but then again, Sir Preston is not ill. It will be interesting to see what Revi's mind will reveal."

"Shall we return?"

"Not just yet. We should examine the entire area to see if there's anything else of note."

"As you wish," said Kraloch.

They continued their examination until Aubrey felt there was nothing else to see.

"Time, I think, to return," she said.

"Very well," said Kraloch, "let us leave this place." He closed his eyes, reciting words of power, then his body vanished, as though he had never existed. When Aubrey dismissed her own spell, she felt a lurching sensation as her mind raced back to her body.

A severe attack of vertigo left her struggling to keep the contents of her stomach intact. When she finally opened her eyes, the room spun, only abating as her eyes adjusted to being back in the physical world. She noticed Sir Preston sitting up, watching her closely.

"Are you well, Lady Aubrey?" he asked.

"I will recover, but the spell was disorienting. How was it for you, Kraloch?"

The Orc, who was a lighter shade of his usual green, looked back at her sheepishly. "I would concur with your assessment," he admitted.

"And you, Sir Preston?" she asked.

"I didn't feel anything. I wasn't even sure that your spell worked until you returned. You two were just sitting there doing nothing."

"Great, another spell that leaves me defenceless," said Aubrey. "Tell me, Kraloch, are there more Life Magic spells that leave us so vulnerable?"

"There are, I'm afraid. Almost all the ones associated with the spirit realm are that way."

"Are you suggesting that this spell was spirit-based?"

"In a sense, yes," said Kraloch. "After all, our minds did leave our bodies, did they not?"

"I suppose they did," she replied.

"Then, you have your answer."

"Well, one thing's for sure," said Aubrey, "we'll need to rest before we try that on Revi."

"Yes," the Orc agreed, "and that is only to diagnose his illness. Once that's done, we need to figure out how to actually heal him."

"I've been giving that some thought," said Aubrey. "When I heal someone, let's say a knife wound, I picture the healed flesh in my mind. Is it the same for you?"

"It is," said Kraloch, "I suppose that means you'd need to picture Revi's mind in a healed state."

"Yes, but we don't know if his mind will look anything like Sir Preston's."

"That's true. Could each person's mind look different?"

"I'm sure it would be similar," said Aubrey, "else the pictures in my great grandmother's book wouldn't match what we just saw."

"An astute observation," said Kraloch, "but now we need to recover our strength if we are to help Master Bloom. I will go and rest."

"My magical energy is low, that's true," said Aubrey, "but I'm wide awake. I think I'll make some sketches of what we saw. It can only help me visualize a healthy mind for Revi."

Kraloch nodded his head. "As you wish."

It was late the next day before they had the chance to visit the poor Life Mage. He lay in bed, the sheets soaked in sweat, his whole body tossing and turning as he mumbled incoherently.

"The magebane has been administered?" asked Aubrey.

"It has," said Kiren-Jool, "though I fear it does him no good. Prolonged exposure to it may have long-lasting effects."

"Then we must cure him quickly," she replied. "Has he taken any food?"

"Only a broth," the Enchanter replied, "and even getting him to take that has been a chore. Do you really think you can help him?"

"We are hopeful," she said, "but we are only here today to investigate, not cure. We must get inside his mind and determine where the illness lies. Only then can we begin to formulate a plan to cure him."

"Then I shall pray to the Saints that you are successful," said Kiren-Jool. "Perhaps, with their help, you will see a way through this for poor Master Bloom." He rose, backing away from the bed.

Aubrey looked down at Revi. His hands were still bound to the bed, limiting his movement, but the risk of the mage releasing his magic was a very real threat, for even magebane wears off in time.

"Shall we begin?" asked Kraloch.

"Yes," said Aubrey, taking a seat beside the bed. The Orc did likewise, sitting across from her, their patient between them. Revi, as if sensing their presence, calmed.

Aubrey closed her eyes, placing her hands on the bed before her, palms down. She waited until Kraloch's voice reached out, echoing through the room, then joined in, creating the eerie harmonic that would release their inner power.

The air in the room crackled with energy, and she felt the hair on her arms standing upright. On and on, they both intoned, the words spilling from their lips faster and faster until they became but a jumble of sound. The pressure mounted in her eyes, and she waited for the sharp jab of pain, but this time, she opened herself to it, and instead, she felt a rush of air on her face.

She opened her eyes to see Kraloch sitting across from her, his own eyes closed to his surroundings. As she watched, the entire image was washed away as if a wave of water had taken her sight.

For a moment, panic consumed her, and then her surroundings took shape. No longer was she in the room. Instead, she stood in a tunnel, surrounded by thick green strands that reminded her of vines. As she reached out, touching one, it clung to her hand. Heat radiated off of it, not a fiery inferno, but a comforting warmth. Pulling her hand back, the vine tried to follow but eventually released its grip.

"Fascinating," said Kraloch.

"What is this?" said Aubrey.

"Some kind of growth," the Orc replied. "Could it be caused by the flame?"

"It IS the same colour," she mused, "but I'm at a loss to explain how the two are connected. Maybe it's just a coincidence. Could Revi have contracted something in the tower? A disease of some type?"

"The rest of us returned unscathed, so I think that unlikely."

She turned to face Kraloch. "Tell me everything you know about the flames," she said.

"They were discovered by the Saurians, many generations ago when my people still lived in cities. They used them to travel great distances."

"Did Orcs ever use them?" Aubrey asked.

"Our shaman's never learned the secret of their use," he replied, "but there are stories of the Saurians taking Orcs with them on occasion."

"And none of your race suffered any detrimental effects?"

"Not that I'm aware of," said Kraloch, "but our shamans believed that pale skins, like you Humans, could become obsessed with the flames. I wonder if this might be the result?"

Aubrey studied the strange tendrils. "Our minds interpret what the magic reveals, I firmly believe that. That being the case, these strands would definitely represent some type of infection. Could it really be from being in proximity to the flames?"

"Can a person become sick by being near others that are ill?" he asked.

"Of course, but how does that explain this?"

"It means," Kraloch continued, "that illness can be borne through the air. I suspect the flames are similar."

"But a flame can't make you sick."

"No," he agreed, "but they emerge from beneath the ground. Perhaps, when the flame rises, it brings with it something that carries the sickness?"

"I've never heard of such a thing, have you?"

"It is said that the Dwarves have, in times past, discovered strange rocks that can make people sick by their very presence."

"And what do they do in such cases?" Aubrey asked.

"They bury the rock beneath layers of stone to keep it at bay. Those that sickened sometimes got better, but most usually died."

"So, they have no cure?"

"Not that I'm aware of," said Kraloch, "but then again, I only know what I've been told."

Aubrey reached out, touching a tendril again. This time she tugged it, feeling resistance. "I don't suppose we could just pull these out?"

Kraloch grasped one, pulling on it with some force. "It appears not." As he removed his hands, Aubrey noticed something.

"Do that again."

The Orc grasped a tendril once more, ready to pull.

"Now let go," said Aubrey.

He released it, looking at her in puzzlement.

"What is it?" he asked.

"Watch," she said, grabbing a strand. She held it only a moment, then let it go, but it stuck to her hand until she pulled it away.

"Interesting," the Orc noted. "It seems to have a different effect where Humans are concerned."

"Earlier, you said that pale skins could become obsessed. What if that obsession is really the mind being taken over by these strands?"

"It's possible, I suppose."

"And what if," Aubrey continued, her mind racing, "the Elves experimented with using the flames?"

"But how would they have had access to them?"

"Revi mapped out the location of all the confluences in Merceria," she said, "and one of them falls within the Darkwood." She stared at the tendrils. "Could these have contributed to the downfall of the Elves?"

"You think these green strands might have caused them to turn to Necromancy?" Kraloch asked. "I see no evidence of that."

"But we know that Revi was acting strange and that Orcs and Humans react differently to these things. Do you think it could even have a different effect on the Elves?"

"I suppose it's possible," the shaman noted, "but at this point, it is only speculation. We would need an Elf that was infected to know for sure. In any case, it's irrelevant at the moment. We are here to find a cure for Revi, not help the Elves."

"You're correct, of course," said Aubrey, "though I must remember to bring my theories to the queen. I'm sure she'd be most interested."

"And these things?" said Kraloch, indicating the strands.

"Now that we've seen them, I must do further research. We can't simply pull them down, that much we know, but I suspect it's our own minds that are restricting us."

"How so?" he asked.

"We are not physically inside his head," she replied. "Rather, our minds are probing his and trying to make sense of what they see. We cannot pluck these vines from a picture, that would be like picking flowers from a painting."

"I see what you mean," said Kraloch. "What, then, is the answer? Some type of healing spell?"

"That would be my guess, but which? We've tried healing flesh and neutralizing toxins. I even tried using regeneration."

"Those spells are all similar," said Kraloch. "Might there be a variation of which we are unaware?"

"Yes," said Aubrey, "one that targets the mind."

"Mutations," said Kraloch.

"Mutations?"

"Yes, it occurs to me that is the term we are looking for. Every once in a while, word comes from our tribemates of an Orc youngling born with unusual features."

"Like what?" she asked.

"The one that comes readily to mind is a colourless skin. We call them ghost-walkers. Instead of a healthy green, they will appear pale and ghost-like, with unusual eyes."

"My grandmother's notes make reference to it in Humans as well, but she called it albinoism."

"Our elders refer to it as a mutation," explained Kraloch. "Though in our society, it is often seen as a mark of distinction. Could the effect we see here today be something similar?"

"An interesting thought," said Aubrey. "Mutations generally occur before birth, but if what you're saying is true, then this infection, or whatever it is, is mutating people that are already born. Perhaps that's the key?"

"So, we need some way to reverse its effects, that is our way forward."

"I agree. Let us return to our bodies and continue our research."

Dismissing the spell, Aubrey felt her mind drifting back to her body.

Everything went black, and then the room began taking form as if it had been slowly illuminated after being plunged into darkness.

Aubrey looked across at Kraloch, who was blinking as his eyes readjusted.

"Any luck?" asked Kiren-Jool.

"Yes," said Aubrey, "we think we've located the problem. The issue now is finding a way to remove the infection."

"You say infection, I take it, you saw something in there?"

"His mind was covered in strange green tendrils," said Aubrey, "the same colour as the flame."

"Could this be true of anyone who has used the Saurian gates?" asked the Kurathian.

"I suppose it could," said Aubrey. "I hadn't thought of that."

"We know the Orcs are immune," said Kraloch, "and likely the Saurians, too."

"That doesn't help the rest of us," noted Kiren-Jool. "We've sent a lot of people through those gates, some more than others. You, yourself, have travelled by that method, Lady Aubrey, have you not?"

"I have," she said, "and so has the queen!"

Kraloch rose. "Come, we have work to do."

The mages of Merceria rose as one when Queen Anna entered.

"You have news?" she asked.

"We have, Your Majesty," said Aubrey.

The queen sat, indicating that the others should do likewise. "Let's hear it then. The realm is in peril, and I have much to do."

"We think we have determined the cause of Master Bloom's illness," Aubrey said.

"That is good news indeed, but I hardly think that requires a meeting of the entire Mages Council."

"There's more," Aubrey continued. "When we used magic to probe Revi's mind, we found evidence of a strange malady, an infection, if you will. We believe it was caused by his study of the Eternal Flames of the Saurian Temples."

"And..." Anna asked. "We've already banned their use. How is this of any import?"

"There may be long-term effects of even light use," she said.

"And how, might I ask, do you know this?"

"After we returned from examining Revi, we thought to conduct similar tests with others, among them Lady Hayley. She, too, shows signs of being afflicted, though to a much lesser degree than Revi."

"Are you saying we're all sick?" the queen asked. "Are you suggesting we quarantine everyone?"

"No," said Kraloch, "we don't believe the illness spreads in that manner."

"Then how does it?"

"There is reason to believe," said the Orc, "that the flames bring strange minerals to the surface. Minerals that are detrimental to Humans, Elves and Dwarves. As far as we've been able to determine, Orcs and Saurians are immune to its effects."

"How bad is it?" asked Anna.

"Revi's mind was full of long green tendrils, but he's the worst case. Others, such as Hayley, show signs of infection as well, but the tendrils hang from the ceiling, more like small hairs than vines."

"I have been through the gates myself," said the queen, "as has Gerald. Are you saying we're all carrying this malady?"

"I'm afraid it's very likely," said Aubrey, "though we can, of course, confirm through further study."

"We have no time for this, for our very way of life is under attack."

"Though the malady is present," said Aubrey, "it does not appear to have had any detrimental effects on others, only Revi is incapacitated."

"So far, but can you assure me that it won't spread? Even a small cut can turn lethal if left untreated. You know that as a healer."

"I do," said Aubrey, "but we have little information to go on at present. The fact is, we simply don't know for sure. What we do know is that many of us have used the gates in the past, and none have shown any signs of this illness."

"And have you a cure?"

"Not yet, Majesty, but we are working on it."

"Then," said the queen, "I must insist that you give it your top priority,"

"Won't you need our healing services in the upcoming fight?" said Aubrey.

"We shall, but until such time as the army marches, you are to continue your research." Anna turned her attention to the rest of the council. "However, when we march to Uxley, I shall require the full power of this council."

"Of course," said Albreda, "we will be happy to lend what assistance we can."

Queen Anna rose, prompting the rest to do likewise. "Thank you," she said, "this meeting has been most informative. I shall look forward to news of a cure."

She left the room, leaving the mages standing.

"I don't envy you, Aubrey," said Aldus Hearn, "you have the weight of the kingdom on your shoulders. If the queen is sick, it puts us in dire peril."

"We are already in dire peril," said Albreda, "or did you forget the invasion so soon?"

"That's not what I meant," grumbled the old druid.

"Then you should choose your words more carefully," said Albreda. "Aubrey already has enough on her plate without you reminding her of her responsibilities."

"My apologies, Lady Brandon," said Hearn, "I did not mean to give offense."

"And none was taken, Master Hearn," the young Life Mage replied. "But I'm afraid you must excuse me, Kraloch and I have much to discuss."

"I, too, must depart," said Kiren-Jool, "for I must give careful consideration as to how I might assist in the upcoming battle."

"You plan that far in advance?" said Hearn.

"Naturally," the Kurathian replied, "doesn't everyone?"

"I prefer to adapt as the battle progresses," said Hearn.

"What of you, Albreda?" asked Kiren-Jool. "Surely, as the most powerful among us, you must take great pains to organize your spells."

"I'm afraid I'll have to agree with Master Hearn on this," she replied, rising from her seat. "I seldom plan such things in advance." She made her way to the door, then stumbled, reaching out to steady herself with the back of a chair.

"Something wrong, Albreda?" asked Hearn.

Albreda stood there, shaking, her eyes squeezed tightly closed. "I see a battlefield," she said, "with the dead strewn all around. We shall lose this war unless...." her voice trailed off.

"Unless what?" asked Hearn.

Albreda held up her hand to silence him. She was evidently struggling, searching for something no one else could see.

"There, I see it," she said, her eyes finally opening. "Yes, that's it, we must seek the woods."

"I beg your pardon?" said Hearn. "You're making absolutely no sense."

Albreda looked directly at him. "There's only one way we can win the coming battle, Aldus, but we must be quick."

"Where are we going?"

"To the Whitewood," she said, "for there, we shall find the answers we are looking for."

"The Whitewood? That's your domain. Why in this world would you require my help?"

"Let's just say you have a way with...dirt."

"Dirt?"

"Yes," said Albreda. "Now come, I shall explain on the way."

They left the chamber, leaving Kiren-Jool to stare after them. "Earth Mages are a strange breed," he muttered, "powerful, but maybe just a little too...feral for my taste."

THIRTY

Home

Fall 964 MC

An ominous mist covered the open terrain before them as the Mercerians plotted their next move. The forest had been a mixed blessing, giving them an ample supply of berries, plants and the occasional stream to fill their water skins. Hunting had been challenging, armed as they were with swords and axes rather than bows, but they had made do, bringing down a couple of deer by chasing them with their horses. Now, however, they must leave the protection the woods offered to make their way south, to the land they called home.

The chill in the air made all aware that winter was almost upon them. Beverly sent the Guard Cavalry out first, scouting the area for any sign of the enemy. They soon returned, declaring the area safe, at least until the mist cleared, for they were hampered by it as much as the Norlanders. Those on foot marched next, with a small detachment of riders bringing up the rear.

When the mist finally cleared, the forest had become a distant memory. By looking at the sun, Beverly knew she was heading south, but was unable to determine their exact east-west position. Having neither a map nor any detailed knowledge of the area, she had to hope they would eventually reach the river that separated their two realms.

The sun was high when they noticed a small group of warriors some distance off to their southwest, the sun glinting off their helmets. The Mercerians kept their eyes on them, but the interlopers soon rode off.

"That doesn't bode well," said Arnim.

"No," said Beverly, "I think they've gone to get help."

"I hate to say it," said Arnim, "but I hope the army is much farther south. I wouldn't want to run into it here, north of the border."

"I'd have to disagree," she replied. "I'd much prefer to find them here. That would at least tell us that our homes are safe. Where do you think that lot came from?"

"The patrol?" said Arnim. "Likely Brookesholde. It's a small village, about the size of Wickfield if you remember?"

"Oh, yes," said Beverly, "we passed it on our way north. Do you think they have a garrison?"

"Likely," he replied, "though how big it might be is anyone's guess. Their soldiers may have gone south with the army, for all we know."

"Let's hope so, for all our sakes."

The day wore on as Beverly set a gruelling pace, only stopping once at a stream mid-afternoon, then continuing on their way. When the Norland village of Brookesholde was finally spotted to their west, Beverly knew they were getting close to the border.

By late afternoon, the Norlander warriors had returned, this time a dozen horsemen in all. They rode out of the distant village, heading directly towards them, despite being outnumbered.

Beverly, prepared for just such a development, ordered their group to take up a position on a slight rise. It was certainly no defensive mound, but at least it gave a better view of their enemy's approach.

The makeshift spears, which she had insisted they make, were now half-buried in the ground, presenting a reasonable deterrent against the enemy horsemen. Beverly organized the defences in the same triangle pattern that Gerald had adopted in their first encounter with their pursuers, keeping the Guard Cavalry outside the defensive ring, ready to counter-attack should the chance present itself.

The enemy rode towards them, but the sight of the spears was enough to give them pause. Beverly ordered the Mercerian horsemen to charge, but it proved futile, for the fleet-footed mounts of the Norland light cavalry simply kept their distance, running away when threatened.

She led her men back to the 'mound' as they were calling it, a look of distaste upon her face.

"We are trapped," she said. "We cannot bring our weapons to bear, and yet if we move from our position, we open ourselves to attack."

"What do you suggest we do?" asked Arnim.

"I'm open to suggestions. How close do you think we are to the border?"

"Not far, but we'll need a ford to cross, and that means Wickfield."

"Not necessarily," said Beverly. "There may be crossing points to the west."

"None we can count on, and without knowing for sure, we can't expose ourselves."

"Then we'll have to move at night."

"That will be tricky," said Arnim. "It'll be a moonless night tonight, making navigation extremely difficult."

"True," said Beverly, "but at least it will give us some protection."

"I have an idea that might buy us more time."

"Speak up, Arnim. Let's hear it."

Arnim rubbed his hands, warming to the task. "Here's what we'll do..."

Captain Dirk Kendall had spent years in the saddle. As a low-born member of Norland society, he had struggled to make a name for himself. Now, with war finally upon them, he had managed to earn a command, even if it was only a small village in the wake of the invasion force.

He looked around at his men, all fifty of them, their faces lit by torchlight. "The enemy is not far from us," he said, "just east of our present position. We shall ride out and eliminate the threat."

"How did Mercerians get this far north?" asked Phelps, an older warrior.

"That we do not know," said Kendall, "but we must do our duty and defeat, or at least capture them. Their very presence could upset our leader's plans."

"So, we're to attack them in the dark?" asked Phelps.

"Of course," said the captain, "this is our land, and I will not suffer them to occupy it. We will strike swiftly and overwhelm them while they sleep."

"And how do you expect us to do that, sir? If I may be allowed to ask?"

"We shall move slowly, riders with torches in the lead."

"I beg your pardon, sir," said Phelps, "but won't that give our position away?"

"It likely will, but our scouts report that the majority of these interlopers are on foot. Once we brush aside their horses, we can concentrate on their footmen," he said, glaring at his men. "Any more questions?"

They all looked downward, intimidated by the captain's ill-humour.

"Good!" Kendal said. "Then, let's ride!"

The captain, spurring his horse, urged it onward, and his men duplicated his efforts. It was a cold night, and as the small detachment began moving east, their breath frosted in the air. Captain Kendall took the lead, his men strung out behind him in pairs.

It was just after midnight when they spotted the light, flickering in the darkness.

"That must be their camp," the captain said. "Spread out."

He watched his men disperse, a line of torches marking their positions. As they drew closer to their destination, he could just make out figures moving about the fire.

"They don't seem to have noticed us," said Phelps.

Kendall was about to reply when a distant figure halted, pointing at them. He cursed his luck and urged his men into a faster trot. The campfires grew brighter, but the figures had disappeared.

"Where did they go?" asked Phelps.

"Likely skulking in the dark," said Kendall, "so be careful."

He slowed the line, no longer sure of his actions. He had expected the enemy to make a stand, but now, with naught but campfires before him, he was starting to have doubts.

"'Ware the flanks," he stammered out. Damn, this was not the image of command he wanted to project!

"Stakes!" called out one of his men.

"We were warned of them," replied Kendall. "Proceed at a slow trot, shout out if you spot anyone."

He halted before one of the spears and dismounted. It was, on closer examination, of very crude construction, and he pulled it from the ground, tossing it aside in contempt.

"There's no one here," he called out, "they've all left."

Phelps halted beside him. "Someone was here, sir. They can't have gotten far."

"True," the captain agreed, "but in what direction have they fled?"

"We shall have to wait for daylight. There's no telling where they might be."

Kendall fumed. "We just saw them moving around their camp, for Saxnor's sake!"

"I'm sorry, sir," said Phelps, "but we can't see anything in this gloom. We'll have to wait for morning if we were to follow."

"Very well, have the men dismount. Mount a picket and rest the horses."

"We could always return to Brookesholde?"

"And lose the trail? I think not."

. . .

Arnim looked back at the camp, absently rubbing his broken arm. It ached terribly, but at least he could ride, a skill that had proven valuable this night. He and a small group had delayed their departure, the better to give the illusion of a busy camp, then fled east, hoping to draw the Norlanders away from the others, should they choose to pursue.

"It doesn't look like they're taking up our trail," noted Harper. "Your ruse didn't work, they're not following."

"No," said Arnim, "but I suppose we should consider ourselves lucky, at least we've bought some time for the others. No doubt by morning, they'll be after us again, but we've left a trail heading east, perhaps that will be enough."

"Orders, my lord?"

"We'll turn south now that we're clear of the camp. We can rejoin our companions once the sun reveals their location."

"Won't it also reveal them to the Norlanders?"

"It will," said Arnim, "it will indeed."

Beverly heard a noise just as the sun appeared on the horizon, the sound of running water. Glancing to the north, she hoped for some sign of Arnim and his men but could see none.

She brought Lightning to a halt, waiting as the rest of her people struggled past. The exhaustion on their faces was plain to see, the night's march having taken its toll.

"Head towards the sound of the water," she called out as she stared north, silently praying to Saxnor to lead her people to safety.

A horseman appeared in the distance, followed by three more. They were riding hard, their reins thrashing left and right, driving their mounts for all they were worth. She recognized the lead rider, the sling on his arm easy to spot. Moments later, the cause of their rush came into view as a large group of horsemen followed behind them.

She turned in the saddle. "Guard Cavalry to me!" she called out. "The rest of you make for the river as fast as you can!"

Her horsemen galloped to her position and stood waiting. There were twenty-four horsemen with her, while the rest of the guards, minus those with Arnim, protected the servants.

Beverly counted off ten men and sent them to guard the others. She drew her hammer, holding it aloft, the sun catching its sky-metal head.

"For Merceria!" she shouted.

"For Merceria!" her men echoed.

Urging Lightning forward, her men fell into line to either side of her.

"Spread out," she ordered, and the cavalry responded with precision, opening up a gap to allow Arnim's men through the line. The new arrivals slowed as they passed through, Arnim nodding his head in greeting.

"There's plenty behind us," he said. "An entire company as far as I can tell."

"Get back to the others," said Beverly. "We'll do what we can to hold this lot at bay." She turned to her command. "Close up, and prepare to charge!" The Guard Cavalry shrank the line, closing the distance till they were almost stirrup to stirrup.

The enemy rushed down at them, their horses whipped into a frenzy. Beverly ordered their counter-charge as soon as they completed their own manoeuvre, and now the two lines collided together in a clash of steel.

Beverly struck out with Nature's Fury, a wicked overhead swing that tore into a Norlander's collar bone. She pulled the weapon free just as Lightning reared up, kicking out at a rider with his front hooves. Horseshoes struck metal, ringing out loudly, then the horse ran off, his rider tossed from the saddle.

A sword struck her leg, glancing off the metal plate, and she pushed out with her shield, using its edge to drive her opponent back. Following up with another swing, she felt the hammer penetrate his shield, then pulled it back, watching her foe, his arm now limp, struggling to escape the fray.

All around her, the riders of the Guard Cavalry struggled in this desperate battle against overwhelming odds. These men of Merceria were no knights, yet they fought with the same determination, dedicated to wreaking what havoc they could.

Unexpectedly, the Norland horsemen retreated, galloping off to the north.

Beverly turned to her men. "Withdraw," she commanded. They all about-faced and trotted south, towards the distant sounds of water, but she looked over her shoulder, concerned the enemy might make another attack. The Norland cavalry, seeing their opportunity, whipped their horses around and spurred them on.

"About face," Beverly called out. Once more, her men pivoted, maintaining their formation. The enemy crashed into them, intent on mayhem, but the discipline of the Mercerians held, once more dealing a savage blow to their opponents, and sending them fleeing.

She looked over her men. Two had been wounded, one severely so, and she ordered him back to the river. The rest she held steady, watching the distant Norlanders for fear they might attempt to repeat their tactics.

The morning wore on and still, she watched, intent on holding their position and keeping the enemy from the rest of the Mercerians. A horseman returned from the south, and she recognized Arnim.

"Wickfield has fallen to the enemy," he said, "so I've sent everyone westward. How are things here?"

She pointed at the distant horsemen. "You tell me. All they do is sit and watch."

"Could they be waiting on reinforcements?" offered Arnim.

"I hope not, it's difficult enough keeping track of this lot."

"Have they attacked?"

"Twice," she said, "and both times we've driven them back. The problem is, we can't withdraw without them sallying forth."

"Your men have been awake all night, they can't keep this up forever."

"I know," said Beverly, "but at least the rest of our party is safe for the moment."

"Not for long, though, unless we can find a new ford."

"You should return to them," said Beverly. "They need you now more than ever."

"What will you do?"

"Delay our friends here as long as I can, then make a run for the river."

"They'll catch you," he warned. "They have faster horses."

"Then we'll sell our lives dearly."

Arnim drew his sword and saluted her. "Be valiant, my friend, and take as many with you as you can." He turned his horse around and rode off at a gallop, back to the south and the escaping Mercerians.

Noon came and went, and still, the enemy watched. Beverly finally resorted to retreating in stages, sending half her men back the distance of an arrow's flight, and then galloping the other half to join them. The tactic proved quite useful, for the enemy failed to attack, contenting themselves to merely move up and keep the range constant. The Guard Cavalry drew closer to the river, though the progress was slow.

It was late in the afternoon when Arnim reappeared.

"We are crossing the river," he announced. "There is a rocky shelf to the southwest forming some rapids. It's navigable, but the current can be fierce. We're using the captured horses to help people across. The other side of the river is rough looking terrain, but it should be more than capable of hiding us from our pursuers should the need arise."

"How long before they're all across?" she asked.

"The last of them were crossing as I left. You'll need to hurry if you want to reach the crossing before nightfall, you've some distance to cover."

"Providing the enemy allows us," reminded Beverly.

"I don't envy you your task," he said. "In the meantime, I must return. I look forward to seeing you south of the river."

She absently watched him ride off, her mind occupied by thoughts. Turning to her men, she gave the command and once more, they began to fall back in stages.

The sun was low in the sky, and Beverly knew it was now or never. Her men had just completed another fall-back and stood, facing the enemy. It had been the same thing all afternoon, fall back and then watch as the enemy slowly advanced. They would then sit for some time, staring at each other across the fields. This time, however, she hoped to surprise them.

"Guard Cavalry," she ordered, "retire."

She wheeled Lightning around and headed southwest at a brisk trot. Her men, eager to obey, followed suit, and the entire line began their retreat.

"They'll be watching," she called out, "so let's keep them guessing." She knew the Norlanders would wait until they halted before advancing and hoped to use that against them. After falling back the requisite distance, she ordered her men into a gallop. The horses, having been tightly reined in all day, were given their head and surged forward. On she drove them, heedless of their formation. The line began to waver as the faster horses stretched their lead.

Beverly risked a glance over her shoulder to see the distant Norlanders. Their horses were now advancing at a gallop, eager to take advantage of the Mercerians' break in formation. She slowed Lightning, letting her men out-pace her.

"Keep going," she shouted, "and get across that river!"

As they galloped off, she brought her mighty Mercerian Charger to a halt. Lightning turned, pivoting in place to allow his mistress to face her enemies.

Beverly drew Nature's Fury, taking a moment to examine the head of the war hammer. Crafted in Sky Metal, it caught the sun's rays, and she couldn't help but think of the smith that had crafted such an exquisite weapon.

"Come, Lightning," she said, "it's time we ended this once and for all."

Beverly felt herself pushed back into the saddle as the great warhorse exploded into action. The enemy, surprised by the lone rider, had slowed, though she could see weapons being drawn. Releasing the great beast's reins, she freed up her left hand to draw her sword. Now, she held both weapons, riding forward with grim determination, ready to bring death and destruction like a messenger of the Gods.

She aimed straight for them, riding between two of their number. Nature's Fury sang out, whipping through the air to strike its target full in the face. She felt the weapon penetrate steel and then tugged it free, just as her sword slashed out to her left. The blade cut deep, slicing through another's leg brace. Lightning didn't stop. Instead, he continued north, eager to deliver his rider to another target.

Beverly's mind focused on the soldier before her, and she swung the hammer upward, striking a Norland horse, sending it rearing up. At that very moment, she stabbed out with her sword at the beast's eye. It turned aside in a desperate attempt to avoid the blow and fell, crushing its own rider beneath its body.

Something smashed down on her back but deflected off the metal plates, and she quickly used her legs to manoeuvre Lightning around. Up came her sword once more, slashing viciously, while her hammer blocked a counterswing. She felt the power building within Nature's Fury, her swings becoming faster and faster, while all she could do was let it flow through her. The hammer drove into a chainmail sleeve, and then she backhanded someone else, flesh giving way before the massive onslaught.

Surrounded by Norlanders, their weapons stabbing forward in a constant push, she parried their blows with her sword, allowing Nature's Fury to wreak its full havoc upon her enemies. Time appeared to slow as she let loose with all the vengeance she could muster.

She struck out yet again but met only empty air. Looking around, she saw them fleeing to the north, leaving their wounded comrades behind. Beverly fumed, unable to come to grips with their retreat, so intent was she on delivering them to the Underworld. Finally, she came to her senses. Her heart pounded in her chest, the blood coursing through her veins, and then she closed her eyes, willing it to slow.

When her mind cleared, she opened them again to view the devastation around her. Scabbarding her sword, she turned towards the river. Moments later, she was riding as fast as Lightning could take her.

The river soon came into view. Arnim was there, watching from the other bank as the Guard Cavalry made their way across the rapids. Beverly's recent fight had left her drained, and she struggled to remain in the saddle, exhaustion threatening to overwhelm her.

As Lightning finally stepped into the water, she felt relief wash over her, but it was not to be. Off in the distance came the sound of horns, and she looked back to see what was left of the entire Norland force descending upon her. She knew, in that instant, that she would never gain the south bank in time.

Beverly turned Lightning around, ready to make one final stand, but before she could draw her weapons, the ground shook, only a minor tremble, but it appeared to be coming from the northern bank. Casting her eyes downward, she watched the ground shake and split as strange tendrils broke through its surface to crawl across the ground and entwine themselves into a wall of thorns.

Instinctively, she turned south to see Albreda. The druid was standing on a rocky outcropping, her hands still tracing arcane symbols in the air, her attention riveted to the enemy horsemen.

Beverly resumed her crossing, finally making the south bank.

THIRTY-ONE

The Old Oak

Fall 964 MC

The winds coming in from the north were strong and cold, promising an early snowfall. Sergeant Garrick pulled his cloak closer, trying to ward off a chill that penetrated deep into his bones. As a Norland scout, he was mounted on a fleet horse, but, like his companions, they were only lightly armoured, the better to maintain the fast pace of their advance.

He looked to his left, to where Talmus rode beside him. "'Tis a cold day," he said.

"So it is," Talmus responded. "Far too cold to be out here in the middle of nowhere."

"You forget," said the sergeant, "we are close to a village called Uxley. There'll be warm shelter there, you can be assured."

"I hope so, for my fingers are growing numb."

They had gone no more than a mile when the flakes began to fall, drifting down from on high to swirl around them. Talmus grunted, causing Garrick to glance at his companion once more.

"Cheer up, Talmus, it's melting even as it falls. Winter's not here yet."

"No, but it's close."

The road meandered slightly to the east and then turned south once again, revealing a sleepy little village in the distance.

"There, you see?" said Garrick. "We're almost there."

"Finally," said Talmus, reaching for his sword.

"Hold," said Garrick, "they may be friendly."

"Friendly? They're Mercerians, for Saxnor's sake!"

Garrick smiled. "They rose in rebellion against their queen. We are the liberators here. Merceria will be ours without bloodshed."

"You really believe that?"

Garrick shrugged. "Perhaps, but I shall be on my guard nonetheless."

"A wise move. Now, let us ride into this place and see what they have to offer."

The sergeant looked back over his shoulder. "Come on, men, there's warmth ahead."

The road ran by a small stream, leading them past a series of houses with closed doors and drawn shutters.

"They must have seen us coming," said Talmus.

"Can you blame them? It's not every day an army comes through. Do you see any signs of movement?"

"No," said Talmus, "but I see smoke coming from a chimney." He pointed towards a large building, sitting beside a giant oak tree.

"Looks like a tavern," said Garrick.

They moved closer to see two men sitting beneath the great tree.

"Welcome, strangers," said the older man, "and welcome to Uxley village. Are you the queen's men?"

"No," said Garrick, "we're Norlanders."

The old man slowly smiled. "All the better for us," he said. "Come inside, friend, and let your men warm up. I'll have Sam, here, lead you to the stables."

The sergeant called his men to a halt. "Dismount," he ordered, then detailed two to escort the horses. The rest filed inside to find a cozy and warm tavern.

"Come, sit," urged the old man. "I'm Arlo Harris, proprietor of the Old Oak. Let me get you gentlemen a drink. It's not every day we get to meet our liberators."

"Liberators?" said Talmus.

"Oh, yes," said Arlo, "they told us you'd be coming."

"Who's they?" asked Garrick, growing suspicious.

"Agents of King Valmar," said Arlo. "They said you lot would be coming to keep the peace. Is that not so?"

The sergeant's shoulders relaxed. "Yes, that's us, my friend."

He took a seat, his companion sitting across from him. There were only eight others here, locals keeping their own counsel, but the entrance of the Norlanders had quieted them.

Arlo went behind the bar, pouring drinks as the other scouts entered.

The old tavern keeper brought over two tankards, dropping them onto the table with a flourish. "There you go, a nice mulled cider to ward off the first chill of winter."

"Thank you, my good man," said Garrick.

"Have you ridden far this day?" asked Arlo. "You look chilled."

"To the bone," replied Talmus. "This is not the time of year I'd choose to be out riding."

Arlo looked around. "Only a dozen? Is this all your men, or are others on the way? I only ask because I'm preparing food."

"You seem very welcoming for a conquered people," said Talmus.

"Conquered?" said Arlo. "More like rescued. The queen was an overbearing despot, much like her father. We're well pleased to be rid of her."

Talmus couldn't help but smile. He took a drink, tasting the thick, rich flavour of the cider.

"This is good," he said, draining the cup. "I'll have some more."

"As you wish," said Arlo. He nodded to a brown-haired waitress who was serving the other Norlanders. Arlo made his way across the room, stooping to gather more tankards from beneath the bar.

Garrick felt his body begin to relax as the drink settled into his stomach. "W'as this?" he said, his words slurring. He blinked, then tried to speak once more. "Wh'"

He felt the grip of fear and tried to stand. The tavern keeper was staring at him from behind the bar, a smile growing on his face.

The sergeant's legs wouldn't work. He looked over at Talmus, but the man had fallen head first onto the table. Garrick's mind started racing as the brunette made her way across the room. Something about her demeanour shook him to his core and then, from somewhere, she produced a sword.

The last thing he saw was the iron blade plunging into his chest, and then he collapsed as everything went dark.

Sam Collins led the two warriors north, across the bridge.

"The stables are just up here," he said, "on the right. Once we've got your horses taken care of, you can return to the tavern, if you like."

Each of them led two horses, the intent being to return for the rest once the first group was settled.

"Here it is," said Sam. He directed them through a large door and into the stables. "Take the stall on the end there," he said.

Sam watched as one of the Norlanders walked his horses to the end of the structure. The warrior held the two reins in his left hand while he opened the stall door with his right. He never saw inside the stall, for as soon as he unlatched the door, an arrowhead blossomed from his chest, followed by a second which struck him in the throat.

The Norland scout fell to the ground without uttering a sound. His companion, busy with his own horses, suffered a similar fate for he too appeared to sprout arrows. He was standing there one moment, looking down at the door handle, then the next he was staring at an arrow that had gone straight through him, its head emerging from his chest. Only a gurgle escaped his lips, then he collapsed.

Gorath emerged from the hayloft, along with his ranger companions.

"Good shots," said Sam.

"We aim to please," replied the Orc.

"Now we must hasten back to the Old Oak," said Sam.

"I'm sure Hayley has things under control," said Gorath.

"Still," said Sam, "I'd feel better knowing for sure."

Hayley looked around the common room. "They're all dead," she announced.

"And justly so," said Arlo. He spit on the dead Norland sergeant. "Filthy invaders. How dare they come into Merceria!"

"I might remind you there's still plenty more where they came from," said Hayley. "We need to get moving. Can you take care of the bodies?"

"Consider it done," said Arlo.

"Good, now it's time for phase two."

"Phase two?"

"Yes, we have blinded their army by taking out their scouts. Now we must move in and nip at their ankles."

"That doesn't sound very devastating," said Arlo.

"Nor is it meant to be," she replied. "But we must slow them down to allow others to get into position. Make sure you bar the doors as I leave."

"You don't have to tell me twice," replied the tavern keeper.

Hayley watched from the rooftop of the church as the next group of Norland cavalry approached. She was lying just behind the peak, safe from discovery.

"What do you make of it?" she asked.

"I'd say almost thirty men, this time," said Gorath. "I doubt we'll see many more."

"I suppose we'll have to take what we can get," she replied. "Give the signal."

Gorath climbed down to the edge of the roof and waved to a distant sentry, while Hayley rolled over onto her back and strung her bow.

"Any time now," she muttered.

Hearing the calls from below, she knew it was time. She stood as best she could and advanced to the peak of the church, nocking an arrow. Down below, just in front of the old oak tree, the large group of riders halted. Several of them had dismounted and were heading towards the main door of the tavern when the first arrow struck, hitting a rider in the lower back, sending him sprawling to the ground, wracked in agony.

It was followed up by more, as Orcs appeared from between the buildings, their warbows easily penetrating the thin armour of their foes.

Hayley let loose with her own arrow, and it sailed across the distance to strike a rider in the back of the head, penetrating his helmet. As the man slumped forward, she reloaded and let another fly forth to strike a soldier's arm, eliciting a cry of agony. The Norlanders tried to react, they really did, but the Orc archers loosed their volleys with such ferocity that it cut them down like chaff.

It was all over in an instant. Hayley pulled a horn from her belt and blew two long notes.

Telethial peered out from among the trees. The enemy forces were trotting down the road, heedless of her presence. She heard the horn sounding in the distance and gave the command. Elven archers stepped from cover, their bows held at the ready.

A shout of alarm rang out among the Norlanders. Several of them urged their horses off the road, hoping to neutralize the threat.

The Elves let their arrows fly, and they raced across the gap in a single volley, striking riders and mounts alike. Many fell, but the rest responded with surprising speed. Orders were shouted, and the entire column turned in place, then rushed for the wood line.

Telethial saw the threat, even as she loosed another arrow. "Back," she commanded.

Her archers moved as quickly as they could, but the Norland cavalry descended on the Elves with a fury. The Elven leader saw a rider take the head off of one of her archers and swore. Turning, she let loose with another arrow, smiling as it hit home.

Suddenly, a rider appeared to her left, and she dove out of the way just as it rode past, hoofbeats heavy in her ears. Getting to her feet, she drew her sword, the Elven blade glowing faintly with magic.

Another horse came at Telethial, and this time she stood her ground, holding her sword two-handed. Closer, the enemy came until finally, she slashed out, the blade humming as it cut through flesh and bone, taking the horse's legs out from beneath it, but the beast fell towards her. Telethial felt the great bulk strike her, and then all went black.

Herdwin waited, listening to the sound of the distant battle. It was hard, sitting and doing nothing while others fought, but he knew that he must do his part. He looked down his line of Dwarves, their heavy arbalests ready to strike fear into the enemy. Behind them stood the axe wielders, prepared to leap forward should the enemy choose to close the distance. If things went badly, he would have little choice but to fight and die, for Dwarves were slow, and they would easily be overrun.

He watched as the enemy column rode past, riders out to the side, guarding the centre column with its heavily armoured warriors. Off in the distance, a horn sounded, signalling the attack.

Farther south, he knew the Elves would be doing their part, and so he readied his soldiers, holding his hand up in a fist to call their attention.

The Dwarves fell silent, each one watching his every move. First, he opened his hand and held up two fingers, signalling his intent for them to target the outriders, then he lowered his hand quickly, the signal to attack, and bolts flew from the steel bowed weapons.

The first volley cut down five riders, many with multiple hits. The arbalesters then stood, using their winches to reload the bulky weapons.

The Norlanders, surprised by the initial volley, hesitated, unsure of what was happening. Then, someone in the centre of the column shouted out orders. The armoured warriors began spreading out to the left and right of the road, moving slowly to maintain their discipline even in the face of the enemy volley.

Herdwin glanced at his warriors. Most of them were still reloading, but a small portion were poised for another shot. He gave a sharp whistle, and the axe wielders moved up to stand closer, barely three paces behind their comrades.

The enemy cavalry began turning to face outward, half of them directly at the Dwarves. The officer's sword came down, and the line trotting forward, straight towards them.

"Three," yelled Herdwin, in the Dwarven tongue. His arbalesters knelt, ready to let loose.

"Two," he called as the ground began to tremble. Bolts flew out, striking down six enemies.

"One," he shouted.

The axe wielders took five paces forward and raised their shields to present a wall of steel, then a second rank came forward, placing their shields over the heads of those in front.

Herdwin took his place in the third rank, ready to cut down any that might penetrate the shield wall. He drew his hammer, noting the dents and scratches it had accumulated over the years, suddenly struck by the idea that he needed to forge himself a new one.

The horsemen smashed into the Dwarven line with a thunderous crash. One of them reared up, striking the shields, the sound of horseshoes ringing out as the beast struggled to climb the mountain of steel.

The top of the wall began to collapse under the weight, and Herdwin saw disaster looming. He ran towards the horse, calling out in his native tongue. One of the Dwarves in the rear rank saw him coming and cupped his hands. Herdwin planted his foot as the warrior heaved, and he catapulted to the top of the shield wall, now held aloft by his compatriots. He struck out, driving his hammer into the panicked horse. The Norland rider, thrashing his horse mercilessly, ignored him, concentrating on collapsing the top of the wall, but the Dwarf had no such worries. He struck out with his hammer again, smashing it into the hapless rider's thigh. The chainmail held, resisting penetration, but Herdwin felt bone crunch beneath the blow.

The horse, already panicked beyond measure, fell to the side, crashing in among the hapless Dwarves. Its rider, crushed beneath the weight of his horse, screamed in agony.

Now there was a hole in the Dwarven line, and the Norlanders were quick to take advantage of it. They were experienced horsemen and used the bulk of their horses to force in against the gap. Wider and wider it became until five men could ride abreast.

Herdwin ran across the remains of the shield wall and leaped, screaming, his hammer held two-handed over his head. He struck a rider on the helmet and heard a pop, then fell in amongst the horse's legs.

He rolled, desperate to free himself from danger, but hooves stomped all around him. His hammer struck out, and he felt bone give way as a horse screamed in agony and fell to the side, clearing his view for but a moment.

A sword struck his helmet, glancing off the metal and ringing out loudly. Herdwin, shaking his head, tried to clear his vision, counter-attacked, swinging high. The tip of his weapon caught a wrist, and then he saw a hand fly through the air, still grasping a sword.

A volley erupted somewhere behind him, and he turned to see three riders go down, their mounts riddled with bolts. His head was swimming now, his eyesight blurred, and he struggled to focus on the melee before him. He struck out once more, feeling his hammer scrape along a sword, but then his weapon was knocked aside, and he felt pain as steel bit into his side, penetrating his chainmail.

Staggering to his feet, his hand instinctively went to his wound, but then the world spun, and he fell, his eyes staring up as doom loomed over him. A Norlander raised his sword in triumph just as a bolt took him in the back of the head, its point protruding from his eye socket. The now-dead warrior fell forward, burying the hapless Dwarf.

∼

Victor Marsh was an experienced warrior. Years of raiding the fields of Bodden had taught him much, and his heart jumped in excitement as he heard the enemy horns sound. This was it, he thought, the moment of truth, a test of steel on steel that would determine the fate of two kingdoms.

The column slowed, and he ached to race forward, but discipline held him in place. From in front came the sounds of battle, the clash of weapons as enemies met. He yearned to ride forward, but his captain simply halted them, looking south towards the expected danger.

A thin mist was drifting up the road, a mist that couldn't possibly exist. It wafted towards them, thickening as it came, and he strained to see what was held within. It drew closer to the front of the column and then a strange whistling sound came to his ears. Soldiers started yelling out in pain, and he rose in the stirrups to try to see over the heads of his comrades.

Before him, riders began to fall, as if brushed from the saddle by some strange wind. The whistling noise continued, then something small flew past his face, cutting his cheek. He turned, looking behind him to see another warrior, a strange fragment of bone protruding from his eye. All around him, his comrades began to drop, while horses reared up in a panic, and then the strange mist enveloped everything.

Victor drew his sword as his eyes tried to penetrate the thick white blanket. Something small brushed past him, like a child, and then another. He had a brief sense that it was a lizard, but he dismissed the thought, for surely such a thing could not be!

A sharp pain caused him to look down to see a bone dart protruding from his leg, and he absently plucked it free, holding it up before his face. As he did so, another struck his chest, digging deep into his padded armour. Pain lanced up his leg as yet another struck him and then his horse collapsed, throwing him to the ground.

Years of riding had taught him how to survive, and so he kicked his feet clear of the stirrups to avoid being crushed. Rolling over, he saw what appeared to be a lizard man looming over him, a vicious-looking spearhead staring him in the face. Victor struck out wildly, desperately trying to deflect the attack, but the diminutive creature simply pulled back his weapon, allowing Victor's blade to pass harmlessly through the air.

The lizard-like creature stepped forward once more, driving the spear into Victor's chest. The Norlander felt it penetrate his armour, felt the bone tip dig past his ribs, and then his lungs collapsed. The whole world was in chaos as he struggled to understand what was happening. His opponent ran past him, ignoring his pleas for help.

THIRTY-TWO

To Battle

Fall 964 MC

Baron Fitzwilliam pulled his horse to a stop. "Do you hear that?" he asked.

"The sound of battle," said Heward. "It seems the fight has begun."

"Get the men into formation," ordered the baron. "You know what to do."

"Yes, my lord."

Heward turned his horse, calling out orders. The men began spreading out right and left, their spears held high, the tips reflecting the morning sun. To their rear, the heavier knights trotted into position behind the rapidly forming front line.

"Keep the archers in the middle," said Fitz. "I don't want them exposed on the flanks."

"Yes, General," said Heward. The knight spurred his horse, galloping off to issue yet more orders.

"I wish Albreda were here," Fitz said.

"Where is she?" asked Aldwin.

"I'm not sure, but most likely where she is needed most."

Aldwin looked back at the army. They were marching smartly into place, their faces masks of confidence.

"They seem calm," the smith remarked.

"Appearances can be deceiving, my boy. Most of them are dreading the coming fight, but we, as leaders, give them something to keep their minds busy."

"Such as forming up?"

The baron smiled, "You learn quickly, Aldwin. You do the family proud."

"I still don't understand why I'm here," he said. "What can I possibly add?"

Fitz turned to him, looking him directly in the eyes. "One day," he said, "Beverly will rule Bodden, and you shall be tasked with running the place when she's not around. Every leader should know the horrors of war if only to keep them at bay. Do you understand?"

"I believe I do," said Aldwin, "but this isn't my first battle if you remember."

"True, it isn't, but it may well be my last, and it's comforting to have family close at hand."

"Your last? Are you ill?"

"No," replied Fitz, "but I'm getting far too old for all of this. War is for the young, not ancient men like me." He looked at Aldwin, noticing his look of alarm. "Fear not, my boy, I shall do my duty this day."

"Will that be enough?" asked Aldwin. "The enemy outnumbers us significantly."

In answer, the baron smiled, "It is not the first time it has been thus. It seems to be our lot in life to be constantly outnumbered by our enemies, and yet still, we prevail."

"Why is that?"

"We are a warrior culture," said Fitz, "and cannot contemplate defeat."

"And how shall we defeat them today?"

"The head of their column is under attack even as we speak," said Fitz, "hence the noise in the distance. They will withdraw back this way to get clear and regroup, but when they do, they will spot us here, with the army from Tewsbury."

"But our men are tired," said Aldwin, "they've marched for days with little rest."

"True, but we will be defending."

"You're sure of that?"

"Our foes cannot leave us in their rear, especially when they cannot advance. They will have no choice but to attack."

"How will you defeat their cavalry?" asked Aldwin.

"By neutralizing their mobility," said Fitz. "Tell me, how would you deal with the threat of their horses?"

"A shield wall?" offered the smith.

"A good tactic. We used the very same thing against the Knights of the

Sword at the Battle of the Crossroads during the civil war, though it almost ended in ruin."

"But you think it'll work here?"

"I do. At the Crossroads, we had to repel knights, but here, the Norlanders are a different foe. Their horses are lightly armoured, and it is they that shall be targeted."

"A horseman without a mount is a prime target," said Aldwin.

Fitz smiled, "You seem to have picked up Beverly's appreciation of tactics. Maybe you'll become a general one day."

"No," said Aldwin, "I'm content being a smith. I've far more interests than war."

"Good, leave the fighting to Beverly. There's no sense in having more military officers in the family."

"I'm worried about her."

"So am I, my boy," said the baron, "but we must trust that the Gods will watch over her."

"I didn't take you for the religious type, my lord."

"I'm not, but looking back on the past few years, I have to wonder if someone up there isn't watching over us. An all-seeing creature of some type. I'm sure that fits the definition of a god, don't you?"

"And here I thought we all managed to make our own fate."

"Perhaps we do," said Fitz, "who's to say? The Kurathians believe in the Saints, but the Orcs follow the advice of their Ancestors. We can't all be right, can we?"

"I'm afraid I'm not educated in such things," said Aldwin, "but I know people. You'll win today, that much I know, and Beverly will return to us, for it must be so."

"Why would you say that?" he asked.

"Because to think otherwise is unacceptable," said Aldwin.

The baron returned his gaze to his front. "Ah," he said, "it appears we have been spotted."

In the open field that sat before them, a distant group of horsemen, no more than a dozen, appeared from the far trees. The effect of the baron's forces was pronounced, for they quickly turned, riding back into cover.

"I expect we'll see more of them soon enough," said Fitz, then turned to examine his lines. His own men had formed up in tightly packed rows, with his footmen in front and the archers just behind, in a second rank. Heward sat among the horsemen, along with Prince Alric.

"Now, we must be patient," he said.

～

Chief Urgon stood amongst his hunters. "I wish we could have brought more," he grumbled.

"There was insufficient time, my chief," said Tarluk, "and we had to leave a garrison to protect Hawksburg."

"True enough, and yet I wish Redblade were here. Long have I yearned to fight at her side."

"The Ancestors will watch over us," said Tarluk.

"So they shall," agreed Urgon.

They waited on a slight rise, on the left flank of the baron's forces, watching the horsemen in the distance. The Norlanders, reacting to the sight of the Mercerians, were now forming up in the distance, a massive line of cavalry that made for an intimidating sight.

"They outnumber us," said Tarluk.

"So they do," said Urgon, "but their leader seems lacking in his tactics. See how he masses his horses for a straight-on attack?"

"Why does he not flank us?" asked Tarluk.

Urgon scanned the tree line, looking east. "There," he said, pointing, "he has moved his horse archers to allow them to outflank the Mercerians."

"Their arrows will destroy the line!" said Tarluk.

"No," said Urgon, "for we shall save them."

More than five hundred Norland cavalry advanced slowly, in two lines, opposed by little more than half that number.

"Where is their cavalry?" demanded Lord Hollis.

"I have no idea, my lord," said Lord Rupert of Chilmsford.

"Have you any idea of their numbers?"

"Our information says they have no more than three hundred men, my lord, the bulk of which we see before us."

"Then who attacked our advance guard?"

"Skirmishers. Nothing more than a nuisance, really."

"Enough of a nuisance that we had to regroup," said Hollis. "I need that village taken, even if we have to burn it to the ground. It blocks our way to Wincaster."

"I shall redouble our efforts, my lord."

"See that you do, Rupert. In the meantime, I will assume direct command of this northern group. We shall sweep these Mercerians from the battlefield as quickly as we can, then swing south to press on to the capital."

"Yes, my lord," said Lord Rupert, turning around.

Hollis watched him head south, then turned his attention once more to the thin line of Mercerians to the north.

"I admire your bravery," he said aloud, "but it will not save you. I shall have my horse archers rain down a hail of arrows, then break your precious shield wall."

～

Captain Galway smiled at the distant sight. As the commander of the Norland horse archers, he was confident, for none of the Mercerian cavalry could match the swiftness of his horsemen.

He began the advance, his men's bows already strung. They would proceed to within a hundred paces, then fill the sky with their arrows, and if the Mercerians moved to threaten them, then so much the better. He and his men would turn tail and ride off into the distance, only to repeat the tactic.

Galway looked again to the distant Mercerians. A slight rise stood to the east of the enemy line, yet their fool of a commander had failed to place men there, meaning they were drastically short of soldiers. He nodded to his signalman to sound the horn and the line sped up, rapidly drawing nearer to their prey.

Closer and closer they came until he felt they were at the optimum range for a volley. Halting, he waited to see if the enemy showed any signs of reaction, but they held firm.

"Ready arrows," he called out.

All down the line arrows were nocked.

"Loose arrows," he commanded.

Bowstrings snapped, sending their volley flying towards the thin enemy line.

～

"Now!" shouted Urgon. "Now is our chance!" He stood, holding his sword aloft, the blade gleaming with magic. "For the Ancestors!"

Orcs erupted from the long grass, streaming down the small hill in a mass of roaring and screaming. The enemy horsemen, intent on the effects of their volley, were staring at the distant Mercerian line when the yells of the Orcs drew their attention. Several of them managed to loose off arrows, but they were hastily aimed with most landing wide of their mark.

Urgon led the Orcs directly into the Norland archers. His sword rang out, slicing through an archer's leg and cutting into his mount. The creature reared up, and the man fell from the saddle. Ignoring him, Urgon kept running, slicing again, his blade lopping off some poor fool's hand. He felt the power of the Ancestors flowing through him, driving him forward in the ancient tradition of a berserker.

A horse went down, kicking and screaming, and the Orc chief leaped up, landing, sure-footed, on its body, his sword striking left and right. An arrow took him in the shoulder, but he ignored it, screaming out a challenge. All around him, the Orcs of the Black Arrow wreaked havoc, cutting down the hapless Norland horsemen and sending their survivors fleeing in fear.

$$\sim$$

Herdwin felt a tug on his legs, and then he was dragged across the ground. He looked up to see a familiar face.

"Dame Hayley," he said, "where did you come from?"

"The rangers have driven the Norlanders out of Uxley," she said. "We saw you go down."

The Dwarf leaped to his feet, but his head spun, and he instantly regretted the action.

"Steady now," said Hayley, "you've taken quite a hit."

"My Dwarves…" he started.

"Are fine," she replied. "They held off the attack and pushed the Norlanders back. The enemy now withdraws to the north."

Herdwin removed his helmet, letting the cool air refresh him. "And Telethial?"

"I have no news," said the high ranger, "but the enemy sent a strong force her way."

"What can we do to help?" he asked.

"Form your troops up here, across the road, and my rangers will take the right flank. We'll advance slowly and keep harassing the enemy."

"I've lost my bearings," complained the Dwarf.

"I'm not surprised," noted Hayley, "anyone else would have been crushed to death." She pointed to the west. "Over there is where Telethial led her ambush while Lily was farther north. The enemy cavalry has withdrawn to regroup. We need to press them to stop that from happening."

"I see," said Herdwin, "it's all about keeping them moving, a clever tactic."

"If we give them time to think, they'll realize we lack the numbers to defeat them."

"Understood."

"Are you sure you're up to this?"

"I'll be fine," he assured her, "just had the wind knocked out of me, that's all."

Baron Fitzwilliam watched as the remainder of the Norland archers withdrew. The Orcs had surprised the enemy, but he knew they wouldn't get a second chance. Even as they returned to their previous position, the enemy was moving more cavalry forward.

"They're getting ready to charge," he said.

"They vastly outnumber us," warned Aldwin.

"Yes, but you have to understand horses."

"I'm afraid I don't grasp what you mean."

"Then, watch and learn."

The Norland cavalry swept across the battlefield. These were not the lightly armoured raiders of the north, but their heavier mounts, intent on destroying their enemy.

The baron watched closely, maintaining a calm demeanour. Only the tight grip on the reins of his horse betrayed any sign of worry.

Closer the enemy came, shaking the very ground with the thundering of their hooves. Fitz watched men walking up and down the Mercerian lines and knew the sergeants were doing their jobs. The Norlanders lowered their spears, ready for the final charge, but at that precise moment, the Mercerians began shouting out orders. Spears appeared all down the line, their butts firmly anchored into the ground.

The men of Norland urged their mounts forward, but the wall of steel broke their resolve. Horsemen began pulling back on the reins, desperate to avoid death at the end of a Mercerian spear. Some horses balked, while some swerved to the side, careening into others. The charge became absolute chaos as riders turned this way or that in an attempt to avoid being run through.

Aldwin saw a horse falter, its rider tumbling from his seat. The great beast pitched forward, smashing into a group of spearmen and opening up a hole in the Mercerian line. The smith was about to call out in warning, but then a knight stepped forward, resplendent in his armour. A Norland horseman rode down on him, but he remained steady, holding tight to a hatchet and shield. As his foe neared, the knight threw the weapon, and it sailed through the air, directly at the horse's head. The great beast swerved as it came close, throwing the rider off balance but only slowing their advance slightly.

"It's Sir Preston," announced Fitz, watching in horror as the rider bore down on the hapless knight.

"He seems calm," said Aldwin. "What do you suppose he's up to?"

"We shall have to wait and see," said the baron.

Sir Preston knelt, grabbing something which lay at his feet. Onward came the horse, and then, seemingly at the last possible moment, the knight raised the spear which lay hidden in the grass. It struck the horse square in the chest, sending its rider pitching forward. A scream of agony erupted from the horse, to be immediately drowned out by the noise of combat. Sir Preston moved to the side, drawing his sword in a smooth, practised manner. As the Norland rider fell to the ground, the knight took two steps forward and drove his blade into the hapless man's chest.

"A remarkable display of bravery," said Fitz, as Mercerians scrambled to fill the gap in their line.

Norlanders rode up and down the wall of spears, hacking away at the tips, cursing at their enemy. Finally, they gave up in frustration and began making their way south, to rejoin their companions.

Fitz drew his sword, raising it high in the air. He held it only a moment, then swept it down. No sooner had he done so than horns sounded behind the Mercerian lines.

"Now," said Fitz, "we shall teach them the folly of their ways."

Hundreds of arrows sailed out from behind the Mercerian lines. The archers had aimed high, and their missiles arced over their own men to come crashing down onto the retreating Norland horsemen.

The arrows had little effect on the armoured enemy, but their mounts were an entirely different matter, as they plunged down from the sky, sinking into soft horseflesh. Animals wailed in distress, causing Aldwin to wince in sympathy. He saw one such beast rushing eastward, dragging its unfortunate rider along the ground by the stirrups.

A second horn sounded, and Aldwin watched as the Mercerian lines parted, creating a gap. Through this space poured horsemen, led by none other than Prince Alric. At his side rode Jack Marlowe, his blue cape billowing behind him. It was a magnificent sight, for they were followed by the Prince's own bodyguard, fierce men of Weldwyn, determined to show their courage this day. The enemy had been withdrawing slowly, their horses tired from their earlier exertions. Alric's troops sliced into their lines, penetrating the undisciplined mob deeply, cutting down riders left and right.

The baron's attention was solely on the prince, for he was deep into the mass of Norland cavalry now, standing in the stirrups as he raised his sword high. Lord Jack was beside him, slashing away with quick, deliberate strikes, cutting down enemies as they went.

Fitz raised his sword once more, twirling it in the air. Three blasts from a horn sounded, signalling the cavalry to withdraw. He watched carefully, concerned his call might not be heeded, but his worry was for naught. The men of Weldwyn answered the call and broke off their engagement, sending the remaining enemy horsemen fleeing in panic. Turning around, they trotted back to the Mercerian lines.

Aldwin watched as they passed by the footmen who closed up the gap. "That was neatly done," said the smith.

"It shows what disciplined cavalry can do," said Fitz. "These Norland warriors are brave, but they seem to have little experience in set-piece battles."

"Could it be their leaders?" mused Aldwin.

"You may be right," said Fitz, "but we'll soon see if their commander learns from his mistakes."

"You think they'll attack again?"

"Of course," said Fitz, "this battle is only just beginning." He turned to an aide. "Have Sir Preston come and see me," he said, "I would like to talk to him."

"Yes, my lord," replied the man, riding off.

"You intend to rebuke him?" asked Aldwin.

"No, I intend to congratulate him," said Fitz. "We seldom see such individual bravery on the battlefield."

"I didn't notice Sir Heward," remarked the smith.

"He's in reserve," said the baron. "I am not yet ready to commit all of our horse. The sun has yet to reach its full height, and there will be much more fighting to come."

Aldwin looked at the blood-soaked field before them. "Such destruction and death," he said.

"Yes, with more to follow. How many dead would you say?"

"More than fifty," said Aldwin, "perhaps as many as a hundred?"

"And yet they still outnumber us," said Fitz. "We must kill three for every soldier we lose if we hope to win this battle."

"They don't outnumber us by that much, do they?"

"No, but our survivors will still have to march to Eastwood, or did you forget there's another army on the loose."

"I wish Beverly were here," said Aldwin.

"As do I," said the baron. "She's worth a hundred men on the battlefield."

"My lord," came a voice.

"Ah, Sir Preston," said Fitz, "you have displayed remarkable courage this day."

"I am only doing my duty," said the knight.

The baron looked at him, noting the blood-encrusted armour. "What's this, Sir Preston?" he pointed at the man's arm, which had a cloth wrapped around it. "Tell me you're not injured!"

The knight blushed. "No, my lord, it is a lady's favour."

The baron sat back in surprise. "A lady, you say? Tell me, noble knight, who might this woman be, that has so captured your heart?"

"The lady Sophie, my lord, handmaiden to the queen."

"Indeed?" said Fitz. "Then fortune has smiled upon you, young knight, for you have proven yourself worthy of such affection this day. Continue your good work, Sir Preston."

"Thank you, my lord," replied the knight. "And now, with your permission, I shall return to my men."

"Of course," said Fitz, "and give them my thanks for their bravery this day."

"Thank you, my lord. I'm sure your words of encouragement will be well met." He turned, riding off.

"He's very formal," said Aldwin.

The baron laughed, "Yes, he is. Let's hope he'll learn to relax a little now that he has a woman in his life."

THIRTY-THREE

Fate

Fall 964 MC

"How did you find me?" asked Beverly.

"You forget," said Albreda, "a part of me is in that hammer of yours. We are connected, you and I, by powers that few can understand."

"We must get our injured to help," said Beverly. "Did you happen to bring Aubrey with you?"

"I'm afraid not, and the situation is perilous, to say the least."

"Why, what's happened?"

"Even as we speak, Norland troops are outside of Uxley," said Albreda.

"Uxley," said Beverly, "that far? What of Hawksburg and Tewsbury?"

"Bypassed. It seems they planned this invasion very carefully. They took us quite by surprise."

"Shouldn't you be there, with them?" asked Beverly. "After all, you're our most powerful mage."

"I'm flattered that you think so," the druid replied, "but the truth is that the battle of Uxley is lost unless your men can be brought to bear."

"My men? You mean the Guard Cavalry? How can that be, we've less than two dozen left."

"They will not be alone," said Albreda, "but we must move quickly, it will take some time to get them all through the gate."

"What about Gerald?"

"His best chance of survival is to bring him with us," Albreda replied, "for all our healers are gathered there."

"Then let us not waste another moment," the knight replied.

It took quite some time to reach the gate. The Mercerians that had fled Galburn's Ridge collapsed in exhaustion as they entered the Saurian temple.

"Rest your men," bid Albreda, "for the battle begins tomorrow, and they must be ready."

"How can you be sure?" asked the red-headed knight. "Did you have a vision?"

"I did," said Albreda, "and it boded ill for the realm."

"How so?" asked Beverly.

"I saw a great defeat," explained the druid, "with many dead littering the battlefield and above it all flew the flag of Merceria."

"Your prophecies have proven accurate in the past."

"Yes," the druid admitted, "but not always in the way I interpret them."

"Do you think it's as dire as your visions seem to indicate?"

"I do," said Albreda, "and yet I sense that we can turn the tide, providing the timing is right. In order to do so, we must arrive with time to strike."

"By my estimate," said Beverly, "it'll take the best part of a morning to move my horsemen through." She paused, suddenly struck by a thought. "What of our horses?" she asked. "The gate in Uxley is down a well."

"Did I not mention Master Hearn?"

"No," said Beverly, "why, what has he to do with all of this?"

"While I have been searching for you, he has been moving dirt. By the time we arrive, he should have an exit tunnel ready for use."

"And if he doesn't?" asked Beverly.

"Then we shall be no worse off than if we hadn't tried," mused the druid. "Now, get some rest, it will be a busy day tomorrow."

Beverly stood watching as the last horsemen entered the magic portal. The flame diminished, and she waited as it recharged.

"Almost done," she said. "The wounded are through as well as our horses."

"The rest will have to remain behind for now," said Albreda. "I must hasten to Uxley to oversee the battle and cannot remain to activate the gate."

"Are you sure they will be safe?"

"The temple here is ample protection against anything they might encounter."

"I wish we could use your recall spell."

"So do I," said Albreda, "but the fact is that Uxley has no magic circle to travel to, not yet at any rate."

"I imagine the queen will be eager to build one there, after this," said Beverly.

"She will, but there are a lot more important places where one is needed first. I'm afraid it will have to wait."

The green flame leaped to life once more. Albreda uttered words of power, pressing the runes at the base of the fire.

"It is time," she said.

Beverly stepped forward, touching the surface of the flame, and then vanished, reappearing a moment later on the other side, briefly lit by its glow, then the flame diminished, and she was gone from sight.

Albreda turned to Lightning, holding out her hand. The great stallion moved forward, nuzzling her palm.

"There, there," soothed the druid, "you will be with her soon enough. We have only to let the flame recharge, and then you can step through." She placed her hand to the horse's forehead and closed her eyes. "See her safely through this," she said, "for the fate of the realm may count on it."

The flame returned to its natural state and Albreda released Lightning. She uttered the magic words once more, touching the runes. Moments later, the flame sprang to life. She could see Beverly on the other side, peering back at her and smiled as she sent Lightning through. The great beast appeared beside Beverly, then the flame once more went dormant

"There," said Albreda, "I have now put events into action. Let us hope it is enough."

∼

The Norland cavalry came into view once more. They were a wall of horse-flesh, two hundred strong, forming a line that stretched to either side as far as Herdwin could see. This, he decided, must be their last attempt to force the Dwarves from the road and clear the way to Uxley.

"Stand by," he called out. The Dwarves brought their weapons to the ready position. They were heavily armoured, these doughty warriors of the mountains, and renowned for being fearless. He fought back the urge to tell them to stand firm. These were professional warriors, there was no need to restate the obvious. The Norlanders had charged three times so far, the last just before noon. Now, with the day wearing on, they had reappeared, determined to push through regardless of opposition.

Herdwin smiled in grim satisfaction. "Let them come, and we shall teach them again the folly of attacking the mountain folk!"

Hayley peered over the ranks of the Dwarves. "We're all set," she said.

The horses came closer until Herdwin could make out individual faces. He raised his arm, holding his weapon high. "Just a little closer," he said to himself.

They were less than ten horse lengths away when the ground caved in. The Dwarves had used their time wisely, digging small holes across the field and then concealing them with the help of the rangers. Now horses pitched forward, throwing their riders from the saddle.

Herdwin swept his arm down, and the Dwarven arbalests sprang to life, sending forth a volley of steel-tipped bolts that ripped through the enemy's armour. When the Dwarves started reloading their cumbersome weapons, Hayley gave the order for her rangers to move up. They loosed off a volley of arrows that dug into the survivors. More horses went down, clogging a field that was already cluttered with the injured and dead.

Hayley saw a group of horsemen to the enemy's rear starting to head east, trying to bypass their defensive position.

"'Ware the flank," she called out.

Gorath moved his Orcs eastward, using the cover of the trees to hide their movements.

"Their numbers are starting to tell," said Herdwin, "they're going to overwhelm us."

"We must do what we can," said Hayley, "and hope that the baron can hold out."

∾

Baron Fitzwilliam saw the enemy massing for another attack.

"Here they come," he said.

Aldwin watched as the enemy drew closer. "Saxnor's beard," he said, "there must be a thousand of them!"

"If not more," replied the baron. "Tell Heward to prepare his men."

An aide ran off to deliver the message while Fitz focused his attention on the troops before them. A massive push was coming, and he began to doubt that his men would survive it.

"Where is the queen?" Fitz asked.

"Still getting into position," said an aide. "Shall I send her a message?"

"No," said the baron, "we'll just have to weather the storm and hope she arrives in time."

~

The Queen of Merceria looked at Captain Montak. The Kurathian was an immense man, even larger than Sir Heward, but whereas Heward looked dangerous, this man looked friendly.

"You may release when ready," she said, nodding her head to him.

Montak spoke little of the common tongue but understood the command. Placing a whistle to his lips, he blasted out three notes.

In front of them, the dog handlers echoed the command, and then the Kurathian Mastiffs were released. The great beasts, the size of ponies and trained to bring down warhorses, surged across the field, quick to pick up the scent of their quarry.

Anna turned in her saddle. "Captain Jaran?"

The archer bowed. "Yes, Your Majesty?"

"Move your bowmen up. You know what to do next."

"Certainly, Majesty."

The Kurathians had been mercenaries, sworn to the service of the Twelve Clans, but defeat on the battlefield had given them a chance at a new life. When they had served the princess during the civil war, she had rewarded them with the one thing that Kurathians prized above all else: Land.

Jaran called out to his men in their native tongue. The archers moved up, following in the wake of the hounds. The mastiffs would tear through the enemy horse, while the job of the bowmen was to finish off the wounded horses and take prisoners. They would use their bows to keep the enemy at bay, but long knives were their preferred method of plying their trade.

Off in the distance, the Norland horses were swarming the baron's lines. The hounds closed the gap quickly and began baying as they picked up the scent.

Jaran held his breath as they struck the enemy. He always thought it strange that such devastation could be so enthralling. The mastiffs flooded across the plain, laying waste to the enemy's horses as if they were a high tide washing away all before them.

~

Heward heard the hounds and knew his time was up. He looked around, spotting Prince Alric in the distance. The prince's horsemen were surrounded by Norlanders, and Heward pushed towards him, cutting down any who stood in his way.

He called to his aide to signal the retreat, for he knew the mighty Kurathian hounds could not distinguish friend from foe. Swinging his axe as he rode, he cleaved through a Norlander's arm, then backhanded his weapon into the man's spine.

The press of horseflesh grew worse, and he slowed, unable to make progress. He could see Alric swinging left and right, his practised, measured strikes clean and efficient. Beside him, fought Lord Marlowe, the Weldwyn cavalier, every bit as brave as his master.

Heward had spent a lifetime in combat, knew the sounds of battle intimately, but there was one sound he feared, and now he heard it as a mastiff's jaws bit down on bones with a sickening crunch. He was willing to fight any foe and had fought countless battles, but the thought of such wanton destruction chilled him to the bone.

"Back, back!" he called out, trying desperately to be heard above the sound of battle.

At last, he caught the attention of Lord Marlowe. The cavalier must have realized the danger, for suddenly he struck out, clearing the opponent before him and then smartly pivoting his horse to face the Mercerian lines. The prince reacted just as quickly, and soon they were retreating. Heward spurred on his horse, dashing for safety as the Norlanders, confused by the sounds, began to seek the source of such a clamour.

The Norland riders were brave, many of them experienced warriors, but never before had they fought such a foe. The mastiffs ripped into their lines, tearing legs from horses and bringing them crashing to the ground, their riders flailing about helplessly, unable to adapt to this new menace.

Heward made for a gap in the lines, his men riding through behind him. As soon as they were safely past, the ranks closed, presenting a wall of shields and spears once more.

The huge knight trotted his horse over to Prince Alric, who was wiping his blade. "My Prince," he said, "you fought well this day."

"As did you," replied the prince. "It was well you warned us, else we would have been caught up in the slaughter." He nodded towards the battlefield.

Heward swivelled his gaze. It was a strange sensation, for from his vantage point, he could see no dogs, but the rear ranks of the enemy horsemen were falling, cut down like wheat by a scythe. The great knight felt the contents of his stomach revolt at the very thought, and bile rose in his throat. He fought it down, then looked away, unable to watch the ruination of a proud army.

"Serves them right," offered Jack Marlowe. "They should have known better than to invade Merceria."

"Who would have thought," said the prince, "that the very animals that were used against us in Weldwyn should prove so useful to us now, in our time of need?"

"I might remind you," said Heward, "that there's still plenty more Norlanders waiting to finish us off."

"So there is," said Alric.

The rangers streamed back from the woods. "There are too many of them," shouted Gorath.

"Form square," called out Herdwin as he turned to Hayley. "Get your rangers behind us, we're going to enclose you."

She watched in amazement as the Dwarves began their intricate manoeuvre. The rear ranks about turned, marching some ten paces and then halted. As this was going on, other Dwarves were moving left and right, forming a thin line to either side. They left a gap, through which the retreating rangers entered the new formation, then Herdwin ordered the ranks closed.

"It's a thin square," said Herdwin, "only two ranks deep. Place your rangers at their backs, and let loose arrows when you can."

Hayley moved up, standing between and slightly behind two Dwarven arbalesters. The metal crossbows were highly effective weapons, but slow to load, and Hayley found herself letting off six arrows for every bolt that sailed forth.

She went to select another arrow and realized she had none left. All around her, the rangers found themselves in a similar state. She drew her sword, preparing for a last stand.

The enemy horsemen had ridden close and were stabbing down at the Dwarves, desperate to break their shield wall.

Off to the east came the sound of horns and Hayley perked up. "What's that?" she called out.

"It sounds like cavalry," said Gorath.

"All our horse are to the north," said Hayley, "with the baron."

The sound rang out again, loud and clear, echoing off the trees, and then horsemen rounded the woods, the banner of Merceria streaming proudly in the chill afternoon air. They were few in number, but beside them ran dozens of ghostly Orcs, their bodies pale and translucent.

"Spirit warriors," said Hayley. "Kraloch has come!"

She watched the new forces slice into the Norland cavalry. There was a titanic clash of steel, and then the Norland troops wavered. Hayley, straining to see what was happening, noticed someone hefting a war hammer on high, the head of it catching the sun before it came crashing down. Only one weapon could have such an effect, and in that instant, Hayley knew that Beverly had come to their rescue.

≈

As panic erupted all around him, Lord Hollis craned his neck, trying to make sense of everything.

"What is happening?" he called out. "Why has our attack stalled?"

"Our men are broken, my lord," said his aide. "They have unleashed great beasts upon us!"

"What are you talking about, man? Come to your senses!"

His aide opened his mouth to speak, but his horse suddenly lurched to the side and then collapsed, taking its rider with it. The Norland lord's eyes went wild in fear as a great beast of a dog tore flesh from bone, then turned its attention on him. It looked like the queen's great mastiff, and he wondered, for a moment, how such a beast had come to be here, instead of in Norland, but then it all became clear as he saw others running amok on the battlefield. It appeared the Queen of Merceria had a secret weapon!

He tore his gaze away from the grisly sight and galloped off as fast as he could manage, fear and adrenaline coursing through him.

≈

"Shall we advance, my lord?" asked Sir Preston.

"No," said Fitz, "we must wait until the mastiffs are once again leashed. They are an effective weapon, but difficult to control. Any sign of the enemy commander?"

"I saw a glimpse of him," offered Aldwin, "or his standard, at least, but once the dogs arrived, it disappeared in the fray."

"Find Heward," ordered the baron. "We'll send his men out once the handlers have arrived."

They watched as Captain Jaran's archers picked their way through the battlefield. They had trained extensively with the mastiff handlers and walked among them with little concern for their welfare. The captain stooped by a fallen Norlander, feeling for a pulse, then slit the man's throat with his long knife.

"Was that entirely necessary?" asked Sir Preston.

"He was likely dying," said Fitz, "and we have few healers to aid the wounded."

"It's still rather distasteful," noted the knight.

The baron turned to him in surprise. "Would you have them suffer on the battlefield?"

"I suppose not, my lord, but it seems so unchivalrous."

"Don't talk to me of chivalry," said Fitz, "this is war, and war is a messy, stinking business."

"Did you hear that?" said Aldwin.

"Hear what?" said Fitz.

"Listen!"

The baron concentrated on the sounds of battle and then heard it. "Saxnor's beard," he said at last. "That's a Mercerian signal. It's calling the cavalry." He looked over his shoulder to where Prince Alric and Heward were chatting.

"But all our cavalry's here," said Aldwin.

"No," said Fitz, breaking into a smile. "No it's not, look," he pointed.

Aldwin looked to the south, where a small group of cavalry rode across the battlefield. Their leader held a hammer high, light glinting off its surface.

"Beverly!" he shouted.

"Saxnor's beard," said Fitz, "I don't know how she got here, but it seems the Gods saw fit to deliver her just in time."

They watched as her men dispatched a group of Norland horsemen. Ghostly figures ran at their sides, and Aldwin rubbed his eyes, not quite believing his own senses.

"What are those?" he asked.

"I have no idea," said Fitz, "but they seem to be on our side."

"They look like Orcs," said Aldwin, his eyes finally focusing.

"Some magic of Kraloch's, no doubt," said the baron.

The mastiffs were starting to settle, many dropping to the ground in exhaustion. The handlers moved forward with leashes to begin the laborious process of collecting them.

"It's over," said the baron.

"Over?" Aldwin replied.

"Yes, the battle. It appears that we've won, despite the odds being against us."

"Perhaps the Gods have favoured us after all," said Aldwin.

"Perhaps," said Fitz, "but I should like to think we won this day because of the superior training of our troops, not by some whim of the Gods."

Beverly struck out with Nature's Fury, collapsing a helmet. The Norland horseman fell, his horse galloping off, riderless. She pivoted to strike again, but the enemy was in full retreat. Small pockets of men were throwing down their weapons, the fight gone out of them. Many looked underfed, and she wondered, briefly, if the rapid advance from Norland had taken too much out of them.

She halted Lightning, then turned in the saddle. Kraloch and Albreda were following along behind them, though still some distance off. Glancing at her hammer, she thought again of the druid's words. Was she connected to Albreda in some strange, mysterious way? She had to admit the thought gave her some comfort. Nature's Fury was forged with heart, but it was the magic of the Whitewood that imbued it.

She urged Lightning into a slow trot and turned towards the Dwarven square. Hayley's archers, emboldened by the charge, had moved forward and were even now picking off stragglers that refused to surrender. Weaving her way through the mass of bodies, the red-headed knight wondered how her allies had survived such a savage assault. Closer she drew until she could see the many bodies of Dwarves who had given their lives this day.

Beverly felt her throat constrict, and tears came to her eyes. "All this death," she uttered.

"Bev!" came a familiar voice.

She spotted Hayley, making her way through the destruction.

"Surprised?" asked the red-headed knight.

"And then some," said Hayley. "How in the Gods' name did you come to be here? Last we heard, you were off in Norland."

"This was Albreda's doing," Beverly replied. "She met us in the Wickford Hills and led us through the gate to Uxley."

"The gate?" said the ranger. "Hasn't she told you it's dangerous?"

"Yes, but we had little choice. Albreda had one of her visions. She saw defeat on the battlefield."

"And so she decided to stack the odds in our favour?" said Hayley.

"So it would seem, and yet I wouldn't have thought such a small group of horsemen could make such a difference."

"But they did," said Hayley.

"It wasn't just us, Kraloch conjured some sort of spirit warriors."

"Yes," said Hayley, "I know, I've seen it before, at the mines near Redridge."

"We'll have to get him to teach it to Aubrey. Speaking of which, where is my cousin?"

"Up at Uxley Hall," said Hayley. "We thought it the best place to treat the wounded. You mentioned Albreda, but have you seen Master Hearn?"

"As a matter of fact, I have, though I imagine he's quite tired. He used his magic to create a tunnel out of the Saurian Temple. Tell me, how is Revi doing?"

"Still sick, I'm afraid, but Aubrey feels she may have a cure in hand."

"A cure? So he hasn't lost his wits?"

"No," said Hayley, "something about the magical flames has infected him. That reminds me, she'll have to check you and your men, as anyone who uses the flames is affected."

"Not seriously, I hope."

"No, those that have only used it a few times seem to suffer no ill-effects. Revi, however, spent days on end staring at the flame, trying to understand it. She would have healed him already, but with the battle looming, she had to conserve her energy."

"So a happy ending for you after all," said Beverly.

"I'm hopeful," said Hayley, "but I've been kept extremely busy myself, planning this battle."

"You planned this?" said Beverly, looking around at the devastation.

"Well, the basic tactics, yes," said Hayley. "Though I didn't know it would be this bad. I tried to think what Gerald would do." She suddenly wore a look of shock. "Saxnor's beard, I just realized he wasn't with you. Is he all right?"

"He'll recover," said Beverly. "He was badly wounded in our flight from Norland. Aldus Hearn placed him in some sort of hibernation until we could get him to a healer. I left him in the good druid's care when we attacked."

"Then you'd best get back to him," said Hayley. "Don't worry, I'll look after this mess."

THIRTY-FOUR

Victory

Fall 964 MC

"Are you sure this will work?" asked Kraloch.

They were in Uxley Hall, looking over the sleeping form of Revi Bloom.

"It should," said Aubrey. "My great grandmother's notes indicate as much."

"You don't sound entirely confident," said the Orc. "Did she have a spell that would help or not?"

"She did," said Aubrey, "but she never got a chance to actually use it."

"Why is that?" he asked.

"She never had need of it. How often do you think someone suffers symptoms similar to Revi's?"

"I suppose I never thought of it that way."

"Now, let me continue with this spell. If it works, I shall have to teach it to you, for there are many people requiring treatment."

She closed her eyes, concentrating. The old familiar tingle buzzed in the air as she began intoning the magical words of power. Warmth spread up her arms and appeared to concentrate in her hands. She opened her eyes to see them glowing a brilliant purple colour, and then she leaned down and touched the still form of Revi Bloom.

The mage's body began to twitch as the light entered him, lingering in his head, then dissipating. He lay still, and Aubrey leaned closer, examining his face.

"Revi?" she said. "Can you hear me?"

His eyes snapped open then looked around, struggling to focus. "Hayley," he said, "is that you?"

"No, it's me, Aubrey. Can you hear me?"

"Of course I can hear you," snapped Revi Bloom. "I'm not deaf, you know." He struggled to sit up on the bed, but his head swam, and he lay back down. "Where's Hayley? I need my lucky charm."

"I'll get her," said Kraloch, making for the door.

"You had us all worried," said Aubrey. "It took a lot of effort to find a cure for you."

"Why?" he asked. "What happened?"

"You became obsessed with the magic flame," she said, "to the point at which you weren't thinking clearly. What can you remember?"

"I remember my mind wandering, free of my body." He struggled to rise again, reaching out for Aubrey's arm. She raised him up until he was sitting comfortably. "I saw things I couldn't explain," he said, "as if my mind was travelling to the ends of the world."

Suddenly, he gripped her arms tightly. "I saw them, Aubrey, I saw them all."

"Saw what?" she asked.

"All the lines of energy, the ley lines."

"And?"

"And I have the answer at last," he said.

"The answer to what?" Aubrey asked.

"We knew there were unused runes in the temples, and now I know what they're for."

"Which is?"

"They can be used," Revi explained, "to reach any area where there's an intersection of the ley lines, whether there's a temple there or not."

"You're saying you can use the flame to travel to any confluence?"

"Yes," he said, "though you can't return, of course, unless there's a temple present. Not only that, but there's no limit to the distance one can travel."

"Oh, but there is," said Aubrey.

"What do you mean?"

"We discovered that even infrequent use can lead to a type of infection in one's mind, that's what affected you."

"But surely you can cure that now," Revi said.

"Theoretically, but it will take time, and we still have much to learn of this strange malady."

"I'm confident in your abilities," said Revi.

"As am I," said Aubrey, "but there are far greater things weighing on my mind at present. While you slept, we were invaded by Norland."

"Typical," said Revi, "wars always crop up to disturb my research."

The door opened, revealing Lady Hayley.

"Revi?" she asked.

"I'm here," he said. "Come to me, I would feel the warmth of your hand."

The ranger moved to the side of the bed, taking the mage's hand and sandwiching it between her own. "I missed you," she said, tears coming to her eyes.

"I am here now, safely returned to your side."

"There's so much I want to say to you," she began.

"And that's my cue to leave," said Aubrey. She made her way to the door, looking back to see the two of them deep in conversation.

Gerald opened his eyes. He was in a strange room that somehow looked familiar while a figure leaned over him, the face slowly coming into focus.

"Gerald, are you with us?"

"Anna, is that you?"

As the image in front of him became clearer, the distinctive blond locks brought a smile to his face. "Where am I?"

"In Uxley Hall," she said, "in my old room."

"Your room?" he said. "Then, where are you sleeping?"

She chuckled, "Alric and I have taken the king's room. Now, you must rest, you've had a bad time of it."

"What happened?" he asked. "How did I get here?"

"Beverly brought you back, and Master Hearn used some kind of spell to preserve you. You were very near death, I'm told."

"The Norlanders..." he said.

"Have been defeated, but not without cost. We took many casualties, many more than we could afford, and we still have to march to Eastwood."

"Eastwood?" Gerald said.

"Yes, they launched a two-pronged invasion. They didn't even stop to take Tewsbury, it caught us completely off guard."

"So you fought them here, in Uxley?"

"We did," Anna confirmed.

"And the others?"

"I'm afraid Telethial is dead, along with a great many of her Elves. Herdwin survived. He sends his regards, by the way. Did I mention he's now on the Nobles Council?"

"Herdwin is?"

"Yes, he's representing the King of Stonecastle."

"Well, I never," said Gerald.

"That's not all. Much has happened in your absence, but I'll fill you in once you've rested."

"You said there's another army to fight?"

"Yes, but I know we'll defeat them," Anna declared.

"How?" Gerald asked. "You just said we took more casualties than we could afford?"

"Yes, but now we have our secret weapon back. You!"

"Me?"

"Yes, with you at my side, I know we'll win."

"I wish I had your confidence," he said, "I tend to be more cautious."

"It's that caution that makes you a great leader," said Anna.

"Did you command the battle?"

"No," she replied, "I relied on my experienced warriors."

"Fitz, then?"

"No," Anna said, "it was Lady Hayley. She proved herself a great leader. By putting down a rebellion and planning this battle, she has proven herself a true defender of the crown."

Epilogue

Winter 964 MC

The Elven Necromancer Kythelia, recently known as Lady Penelope Cromwell, gazed across the windswept land before her. The wind blew in from the west, driving snow through the ruins to settle against the small stone walls that still remained.

"Do you know where we are?" she said.

Her companion, Princess Margaret, cast her eyes around, taking in the bleak landscape.

"No?" she said. "Why, should I?

"Centuries ago," said the Elf, "there was a great battle here between the Elves and the Orcs of this land. The Elves carted off their dead, but the Orcs, vanquished, were left to rot, their bones bleaching in the sun." She gazed up at the winter sky. "Of course, it was summer when they fought, but that matters little for our purposes."

"I see no sign of bones," said Margaret.

"Nor would you," the Elf continued, "for that was long ago. They have returned to the ground and no longer exist within this mortal realm."

"Then why are we here?"

"When a person dies, their spirit is linked to the place of their departure. We shall use that this day to conjure forth the dead."

"We are to animate them?" said Margaret. "They would, I think, make poor warriors."

"No, we will not animate their corpses. They would be, as you said, rather ineffective, and their mortal remains exist no more, in any event. No, instead we shall call forth their spirits and bind them to us."

"But won't they disappear when the spell ends?"

"We shall be using Blood Magic," said the Elf. "They will remain active until we dismiss them."

"I'm not sure I understand," said Margaret.

"The calling of spirits is not unknown to you," said Penelope.

"Yes, but all spells expire."

"In this case, the spells can be maintained."

"For how long?"

"Indefinitely," said Penelope, "though each such spirit raised will consume some of your power."

"How many can I raise?"

"That will depend on the power level you have reached, but likely in the range of six companies."

"Six companies? That's only three hundred souls. How do you expect to create an army with such few numbers?"

In answer, Penelope waved her hand, indicating the robed individuals that roamed the field. "These are my followers," she said, "dedicated individuals who can each raise a hundred or more warriors."

Margaret counted heads, giving up as she reached fifty. "That's quite an army."

"Yes," said Penelope, "an army the likes of which has never before been assembled. Now, are you ready to begin?"

"I am," said Margaret.

"Remember your training. Concentrate on the task at hand and put all else from your mind."

"Yes, Mistress."

Margaret closed her eyes, thinking back to her training. She sought the darkness within her and started calling forth the words that would unleash the power. As her pulse quickened, she felt the rush as her heart started beating rapidly. Energy coursed through her and then she opened her eyes to see the world in shades of grey.

Feeling the presence of spirits all around her, she began the incantation, releasing the magic to flood across the ground in a wave of energy. Snow circled high into the air, driven by unseen forces, and then figures began to materialize. They looked vaguely Human at first, wispy outlines that quickly took the more solid form of Orcs. Then more appeared, dozens of them, and she focused her attention on them, gathering the threads that linked them to the spirit realm.

"Good," said Penelope, "you've done it. Now anchor them in the physical realm."

Margaret did as she was bid. She imagined the threads of their souls and tied them off, keeping them from returning to their natural state of spirit energy. The spell ceased, and she looked at those before her. More than three hundred Orcs stood ready to fight, their faces devoid of emotion, their bodies appearing ghostlike and pale.

"Now," said Penelope, "with the three kingdoms in ruins, the time to strike is nigh!"

<<<<>>>>

Share your thoughts!

If you enjoyed this book, I encourage you to take a moment and share what you liked most about the story.

These positive reviews encourage other potential readers to give my books a try when they are searching for a new fantasy series.

But the best part is, each review that you post inspires me to write more!

Thank you!

Ashes - Chapter One

FROM THE ASHES

Spring 1102 SR* (Saints Reckoning)
(In the tongue of the Orcs)

An arrow sailed through the air, digging into a tree near a deer. Alarmed by the sound, the creature bolted, disappearing deeper into the woods.

A bellow of rage exploded from a nearby bush. Its occupant stood up, his green Orc skin blending in well with the surrounding forest. "I should have had him," he growled.

"There will be more," called out his Orc companion. "To be honest, Laruhk, I am surprised you got so close. I would have heard you at twice the distance."

"You mock me, Kargen," he replied. "My skills are just as good as yours."

"And yet the deer escaped," stated Kargen, his face breaking into a grin, "but it is of no consequence, we shall merely have to find another."

"Had you not given our last deer to Athgar, we might be back at our village, enjoying the smell of roast venison."

"He needed the kill," defended Kargen, "and we are sufficiently skilled that we shall not return empty-handed."

"Bah, you favour the Human too much. What is it about him that you find so interesting?"

"He is not like the rest," asserted Kargen. "He treats us with respect, and in turn, I offer the same to him."

"Athgar is not much of a hunter," observed Laruhk.

"Neither are you if your last arrow is any indication." Kargen wandered over to the tree, pulling the shot loose. "The tip is undamaged," he said, offering it back to his companion.

Laruhk tucked it into the quiver that hung from his belt. "Where shall we look next?"

Kargen didn't answer, he was too busy sniffing the air.

"What is it?" asked Laruhk.

"Something on the wind, smoke I think, coming from the west."

"A nearby hunter?"

"No," said Kargen. "It is too strong for a simple campfire. This is something bigger."

"An army camp, perhaps?"

"Here, in this part of the woods?" asked Kargen. "Humans know this is Orc territory, they would be fools to enter."

"And yet, it has not stopped them in the past," said Laruhk. "It is the reason we built a palisade around Ord-Kurgad, remember? I can think of no other explanation for the smoke, can you? The only other thing nearby is the village of Athelwald."

"Perhaps it is under attack?" suggested Kargen.

"Who would attack the Therengians?" asked Laruhk. "They form a buffer between the duke and us. Without them, there would be trouble on the border."

"Perhaps that is someone's intent?" supplied Kargen. "We know so little about the ways of Humans, but they are said to be devious."

"You think that outsiders mean to invade us?"

"It is a distinct possibility," said Kargen.

"And so Athgar's people, these Therengians, would they fight?"

"They would not fight us," replied Kargen, "for we are the only ones to trade with them, but they would, I suspect, fight to defend their village."

"If that is so, then what are we to do?" asked Laruhk.

"We must investigate further," his friend decided, "and try to discover what has befallen them. Let us see if we can solve this mystery."

They made their way upwind, following a westerly path until they emerged from the trees onto a slight rise, the Therengian village of Athelwald visible some distance off. Even from their current position, they could make out flames. Thick, black smoke poured from the dwellings, while horsemen rode about, torches in hand, their armour glinting in the sun.

"Your suspicions are correct, they are under attack!" called out Laruhk.

"Yes, but by who?" asked Kargen, shielding his eyes, straining to make out what details he could.

"Armoured riders on horseback, it would appear," said Laruhk.

"I can see that, but who are they? Mercenaries? Agents of the duke?

Soldiers from Krieghoff? They wear heavy metal armour, perhaps a war has broken out, and Athgar's village has been caught in the middle?"

"What shall we do?" asked Laruhk.

"There is not much we can do. If we were to go down there now, we would be slaughtered along with the rest of Athelwald. No, we must wait and watch. With any luck, we shall be able to identify the attackers."

"Why? To seek revenge?" asked Laruhk.

"No," Kargen replied, "this is not our fight. To intervene would be to invite disaster for our own people."

"As usual, you are in the right, my friend. We shall let them kill each other, and then there will be fewer Humans to threaten us in the future."

"You misinterpret, Laruhk. We shall wait until the riders have left and then enter Athelwald. There may be survivors."

"I thought you said it was not our fight? The Orcs of the Red Hand have been left alone by the duke. Are we to change all that with our actions this day? Surely, if we interfere here, there will be repercussions?"

"I cannot stand by and do nothing," said Kargen. "We Orcs exist in a precarious position, surviving only so long as the Duke of Holstead does not see us as a threat. I would have thought the same of Athgar's people, but something has altered that relationship. Change is coming, whether we want it or not."

They watched the riders as they torched the village. The dead lay scattered about, while others, cut off by the horsemen, cowered before the display of weapons.

"They mean to take prisoners!" announced Laruhk.

A drop of rain fell, landing on Kargen's face. "Our ancestors weep," he observed. "Mark this day well, for something has started here that will have a great effect on our people, I can feel it."

"Surely you jest, Kargen. The Therengian's are a minor people. How could the loss of this one village affect our tribe?"

"Just as the loss of a single hunter can change the fortunes of the hunt, so too, can the loss of a single ally leave ripples in the lives of others. I do not know what has happened this day, but I feel it has changed our future."

They watched in silence, the raindrops increasing in frequency till they became a heavy rain, obscuring their view of Athelwald.

"Come," said Kargen, "it is time we approach."

They made their way down the hill. The rain had soaked the ground, yet smoke still poured forth from the buildings. As they drew closer, a quiet settled over the area, lending an eerie feeling to their journey. Arriving at the edge of the village, they paused, listening intently, trying to ascertain if the enemy horsemen remained.

"They are gone," announced Kargen, advancing.

Slowly, cautiously, they walked into the remains of Athelwald. The thatched roofs had, for the most part, been burned away, while little was left of the buildings save for some scorched timbers and mud.

Laruhk stopped, gazing down at the body of a villager. "This was no battle," he declared, "this was a massacre."

Kargen swept his gaze across the area, taking in the footprints that were yet to be washed away by the rain. "Yes," he finally said, "and yet I fear killing was not their objective."

"How can you say that? Look at all the bodies!"

In answer, Kargen ran forward, then paused, pointing at the ground. "There, you see? They were taken from here in a large group, herded, like the Humans herd cattle."

"But why would someone do such a thing?" asked Laruhk.

"There is only one reason I can think of," replied Kargen. "They were taken as slaves."

Laruhk made a face. "How barbaric," he spat out in disgust. "Have they no sense of decency?"

"No, they do not, whoever they were. I suspect these people fought back," he waved his hand to indicate the dead, "but they had little chance against armoured horsemen."

"Poor Athgar," said Laruhk, "I shall miss him."

"I doubt he was taken," offered Kargen. "He is not the type to surrender without a fight."

"Then he is likely dead," said Laruhk, "and yet I do not see his body."

"Let us look around some more, perhaps we will be able to find him, and let his spirit rest."

They poked their way through the burned-out huts, ignoring the rain. It was Kargen that finally found what he was looking for. "Over here," he called out.

Laruhk came running, "What is it?"

"This is what is left of Athgar's hut," said Kargen. "The rain must have extinguished the fire."

"Is he in there?"

"I do not know," Kargen replied. "The timbers that formed the roof have collapsed. Help me move them, and perhaps we can find his body."

They quickly got to work, hefting the timbers and tossing them to the side. As they moved yet another one, Kargen tripped on something, sending the wood toppling to the side. He looked down to see a boot, still attached to a leg.

"A body," he called out. "It must be Athgar, buried in the debris."

Laruhk moved forward, crouching to wipe ashes from the body, revealing Athgar, the human's brown hair framing a face with a patchy beard. The Orc pried open an eyelid to look into the human's grey eyes. "He is dead," he declared.

"No, he is not," said Kargen. "Note how the rain bubbles around his nose? Quickly, we must pull him free."

Kargen lifted the man's head, shielding him from the rain with his massive green body. "Grab his legs, let us pull him from the remains of this hut."

They dragged him out, laying him on the ground. As they did so, the rain slackened, then suddenly stopped. Kargen looked up at the sky in surprise, "The ancestors look kindly upon us."

"It is just rain," offered Laruhk, "not the ancestors."

"Do not be so sure to dismiss things," retorted his companion.

Laruhk looked over the body. "He seems to have taken a rather nasty hit to the head," he observed, "and there are several cuts to his arms, along with burns."

"Strange that he would have taken refuge in a burning hut," observed Kargen.

"I suspect he fought back, but something must have forced him into the hut. Perhaps he was driven back by a horseman?"

"Perhaps," said Kargen, "but we will not know for sure unless we can save him. He looks to have suffered quite a few burns."

"He is young, is he not?" asked Laruhk.

"He is," agreed Kargen. "Only twenty years of age, if I am not mistaken. Not even old enough to have a full beard, see how patchy it is?"

"Even more so with his burns," noted Laruhk. "It is a shame that Uhdrig is not here to heal him."

"Then we must transport him," said Kargen.

Laruhk turned to his companion with a look of surprise, "Are you suggesting we take him back to our village?"

"How else would we save him?"

"But we cannot," Laruhk objected. "A Human has never entered Ord-Kurgad."

"There is a first time for everything," stated Kargen, "and I will not leave him here to die, unless you have a better suggestion?"

"No, I do not," said Laruhk.

"Then, it is settled. Now, how do we move him?"

Laruhk swept his gaze around the remains of Athelwald. "We could carry him dangling from a pole?"

"Very well, let us bind his hands and feet, then slip a pole between them. We shall carry him back like a prize deer. It will allow us to move swiftly."

Kargen pulled strips of leather from his satchel and bound Athgar's arms and legs firmly while Laruhk dug around the ruins of the village, finally returning with a spear.

"How about this?" offered Laruhk.

"It will have to do," said Kargen, "for we have little else."

They threaded the pole between Athgar's arms and legs then hefted him into the air, each Orc bearing one end of the spear.

"He is lighter than I expected," said Laruhk.

"He is a Human," reminded Kargen. "They are slighter of frame than us. We must remember that he is not as hardy as an Orc, so try not to jostle him too much."

They began moving eastward, soon clearing the remains of Athelwald, and making their way towards home.

Sometime later, they came into view of the palisade that marked their home. They were spotted almost immediately, and Kargen recognized the two Orcs that ran out to meet them.

"What have we here?" asked Korsune.

"It is a Therengian," declared Kargen. "We found him in the ruins of his village."

"Is he alive?" asked Durgash.

"He is," confirmed Laruhk, "though he is badly burned. He will need the healing touch of Uhdrig."

Korsune stood still, looking at the Human suspended from the spear.

"What are you waiting for?" asked Kargen. "My arms are tired."

"We cannot take him into Ord-Kurgad," defended Durgash, "it is forbidden."

"This is Athgar of the Therengians," Kargen reminded him. "Have you forgotten the arrows he has made for you over the years?"

"No, but Gorlag will not be happy."

"Gorlag can kiss my ancestors."

"Kargen," Durgash admonished, "you cannot speak that way of our chieftain."

"Help or get out of our way," warned Kargen. "I shall take responsibility for everything."

"Very well," said Durgash. "Korsune, grab the other end."

They transferred their burden, and then all four Orcs continued on. The palisade ran around the entire perimeter, save for a small gap. To cover this, a secondary wall had been constructed outside of the main wall, forcing everyone to walk parallel to the wall for some distance before entering.

They passed through quickly, revealing the village beyond. Huts made of wood and mud were built close to the palisade, leaving a large fire pit in the centre, much like the Therengians. The structures themselves, however, differed significantly. In place of the small dwelling of the Humans, Ord-Kurgad was more communal in nature, for the vast majority of the Orcs lived in longhouses that held anywhere from twenty to fifty hunters. Only the old Orcs, or those who had bonded, lived in smaller huts. The largest one of all was that of the chieftain, the mighty Gorlag, who was exiting the building, lured, no doubt, by the commotion.

"What is the meaning of this?" he called out.

"It is a Human," offered Laruhk, as the party halted.

"I can see that," replied the chieftain, "but what is he doing here? It is forbidden!"

"He is injured," defended Kargen, "and requires the help of our shaman. Where is Uhdrig?"

The old shamaness stepped out from behind Gorlag. "I am here," she said, moving towards Athgar. The Orcs carrying him lowered his body to the ground and removed the pole while she knelt by the Therengian, casting her eyes over his wounds.

The chieftain opened his mouth to speak but was forestalled by the shamaness, who raised her hands, taking the attention from him. "What happened here?" she asked.

"His village was attacked," explained Laruhk, "and we found him in the ashes."

"You say you found him in the ashes?" repeated Uhdrig.

"Yes," said Kargen, "that is right. Why? Is it important?"

In answer, she returned her attention to the Therengian. She pulled out a knife, slicing through the bonds that held his wrists and ankles together.

The chief, Gorlag, moved closer, his shadow falling across Athgar. "He must be taken from here immediately!" he ordered.

"No," objected Uhdrig, "he is marked by fire."

There was a collective gasp from the assembled Orcs.

"Surely you are mistaken," said Gorlag, "it cannot be!"

"Do you doubt my proclamation?" asked the shamaness.

"No, of course not," said the chieftain, "but he is a Human."

"Human or not, he has the mark." She pointed with her finger. "See how his burns already begin to heal?"

"But-"

"But nothing, Gorlag," she retorted. "You know our ways as well as I. We cannot refuse one who has been marked by flame, it is the very essence of our tribe."

"Those rules only apply to Orcs," objected Gorlag.

In answer, the shamaness raised Athgar's right hand. "Can you not see the blood-encrusted on his hand? He has been marked as a member of this tribe. Where is Artoch? He is the master of flame, he can tell us more."

"Very well," said Gorlag, turning to those behind him. "Go and fetch him, he will see the wisdom in my orders."

A couple of hunters ran off to locate the master of flame while the others turned back to the body before them.

"Will you heal him?" asked Kargen

"I shall," replied Uhdrig, "but it is not for me to decide whether we expel him. That will be the decision of the tribe."

"What have we found?" called out a voice. A relatively short Orc pushed his way forward, his light green skin in stark contrast to those around him.

"Master Artoch," said Uhdrig in greeting. "Come, tell us what you think of this... Human."

The master of flame knelt, lowering his head to examine the burns on Athgar. "He lives," he announced, "though he should, by all rights, be dead."

"He was found in ashes," offered the shamaness.

He looked to her in surprise, "Found in ashes, and yet alive. This is the mark of one touched by fire. Can you heal him?"

"I can," she admitted, "though it will take some time. The skin must be regenerated. It will take several days at the very least."

"We must first determine his fate," declared Gorlag.

"And so we shall," replied the master of flame, "but he must be fit to stand trial."

"Trial?" asked Kargen.

"Yes," said Artoch, "the tribe will sit in judgement to determine if he will stay or be banished."

"Very well," said Gorlag, "we shall let our... guest recover from his wounds. In three days, we will determine his fate. In the meantime, who will speak on his behalf?"

"I will," declared Kargen, meeting the chieftain's stare with a steely gaze.

"Very well," Gorlag replied, "and I shall speak against him. The will of the tribe will decide what is to be done with this Human."

The sword struck downward, cutting into the wood. Athgar felt the shudder as the bow absorbed the blow, narrowly missing his fingers. The rider's massive horse forced him back.

As his vision blurred, he saw his sister, Ethwyn, staggering forward, blood pouring from her forehead. Another rider loomed over her, striking her down with the flat of his blade.

Again a blur, and then he felt his chest tighten as the horse's hooves impacted, knocking him backward. When his enemy opened his visor and laughed, Athgar saw the man's face, one he would not soon forget; the long scar running down the left cheek, cutting through the thick black beard was forever seared into his memory. The Therengian staggered back as all turned dark.

Athgar opened his grey eyes. Everything around him was fuzzy, and out of focus, then a green face loomed over him. Sounds started coming to his ears, the language of Orcs.

"Where am I?" he asked, using their tongue.

"You are in Ord-Kurgad, our village," replied the face, finally coming into focus.

Its wrinkled countenance identified it as an elderly Orc, or at least that's what Athgar assumed. "My name is Uhdrig, I am the village healer," the Orc said.

"I am Athgar," he murmured, his voice weak. "What happened?"

"You were found in Athelwald, buried in the ashes," she replied. "What do you remember?"

The images once again came flooding back to him in a rush. "There was a battle, we were attacked. Men on horses burning the huts," he coughed out.

"You must rest," Uhdrig advised. "You were badly burned. I have used magic to heal you, but the burns will take longer for the spell to have an effect."

"How long has it been?" he asked.

"More than a day, why?"

"I must find the survivors," said Athgar, trying to sit up.

"There were no others," she said, pushing him back down. "Kargen told us you were the only one they found."

"They were all slain?"

"No, but Kargen will explain later. For now, you must rest and recover your strength. Once you are better, we have much to discuss."

Another Orc loomed over him. "How are you feeling?" the newcomer asked.

"Sore," replied Athgar, "and my skin feels like it's on fire."

"That is to be expected. I am Artoch, Master of Flame. Tell me, how long have you held the spark?"

"What spark? I don't know what you're talking about."

"You have an affinity for fire," continued Artoch. "You have been touched by it. With patience and training, you can be taught to harness that spark, to control the flame."

"I don't understand," said Athgar. "Are you saying I have the makings of a Fire Mage?"

"You have, as long as it does not consume you. This gift can be controlled, and even directed if you wish, but it will take great mental discipline."

"I don't understand," said Athgar, "if that was true, shouldn't I have shown some affinity for fire in the past?"

"The gift of fire can be a fickle thing," said Artoch. "While some show an aptitude as they grow, others only have their power unlocked through great suffering. I believe you fall into the latter."

"This is all too much for me," the Therengian replied. "I remember fighting the horseman, and then waking up here, and now you're telling me I'm a Fire Mage?"

"You have the potential to be one, yes," said Artoch

"Who found me?"

"Kargen and Laruhk. They were out hunting when they detected the smoke from your village. I am sorry to tell you it has been burned to the ground."

Athgar tried to sit up again, but firm hands pushed him back down. "You must rest and heal," said Uhdrig. "The time for questions will come later."

"But I have to track down the attackers," insisted Athgar.

"It is far too dangerous," said Artoch. "Without learning to control the fire within you, you would perish."

"I don't understand," said the Human.

"You have great magical potential," explained the Orc, "but you are untrained, making your days dangerous and numbered."

"Nonsense," objected Athgar, "I've never had that problem before."

"No," said Artoch, "I do not suppose you have, but it has been released now, and it can only grow, putting your own life in danger unless you learn to control it. And it is not just you that you must consider."

"What do you mean?" Athgar asked.

"You might find survivors, only to burn them to death in your sleep. Is that the fate they deserve?"

"No, it's not," Athgar agreed, "but I must begin my search before it's too late!"

"You may go if you wish," the elderly Orc replied, "but you would likely not live out the week."

"It's that dangerous?" asked the Therengian.

"It is," said Artoch. "If you would permit me, I would teach you, provided the tribe agrees to let you stay, of course."

"In any case," added Uhdrig, "it is too late. They are long gone, their tracks washed away by rain. One day, perhaps, you will find them, but the ancestors have clearly spoken, that day is not today."

Athgar closed his eyes, his head in turmoil, trying to make sense of everything, until sleep finally claimed him.

CONTINUE READING ASHES

How to get Battle at the River for free

Paul J Bennett's newsletter members are the first to hear about upcoming books, along with receiving exclusive content and Work In Progress updates.

Join the newsletter and receive *Battle at the River*, a Mercerian Short Story for free: PaulJBennettAuthor.com/newsletter

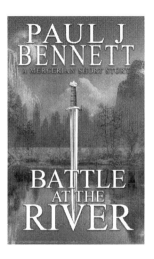

An enemy commander. A skilled tactician. Only one can be victorious.

The Norland raiders are at it again. When the Baron of Bodden splits their defensive forces, Sergeant Gerald Matheson thinks that today is a day like any other, but then something is different. At the last moment, Gerald recognizes the warning signs, but they are outnumbered, outmaneuvered, and out of luck. How can they win this unbeatable battle?

If you like intense battle scenes and unexpected plot twists, then you will love Paul J Bennett's tale of a soldier who thinks outside the box.

A Few Words from Paul

Defender of the Crown parallels Heart of the Crown in a couple of ways. While both deal with a diplomatic journey to a foreign realm, the results are far different. In Heart, Anna was a young girl, a pawn of King Andred in a game of politics. Despite this disadvantage, she completes a very successful mission. In Defender, however, she is now queen, a far cry from the young girl that travelled to Weldwyn.

The court of Merceria remains weakened due to the events that took place in Burden of the Crown, and there is still much opposition to the queen's policies. Anna, now faced with another diplomatic challenge, must decide who will rule the kingdom in her absence. Despite obvious villains who plot and connive, this time, some of her most stalwart supporters balk at the thought of the queen travelling into the heartland of Norland, their traditional enemy.

Ultimately, though, this tale is about people. Heir to the Crown now has a large cast of characters, and inevitably, some will receive a little less attention than others. In Defender of the Crown, the emphasis is on Hayley as she struggles to deal with her newfound responsibilities, both as High Ranger and as the queen's steward. It also delves into magic in more detail, giving Aubrey a more prominent place.

After reading this book, some questions are still left unresolved. With a foreign army threatening Eastwood, the military might of Merceria, now bolstered by its allies, must repel this force and then take the war to Norland territory. All this, while a new threat demands that Gerald and Anna march again in Fury of the Crown.

I could not have completed a work of this magnitude without the help and support of my loving wife, Carol. These stories, indeed all my books, are due in large part to her tireless efforts in editing, promoting and inspiring these tales.

I would also thank Christie Kramburger for once again providing us with an outstanding cover, along with Stephanie Sandrock and Amanda Bennett, for their encouragement and support. Though their characters do not appear as often in this tale, I must thank Brad Aitken, Jeffrey Parker and Stephen Brown for their inspirations.

My BETA reading team continues to provide valuable feedback, as usual, catching plot holes and inconsistencies. Their assistance in the editing process is very much appreciated. Thanks to Rachel Deibler, Tim

James, Stuart Rae, Michael Rhew, Phyliss Simpson, Don Hinkey, James McGinnis, and Shelley Heddings for giving of your time!

And a quick shoutout to Dianna-Lynn (Dee) Lundgren and Cody Anne Arko-Omori, who, after Carol is finished with the manuscript, give it that final polish!

Lastly, I must thank you, the reader, who has made this series a success. Your emails and book reviews continue to inspire me on this quest.

About the Author

Paul J Bennett (b. 1961) emigrated from England to Canada in 1967. His father served in the British Royal Navy, and his mother worked for the BBC in London. As a young man, Paul followed in his father's footsteps, joining the Canadian Armed Forces in 1983. He is married to Carol Bennett and has three daughters who are all creative in their own right.

Paul's interest in writing started in his teen years when he discovered the roleplaying game, Dungeons & Dragons (D & D). What attracted him to this new hobby was the creativity it required; the need to create realms, worlds and adventures that pulled the gamers into his stories.

In his 30's, Paul started to dabble in designing his own roleplaying system, using the Peninsular War in Portugal as his backdrop. His regular gaming group were willing victims, er, participants in helping to playtest this new system. A few years later, he added additional settings to his game, including Science Fiction, Post-Apocalyptic, World War II, and the all-important Fantasy Realm where his stories take place.

The beginnings of his first book 'Servant to the Crown' originated over five years ago when he began a new fantasy campaign. For the world that the Kingdom of Merceria is in, he ran his adventures like a TV show, with seasons that each had twelve episodes, and an overarching plot. When the campaign ended, he knew all the characters, what they had to accomplish, what needed to happen to move the plot along, and it was this that inspired to sit down to write his first novel.

Paul now has four series based in Eiddenwerthe, his fantasy realm and is looking forward to sharing many more books with his readers over the coming years.

Made in the USA
Monee, IL
01 March 2021